# THE BATTLE OF
# HALF MOON MOUNTAIN

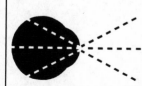

This Large Print Book carries the
Seal of Approval of N.A.V.H.

FIVE TRAILS WEST, BOOK II

# THE BATTLE OF
# HALF MOON MOUNTAIN

## ONE FAMILY'S WESTERN ODYSSEY

## JAMES D. CROWNOVER

**THORNDIKE PRESS**
*A part of Gale, Cengage Learning*

GALE
CENGAGE Learning·

Farmington Hills, Mich • San Francisco • New York • Waterville, Maine
Meriden, Conn • Mason, Ohio • Chicago

GALE
CENGAGE Learning®

LIBRARY OF CONGRESS CATALOGING-IN-PUBLICATION DATA

Names: Crownover, James D., author.
Title: The Battle of Half Moon Mountain : one family's western odyssey / by James D. Crownover.
Description: Large print edition. | Waterville, Maine : Thorndike Press, 2016. | © 2015 | Series: Thorndike Press large print western | Series: Five trails west ; book 2
Identifiers: LCCN 2016003772 | ISBN 9781410488701 (hardcover) | ISBN 1410488705 (hardcover)
Subjects: LCSH: Families—Fiction. | Frontier and pioneer life—Fiction. | Large type books. | GSAFD: Western fiction. | Historical fiction.
Classification: LCC PS3603.R765 B38 2016 | DDC 813/.6—dc23
LC record available at http://lccn.loc.gov/2016003772

Published in 2016 by arrangement with James D. Crownover

Printed in Mexico
1 2 3 4 5 6 7 20 19 18 17 16

*To Carol*
*for her*
*encouragement & patience*

Ruth Harris
Born: 1790
Place: Tennessee
Married: Tom Finn 1806
Married: Samuel Meeker 1815
Place: Village on the Middle Fork

Hiram Harris
Anglo-Saxon
Born: 1767
Place: South Carolina

Samuel Harris
Born: 1794

Sarah Fourkiller
Cherokee
Born: circa 1774
Place: Tennessee

Jerry Harris
Born: 1796
Place: Tennessee
Married: Kansas 1822

Joseph Harris
Born: 1805
Place: Tennessee

John (Pony) 1833
Jacob 1835
Luzina 1838
Parlee 1842
Zenas Leonard 1844
Born: 1844
Place: Arkansas
Married: Sophia
Maria Gomez 1876

Jesse Meeker, nee Finn
Born: 1807
Place: Pirate's Island
Married: Amira Dreadfulwater 1831
Place: Chewey, Cherokee Nation

Sarah Fourkiller Meeker
Born: 1816

7

# PROLOGUE

I met Zenas Leonard Meeker while working
on the Federal Writers Project in 1937 and
after we became well acquainted, I convinced him to let me write his biography. To
my surprise, he began with his grandfather
and related the experiences of four generations of his family before he got to his
personal story.

This is the second book of his recollec-
tions of the migration of his family west
from Tennessee. Zenas, when he stood, was
slim, erect, and square shouldered, about
five feet nine inches tall. He had a clear eye
and firm grip when we shook. He still
walked with a sure step though he occasionally carried a cane; "Not because I need
support, but so's I can keep the dogs out
from underfoot," he explained. His hair,
though thinning, still held a lot of the black
color it must have been in his younger days.

Mrs. Meeker, his wife of sixty-two years,

was tall and erect for a woman of her age and her graying hair and fair skin bespoke of someone with Castilian bloodlines who had once been blonde or red-headed. She looked to be some years younger than her husband.

There were a couple of horses in the corral, a few chickens in a wire pen, and I heard a pig squeal behind the barn. A milk cow grazed on the sparse grass nearby. "Sophie makes me keep a milk cow for cooking and the grandkids when they come by," he said with a smile. "And I like a little buttermilk with my cornbread, too."

James Daniels

Surviving the New Madrid earthquake of 1811–12, Ruth Finn, her son, Jesse, and her brother, Jerry Harris, the second and third generations, traveled west with the Fourkillers to their home on the Middle Fork of the Little Red River where Ruth and Jerry established their home.

The third trail the family was involved with was the southern route to California as marked out by Captain Randolph Marcy. Originally called the California Road, it was later called the Southern Route.

The fourth trail the family followed was the Cherokee Trail. It was established by the Cherokees on their way to California in 1849. It ran west from the Arkansas–Indian Territory border and was the preferred trail for Arkansas drovers and Indian Nation travelers, having plenty of water and grass and avoiding the overgrazed trails and passes of the Oregon Trail to the north. A man named C. C. Seay took a herd of cattle, quite possibly white faced, over this trail from Cincinnati, Arkansas, to California in 1853.

*The Battle of Half Moon Mountain* tells about the life and adventures of Ruth, Jesse, and Jerry and how the family changed their name from Finn to Meeker. Of course, that is only a minor part of the story and it is safe to say that their life does not become quiet and sedate . . .

# Chapter 1
## Samuel Meeker
# 1814

---

*"Awhile back I mentioned that Riley had said that someone called Big Sam was at th' cabins on Weaver's Creek,"* Zenas said when next we met. *"I'll tell you about him in this tale, as Grandma told to us."*

It was sometime in December 1813, before the men returned from their hunt that we were sewing some clothes before th' fire in the Fourkiller cabin when we heard a hale from the yard. Lydia opened the door a crack and peeked, then flung it wide open and called, "Come in here, Sam Meeker, what are you doing this far from home?"

"I've come west to seek my fortune and see that Lonza Fourkiller is treating you well!" a deep voice boomed across the yard. In a moment, a shadow fell across the floor and a large man in the dress of the Cherokees stepped through the door. He was not much taller than Lydia, but he was very

13

broad in the shoulders, deep-chested, his arms large and muscled. Lydia threw her arms around his neck and hugged him. "I'm so glad you have come, for he has left me here alone and gone off on a long hunt." She laughed and stepped back, flushed and a little flustered.

Riley ran across the room yelling, "Big Sam, Big Sam!" He fairly flung himself at the man, this Sam grabbing him in his free arm and folding him into a bear hug, "Where is Riley, and who is this big boy jumping on me?"

"*I'm* Riley all grown up, see?" the boy yelled, squirming to be released from the hug so the man could see his face.

"No, you're too big to be Riley, why you are almost grown and Riley is a little boy!"

"Big Sam, you know I'm Riley," he scorned.

The man laughed a deep rumble as he sat the boy down and leaned his rifle against the wall. "Well, I think you *are* Riley, but I hardly knew you all grown up like you are, how'd you get so big?"

"I growed up coming 'cross the country!" Riley crowed.

Laughing Brook had risen and taking a bowl had dipped out a large serving of the food warming by the fire. "Welcome, Sam

14

Meeker, won't you have something to eat? I am Laughing Brook, Lydia's mother."

"Thank you very much, Laughing Brook, I have heard much good of you and Wash Fishinghawk." His eyes twinkled as he removed his hat and bowed.

"Oh, and this is Ruth Fourkiller, who came with us from New Madrid." Lydia had recovered from her excitement, though her cheeks were still pink. "Samuel Meeker is Lonza's best friend from the east. They grew up together," she explained.

"And this is my son, Jesse," I added, patting Jesse's shoulders as he stood quietly before me.

"I'm glad to meet you both," Sam Meeker said with that little bow. "I am puzzled why these two big boys didn't go on the long hunt with the rest of the men," he said, taking the proffered seat and addressing the food before him.

"We stayed here to watch the women folk and take care of Rising Sun," Riley crowed, his chest swelling.

His spoon stopped and his eyebrows rose. Samuel asked, "Who is this Rising Sun?"

Lydia had lifted the sleeping baby from his crib and held him down for Samuel to see. "This is Rising Sun, my child," she said. "He was born the day after we arrived from the east."

Big Sam's eyes grew large with the realization of the ordeal Lydia had come through and the surprise of the new child. "Ohhhh," was all he could say as he looked at the now robust child, "Ohhhh." When he had regained his composure, he said, "Where's that Lonza Fourkiller? I'll fry his gizzard for dragging you across the country like that!"

Lydia laughed. "Oh, he didn't know until we were well on our way back and by then there was nothing more to do but to travel on. Ruthie and her brother, Jerry, helped us greatly and I could not have done without them."

"You came through the quaking lands?" he asked.

"We were there when the Hard Shake hit, it was the third and the worst they had seen," she said solemnly. "They got better the closer we got to here."

"They were still shaking a little when I came through, but not near so bad. I came across from the Shawnee towns upriver from the mouth of the Ohio."

*[At this period in time, the Shawnee lived around Cape Girardeau. — J.D.]*

"That makes the trip longer, doesn't it?" she asked.

16

"A little, but the rivers are smaller and easier to cross." Sam Meeker had been wishfully eyeing his plate and with a wave of her hand, Lydia turned her attention to Rising Sun so the man could eat. Riley could hardly contain himself and kept dancing around the table chattering to Sam Meeker, who tried his best to pay attention and eat at the same time.

"Riley, slow down and let Big Sam eat!" Lydia scolded. "Why don't you and Jesse go unload Sam's horse and put him in the corral? Show Big Sam what a man you have become."

Riley's chest swelled and with an air of authority he called, "Come on, Jesse."

I hurried to the door and saw that the packs on the horse were too big for the boys to handle, so I stepped out and helped them unload the horse. "You boys give him some grain — not too much — and rub him down before you put him up," I called after them.

"OK, Ma," Jesse called and ran ahead to get the corn.

As I entered the house, Laughing Brook was setting a second bowl of food before Sam Meeker. "That sure is good stew, Grandmother, I guess I could eat the whole pot."

"You may have all you want, Samuel," she

17

replied, smiling.

I couldn't say that Sam Meeker was a handsome man, but the openness of his countenance and his ready smile assured me that
he had a kindly nature and I felt at home in
his presence from the start. He wore his
auburn hair long in the fashion of the
frontier, tied back in a queue most of the
time, even in winter. His features were
Indian, the color of his hair a result of the
infusion of Mandan blood a couple of
generations before him. Later on, I learned
that he was called Big Sam to differentiate
him from another boy he and Lonza grew
up with, who was called Little Sam. It
turned out that as the boys grew, Little Sam
grew to be taller than Big Sam by head and
shoulders. Still, the names stuck, much to
the amusement of the community.

If he wasn't tall, Sam Meeker was a big
man in other ways. He had broad shoulders
and a deep chest that tapered only slightly
to his waist. His arms and legs were large
and heavily muscled. He had broad strong
hands that fitted well with his arms. His feet
seemed a little large, though they would be
so of necessity to carry the weight of his
body. Trackers acquainted with him could
identify his trail, though he was such a good

woodsman that signs of his passage were seldom seen if he so wished.

For all his size, he could move like lightning and I learned to be aware when he began to bounce up on his toes, for some kind of action was about to explode. His short coupled arms and legs gave him extraordinary leverage and he loved to wrestle. An Englishman, in later years, taught him to box and after that, he was never beaten in single combat, be it friendly or deadly.

Children were drawn to him and he loved children. He had a special way with them. Nothing raised his ire quicker than to see a child mistreated and pity the one who mistreated the child! Seldom did I see him punish a child for misbehavior, but a word or look would bring the child back into line. More than once, a sharp word or look has brought tears, not from fright, but merely from the thought that the child had displeased Big Sam. Even his own children called him Big Sam and their relationship to their father was especially close and loving. He had a deep voice and hearty laugh that put everyone around him at ease.

Like Lonza, he was well educated and loved to read. His hand was legible, though he tended to hurry and scrawl his words.

He was patient and tolerant with others, but impatient with himself if he felt that he could do better.

The evening passed quickly with Lydia and Big Sam in conversation about the people back east and stories of their two lives since parting. Laughing Brook and I mostly listened, though Big Sam drew us into the conversation often. The boys grew quiet and sleepy, Riley sitting on Big Sam's lap and nodding off.

"It looks to me that these boys have had a big day caring for the place and all," he said. "It's time we went to bed, tomorrow will come early."

There was a moment of hesitation while we thought about sleeping accommodations with three unescorted women and a strange man in our midst. "I've slept outside so long, I wouldn't be comfortable under a roof, so I'll just roll my bed out in the yard," Sam said.

"There's a shelter by our chimney where my brother, Jerry, sleeps," I suggested.

"Sounds just right, Mrs. Fourkiller, that's where I'll bed down."

"Me too," Riley chimed in. "Me and Jesse and Sippie sleep there all the time. Sippie's our guard dog."

"Well, you're welcome if you don't have fleas," Big Sam teased.

"I don't, but Sippie might. We make him sleep on top of the covers anyway."

Big Sam chuckled. "Are you going to sleep by the chimney with us, Jesse?" he asked.

Jesse hesitated, looking at me for direction. "It's OK, Jesse, you can sleep out if you want to. We can get your bedroll from the cabin," I said, rising.

"That's OK, Aunt Ruth, I'll share mine with him," Riley said. He was rubbing his eyes and we could tell he wouldn't last long.

Laughing Brook and I gathered our things and prepared to leave while the boys dug out their bedroll. Big Sam was rummaging in his packs by the door and we left together, the boys showing Big Sam the shelter by the chimney.

"We will meet here for breakfast after sunrise," Lydia called from the door.

As I returned the next morning, I heard the axe at work chopping wood. Instead of one of the women, Big Sam was wielding the axe on the woodpile. He stopped and grinned as I approached. "Good morning, Mrs. Fourkiller," he said sheepishly, rubbing his hands on his shirt. "I thought to earn my breakfast by chopping some wood." In the tribes, it was left up to the children

21

and women to gather firewood. Somewhere along the way, Big Sam and Lonza both learned that the white man's custom was for the man to take care of the firewood, though many a lazy white man had adopted the Indian custom.

"By the size of that stack of wood, I would say that you have earned breakfast and dinner and gone a ways toward earning your supper," I replied. "Sippie, go get the boys," I called to the dog as I hurried into the cabin with a side of bear bacon. Even as I closed the door, I could hear the boys squealing as Sippie rousted them out of the covers. In a moment, the three of them came bounding in the door, Jesse with one moccasin on and the other in his hand. "When's breakfast, Ma?" he called.

"You mind your manners, young man, breakfast will be ready when it's ready and not before. Now go wash up."

"I was gonna ask the same question," Big Sam whispered, piling a big armload of split wood on the hearth.

"As soon as the bacon is done, we can eat," Lydia called. I could see the Dutch oven was already in the coals baking biscuits and Laughing Brook was stirring the gravy. Loud protests were coming from the gallery about the icy water in the wash bowl and I

22

handed Big Sam the kettle of hot water.

"Hold on, boys, I'll warm the water," he called.

When all was ready, we sat down to eat.

"That certainly was good, ladies," Big Sam said, pushing back from the table. "I noticed you are getting low on fresh meat, how about if I go out and hunt a little today? Maybe I can find a fat bear or a deer to tide us over."

"That would be welcome," Laughing Brook said. "We are getting low and it will be some time before the men return. Some of the other hunters have come in but our men will be curing their own meat, so they will be away longer."

"Won't be much game close in to the village, so it may take me a couple of days to find something, but I won't come back without meat," he said. With that, he got up, stretched, and thanked us for the meal.

"Your horse needs to rest," I said. "Take one of the others with you, but leave Jobe, the mule, for us to use. The boys can tell you about the horses."

Big Sam grinned at me, "Why thank you, Mrs. Fourkiller, I'll do just that. Now, where did those two scamps get off to?"

"They had better be out there pitching hay to the horses," said Lydia.

23

"I'll go see to them, shore thank you ladies for the feed."

"You're more than welcome, Sam, it's surely good to have you here. I can hardly wait to see Lonza's face when he sees you."

He left and we busied ourselves cleaning up the table. Soon he was back to the front door with his bedroll packed behind the saddle. Retrieving his gun from the pegs over the door, he was just stepping out when I called to him, "Here is a pack of food that will do you for a couple of days. Hopefully by then you will have fresh meat," I said.

"Thank you again, Mrs. Fourkiller," he smiled.

"Please call me Ruth," I said, then for some reason I began to blush and quickly turned away.

Jesse and Riley rounded the corner, each on a horse and their bows in their hands. "We're going with Big Sam," Riley called as he passed the porch.

"No you are not!" Lydia and I said in unison. They stopped and turned toward the porch. "Ma . . ." Jesse began.

"This is not the time for you to be leaving with the men gone," I said. "You need to be here to do your chores."

"Sam won't be away long and you can go later when there will be a longer hunt,"

24

Lydia added.

"But . . ."

"Don't argue with your mothers," Sam put in. "When I get back, I will take you both and we will have a good hunt. But not before the men return from the long hunt," he added.

"Awww . . ."

"No more argument," I cut in. "We need you here and that's that!"

Sam turned and wiped imaginary sweat from his brow. Laughing Brook chuckled.

With downcast eyes and lips they turned back toward the corral. Lydia looked at me and I nodded. "You could ride with Sam to the end of the road if you want to, but not one step beyond, do you hear?"

"Yes, Ma." Their faces brightened some and they turned to wait on Big Sam.

On the front step, Laughing Brook and Sam talked a moment about where the best hunting would be and it was decided that he would hunt southeast below the mineral springs by Round Mountain, since the village hunters had gone west and north for the fall hunt. Presently he was up and away, riding down Weaver's Creek to the river.

Laughing Brook watched him till he was out of sight, then turned to the house, rubbing her hands in her apron. "He seems like a nice man, Lydia."

"Yes, he is," she replied. "His parents died early and he grew up in the Fourkiller home with Lonza. They were inseparable, but he had said he would never leave the Tennessee Valley and he stayed there when Lonza came here. I wonder what made him change his mind."

"Many things can happen in this life to change the things people do," Laughing Brook said and busied herself with the chores of the day.

It was almost an hour before the boys raced by on the road. They were both lying down on the ponies and racing for some finish line. Soon they were walking the winded horses back and arguing over who had really won the race.

*Zenas thought it would be fitting to interrupt Grandma Ruth's narration here and insert Sam's story of his first hunt in the Little Red River bottoms.*

# CHAPTER 2
# THE BEAR FACTS

*"I heard Grandpa Sam tell this story a time or two when I was a tad and again after I had been on a bear hunt or two with him and could appreciate the tale from the perspective of experience," Zenas said.*

By our reckoning, it was December 5, 1814, the day I got to the Fourkiller place. The men were away on the long hunt and the women and children were left at home. I had been on the trail two months, more or less, and was glad the trip was over. I liked Laughing Brook right off. It was obvious she was held in high esteem by Lydia and the children. They sure made me feel welcome, and I felt right at home.

Lydia introduced me to a widow by the name of Ruth Fourkiller, who had traveled with them from the Mississippi. She and her brother had built a cabin nearby. She had a son about the age of Riley and the

27

two were the life of the households.

We ate the last of the meat they had for breakfast the next morning and I determined to make a little hunt. The boys set up a howl to go, but their mothers put a stop to that and following directions from Laughing Brook, I headed south in hopes of finding something quickly. But that wasn't to be, for the land had been hunted over pretty good.

Laughing Brook had said that I wasn't likely to find game bigger than a squirrel until I crossed a river some six miles south of the settlement and she was right. Even then, it was some distance south of High Top Mountain before I saw any sign of larger game. I followed the tracks of a herd of deer until they disappeared into the bottoms of Cadron Creek. It being near dark, I decided to camp above the bottoms and continue my hunt in the morning. I made a cold camp, eating from the food Ruth had sent with me. Tying the lead rope to the horse's hobbles and to my wrist, I slept on his blanket while he grazed through the night.

As soon as it was light enough to see, I picked up the deer trail and followed it into the bottoms and almost as quickly lost it in the heavy brush. It was no use thrashing around in that on a horse. It would only warn the game that we were there and I would get neither sight nor sound of any critter bigger than a possum so we pushed on through and across the creek. Out of the bottoms, I turned the horse east and we rode to the bluffs above the Little Red River.

A mile or two east of where we hit the bluff, it took a sharp turn to the right away from the river. I rode on, looking for a way down to the bottom and back toward the river where I might find game. We came to a small creek that ran into the river and, though it was steep and rough, made our way to the bottom. The ground opened up into a valley maybe three miles wide tapering down to the river. One side of the valley was drained by the creek we had come down and the other side by another branch from the east. They met about two thirds of the way to the river and the land in between was open enough to provide good browse for deer.

Although there was abundant sign the deer had been there, it was all old and there wasn't a deer to be found in the whole bottoms. Something or someone had scared them away. I tried riding upstream but the bluffs soon came right down to the water's edge and I had to turn around or swim the

29

river, something I didn't want to do there. It looked like we would have to go back up on top the way we had come and I didn't want to share that information with the horse until I had explored all the alternatives.

Just before we got to our trail down the branch was a steep and narrow gully that split the rock cliff and as I rode past the mouth, my eye caught some movement up on the side of the bluff. I would have passed by, but some gravels rattling down the gully side confirmed my sighting and I tied the horse to a bush and climbed as quietly as possible. About halfway up the bluff on the north side was a rock bench and I couldn't tell what was there, so I climbed the south side of the gully until I was above the bench. It was only five or ten feet wide and nestled under the cliff was a shelter such as is found in the bluffs of that country.

I couldn't tell how deep it was but it obviously made an ideal den for critters and I hoped the critter I had heard and glimpsed was a bear. There was a hackberry sapling about six inches through near me, and working my way up above it, I could brace my feet against the base of the tree and lock my knees and have a fairly comfortable perch to hide behind and watch the shelter.

The hillside was so steep that sitting on the ground, I was almost standing up. I propped my rifle barrel on a small limb and had a good place for sighting a target in the shelter with minimal movement. All that was left was to watch and wait.

The longer I sat there, the more uncomfortable I became and I was near the end of my endurance when I thought I detected movement in the dark shelter. Sure enough, there eventually appeared a bear who came out of the shelter and lumbered upstream on the ledge. I took careful aim at the base of his ear and fired. He fell like a stone and the recoil of the rifle caused me to lose my footing and I slid down astraddle the tree and received a "grievous wound" as it is sometimes called.

*"Grandpa Sam never told about the 'grievous wound' part in mixed company," Zenas interjected.*

Luckily, the butt of the rifle caught on the ground and when I had caught my breath and wiped the tears out of my eyes, it was leaning up against the tree and limb as if I had carefully set it there. I scrambled around the gully and when I got to where the ledge tapered off into the bluff, I stopped and reloaded my rifle. Then I cautiously approached the bear. I poked it a time or two with the end of the rifle and seeing the blood on its head was satisfied it was dead.

There was no way to haul the carcass up the bluff and my only recourse was to lower it down to the bottom. To do that and not ruin the pelt or meat, I would have to butcher the bear where it lay and lower it a part at a time. I started to turn the carcass on its back and got it far enough on its side to note that it was a sow when she suddenly swiped me across the face with her paw.

The blow knocked me down and an enraged bear was suddenly standing over me on her hind legs, her eyes glowing red with anger. She was between me and the rifle I had leaned up against the rock wall and as I started to roll over, she swiped me in the chest right down my rib cage. My head slammed into the rock floor and everything went black for a few seconds. I could hear her grunting and feel her breath but couldn't see anything. As my vision returned, she was down on her all fours astraddle me and I was looking up at her underside. She must have been satisfied I was dead for she just stood there swaying back and forth and looking from side to side. She roared to tell the world she had made a kill and bent down and bit into my left shoulder to drag me to her den.

I pulled my knife from my belt and as she dragged me along, I swung for her ribs as hard as I could and buried the knife to the hilt. That caused her to drop me and she swung around trying to grasp the knife buried in her lung. Her first circle she clawed me from my buttocks to my ankle and her third circle carried her over the bluff and down to the bottom of the gully.

I blacked out again and this time I didn't hear or see anything for some time. When I came to, I was lying in a pool of curdled blood and I was pretty sure it wasn't bear blood. I was a mess. I carefully felt of my leg and it didn't feel very wet, though my hand was bloody when I drew it back. Most of the blood came from my chest and possibly my shoulder, though I couldn't see that. I pulled my tattered shirt together and pressed it tightly against my chest and holding it there with my left arm, I rolled on my right side and with my good arm began to drag myself backwards to the rock wall.

It was a long painful six feet to that wall and I thought I would never get there. Propping myself up against the wall made me a lot dizzier and only the necessity of taking stock of my condition and tending my wounds kept me from lying back down. My trail across the ledge was marked by a big smear of blood and it scared me into action. Somehow I got my leggings off and pulled the right leg on to my left leg. Then I cut the remains of the left legging into strips and tied the leg tightly from top to ankle. I wrapped other strips around my body and tied the bunched-up shirt tight against my torn chest.

There was a trickle of blood from my shoulder and feeling gently I discovered two puncture wounds in the front of my shoulder and knew there were at least two more behind. They didn't seem to be bleeding much so I stuffed the two wounds I could reach with bits of cloth and hoped the ones on the back of my shoulder would not bleed too much.

It was past midafternoon and cool there in the shade of the bluff. I could feel a cool breeze blowing down the gulch and knew it was going to be a cold stay on the ledge if I stayed the night there. After a long rest, I got my feet under me and at the risk of reopening the wounds on my leg, inched my way up the wall until I was standing. To my surprise I could reach my rifle and using it for a crutch, I limped to the rock shelter. As my eyes grew accustomed to the gloom, I could see a pile of leaves where the bear had denned up. If I could not get down tonight, it would make a good bed for me. I only hoped the old gal didn't have a mate that would show up.

Carefully, I shuffled over to the edge of the ledge, but not too close in case I had a dizzy spell and tumbled off. It must have been 150 feet to the bottom and most of it nearly vertical and rocky. The only hope I had of getting down was back the way I had come and down the side to the bottom of the gully, then down to the valley bottom. It was a long trip for a one-legged, one-armed man and I didn't want night to catch me on the way down. The sensible thing to do was to hole up and wait for morning.

I retraced my steps to the shelter and crawled into the pile of leaves and immediately slept. When I next awoke it was the darkest black I had ever seen. For a moment or two I wondered if I had died, then I turned my head and saw the outline of the mouth of the shelter by the dim light of the sky. I was cold and burrowed deeper into the pile of leaves and slept.

The sun was full up when I awakened and it must have been at least midmorning. I lay there a few moments gathering my wits and testing to see what was still working on my body. My left leg was stiff and when I drew my leg up, I could feel the pants leg pulling where it had stuck to the scratches. The most sore part was my shoulder and I wondered if that bear had broken a bone when she bit into me. All in all, I was in for a lot of pain the next few days, but I had to move or be in real trouble.

When I tried sitting up, pain shot from the base of my neck up into my head and I had to lie back down. I was dizzy and closed my eyes for a few moments. I lay staring at the ceiling of the cave and thought I must be hallucinating, for I saw plainly written there an L. Focusing on the letter shape, I saw next to it an 8, then a 9 and a 1. I closed my eyes and thought hard a moment, "L891, L891, what in all creation could that be? It sure doesn't make sense." Yet, there it was, almost close enough to touch. L891 had been written on the ceiling with the smoke from a torch. When I looked again, I could see other writing in some very strange shapes that I could not decipher. Beneath the L891 line was another row of letters of some kind that I had never seen before.

This was very puzzling to me and I lay there with my eyes closed thinking about what it could mean. Obviously *someone* had written those strange letters there, I'm sure the bear didn't. I laughed at the image of the old sow laboriously writing on the ceiling of her den with a smoking brand.

I must have slept some and in my dreams I saw the letters over and over again until suddenly my thoughts said, *Maybe what you saw was upside down.* I opened my eyes and looked again. In my addled condition, I debated on which was upside down, me or the writing, but I could not read it as though it was upside down. *I'm gonna have to turn myself around if I want to read this thing,* I thought.

So I began the laborious process of spinning myself around so I could look at the writing from the other viewpoint. I got turned and looked up and the writing had disappeared! I almost panicked, it *had* to be there. I could not have imagined it! I looked all around the ceiling and finally to the right a little way, I could see the letters. In spinning around, I had moved away from where my head had lain and the letters were no longer directly above me. In spite of the pain in my neck and head, I scooted over under the writing and lay there awhile with my eyes closed. I started drifting back to sleep, but woke with a start when I remembered why I was there.

When I looked up at the ceiling, I could see plainly what the writing said:

Mai 29 1687
Morte de Marle

*So there it is,* I thought. *In 1687 someone named Morte de Marle wrote his name on this ceiling!* And I marveled at that. What a relief to finally know what the writing said. It was as though it was the most important thing in my life to learn and meant the difference between life and death to me. I now know that that blow on the back of my head had injured my brain and I was partly out of my head. My thirst was agonizing.

"Well," I said to myself, "now that's solved, get on with leaving this place." By rolling onto my right side, I could push myself up a little and gradually sit up. With my hand, I could measure that the ceiling was just a few inches above my head and I could not stand up here. By scooting backwards, and trading leg pain for shoulder pain for head pain and back to leg pain, I moved out to where the ceiling was higher and I could stand. It was then that I realized that my crutch, the rifle, was still lying in the bed, so I went back until I could reach the gun, then back out again, dragging the gun with me.

I'm still not sure how I got into the standing position. It must have been that I climbed the rifle, and found myself standing and leaning heavily on the gun. My head ached something terrible and I braced myself to not fall again. There had been thoughts of feeling sorry for myself, when a voice in my head asked, *You're going to let some scratches from an old she-bear and an aching head keep you from climbing down from here and getting that meat back to those people? You sissy girl! What a baby you turned out to be!*

It made me angry and with that, I began limping toward the upper end of the ledge and the bottom of the gully. "I'll show you," I said to the voice and sitting down with the rifle in my lap began scooting feet first down the hill. I don't remember much about that trip, only once or twice did I find myself maneuvering around boulders and sometime near high noon, I bumped into ol' Sow.

From there, things got clearer. My horse was still tied to the bush and we walked down to the stream and got a long drink. I could travel pretty good hanging on to the horse and we went back to the gully. It was fortunate that I had a rope long enough to reach the bear where she lay and tying her two hind legs together, we pulled her out into the open. The weather was very cool and the carcass had not spoiled.

The knife had disappeared and seemed lost until I looked at the wound and saw the end of it sticking out between her ribs. She must have landed on it sometime in her fall and driven it all the way into her gut. It took some time to work it out.

A tug on the rope reminded me that the horse was still tied to the bear. He was trying to reach more grass. My head spun and we made another trip to water. Horse didn't drink, but I made up for him. Thirst made me desperate for more water and this time I remembered to fill the water bag.

With the horse staked on some grass, I hobbled stiff-legged to the bear. Butchering her took the rest of the afternoon, and by the time it was done, the water bag was empty and I was starving. A long drink at the branch and a gathering of wood and fire later, the heart and liver were roasting. They almost burned while the horse was being relocated closer, but I got to them in time and it didn't take long until they were devoured.

In my exhausted condition, I gave that voice in my head a tongue lashing for calling me those names and didn't awaken until sunrise. Now, there was an urgent need to get out of that valley and back to the settlement for some reason I could not quite fathom. Horse didn't like the idea of a bear being tied on his back but I convinced him it was all right and he allowed me to load him.

It was a long hard pull up that gully. Sometimes the horse's belly was almost dragging the ground, but he made it. We both stood at the top huffing and puffing, then sensing that we were on our way home, he started off and I let him have his way. I hung on to him and if I could have, I would have made that bear walk a ways and let me ride. There were a lot of rest stops that day, me and Horse being in the shape we were in. I didn't dare unload him and by evening he was tired out. We camped between Sugar Loaf and High Top and he was sure glad to get that load off. After he rolled and drank his fill, I staked him out and built a fire. That may have been the biggest steak I have ever eaten and as soon as it was gone, so was I.

There was just a crack of light in the east when I awoke. My head still ached but it didn't keep me from hurrying around and moving on. We had a river to cross and still some distance to the village. It would be a long day.

Not far above Sugar Loaf, we crossed in the riffles where it hardly got to Horse's belly. We both had trouble keeping our feet in the current, but eventually made it to quiet water. He stood and drank while I soaked some and watched water turn brown from the dried blood all over me. It sure attracted the minnows and they nibbled on me. Even my hair was caked and crusted over. I was glad we had to wade the river. It would have scared the life out of those women to see me that bloody.

It was time to get out when the bandages loosed from the wounds and I began to see fresh blood. On the bank, I cleaned up some and put the tattered shirt on since the scratches had mostly stopped bleeding. The scratches on my face washed clean and bled some. My face felt tight and sometimes when I stepped into a little hole, it jarred and hurt.

Horse was more and more anxious to get home and we hardly stopped all day. Near late afternoon we came in to the Fourkiller yard and haled the house.

*I was quite curious about the inscription on the shelter ceiling, especially the 1687 date, which is supposedly many years before any*

*Europeans were in the area. It took some searching, but I discovered the account of La Salle's attempted colonization in Matagorda Bay on the Texas coast. Due to bad luck and shipwrecks, they found themselves stranded and low on provisions. In 1686 La Salle set out for his fort in what is now Illinois and thence on to Canada for help and to resupply the colony. The defection of several members of his party caused him to abandon his trip and return to Matagorda Bay. In early 1687 he again set off for Canada, but his nephew and two of his Indian servants were murdered by members of his party and when he went to find them he was assassinated also.*

*The remainder of his party killed the assassins and a portion of them continued their journey. Somewhere in Arkansas, one of the men named de Marle drowned. So the inscription Sam found would read in today's language: de Marle died May 29, 1687, I suppose somewhere near the shelter. — J.D.*

# CHAPTER 3
# THE HUNTER'S RETURN

*Zenas leaned over and tapped my knee. "That was the story up to the time Sam returned, now I'll tell you what Grandma Ruth told us.*

I had much to do at the cabin and soon was busy with my own chores. Nothing much was said about the hunters or Big Sam until midafternoon of the fifth day he was gone when he walked into my yard leading his horse laden with bear meat. "Hellooo the house!" he called and I knew his voice.

When I looked out, there he stood, his face with long scratches down the left side and his bloody shirt in tatters, one leg bare and the other covered with a bloody legging.

"Gotcha some bear meat." He grinned.

"Looks like you got more than that," I said. "Isn't it easier to *shoot* your meat rather than wrestle it to death?"

"S'pose so, but it isn't near so much fun."

He grinned sheepishly, tugging at the tattered shirt.

"Come in here and sit yourself down while I get some help. Where *are* those boys when you need them?" They appeared the third time I called. "Go tell Lydia and Laughing Brook that Samuel is here at my house and we need some help."

"Big Sam's back!" Riley yelled, starting for my cabin on the run.

"*Stop,* Riley, and go get your mother *right now!*" I called and the tone of my voice turned him around to follow Jesse up the path.

I turned to go to the house and there stood Sam Meeker on the porch grinning at me. "I said for you to get into the house, now git!" I ordered a little flustered and concerned. "Sit down on that stool while I get some cloths and hot water."

He obediently sat and began tugging at his shirt, trying to remove what was left of it. I quickly got some cloths and the kettle of hot water that always sat on the hearth. Mama's sewing basket was on the table and I cut the rest of the shirt off him with the scissors. The scratches on his face and chest didn't look too bad, just deep enough to draw blood, but there were four puncture wounds on the front and back of his right shoulder where the bear had gotten his teeth into him and they looked awful deep.

There were steps on the porch and Laughing Brook called, "Those packs look like they are really loaded with . . . oh my!" she exclaimed as she came through the door and beheld Big Sam sitting there.

"Good morning, Laughing Brook, how are you?" he said cheerfully. "I brought you some fine bear meat, but the old gal didn't want to come along with me." He grinned at her. The mauling didn't seem to affect him much and he shrugged offhandedly as we fussed and cleaned on him.

Jesse and Riley were wide-eyed and full of a thousand questions. "Boys, boys, that horse needs caring for," Lydia said over their din. "Go unload him and take him to the corral. He needs some feed and rubbing down. Big Sam will tell you all about it when we get him cleaned up!"

They just stood there watching until I stamped my foot and said, *"Go!"*

"The scratches on his face are OK, but we will have to stitch some of the ones on his chest," Laughing Brook said. She began to pull the ripped legging away and he quickly pulled it back over his hip.

"They're OK," he said.

"Don't be silly, Sam Meeker," Lydia said.

"We've all seen bare buttocks before and yours are no different, now let us see!"

He protested weakly, pink rising from his neck. I smiled to think that he was embarrassed.

"More stitches," Laughing Brook muttered, dabbing blood away from some deep gashes in his hip. The leg was not hurt much, just long scratches that had bled a lot, but the two middle and longest claws of the bear's paw had gone deeply into the skin of Big Sam's hip and they would need stitches. Fortunately, the wounds were clean and there wasn't much more than caked blood on them.

"Did you wash off after the wrestling, or were the scratches always this clean?" I asked.

"I was going to wash them, but it stung too much so I didn't until we crossed the river," he said. "They didn't get too dirty, since she never throwed me." He chuckled a little at that.

Laughing Brook was looking through the sewing box for needles and thread. She found a medium-sized needle and pulling a yard of white thread from its spool, threaded the needle. There was a beeswax candle on the table and she heated the needle, then drew the thread across the soft wax several times.

"I want to get the chest scratches stitched first, then we can do the hip," she said.

I stood by his side and dabbed away the blood so Laughing Brook could see where to put the stitches. Samuel barely flinched when she made a stitch, but I could feel his muscles tighten in his back where my hand rested. The deep scratches were from his shoulder to his pap, then they were only shallow scratches down across his ribs. One scratch required three stitches and the other one needed four.

"Now, if we stitch the hip as you sit, you won't be able to straighten out your leg," Laughing Brook said. "So you need to lie on the table and straighten your leg while I sew."

"Yes, doctor." Big Sam grinned. "Just so I don't become the main dish!"

Lydia had appeared with Rising Sun. After surveying the wreck, she laid the baby on my bed and returned. Her face was pale and her lips drawn into a tight line. "You'd be too tough for that!" she exclaimed.

Sam Meeker still didn't evidence a lot of pain as he sat on the edge of the table, then lay over on his side.

"Scoot to the other side of the table, Sam,

so I can reach the cuts better," Laughing Brook instructed. She walked around the table behind his back and began to work.

Jesse ran to the bedroom and returned with a pillow. "You think I could take a nap while those women work on my b-hind?" Sam grinned at him.

Riley had been watching all this wide-eyed, now he took the opportunity to ask, "Does it hurt, Big Sam?"

"No, not much, Riley, only when Grandmother sticks me with that needle."

"Grandma, don't stick so hard," Riley implored.

"I remember when all we had were bone needles, Riley, and they were big and they really hurt when they were used. This needle is a lot smaller and better." Although her hand was steady, I could tell by her pale face that she was tiring.

"Why don't you rest a little, Laughing Brook, and I can make some stitches?" I asked.

"I think that would be good," she said and handed me the needle.

"I am going to make some tea," Lydia said. "We will all need some when this is done."

So Laughing Brook sat on the stool across

from Sam, talking to him while I began to sew.

"Oowww! your hands are cold!" Sam flinched for the first time when I touched him.

"I'm sorry," I stammered, taking my hands off his buttocks.

He was laughing and, looking at Laughing Brook, asked, "Is she blushing?"

Laughing Brook smiled. "Maybe a little. Where did you get the bear?"

"I spent the first night at those stinking springs you told me about, then the next morning I went on south. I found her trail in the bottom between Round Mountain and the Sugar Loaf hill and tracked her around on the south side of Round Mountain where she was about to den up. Must be a cold snap coming. My shot was a long one and I didn't hit exactly where I wanted to. Naturally, that made us both mad and when I walked up, that possum-playing bear jumped up and said, 'What'd you do that for?' and slapped me across the face. That did it and we set to. While she was setting her teeth into my shoulder and clawing my b-hind, I stuck her in the heart with my knife. Guess I got the best of it, for she just lay down and died. I'm OK except for being sore and losing a lot of blood. I ate most of her liver and that should help with the blood loss. It took longer coming back than it did to get there. I guess the horse was slower with all that meat on his back."

"Not to mention the pace of his companion," Laughing Brook said.

Lydia's tea smelled good and I only had a few more stitches left. She hurried around and cut off steaks from one of the hams and soon had them frying in the skillets. Then she poured a large cup of hot tea and handed it to Laughing Brook with the honey. While she sipped the tea, Lydia brought another cup for Big Sam. When he reached for it, he pulled away from me a little.

"Be still!" I commanded, giving his backside a little slap.

"Now she's gone to beating me, Jesse!"

"Ma . . ." began Jesse.

"I only have one more stitch, Jesse, and I'll be done if someone would hold still for a minute!" When it was done, we all relaxed some. The steaks were ready and on plates.

"If it's OK with you, I think I'll just eat here," Big Sam said.

"Oh no, you won't!" Lydia and I said in unison.

Slowly and carefully, he rolled off the table and stood up. He took a step or two then said, "Now I can't bend my leg for the stitches but it does feel better."

Suddenly we all realized that he was standing there in nothing but his breech-clout and moccasins. What a grand sight he was!

"Jesse, get Big Sam a blanket from the shelf," I said. I turned away, pretending to be busy helping with the meal. Still, when I think of him after all these years, that vision comes into my mind.

*"Grandma Ruth usually paused here in her story and she never told it without blushing,"* Zenas said and chuckled.

Our breakfast consisted only of bear steaks, bread, and the hot tea. Big Sam started to sit down on the stool and grunted. "If you don't mind, ladies, I think I will eat standing, since I can't bend this hip any." And he did. In fact, for several days he either stood or lay on his side because of the stitches in his hip.

"We should put a poultice on those scratches so they won't fester," Laughing Brook said as we ate.

"There's some trout lily growing down by the creek. I'll gather some leaves for a poultice," I said.

52

"Don't we have some slippery elm powder at your house, Mother?" Lydia asked.

"Yes, we do," she replied. "We can make the poultice out of the powder and wrap the trout lily leaves over it if there are enough leaves."

"I'll gather the leaves after breakfast and we will see if there is enough."

"Now wait on there," Big Sam said. "You aren't going to wrap me up in some stinking stuff the hogs won't stand, are you?"

"It doesn't smell bad and it will help you heal and prevent infection," Laughing Brook said.

"Even if it did smell, you would have to wear it if we said so," Lydia retorted. "If we didn't like it, we would send you outside to stay," she sniffed.

We busied ourselves cleaning up the table and scattered to gather up the medicines and wrapping cloths. When we met back at the cabin, Big Sam had disappeared. The boys had been off on some adventure and they didn't know where he was, either. After some searching, I went into my bedroom, and there he was in my bed asleep.

Lydia giggled. "Well, that's a nice present to find in your bed, Ruthie," she whispered.

We left him there and he slept most of the day while we worked up the bear meat and skin he had brought back.

When he awoke, I fed him some sage hen broth and he soon fell asleep again and slept through the night. Laughing Brook sat with me until late in the night. She was pleased that Big Sam didn't have any fever, "He's strong and healthy, I don't think he will have any problems healing," she said. "The hard part will be making him sit still long enough to heal!"

Jesse had laid his bedroll out by the fire and soon after Laughing Brook left, I stoked the fire and lay down beside him and slept.

I had finished milking and was cooking some breakfast when little feet clattered across the porch and Riley burst through the door. "It's snowing, Jesse, get up, get up!" He was dancing from Jesse's pallet to the door and back. Jesse sprang from the covers and sprinted to the door.

"Don't you go out there barefooted, Jesse," I called futilely. In a moment they came bouncing and shivering back with Sippie shaking snow and moisture from his coat.

"Ma, why didn't you get me up when you saw the snow?" he complained.

"Because I didn't know it was snowing much until Riley told us."

Riley suddenly had a thought and ran to

the bedroom before I could stop him. "It's snowing, Big Sam, it's snowing!" he shouted.

"Great!" Sam's voice boomed. "Now we can track rabbits and foxes! Do you have a bow?"

"Sure I do, and arrows, too! Jesse has his own and we hunt all the time!"

"Good, let's get some breakfast and we'll go hunting." Big Sam came through the door pulling his blanket around him. "Good morning, Ruth," he called as he limped across the floor. "I swear I could walk better before you women stitched me up."

"Yes, and you bled a lot more, too."

He looked well, maybe a little better than he did before his long nap, and when I felt his brow, it was cool; no fever was a good sign. "Let me see your shoulder . . ." I pulled the blanket off the right shoulder to look at the puncture wounds, "Just a little bit of bleeding, but now it's dry." We hadn't treated them and I was concerned. They didn't look very good, red and seeping and a little swollen. The blanket had stuck to his back and I had to peel it off. For the first time, I noticed the two arcs of bruises that ran from puncture to puncture where the bear's other teeth had pressed the skin but hadn't broken through. There was the edge of a bruise peeking out from under his arm and when I lifted his arm there was a large ugly black and purple bruise across his ribs. He stood quietly while I pulled the blanket off his back, revealing several more bruises. I touched one lightly and he winced.

"We had a good match there for a while," he grinned at me.

"I thought you said she didn't throw you."

"She didn't throw me *after* she clawed me," he corrected.

"That must be the male ego," I sniffed. "Did she break any ribs?"

"I didn't find any when I dressed her."

"I mean *your* ribs!"

He grinned, "Doesn't feel like it — I guess not."

"Boy, Big Sam, you shore got a lot of bumps!" said a wide-eyed Jesse.

"I suppose that isn't all of them, Jesse, we never have looked at his right leg."

"Oh they are just bruises anyway," Big Sam said, shrugging his blanket back across his shoulders. "I'm hungry!"

I had forgotten the bacon and it was done to a crisp. "Drink some of this broth while I finish up. Riley, have you eaten?"

"No, Aunt Ruthie, Ma and Grandma are making Big Sam's poultice."

Big Sam groaned, "I don't need any . . ."

"Hush and drink your broth," I interrupted.

He started to sit down and winced, "Blasted stitches."

"Be careful, if they pull out, they will hurt a lot more," I warned.

He stood a moment, then spying the pallet still lying by the fireplace, hobbled over and holding his left leg straight out, lowered himself with his right and eased on to the floor. "There," he said with a sigh. "Riley, hand me that cup of broth."

We were still eating when Lydia and Laughing Brook came in with their poultice. They went right to work on the protesting patient and by the time I had their breakfast ready, they had finished.

"Get your bow, Jesse, we're going rabbit hunting with Big Sam!" Riley called as he headed for the door.

"Hold on there, young man!" Lydia called. "Have you looked out at that snow lately? It's so thick you can't see our cabin, and there is a coating of ice under that. The rabbits won't be out until this ends and neither will you!"

"But Ma . . ."

"Look for yourself, Riley, and Big Sam isn't going anywhere until he is better!"

"Awww," Jesse groaned.

"Sure is a bossy bunch of women, aren't they, boys?" Sam grinned.

"That's right, and you better know it," said Lydia.

I had to laugh. "Sam Meeker, you couldn't walk across the room without grunting, much less run around out there in the brush chasing rabbits. I think you boys had better think of something to do inside for today."

There were more complaints, but one look outside at the snow and they were happy to sit by the fire and play and talk to Big Sam. It wasn't long before all three were laughing and cutting up. Sippie lay by the warm hearth and watched contentedly.

We had much to do to work up the bear skin into a robe and being too cold and snowy outside, we decided to do it by the fire. While Lydia and I worked on it, Laughing Brook began sewing on a legging to replace Big Sam's ruined one.

Using it for a pattern, she commented, "My, you have big legs, Sam, I hope I have enough leather here to make another."

"Sometimes, we have to sew a seam down both sides if the hides aren't generous," he replied, looking up from entertaining the boys.

It was a quiet day, with everyone busy and cozy in the cabin. Lydia commented on how

58

tight and well-built the cabin was and I was proud of the job Jerry had done.

Big Sam didn't complain about the inactivity and in the afternoon he slept a couple of hours. When he awoke, he rose stiffly and hobbled around the room a few times to "shake the kinks out" and tease us as we worked. After supper he made as to sleep on the pallet, but I made him go to the bed, saying that Jesse and I would sleep by the fire so I wouldn't disturb him when I put wood on the fire. It was very cold and the snow continued heavy all night and all the next day. About midafternoon the men came in from the hunt, tired and half frozen. We got the horses unloaded and in the shed. Lonza and Sam had a joyous meeting and we settled down to a meal of hot stew and cornbread with cold milk. It was good to have the men home and safe.

Big Sam Meeker healed quickly, a good sign of his health and vitality. We treated the puncture wounds of the teeth with special care, since they were most likely to fester. They seeped for several days, then finally healed up and left four dimples in his shoulder. It was two weeks before we would let him take the stitches out. I looked up from cooking dinner one day because the men were being unusually quiet and found Big Sam cutting the stitches and pulling the threads out of his chest. He couldn't get to the ones in his hip, though, and Lonza and Jerry refused to do it for him out of orneriness. He tried to convince Riley and Jesse to do it, but they tried to take the first one out without cutting it. When Jesse laid the knife on top of the first stitch and started sawing, Big Sam quickly put an end to their helping and had to settle for us women removing the stitches to the merriment and many smart remarks from Lonza and Jerry. The scratches faded and in time the scars on his chest grew dimmer, but never quite disappeared. The scars on his hip never faded. Of course, being the active man he was, there were other scars accumulated over the succeeding years.

Sam and Jerry became close friends and I found Sam at my table as much as he was at Lydia's. Little by little, we told him the story of our experiences with the pirates and the shakes and he told us of his life in the east.

It seems that some enterprising mother had her eye on him as the one to marry her daughter. After avoiding the net she cast to trap him and having to whip her "outraged" sons, he got a big yearning to travel west

and visit his friends rather than to become
the one man side of a feud. Many years later
he met the daughter in Indian Territory. She
had married, had children, and had survived
the Trail of Tears to settle in the Cherokee
Nation.

I suppose it was natural that I would be
drawn to Samuel Meeker, being thrown so
close together as we were. In the spring of
1815 he began to earnestly court me, but I
was reluctant to commit myself to him. It
wasn't that I wasn't attracted to him, quite
the opposite, and Jesse loved him too. But I
was concerned about how Jerry would feel
with another man involved in our household. Other would-be suitors from the village had called from time to time, but I had
no special feelings for any of them.

It all came to a head one day in the early
fall when White Wolf appeared at our door.
In spite of the personal danger, he had come
to visit us. They had reached his people
safely after parting with us and his wife and
mother were doing well. Little Chief had
grown and become quite the helper for his
mother, who was expecting their second
child soon. We had a good visit and after a
few days, Jerry came to me and said White
Wolf had invited him to stay with them for

a while. I was taken aback, for although they had talked about it on the trail, I had not taken it seriously and the thought of being separated from Jerry after all we had gone through together was a jolt. It troubled me for several days and Big Sam noticed my mood.

"Something's wrong, Ruthie, what is it?" he asked.

"White Wolf has invited Jerry to return to Swan Creek with him and he wants to go," I said, near tears.

I remember he was quiet for a few moments, then he said, "I guess that would be the first time you two would be separated, wouldn't it?"

"For any length of time, yes, and I don't know if I could take that very easily."

"You have almost been a mother to him for a long time, and there is one thing you must learn as a mother." After a pause for a moment or two, he went on, "A successful mother has to know when the time is right to turn loose."

With that, he got up and gave me one of his big smothering hugs and left. I thought about what he said and sat and cried for a long time. I was cooking supper when Laughing Brook came to visit and noticed my red eyes and wrinkled apron soaked with tears. "Are you still struggling with Jerry wanting to leave with White Wolf?" she asked.

"Yes, and I suppose it is mostly selfishness on my part, we have been through so much together."

"You have and it's no wonder you feel the way you do. I understand." After a few minutes of talking about the fall harvests and what we would do the next few days, she said, "Ruth, I have been where you are several times with my children. When it came time for them to go out on their own, I was never ready, but very early in our family life, I realized that all of raising children was a process of turning loose. You turn loose of them when they take their first steps alone, you turn loose when they stop nursing and eat food from the table, you turn loose when the boys begin to learn the skills of a man, and on and on. Gradually, that child acquires the ability to stand alone and that is the purpose of it all. Though my children are gone from my house, we are still close and they still love me as I love them. Part of my satisfaction in this world is that I have grown children who are able to take care of themselves and their families with the things I have taught them. Jerry has had to grow up fast and it has been hard for both of you. Now, he's a grown young man that I suspect you depend on more than he depends on you and that's good. It's natural that he should want to try life on his own even though it hurts us to let him go."

"Do you think I am being selfish, Grandmother?"

"No, not at all. In fact, I think that it would be sad if you *didn't* feel the way you do. Some things in life don't feel good, but are necessary. This is one of those times for you."

With that, she gave my arm a pat and made her departure. I was close to tears again, but I realized that what she had said was almost what Sam had said and that they were both right. Over the next few days, I gradually accepted the fact that Jerry needed his independence and made peace with it.

Big Sam and White Wolf had gone off with Wash to look at some horses they were thinking about trading for, and Jerry, Jesse, and I had the house to ourselves for a rare evening.

Jerry was sharpening his knife on the porch and Jesse was playing with Sippie in the yard. I finished the dishes and came out to sit and cool a bit before bedtime.

"When do you and White Wolf plan to

leave for the north?" I asked.

Jerry stopped honing for a moment and without looking up (if he had, I would have cried) said, "We haven't decided yet, but we think we will take the long hunt with the family, then part when the hunt is over."

"That makes sense," I said. "You will need provisions for the winter same as we will." I tried to sound as casual as possible. "Lydia and I are going this year and Laughing Brook will stay and care for Rising Sun. Wash will care for the stock and look after the farms."

"I think you will enjoy it, though it is a lot of work," he said, smiling. "When the women come with us, they say it is much more productive and easier."

"I suppose so, has anyone said when we will start?"

"No," he said rising, "but I should think it won't be long now." He smiled and it was as though a weight had been lifted from his shoulders.

"I can leave knowing you and Jesse will be safe and cared for here, but I don't plan to stay up there. This is where I have a home."

"Always," I whispered.

He laid his hand on my shoulder and patted softly as we watched dog and boy romp in the fading light. I was glad the light was dim, for there was a tear trickling down my cheek.

# CHAPTER 4
# A PROPOSAL

A week later as I was resting on the porch after washday chores, Lonza walked over and sat on the step, looking out at the valley and the river bottoms. He didn't say anything for a few minutes and I was quiet. It was very unusual for him to speak to me in private because he avoided anything that might look improper between us. At last he turned to me and said, "Ruth, Sam Meeker has asked Laughing Brook for your hand in marriage."

At first, I felt the blood rush from my face, then I felt flushed and hot. It took me a minute to gather my wits. "Why would he do that without consulting me?" I asked.

Lonza looked surprised, then he said slowly, "I suppose he is trying to follow the custom of our people as much as possible."

I began to fan myself furiously. "And he sought permission from Laughing Brook because she is the clan mother?"

"Yes. Laughing Brook came to Jerry and I because she didn't know if you felt she was your clan mother and because Jerry is your nearest male kin and I am distantly related to you — and care greatly for your welfare," he added. "Jerry has asked me to talk to you."

I thought for a few moments and my temper cooled. "Thank you, Lonza. I am honored that you feel that way toward us and I would be honored for Laughing Brook to be my clan mother if she also consents. However, after the Cherokee customs, there are others that I am acquainted with and I wish to reserve my decision for Sam Meeker's ears alone, will that be acceptable?"

He was visibly relieved. "That would be *most* acceptable to me and to Laughing Brook," he said with a smile. "I will relay your message to Sam."

A few minutes after Lonza had left, Lydia and Laughing Brook appeared on the path. Both were beaming happily and I rose to meet them.

"It is an honor to us that you want me to be your clan mother," Laughing Brook said as she hugged me.

"I am honored that you have accepted us into your clan," I replied. "Lydia has become as close as a sister to me."

We sat on the porch and rocked and talked for a while.

"Should I give your consent to Sam Meeker?" Laughing Brook asked after a few minutes.

"No, Grandmother, I have told Lonza that Sam should come to me with his proposal after the white man's custom. But I would like you to stand with me in the traditional Cherokee wedding ceremony. That is the way my mother was married and I would wish for the same."

"That is wise, Ruth, and I will be glad to be your clan mother at the wedding."

Lydia fairly danced out of her chair. "So you intend to say yes to his proposal! This is so exciting I can hardly stand it!"

"Oh, please don't tell anyone until Sam talks to me!" I begged, but I knew my request was futile. "I should be the one who decides who I will marry and the man I marry will have to treat me as a person with my own will, then I will give him my answer." I hadn't wanted to let my intentions be known before Sam came to me, but there it was. Lydia would not be able to hide her feelings from Lonza; neither could Lonza hide the knowledge from Big Sam or Jerry.

Laughing Brook nodded hesitantly. This was certainly not the Cherokee custom. The white man had such strange ideas, but she was willing to allow me to have my way in the matter, so long as it did not violate any of the tribe's taboos. I had to act quickly now to avoid more confusion and risk hurting people's feelings.

"Where is Big Sam?" I asked.

"He has gone to Standing Bear's to buy a horse. I should think he is on his way home by now," Lydia replied.

"I will meet him, watch Jesse for me while I'm gone, please." I said this to make plain that I was going to meet Sam Meeker *alone.* In her state of excitement, Lydia was likely to come tripping after me.

I hurried down the dusty road and it wasn't until I stepped on the locust thorn that I realized that I was barefooted. I had slipped my moccasins off when I sat down and in my haste and excitement I forgot to put them back on. It was too late, I could not return now. I hobbled over to the side of the path and sat on a log. Lifting my skirt, I lay my foot on my knee and pulled at the thorn. It was buried deep and hurt like blazes. I pulled harder, but it wouldn't budge. I tried again only to feel the pain shoot up my foot like fire.

"Oh, damnation!" I cried out loud and worked all the more furiously with that stubborn thorn.

"What's the trouble, Ruthie?"

There was Sam Meeker not a hundred feet away, leading a pretty white pony. Quickly I covered my legs, but it was too late, he had seen, his grin told me.

"I stepped on your brother the thorn and he won't come out of my foot."

"Why would he be my brother?" The grin only broadened.

*"Because you're a thorn in my side, that's why!"* I was near tears from pain, anger, and dismay all boiling up inside me. "If you wanted to marry me, why didn't you ask *me* first instead of everybody else in the world? Did you talk to Riley and Jesse, too?"

"Well, I did talk to Jesse a little . . ."

I jumped up. *"SAM MEEKER!"* I shouted. He blinked and stepped back. The pony jumped at the noise and took a step or two backwards. *"Am I some old item you want to buy from everybody without any say-so in the matter?"*

"Why, no, Ruth, I . . ."

"You *did*! You talked to every person in the world but the one you should have been talking to, and that's *ME*!" I was so mad, I stomped my foot and drove that blasted thorn into my foot more. I almost fainted.

Before I was aware, I was back on the log

and Big Sam was sitting beside me and had his arm around my shoulders.

"Let's see that foot." He lifted my leg by the ankle before I could protest. "My word, Ruthie, that's a big thorn! What are you doing out here barefooted, anyway? Be still, I'm going to pull it out!" He gave a tug and it didn't budge, then with his mouth set in determination, he grasped my foot with one hand and the thorn with the other and pulled until it slipped out. A trickle of blood dripped off my heel into the dust.

"No wonder it didn't want to come, the point was hooked." He squeezed my foot hard and the pain subsided. "Just let it bleed some and we will bandage it when we get to the cabins." He lifted me as if I were nothing and set me on the horse's bare back sidesaddle. The horse shied a little.

"He's not used to this sidesaddle thing, but he's gentle enough." He looked up into my eyes and asked, "Now what is this you are so upset about?"

I gripped his shoulders and shook him a little, "Why didn't you ask me to marry you first before you asked everyone else in the world? I shouldn't be surprised if you asked Sippie too."

"Oh, I asked him first," he grinned. "Besides, I knew what you would say without asking."

"Oh, you did, did you? Well, I have something to say to you, Sam Mee . . ."

"Shush, Ruthie," he put his finger to my mouth, "You know I love you and I know you love me, now what can be so bad about that? If saying the words makes you feel better, I'll say them; Ruth Fourkiller will you have me as your husband in good and bad, bears and thorns, and cornfields and kitchens?"

I caught my breath and felt dizzy. It must have been the thorn. With my eyes closed, I lay my head on his forehead, "Yes, Samuel Meeker, I will marry you!" I whispered.

He slipped his arms around my waist and we stayed there just like that a long time, until the horse moved. "Snowflake wants to be getting on to her new home," Big Sam said, releasing me and taking up the halter rope. "I bought her for a wedding gift and almost didn't have anyone to give her to, but now I've got you!" He skipped a step as he led down the path.

I felt light-headed and hung on to Snowflake's mane. *It must be the thorn,* I thought, but I knew it wasn't.

No one was at the Fourkiller cabin and when we rounded the corner in the path, there they all sat on our porch. "Ruth, you forgot your shoes." Lydia scooped them up and started down the step. "What a beautiful pony, Sam" — she spied a drop of blood clinging to the end of my toe — "Oh Ruthie, you've stepped on something!"

"She stepped on a thorn and still has one in her side," Big Sam grinned.

"In your side, Ruth? How . . ."

"Yes, in my side, and I would guess he weighs about a hundred stone!"

"Ohh, you tease me —" she started, then her eyes got big. "He's asked you!"

"Nooo, more like *she* told *me*!" Sam picked me up like a child and carried me to a chair on the porch.

They gathered around us, all talking at once. I glimpsed Wash Fishinghawk rocking in his chair, pulling on his pipe and smiling.

Snowflake began grazing across the lawn. "Riley, will you catch up that horse before she grazes all the way to the river? Bring her up here."

Snowflake followed the child patiently. *She is such a gentle pony,* I thought.

"Jesse," Big Sam's voice boomed, "Ruth has asked me if I will be your father and I have consented to do so!"

"Hoo-ray!" the boys jumped up and down in glee. There was no way I could correct his joke, so I just sat there blushing and smiling while the clan gathered around and congratulated us. Sam was beaming and Jerry, White Wolf, and Lonza were shaking his hand. Lydia flung her arms around my neck. "This is so wonderful." She wiped tears from her eyes.

Laughing Brook was standing beside Wash's chair with her hand on his shoulder. They were both smiling. "We must have a celebration!" Wash called over the noise. "Tomorrow is a holiday and we will eat dinner under the arbor!"

"That's good, Father," Lydia called, "and Ruth and Sam are the guests of honor!"

"First of all, we have to see to that foot," Laughing Brook said, pointing to the little splashes of blood on the stones. "Jesse, can you pick me a couple of trout lily leaves from the spring? Lydia, find us some wrapping and a stocking to put over it."

Soon the bandage was in place and one of Jerry's stockings covered my foot. Just the pressure of the bandage made it feel better.

"The sun is behind the hills and I haven't milked." I started to rise.

"You just sit there, Ruth. I will milk for you tonight." Jerry hurried off to fetch the bucket. "Riley and Jesse, put the pony in the corral."

"I will fix us a bite to eat," Lydia called from the path, and Laughing Brook followed.

It was just Wash and I sitting and rocking. He pulled on his pipe and the pungent smell of the tobacco tickled my nose.

"I wish you and Samuel a joyous life," he said. "You won't know what a valuable companion you have until you have spent many winters with him as I have with Laughing Brook."

"Thank you, Grandfather." It was all I could say at the moment, my heart was so full.

The next day was one of the most memorable in my life. Everyone was so happy and excited and everything was perfect. White Wolf and Jerry must have been up well before daylight, for they returned about midmorning with two fine tom turkeys. Lonza appeared with a huge hunk of buffalo hump meat and ribs that must have cost him dearly.

We didn't eat until midafternoon and most of the village must have come. Each brought a dish and there was twice enough food for the crowd. A wedding was an event for great celebration for the whole village and the end of summer just before the long hunts began was a very good time for celebration. Big Sam carried my chair to the arbor early and I was made to sit and watch and greet the visitors as they arrived. My foot was sore and it hurt to walk or stand on it, but most of the day I didn't feel it at all. Big Sam's grin never left his face and he was everywhere greeting people and being congratulated or teased by all. We talked to the village priest about setting a day for the wedding. Since the time of the long hunt was very near and people would be pressed to leave as soon as they could, it was decided that the wedding should be as soon as possible. The ceremony would be held in the town house and the sacred spot would have to be blessed by the priest for seven days prior to the wedding, so it was decided to have the ceremony in eight days, which was October 15, Jesse's birthday. This was agreeable with all and more than one hunt was postponed until after the wedding. It was near sundown before the last guest left and quiet settled over the arbor. Even the boys had left to drive in Bossy and the horses.

As the excitement subsided, my foot began to throb and Lydia said I looked pale. Big Sam overheard her and insisted on carrying me back to the cabin. He swooped me up and carried me to the porch where he deposited me on the bench by the door and sat down close. "Well, Ruth, how did you like your holiday?"

"It was wonderful, Sam, how did you like it?"

"Great! I didn't expect so many people, did you?"

"No, but Lydia told me that Wash asked Lonza to go into the village and have the Crier announce the feast last night."

"So that's how so many knew about it! I was wondering how the word got around."

"Sam, can we change Jesse's name to Meeker?"

"Why, yes, Ruth, that would be fine with me." He sounded a little surprised.

"His father was not a good man and I would like to wipe his memory out of our lives forever."

We sat quietly for a few minutes, watching the dusk fall over the river bottoms.

"Ruth, I want you to know that I will do everything I can to make you happy."

"I know you will, Sam, and I couldn't be happier than I am right now." I laid my head on his shoulder. He was so strong. We sat like that until a storm came around the corner sloshing milk and fussing at Sippie.

"Jesse, be careful with that milk!" I called.

"Yes, Ma. Sippie was trying to drink out of the bucket." He panted, as he plopped the bucket on the bench and spilled more. Sippie eagerly began licking it up.

"Ma, is Big Sam going to be my pa now?"

"Yes, is that OK with you?"

His face brightened. "Yes, I told him to go ahead and ask you, it was all right with me."

I elbowed Sam sharply in the ribs so that he grunted.

"Well, thank you for your permission, Jesse. Do you remember your father?"

He made a face, "He wasn't *my* father, he was *mean!*"

"Well, do you think when we marry that you would like to change your name to Sam's if he says that is good with him?"

"You mean I would be Sam instead of Jesse?"

"No, she means you would be Jesse Meeker," Sam said.

"We could stand only one Sam in this family." I laughed.

"Would that be all right with you, Big Sam?" Jesse had a quizzical look on his face.

"Yes, Jesse, that will be fine with me."

"And Ma's name would be Ruth Meeker?" He shrugged his shoulders, holding his hands out, palms up.

"We can do that — Ma, can I go tell Riley?"

"Yes, you may, but come right back here, it's bedtime." I had to raise my voice to be heard as he disappeared down the path.

Sam chuckled. "They're full of life, aren't they?"

"Ohhh, yes." I sighed, picking up the milk bucket and limping inside. "I am not hungry, Sam, but I can fix you something if you are."

"No, I'm not very hungry," he said, taking the bucket and setting it on the table. "This is all I will need to tide me over until morning." Then he kissed me full on the lips for the first time.

# CHAPTER 5
## A CHEROKEE WEDDING

*October 15, 1815*

The next seven days were a blur of activity, a hundred things had to be done, the most important of all being the making of three dresses for the wedding. From somewhere, Lydia produced her wedding dress. It was a beautiful white deerskin with fringed hem and beaded designs sewed on it. It fit me well, though I was some taller. Laughing Brook produced a white fringe that we sewed on the inside of the skirt that made it long enough and didn't detract from the overall effect. It was no trouble getting the other dresses ready, Laughing Brook wearing the costume of the clan mother, and Lydia wearing a new dress of silk she had purchased when in the east. I wondered about Sam's clothes, but Lydia said that he was taking care of that, so I didn't worry. I didn't see much of him. He spent a lot of time in the village (having a suit made by

Speaks Softly, I later learned). They were also preparing for the hunt. We were to leave the day after the wedding, along with the rest of the village.

It seemed that the hours flew by, but the days lasted forever. I don't think I slept half of the night before the wedding day and I was up well before daylight with a thousand little things to be done. The men, except for Jerry, had left for the village early, thankfully taking Riley and Jesse with them. Midmorning one of the young girls from the village arrived and took Rising Sun in hand. An hour before high noon, we were ready. Jerry appeared at the door leading Snowflake. He handed me a large ear of dried corn and I wrapped it in the dyed corn shucks we had made for it. I was supposed to ride Snowflake, but for fear of mussing my dress, I walked and Jerry led the horse.

The day was gloriously bright and still, the hills striped with a thousand colors of leaves. I remember it was pleasantly warm and there were little puffs of dust where we stepped in the path. We stopped at Speaks Softly's cabin to freshen up and wait until just before high noon to enter the town house.

When it was time, the women wrapped

me in a blue blanket. Laughing Brook led the procession with me following and Jerry behind me. We entered the town house at the same time that Sam, wrapped in a blue blanket and accompanied by Lydia in the stead of his mother, entered from the other end of the building. Down aisles made through the village witnesses, we met at the sacred spot before the sacred fire.

Sam gave me a ham of venison wrapped in deerskin. This was to symbolize his intention to keep meat in the household. I gave him the ear of corn symbolizing that I would be a good housewife.

Laughing Brook stood on my right as the clan mother indicated her approval and that the wedding was legal according to tribal customs. Jerry stood on my left as his vow to take the responsibility of teaching the children of this union in spiritual and religious matters, as is the traditional role of the uncle.

The priest blessed us, removed the two blue blankets, and wrapped us together in one white blanket. Then he blessed all the rest in the wedding party. Last, he blessed all the guests.

It was my request that, at this point in the ceremony, Lonza would read from the Bible. At the priest's nod, Lonza stood, reading from Pa's Bible, Genesis, Chapter 2, Verses 18 through 24:

*Then the Lord God said, "It is not good that the man should be alone; I will make him a helper fit for him." So out of the ground the Lord God formed every beast of the field and every bird of the air, and brought them to the man to see what he would call them; and whatever the man called every living creature, that was its name.*

*The man gave names to all cattle, and to the birds of the air, and to every beast of the field; but for the man there was not found a helper fit for him. So the Lord God caused a deep sleep to fall upon the man, and while he slept took one of his ribs and closed up its place with flesh; and the rib which the Lord God had taken from the man he made into a woman and brought her to the man.*

*Then the man said, "This at last is bone of my bones and flesh of my flesh; she shall be called Woman, because she was taken out of Man."*

*Therefore a man leaves his father and his mother and cleaves to his wife, and they become one flesh.*

Then a young woman stood on one side

of the town house and sang a Cherokee love song. A young man on the other side of the guests stood and replied in song. Another song was sung and the guests joined in. At the end of the singing, the guests stood and the priest gave the traditional final blessing to the couple:

Now you will feel no rain
for each of you will be shelter for the other
Now there is no loneliness
Now you are two persons
but there is only one life before you
Go now to your dwelling to enter into the
days of your life together and may your
  days
be good and long upon the earth.

Then the priest handed me the wedding vase and Sam and I drank from its two spouts at the same time. The priest removed the white blanket from us and Sam took both of my hands in his. I had never seen him so resplendent in his wedding suit and it took my breath. He looked me in the eyes and smiled. To the guests he said in his booming voice, "This is my wife, flesh of my flesh, whoever harms her harms me, whoever loves me must love her. I am her shelter." Then taking Jesse and holding him high, he said, "I now take this boy as my son. From this day forward he shall be called Jesse Meeker. Now, let's celebrate!"

And celebrate we did! The rising sun found many of the guests still singing and dancing and feasting. In spite of their plans, very few clans left the Village on Middle Fork for the hunt that day, certainly not the Fishinghawk clan.

*"That's how th' Finns came to be called Meeker, an' none of us has ever complained about it," Zenas added. "Sam Meeker was as good a man as Tom Finn was bad. No doubt he loved Grandma Ruth dearly and they had a happy an' eventful life together, raisin' six kids of their own, three boys an' three girls, plus an orphan or two along th' way."*

# CHAPTER 6
# THE LAST LONG HUNT
# 1815

The men had determined to go into the White River drainage north and somewhat east of the village. They thought the game would be plentiful and it would also be convenient for Jerry and White Wolf to get to the Fallen Ash Trail going northwest. We started out up Middle Fork early the second day after the wedding, Laughing Brook holding little Rising Sun and waving good-bye and Sippie howling unhappily on the end of a rope tied firmly to a post.

There were several families following the same trail and we enjoyed traveling and visiting with them. The men were most interested in the hunting, and discussed places and the prospects for a good hunt. They learned where each clan was planning to hunt and adjusted their own plans so as not to interfere with each other. At the same time, knowing where each clan might be would be a great help in case of accidents or need for defense against competing hunters from other tribes, especially the Osage, Delaware, Kickapoo, and others who made their homes on the upper White River country. Considerable friction was building over who controlled the Ozarks hunting grounds. There were very few settlements within the hills and none of them were permanent save for the Village at the Forks, Middle Fork Village, and the settlement at Bear Creek Springs. Being nearer to the White River tribes, the Bear Creek settlement was subject to considerable harassment.

Our neighbors were wary of White Wolf, concerned that he might be a spy or up to some other tricks, but Lonza assured them that White Wolf was visiting as a friend and posed no threat.

The boys were jubilant to be going. They had insisted on packing their own things and Lydia and I secretly went through their packs and eliminated unnecessary baggage. Separately, we supplemented their packs with the items necessary to take for them, like clothing and warm blankets. They were charged with the care of their packs and their own horse, a gentle old pony that they rode together, taking turns riding in front and holding the reins.

We camped the first night at the mouth of Meadow Creek, several families sharing the camp, and we had a good time visiting. Several boys from the village were in this camp and as to be expected, they got into mischief stirring up the hives in the Bee Bluff above camp. One of the men in camp guessed the trouble when they heard the yells and saw the boys racing down the hill. "Bees coming to camp!" he called and everyone dove for cover. In a moment, campfires and food were abandoned and all that could be seen of the camp occupants were lumps under blankets and robes, trying desperately to make their refuges bee-proof. Sam had grabbed a blanket and tucked it around us as we sat on the ground near our fire. He was laughing uncontrollably and I could hardly keep myself covered.

"Bees! Bees are after us!" a half-dozen panicked voices called running into camp. "Jump in the creek!" "Run for the creek!" a dozen muffled blankets called back. "Duck under!" the advisers called. There was the patter of feet followed by splashing and more yells as the cold water took effect.

Somewhere a muffled voice yelped as a bee found a crack in the victim's defenses. "Wait until I get ahold of that boy!" a nearby robe swore.

"You'll have to wait your turn, I'm first," another lump under a blanket growled.

"Ouch! Cover me up and quit wiggling!" came from farther away.

"I can't stay under forever," came a plaintive call from the creek.

"You might after I get ahold of you!" an irate mother replied from somewhere near.

"It's coooolld!"

"Do you want cold water or stings?"

"Go 'way, bees, go 'way!" I could hear Jesse's voice among the others.

"Duck under and hold your breath, Jesse," I called.

A few seconds later, he called back, "They're still here, Ma!"

"Hold your breath longer," Big Sam called between laughs.

Still the angry bees persisted and the boys yelled and Big Sam laughed.

"If you're going to sit there and laugh, Sam Meeker, *I'll* go help them," I said, standing up with the blanket still over my head.

"Hey, come back with that blanket!" he called, but I was well on my way to the rescue. Before I got there, Sam passed me. Wading into the water, he scooped up Riley and Jesse and continued on across the creek. I felt a sting on my leg, then another. They had found me, so I sat down and covered myself again.

Through a small crack, I watched Sam and the boys. When he got out of the water, he ran a few steps, and turned around holding the boys in his arms and talking quietly. "See, there is one crawling on my arm," I heard him say, "but I'm not afraid and not moving, so he won't sting me, but he'll go find someone who's afraid and sting him. There he goes, no sting. Now, don't show fear and don't move and they will go away." They all three were motionless, not moving a hair.

Several people were throwing damp leaves on the fires, making smoke billow and sending the bees away.

"Look, Big Sam, they are going away!" Riley exclaimed.

"Sure, they are," Sam replied and moved back across the creek, a boy in each arm. "Now let's see how many coups those bees counted on you boys."

"I got stung a hundred times, but not once after I wasn't scared," Jesse exclaimed. A tear had streaked his cheek and he wiped it away impatiently.

"I bet *I* got *two* hundred stings," Riley bragged.

"We'll see, boys." Sam sat them down and Lydia and I began stripping them off. A few dying bees fell out of their clothes and they both had a dozen or more stings. We pulled the stingers out that we could find and daubed them with mud Lonza had brought from the river bank. The boys began counting mud spots on their bodies for bragging rights. A nod and wink from Lydia told me what she was doing and by the time we had quit daubing and they had quit counting, they had the identical number of stings.

"Wow, Riley, you got as many as I did."

"Yeah, I guess they knew we didn't start the war and went easy on us."

Jesse's eye was swelling shut and there was a big knot on Riley's ear. Lydia was combing bees out of his hair and I found several in Jesse's. We tried to get the stingers out of their heads, but I'm sure their hair hid several we couldn't find.

Looking around, I saw others going through the same de-stingering process on other boys. It was unusually quiet as everybody concentrated on the job at hand. Lonza and Sam came up from the river carrying several willow switches apiece. Jesse squirmed uncomfortably at the sight. "No, Jesse, these are not for switching, they're for medicine." Big Sam smiled.

I broke off the tender end of one of the switches. "Here, chew this up good. When you're finished with it, spit it out and I'll give you another," I said. Soon, all the boy victims of the bees were chewing on the willow stems and not a few of the rest of us were too. The camp quieted down and we sat down to eat our meal.

"Riley, what possessed you boys to stir up those bees, anyway?" Lydia asked.

"Little Fox dared Jesse to step on the bees coming out of a hole in the rock, but he wouldn't do it, so Cub Bear did, only he forgot he was barefooted and they stung him all over his feet, then the bees started coming out all over us and we ran."

"Is that Cub sitting by the creek with his feet in the water?" I asked.

"Yes, Aunt Ruth, his feet hurt awful bad and he had to run down here on them."

"I wonder how much honey is up there," Big Sam said thoughtfully.

"We could use some for the winter," I said.

"I'm not sure it would be worth the trouble, now that they are stirred up. They won't be in a good mood for a few days now," Lonza said.

"I have robbed many hives without getting stung," White Wolf said. "I will be glad to get you some honey, Ruth, if you wish."

Cub Bear's father was nearby and over-heard the conversation "There would be plenty of honey up there for all of us and the bees, but they are ferocious defenders," he said.

Several of the other campers, hearing the talk, stated their desire to stock up on honey, so it was decided that we would try to rob the bees on the morrow and send the honey back to the village while we moved on to the hunting grounds. The men began preparations for gathering the honey and the women hurried and gathered and made skins to store the honey in. By dark, all was in readiness for the morning's harvest.

Jesse's eye was swollen completely shut and he felt warm to the touch. He seemed listless and soon drifted off into a restless sleep. Riley tossed and turned and finally fell asleep. Lydia or I checked on them several times in the night and both seemed to ease considerably as they slept. Finally, I was satisfied that they would be OK and I lay down and wrapped Big Sam's arm around my waist and slept until he rose in the predawn gray to help harvest the honey. The camp stirred quietly and soon the men left while the women began their morning meals.

Six young boys with lumpy bodies and

faces slept on until the sun peeked over the hills and the girls teased them awake. Jesse's eye was still swollen, but he seemed happy otherwise and ate a big breakfast. He and Riley and a couple of other boys tried to sneak back up to the bluff, but one of the mothers caught them and sent them scurrying back to the camp. Cub Bear's feet were swollen above his ankles and he could hardly walk. Most of the morning he sat with his feet in the creek, chewing willow bark.

About midmorning, the men returned with all the skins filled with honey and combs. "We could have filled as many again and still left plenty for the little bees," Big Sam said. "That White Wolf dipped all the honey out and didn't get a single sting. He's a real honey gatherer!"

All the men spoke of his skill and the women warmed toward him and praised him for his good work. White Wolf was pleased he had won their friendly admiration. Soon, three horses were loaded with the honey bags and three of the older boys including Jerry were sent back to the village with the treasure. Lonza gave Jerry directions on how to find us on his return and on the evening of the third day, he rode into camp.

Another long day brought us into the big neck of the White River between the mouth of the Buffalo on the west side and the Norfork flowing into the river from the north. It was here in the flats and hills of the great neck that the men hoped to find abundant game. Under the north side of the bluffs that marked the south border of the bottoms we found a nice spring and stream and determined to make our permanent camp a little ways down from the spring. This place was later named Farris spring and creek.

Early next morning the men slipped quietly out of camp leaving the boys asleep to their great consternation. They soon got busy exploring the neighborhood and Lydia and I set about making the camp comfortable. Midafternoon, Jerry came into camp with a fat deer over his shoulders. We hung and skinned the doe while Jerry took the axe and cut firewood and saplings for drying racks. Sam, White Wolf, and Lonza had gone west and north exploring the area for signs and didn't get in until nearly dark. They were satisfied with the country, not finding any other camps and having seen signs of deer, elk, and bear. Big Sam said it looked like a good hunting ground. There were also plenty of nut trees around, chestnut, beech, walnut, and hickory. The bottoms had white oak heavy with mast and the boys had come back from somewhere near with their shirts full of pawpaw fruit. The hunting was good and we were busy with curing meat and skins, gathering nuts, and all else that goes into the long fall hunt.

Sam Meeker was most attentive to me and the others teased him about spoiling me, but he only grinned. As time passed, we became more and more comfortable with each other and I was very happy. Though we didn't have as much time together, just the two of us, Jerry and I remained close and we spent many evenings around the fire talking and planning things for the future, some of which actually happened later in our lives.

The days grew shorter and almost before we knew, it was mid-December and time to break camp and return home with our provender. Jerry and White Wolf began separating and packing away their portions and we insisted on adding to it those things Lydia and I had prepared for them. Soon it would be time for our parting and I was dreading it.

We had the packing done and the men were going to make one more sweep through the bottoms for some fresh meat to use on the trail. They left camp before daylight as was their usual custom and we didn't hear more from them until midday when Jerry and Sam came into camp with a deer. We were in the middle of cutting and packing the meat when Lonza and White Wolf hurried into camp.

"There's an Osage hunting party camped by the Sugarloaf hill. They're just setting up camp, but it won't be long before they discover that someone else has been hunting here," Lonza said.

"It would be good to be gone before they discover us," Sam said, rubbing his chin. "We're packed, let's load up and go."

Lydia and I didn't need a second opinion on that notion, we sent the boys for the horses and began gathering the packs for loading while the men made plans.

"I won't see my husband killed and son adopted into an Osage family," Lydia said. Her determination was clear in the way she angrily tied packs on horses. She wasn't scared, only determined. I don't think she gave a second thought about what her fate might be if caught by the Osages.

The thought of a second captivity for me fueled my work. In a few moments, the men were helping us and it wasn't long before our things were loaded.

"Jerry and White Wolf are going to stay

here with their gear until they are found," Sam told me. "White Wolf was sure he knew the group and they will be safe. They are going to say that they discovered us here and ran us off and captured some of our provisions."

"That should give us time to make good our escape," Lonza added.

Lydia had loaded the boys on their horse and was leading the way out of camp with a packhorse in tow, the boys close behind.

"Go on, Ruth, we will be right behind." Sam grinned reassuringly and gave me a slap on the behind.

I didn't have time to even say more than a goodbye to Jerry, but he caught up with me and gave me a big hug. "Go, Ruthie, I'll be all right. I will try to see you about this time next year. Lonza has already said this will be his last long hunt, so you should be at the Middle Fork Village then."

"Be sure you come then, you can see Jesse's little brother or sister," I whispered. *"Don't tell!"* I warned him. *"Sam doesn't know!"*

I left him standing there big-eyed and slack-jawed and hurried after the fast disappearing Lydia. The men caught up with us, Lonza pushing on by to catch up with Lydia and guide us, while Sam stayed behind me, watching the back trail. We traveled well into the night, then suddenly turned off our path into a canebrake and across a creek where we made dry camp with cold jerky for supper and no fire. The boys were rolled up and asleep and Lydia and I lay down on either side of them to nap fitfully. Sam and Lonza took turns on watch.

I wondered at the way things could turn. One moment we were seemingly secure and the next we were in flight. It brought back a flood of memories, the capture and murder of Mama and Papa, the loss of Samuel and Joseph, life on the island and our escape, the shaking and fleeing across the country to an unknown fate. And here I was fleeing again. I was on the verge of tears when just at that moment, the robe on my back lifted and Big Sam lay down and pulled me close, his arm across my middle, so close to the new life stirring within that he was unaware of. I felt a warm flood wash over me. Safe in my lover's arms, I slept soundly.

I awoke to the sounds of the men packing the horses and we were on our way. Weaving through the trees in the deep leaves was noisy, but we had no other choice. Lonza led the way up a draw to the ridge where the wind had blown the leaves clear. Not so noisy, but now our tracks were plainer. All day we trudged on, barely stopping to water the horses and grab a bite to eat. Toward evening we came upon a large camp of our neighbors from the village on their way home after the hunt. Our story of the Osage hunters caused a little stir and the watches were set for the night, but our large number assured us that there would be little danger from a small hunting party.

We cooked supper beside a warm fire and with a happy sigh of relief lay down to a long needed rest. The rest of the trip home was uneventful. Crossing the river at the village, we were met by Sippie, who fairly attacked the poor pony the boys were riding. They tumbled off laughing and rolling with the dog and ran ahead to the house. Laughing Brook and Wash were standing by the door and Rising Sun toddled into his mother's waiting arms. The smell of warm bread and hearty stew greeted us as we entered the Fourkiller cabin. After a huge supper, we carried our packs to our cabin. Opening the door we were met by a breath of warm air from the fire crackling in the fireplace. Laughing Brook had known again that we would arrive that night.

*Sophie had been standing at the door listening to the last of Zenas' story. She handed him the old family Bible, which he laid in his lap unopened, patting it fondly. "Sam and Ruth's first child was born August 12, 1816, a girl named Sarah Fourkiller Meeker. She grew up, married a doctor, and lived all her life in those Ozarks hills. Folks said she delivered as many babies as her husband did!"*

# Chapter 7
# Swan Creek
# 1815

*"When Big Sam and Grandma Ruth left th' great bend huntin' ground, Uncle Jerry and White Wolf stayed behind to divert th' Osage huntin' party from pursuit o' th' Cherokee party. This wasn't too hard t' do, since th' Osage had their families along an' were more interested in huntin' meat than scalps. Uncle Jerry told it thisaway."*

White Wolf an' I discussed what we should do an' decided on two or three possibilities: we could stay in camp an' wait to be found; we could go to th' Osage camp; or we could go on hunting 'til we ran into them. It didn't take long to rule out hunting, since we didn't want to be caught in th' woods at th' business end of a gun or arrow. Our safest option was to just sit where we were 'til they discovered us, since creeping through th' brush around their camp might also prove hazardous for our health. It wouldn't be long 'til we had company, since all fresh trails led to our camp.

After the others left, we rearranged camp an' gear to our liking, then th' next mornin' we started cleaning an' preparing th' deer hide from our last kill. We were keeping a sharp lookout for any activity an' White Wolf saw movement first. "Keep looking behind me, Jerry, you should see someone there," he whispered. In a moment, I saw suspicious movement in th' brush an' nodded slightly to Wolf, "They're here."

White Wolf continued working an' said low, "Don't make any sudden moves." After a moment or two an' without raising his head from his work, he called in a normal voice, "Welcome to our camp, Otter, son of Long Runner!"

After a long moment, an exclamation came from behind White Wolf, "Waugh, could that be the White Wolf doing woman's work?"

"Would Otter say that woman's work is dishonorable while he ate his wife's stan-inca or sat by her warm fire? Does Otter build his own fires on the hunt, or does he take his wife along to do it for him?" White Wolf stood an' turned toward th' source of th' voice, "Come in and eat, my friend."

A handsome warrior stepped out of th'

brush an' strode into camp. He was as tall as White Wolf, both being over six feet an' both well-built men. I turned in time to see another man step into th' clearing from b'hind me. He was even taller an' a little older than Otter an' White Wolf, his neck an' shoulders covered with tattoos, large rings dangled from his ears. "Don't let Otter fool with you, White Wolf, he can dress a hide better than most women I know!"

"We were both taught by the same grandmother, Tall Oak, and taught well! Welcome, my friend!"

There was little formality in their greetings an' I could tell that all three were close friends, which caused me to relax some.

"Tall Oak, Otter, this is Jerry Harris, who saved me and my family when the Frenchmen shot me."

"We have heard much about you, Jerry-harris," Tall Oak said, "thank you for what you have done for Wolf . . ."

"But you should know that some of our people are not so thankful that you saved this scamp," Otter put in, with a big grin.

"I'm pleased to meet you," I said, not feeling familiar enough to enter into their banter.

"This is a large camp for two, Wolf, where are the rest?" Tall Oak asked.

"They have left for home with their provisions," he replied. "Jerry and I are getting ready to leave too. He will return with me to my home."

"That is good," Otter said. "May be that he can keep you out of mischief for a while."

"Morning Starr will be pleased to have someone of her own people to talk to," Tall Oak observed.

"Yes, she was quite taken by Jerry and the Whites at Flee's Settlement that took care of me and rescued Zilkah, Little Chief, and her from those French bandits. Have you eaten?" he asked.

"Not since very early," Otter said.

We busied ourselves fixing meat to go along with our stew while the three friends caught up on th' latest news. "How was Morning Starr when you left?" White Wolf tried to sound casual, but his interest showed.

"Her time nears," Tall Oak answered. "She asked that we send you on to her if we met."

"We have finished our hunt and were preparing to leave when you found us. Where are you camped?" White Wolf asked innocently.

"Right where you found us, you raccoon!" Otter retorted. "Do you think we are so blind that we did not see where you spied on us and could not follow that trail you built coming back here?"

Tall Oak chuckled. "I told him it was you when I saw the track, but he wouldn't believe me. The man with you was Cherokee, wasn't he?"

"Yes, that was Lonza Fourkiller. He and his wife were very kind to us while I was healing."

"I shall remember that," Tall Oak said soberly.

It was a touchy thing between our tribes that we were claiming the same hunting grounds. Trouble was always lying just b'low th' surface. Knowing the suspicions the people in Middle Fork Village had of White Wolf, I expected th' same for me in Osage villages — and I would find it so. For now, these men showed no animosity toward me an' I felt comfortable in their company.

"If you are headed for the Fallen Ash, why don't you move down to our camp and stay?" Otter suggested.

I nodded an' Wolf said, "We will do that. I would like to see the others and visit with you a little. Are you near the end of your hunt?"

"We should be, we had to move from our first grounds and thought the great bend area would hold some game for us, looks like we are a little late, though."

"We can show you where the game is," I said. "We didn't get all of it and there should be enough for you."

"Very good, Jerryharris, we will be glad for your company," Tall Oak said.

It was decided that the two hunters would continue their hunt an' we would pack an' move to the Osage camp at the Sugarloaf hill. We told them where they were likely to find good deer hunting an' began packing.

By midafternoon we were loaded an' on our way. The sun was still an hour high when we hailed the Osage camp. Only the women were in camp an' they were cautious until they recognized White Wolf. Their greeting was warm an' we soon were at home in their camp. By th' time hunters began returning, they had fed us an' I got my first taste of staninca bread with the hominy they called ahuminea. The women had harvested salt at a salt spring near their last camp an' it sure made the food good.

By dark, all hunters were in an' they greeted White Wolf warmly. I was introduced to each newcomer as the savior of White Wolf an' his family an' was so genuinely welcomed that I felt embarrassed by all the attention. The camp took on the atmosphere of a reunion an' the people stayed up later than normal visiting.

I was used to White Wolf's dawn chant, but the event of the entire camp participating in the chant the next morning gave me a start. I woke up just b'fore dawn an' noticed that White Wolf had already left for his chant time. No one else was in sight, an' thinkin' that they were still alseep, I stoked up a fire an' started a pot of coffee boiling. As th' sun peeked over th' horizon, a dozen voices raised in prayer where I had expected one. Hair stood up on my neck an' I got chill bumps. I didn't realize until that moment that the *whole tribe* practiced th' chant. Voices came from every point around me an' I realized that the dawn chant was an individual thing, each person seeking a place alone to chant an' pray.

No use in me trying to describe a dawn chant, it can't be done. It always b'gan with th' highest note possible an' traveled from there singsong down to th' lowest note possible. This was repeated over an' over, interspersed with prayers an' supplications for needs of th' moment. None of it being in unison, there was an awful noise. Even th' dogs joined in.

Th' reason they chant in the morning is

that they b'lieve east represents life, light, an' th' coming of good things. West represents death, darkness, an' evil. This must have affected them somethin' terrible, since they were always being pushed west, to them into darkness an' death, which it very nearly came to be in time.

Gradually, th' chanting ended an' people began wandering into camp from all points. Some had their faces streaked with mud, some were streaked with tears. As soon as they washed, all was normal again an' a new day b'gan.

Tall Oak an' Otter left shortly after eating but some of the other hunters stayed longer to visit with White Wolf. Before long they had all slipped out of camp for the hunt an' we were left with th' women. They chattered away as they worked th' skins an' I paid little attention 'til I heard Morning Starr's name mentioned several times. I looked at White Wolf an' he had a little grin on his face.

"What are they saying about Morning Starr?" I whispered.

"They are saying that she might be delivered by now and they are speculating what the child may be. Some are saying boy, but the elders are saying it's a girl. That old one over by the fire is saying that it is twins and

110

that they were born yesterday about sun-down." He grinned. "What they are really saying is that I should be on my way home to see for myself and be there at the time of birth, but they will not address me directly for it is not allowed that women should tell a warrior what to do."

I thought a minute, then stood up an' said in a louder than normal voice in my broken Osage, "White Wolf, it is time we go to Morning Starr before she delivers her twin daughters."

There was a startled silence for a moment, then someone tittered an' the old woman by the fire nodded her head emphatically. The women resumed their work more intently. There was a very pregnant silence for a few moments.

White Wolf stretched slowly an' said, "I suppose you are right about leaving, but you are mistaken about the child. These loins only produce man-childs!"

At that, the women burst into laughter, most of it derisive. The old one by the fire shook a stick at White Wolf an' let go a string of chatter, little of which I could understand.

"She's telling me that the Cherokee prophet Jerryharris is right, that I should go at once and that if it is twin girls, you should claim the right to name one of them and she should name the other." Wolf was grinning broadly.

I nodded enthusiastically, then went over an' gave Granny a hug. "You are a great seer," I said in Cherokee an' the name stuck at least for a while. They were still calling her the Cherokee name "Seer" when they came in from the hunt.

Wolf gathered packs while I brought in th' horses an' it was less than an hour later when we said goodbye to the women an' headed for th' ford. By noon we were on Fallen Ash Trail headed for White Wolf's home.

It was so that as soon as White Wolf was on his way, he couldn't get there soon enough. We stopped late an' cooked some supper, then pushed hard until full dark. As usual, I was th' tail end of our parade an' I was ready to tie my rope to th' horse in front of me afore I lost sight of him when we came to a creek an' Wolf turned an' waded downstream. Th' gloom lightened a bit when we come out in a little meadow-like clearing.

"Wait here," Wolf called softly, then rode up th' bank an' around th' clearing. When he was satisfied no one else was using the meadow, he rode back an' said, "We'll camp here."

It didn't take long to unload an' turn horses out. They were glad to be free. After rolling, they began grazing across th' meadow. Without so much as a word, our rolls were thrown out under cover of th' trees an' we were soon asleep, depending on our horses to warn us of any visitors that might happen by.

There was just a hint of gray in th' eastern sky when I next opened my eyes. Stars were dimmin' an' Wolf came leading in our horses. "We will stop after sunrise and eat," he said as we began loading. The horses were reluctant to go, being lazy from inactivity in th' hunt camp, but we got 'em in hand an' White Wolf led off uphill into th' woods. We wound around, not followin' any trail 'til we eventually came out on Fallen Ash quite a ways from where we left it, then Wolf set a steady pace. It was nearly noon when he turned off into another meadow. We turned out th' horses an' built a fire in a fire pit for our dinner. Th' horses grazed contentedly an' protested again when we caught 'em up after a couple of hours, but Wolf had a burr to move an' move we did!

I had noticed th' land gradually changing, hills were steeper, an' here an' there, limestone bluffs appeared under overlaying sandstone rocks. Our trail mostly follered ridges, passing from one to another across saddles, sometimes dipping deep into valleys where there was no saddle. Travel got slower because of steep hills an' I could understand why Wolf had pushed us where travel was easy. Gradually sandstone disappeared an' all that was left was limestone. It lay in great sheets where it was bared, in blocks, an' boulders of it were scattered around in other places. Th' woods was still thick an' dark, but there was hardly any pine to be seen. From some high prospect you could foller th' line of bluffs by rows of dark green cedars that grew along them. This was still virgin forest an' species of trees had separated themselves according to their preferred locations and elevations; willows an' sycamores in th' bottoms, mixed hardwoods next up th' sides of th' hills, cedars in rocky soil along the bluffs. Then there were bands of chestnuts, black cherries, hard maples with oaks makin up th' top tier on the mountainsides. This banding was most apparent in th' fall when leaves turned an' th' hills were banded with different colors, top to bottom. On top, th' trees were mostly scrub oak an' cedar mixed if there was any at all.

If I was to describe th' upper hills we came into, I'd say they consisted of about six inches of soil an' six miles of limestone. There was abundant water an' it had leached through th' rock 'til th' land was full of caverns an' sinkholes. A lot of hilltops were bare of trees b'cause th' soil was so thin. All that'd grow there was grass, some prickly pear an' low shrubs. Locals called them knob hills or bald knobs. In later years, a gang of white vigilantes was named after their meetin' place, Baldnobbers, they called 'em.

Somethin' about th' country made you feel you was on top of th' world when you looked across those ridges, though I suppose we weren't very high elevation-wise. Th' sky was high an' near as blue as it is on th' high plains an' mountains of th' west. In summer, great thunderstorms'd build an' sweep across th' hills howling an' roarin' somethin' fierce. Night skies were filled with more stars than I had seen afore an' if there was no moon, th' darkness was so thick th' only way to see hills was where th' stars stopped. Winters were cold an' windy, but th' snow when it came only lasted a few days. Still water froze over an' when it was really cold riffles froze too.

At th' time I first came there, they was

only one or two families of whites. They lived along Beaver Creek, hardy souls that identified more with Indians than with their own kind. They was also a smart number of squaw men living amongst th' tribes, but most of them was more "Injun" than th' Indians. Over th' next few years, a poor brand of white man moved into th' hills. We'd call them outlaws or white trash today. They's more about them later in this tale.

From Lick Creek, th' White River came from westward an' our trail traveled northwest to cut off a great bend in th' river. The third night we camped early an' hunted 'til we got a fat deer to take to th' village. We came back to White River at Beaver Creek an' it was just a jump from there to th' mouth of Swan Creek.

In 1808 the Osage Nation gave up most of th' Ozark Plateau in a government treaty but they took little notice of it an' continued to consider th' region as theirs. It was used mostly for hunting, but some like White Wolf an' his clan lived there year-round in small hunting-type villages up an' down Swan Creek in their case. Their hold was tentative b'cause of other tribes from east of th' Mississip that th' government had shipped in. There was a village of Kicka-

116

poos on th' James River where Springfield, Missouri, is today an' Delawares, Weas, Shawnees, Peorias, an Piankashaws also inhabited th' region. Osage warriors were in constant conflict with these tribes. Eventually, they had to abandon their Swan Creek homes an' move on west to their reservation in Kansas where th' bulk of their tribe lived, but for th' time being, they lived on Swan Creek.

We passed through a village at the mouth of th' creek an' a couple of others further upstream afore we came to White Wolf's village nestled in a crook of th' creek a little ways above th' mouth of Stout Creek. First to spy us was Little Chief, who wasn't so little anymore. He came runnin' an' shoutin'. White Wolf scooped him up on his horse an' he led us triumphantly into a circle of huts. There stood Zilkah with Morning Starr, who was still very much with child. Other relatives that gathered were mostly elders an' women with men still out on th' hunt.

I was mostly forgotten for a moment so while all th' greeting was going on, I unslung our deer carcass an' hung it on th' communal meat rack in the circle of huts. Suddenly I was struck b'hind th' knees by a ball of energy yelling "Jerryharris! Jerryharris!"

Down I went with fifty pounds of boy clambering on my stomach an' pounding my chest in excitement. I gave him a bear hug mostly to stop th' pounding while ever'one laughed. Zilkah came close b'hind chattering away an' grabbed Little Chief off so I could recover my feet an' get a hug from her. She led me back to th' people standing there an' Morning Starr reached me with another warm hug. She led me to th' midst of their circle of friends an' family, Little Chief pulling on th' other hand, an' said something in Osage, enough of which I caught to make me embarrassed. The people gathered round shaking my hand an' patting my shoulders an' I felt warmth in their welcome.

Mornin' Starr's eyes were shining an' she spoke to me in our tongue, "This is the second time you have brought my husband back to me, Jerry, and this in time for the birth of our child!"

I stammered something, I don't 'member what, an' Wolf rescued me by calling for an' evening feast to celebrate his return an' my visit. Th' crowd scattered to do a dozen chores, leaving us to unload horses an' turn them into a large corral where they could graze. Morning Starr supervised us in storing provender while Zilkah joined other women butchering deer an' preparing it for a feast. An' what a feast it was! There was corn made into ahuminea, squash, pumpkin, staninca bread, beans, steaks, ribs, an' more. I ate to excess, I'm afraid, but vegetables were so good after a steady diet of meat that I couldn't help myself. Zilkah kept filling my bowl 'til I hid it to keep her from filling it agin.

Dark settled on us. One by one an' in little groups people began to drift off to their beds. I laid out my bed b'hind White Wolf's hut an' stretched out to relax a moment before sleep. Little Chief crawled under th' covers an' I drifted off to th' tune of his half-Osage, half-Cherokee chattering.

I awoke with a start at th' sounds of th' morning chant an' lay there listening to the mournful sounds saturating th' air. Little Chief stirred, gave me a kick, an' lay quietly, listening. As they died away, he began his chatter an' we lay there a few minutes until th' inactivity overtook him an' he had to wrestle some. He ran away at the call for breakfast, leaving me to gather up th' bedroll an' store it away.

Th' next few days was filled with sorting an' storing food we had brought. Zilkah an' Morning Starr was pleased with the things Ruth an' Lydia had sent an' set about making pemmican an' other things out of nuts an' berries. Then th' other hunters came in an' feasting an' celebrating started over, which didn't displease me at all.

Th' tenth night after we arrived, White Wolf plopped his bed robe down b'side me an' Little Chief, muttered, "It's time," an' went sound asleep. I lay there wondering at his ease while his wife was giving birth but I came to learn that very few Indian women had complications in childbirth an' it was not considered a stressful event. Presently I heard a muffled cry from th' baby an' then silence an' I drifted back to sleep.

There was only a faint glow in th' east when I next woke up. Flipping the robes off, I stirred up a fog of snow that had fallen and was still sifting down through th' trees. Wolf an' his robe were gone an' I slipped out of my bedroll as quietly as possible. I paused at th' hut door an' called softly to be answered by a welcome call from Morning Starr. She lay in a bed piled with robes an' blankets an' in her arms lay th' infant. "We will call her Snowflake because she came with the first snow." Morning smiled as she uncovered the sleeping child for me to see.

I have always marveled at th' birth of an infant an' it seemed to me that this was th' most perfect of babies. Her little hands were the most delicate an' she gripped my finger tightly until sleep returned an' she relaxed. I could tell White Wolf was quite taken by her already, which is a natural thing b'tween father an' daughter. Th' birth caused a stir in th' village an' many visitors came an' went during th' day. I felt in the way so made myself busy gathering firewood an' stacking it by th' door.

About midafternoon, a group of hunters approached an' I spied a familiar face in th' crowd. I hurried into th' hut an' asked to show th' child to newcomers. Stepping outside with Snowflake bundled in my arms, I called out, "Seer!" The old woman looked up surprised to hear her new name called in a strange voice, then smiled broadly as she saw me. The women gathered around me as th' men looked on puzzled an' I unfolded th' blanket from Snowflake's face.

Carefully in Osage, I said, "I have named her sister Snowflake because she has come with the first snow. What would you name this one?"

Seer's eyes widened as th' meaning of my words soaked in an' th' women broke into excited chatter. Seer looked from the baby to me, back to the baby, still speechless.

Morning Starr had come to th' door,

taken all this in an' guessed th' joke I was playin'. "He is only teasing you, Grandmother, this is the only child," she said.

"Ahhh." Seer smiled at my little joke, then whapped me sharply on the leg with her walking stick. "Jerryharris, you're a sly fox and *that* shall be *your* name," she said. "Now I have named the second child!" She turned an' walked away in mock indignation as the crowd laughed.

That night we had another feast an' I paid close attention to Seer, even serving her as she sat by th' fire in th' lodge house. She was very old an' I guessed that this would be her last long hunt. She warmed to my friendship an' we visited as much as we could with our language limitation an' some sign language. There was much merriment at our pranks an' th' fact that we had named each other. From that time on, I became Sly Fox in the Osage tribe an' I have kept th' name among all tribes 'til this day.

This group was only passing through to their reservation out west an' had stopped to visit kin an' rest b'fore going on. Two days later as they were preparing to leave, I gave Seer one of my ponies to ride on the long trip home. She was most grateful an' gave me another tap with her cane, but not so sharp this time.

"You have done a kind thing, Jerry, and those people will not forget it," Morning Starr said as we watched them go.

# CHAPTER 8
# A WINTER HUNT

The next days were busy for th' family with a little one added to their daily routine. Little Chief an' I both felt in th' way. I had piled all th' wood I cared to an' with nothing to do wandered around like a lost goose. Otter lived nearby an' noticing my restlessness proposed that we take a short hunt for some fresh meat. Little Chief an' Otter's son, Otter Kit, were playing nearby an' overhearing our talk, begged to go.

"We will talk this over and decide." Otter said somewhat sternly, "You two big ears go down to the creek and see if you can find any beaver sign. When the sun touches the mountain you can come back and we will tell you what we have decided."

With solemn faces, they turned for th' creek.

"Don't go downstream, go *up* the creek!" Otter called.

Obediently, they reversed course an' trotted off upstream.

"Both boys have been on short hunts before," Otter said. "Do you think we should take them along?"

I nodded. "I will see if White Wolf will allow Little Chief to go with us."

When I brought up th' subject with Wolf, I could see Zilkah nodding her head b'hind him. She had her hands full watching after Little Chief an' helping Morning Starr too.

"I think that would be a good idea," he said. "It would get him out from underfoot" (I wondered why he didn't include *me* in that), "and the experience would be good for him."

So it was set that th' boys would go hunting. Otter called them in an' questioned them sternly on what they would take if we consented for them to go. Both boys considered carefully, knowing that their answers would determine if they were fit to go hunting.

"How long will we be gone?" Kit asked.

"We will return here by noon on the fourth day."

"That would be six meals," said Little Chief.

"Then we should plan on enough food for eight meals in case we are delayed or have guests," Kit said.

"We will take our bows and arrows and fishing line and hooks in case we need to fish," Chief added. "The weather is cold, so . . ."

". . . We'll need *two* blankets apiece," Kit put in. "We should take four horses . . ."

". . . Three for riding and one for packing — Kit and I will ride double," Little Chief put in hastily before Otter Kit could make a mistake and leave out a packhorse.

"Good," said Otter. "Now what else would you take?"

"Extra shirts, pants . . . and moccasins!" Little Chief was thinking hard.

"We will need knives to skin our take, and an axe for the firewood," Kit added.

"I will get some pots from our house to cook in," Little Chief offered.

"No, we take no pots on this hunt," Otter said. "We will learn to cook and do without them."

"Can we take some salt for the meat?" Kit asked.

"That would be good," Otter replied. "Now gather your things and bring them here to pack. We will leave early tomorrow morning."

The boys scampered off on their errands while we watched an' chuckled at their antics. Two piles of gear grew as they gathered all th' things they thought they needed to take. Little Chief wheedled a small bag of salt from Zilkah, set it triumphantly on top of his pile, an' plopped down beside it.

"Is that everything?" I asked.

"Yes," came a breathless answer.

"I suppose you are going to chop wood with your skinning knife?"

He slapped his forehead an' hurried off to th' hut. There was a flurry of chatter from Zilkah and our would-be hunter was hustled out of th' door empty-handed. He stood there perplexed a moment, brightened, an' disappeared around th' hut. In a moment he trotted back with my axe in his hand. "I had to get yours, because Grandmother wouldn't let me have hers," he said.

"You may *borrow* mine, but I will have to carry it on the hunt. Maybe you can save up hides and trade for one of your own next spring."

His eyes brightened. "Do you think we will get some good furs on this hunt? I can trap beaver and mink enough to get an axe *and* knife of my own!" he brimmed with confidence, unaware of th' work involved.

"Who will prepare your pelts?" Otter asked.

"I will get Grandmother to."

"Your grandmother will be too busy to bother with your pelts, you will have to learn to do them yourself."

Little Chief's face fell. "Isn't that a woman's work?"

"All should know how to prepare skins for use or trade," Otter replied. "Then when you get a wife many snows from now, she will prepare the skins for you."

"I will never have a wife, girls are too much trouble." Otter Kit plopped down th' last of his gear an' sat down beside it.

"It may be that you will change your mind when you are older." Otter grinned.

"Not me," came th' firm double reply.

Not too long ago that was my sentiment, but lately I had been giving th' opposite sex some thought, especially since my encounter with Bluebird on that first long hunt. I wondered where she was now an' if she had married. There were a few girls here, but Zilkah an' Morning had warned me that their mothers would not allow me near them. Osage women are very protective of their daughters an' save them in hopes that they will catch th' eye of some great or soon to be great *Osage* warrior. I noticed that when men from other tribes visited, th' girls disappeared. I must have given th' old women fits, being around all th' time an' I let it be known by action an' word that I was not interested in courting right now, which was a lie. It was a long time b'fore they relaxed somewhat, but I noticed that they were always vigilant when I was around. It would have been very hard to carry on some kind of courtship with an Osage girl an' I never tried, being afraid of th' consequences for everyone, especially White Wolf an' his family.

"Now we need to pack the gear so we can get an early start in the morning," Otter said. So with much instruction an' many questions, each boy made a pack ready for loading. It wasn't until th' packs were finished an' stored that both realized that they had packed away their bedrolls, which they would need for th' night.

"No need to unpack, boys, we can find enough for you to sleep in tonight," Otter said.

"I sleep with Uncle Jerry, so it doesn't matter to me," Chief said.

"On this hunt, you will learn how to sleep in your own blankets and stay warm . . ."

". . . And if I can't, Uncle Jerry will keep me warm."

"Me too!" Kit chimed.

The boys couldn't stand still, they were so excited an' told everyone they met that they were going hunting. Their strut was especially apparent around th' few other children in th' village an' there was more than one envious look as they passed on.

The hunters commanded an early supper so they could get to bed early, but their meal was served at th' customary time over their protests. Soon after, Little Chief grabbed up my bedroll an' disappeared around th' hut. I waited awhile in hope he would be asleep, but a couple of hours later, just before turning th' corner, I heard voices an' realized there were *two* young mules in my bed! Quietly, I retreated, scrounged up a robe, an' settled down out of sight. Later when I awoke an' there was no chatter, I slipped around and rolled up next to th' hunters. My sleep ended with an arm slung across my face by a restless sleeper.

"Time to get up and hit th' trail, boys." An' two sleepy heads popped up. It took Kit a few seconds to remember where he was, then he was on his feet an' both were off at a run.

"Hold on there," I called. "Are you going to just leave this bedroll here and let me freeze on th' hunt?"

With sheepish grins, they returned an' rolled up th' bed. Off they went, one on each end of th' roll, heading for our packs.

Otter had already brought horses up an' was loading them. He must have been up some time for a fire burning in a hole he had dug was dwindling down to ashes.

All was ready, boys clamoring to leave, when he said, "Now we will prepare ourselves for the hunt." Taking a pot sitting by his fire, he poured water into th' hole an' stirred th' mixture with a stick. When he was satisfied, he dipped both hands into th' mixture an' smeared it all over his face, neck, and anywhere skin was exposed, nodding to th' boys to follow suit, which they did with gusto. Noticing that I was not participating in th' ceremony, Little Chief dipped into th' pit an' smeared both my cheeks an' forehead with a liberal portion of ashes.

Otter said, "Now we will pray for a successful hunt," as he fell on his face.

I did likewise, not because I particularly wanted to, but as an example to th' boys. In a moment, Otter leaped to his feet with a shout, mounted, an' rode off, with boys scrambling to catch up. I boosted them on their horse an' of course by th' time I could get in th' saddle an' catch up th' pack rope, I was tail end agin.

Otter headed north up a ridge. We rode around to th' top of a bluff that overlooked the valley where we could see our village an' smokes rising from other villages off in th' distant still air. After a moment, we turned an' resumed our journey. Otter's plan was to travel hard most of th' day, find a good camp to hunt from for a day or two, then make a leisurely circle back toward our village, hunting an' lettin' th' boys (and me) get acquainted with th' country. We rode that ridge for a few miles, then dipped down into a hollow an' around one of those bald knob hills sticking up through th' trees. On th' north side, Otter showed us a hole that opened into a cave. Th' boys threw rocks into it an' speculated on how many bears were holed up there. When I suggested they go in an' see, they declined th' offer. Climbing out of the hollow, we struck another ridge dotted with tall pines of th' short leaf variety found in this region. After a while, Otter pointed down a gully where he said there was another cave, but we didn't detour over to see it. This ridge was several miles long running north an' south so we stayed on top 'til it dipped down to a low gap where Otter turned off to th' left an' led us down toward a small stream he called Peckout Creek. On a bench above th' creek he stopped.

"This is where we will make our camp,"

he said as he dismounted. Th' boys took charge of th' horses as I unloaded th' packs. They picketed them by th' creek where they could drink an' graze.

"Let's go fish for our supper," Otter suggested an' we were soon traipsing down th' creek looking for cane poles an' a good hole to fish in. We must have gone nearly two miles b'fore we found cane an' it wasn't much further along that Peckout ran into another larger creek.

"This is Bull Creek," Otter explained. "We should find some good fish here." He pushed a stick into th' soft humus under th' canes an' sawed on it with another stick 'til several worms popped out of th' ground. Each boy grabbed one an' soon had hooks in water.

"Everyone catches his own supper!" Otter whispered as he cast his line. "Catch what you can eat and no more."

"What about breakfast?" Kit asked.

"If you want fish for breakfast, you can catch enough for that."

All was quiet as we settled down to our job. Kit got th' first bite, to Little Chief's dismay, but Chief lost his bait first. There were several trips to th' vibrating stick for bait b'fore they caught a fish an' darned if they didn't both land one at about th' same time. There was a short intense whispered debate about who was first until I "shushed" them, then after a moment, a debate started over whose fish was bigger, Kit's rock bass or Chief's goggle eye. That conversation only ended when I landed a nice rock bass. Otter had only gotten a bite or two an' I suspected he was fishing without bait. I guessed his plan an' when I got another good bite, I left th' line alone.

It wasn't long before th' boys had four fish apiece, enough, they said, for supper an' breakfast. Meanwhile Otter an' I were having a hard time keeping bait an' hadn't landed a thing.

After a few minutes watching our frustrated efforts, Little Chief asked, "Do you want me to catch you some fish, Sly Fox?"

"No way," I answered. "We are to catch our own supper."

After a few more minutes. "I can catch you some fish, Uncle Jerry, if you let me."

"Well, I give up," Otter said in disgust. "I guess I'll just have to do without for supper."

"What if you and Sly Fox fixed the fish we have here and the fire and Little Chief and I caught some more fish, wouldn't that be sharing the work?"

Otter rubbed his chin. "That would be

sharing the work, all right, I guess if Sly Fox says it's OK, it would be OK with me."

"I don't want to miss supper," I said, "and I sure don't have any fishing luck with me today. Do you boys think you could catch enough for all of us?"

"We can for sure," Kit replied. Little Chief was already sawing up more bait an' in a moment they were both diligently attending their duty of fishing.

"I saw a clay bank up the creek a ways, if you start us a fire, I'll get the fish ready," Otter whispered, grinning.

Casting about in for firewood, I stumbled on an old stump hole that would make a perfect fire pit an' soon had a good fire going. Excited half whispers from th' creek bank told me that they were havin' good luck, so I hurried off to help Otter an' met him coming back with an arm load of fish, each encased in clay mud. I led him back to th' fire where there was a good bit of coals built up. We dug back coals an' laid our clay vessels in, covering them with more coals an' adding sticks on top.

The fishermen came in with eight more pan fish of various kinds an' we went to th' clay bank to prepare them. They were fascinated with fish hearts that kept beating after I had gutted them. Otter had piled offal from th' first batch nearby and we added ours to it. Th' boys had a time coating fish with wetted clay. I showed them how to make a uniform thickness so th' meat would cook evenly an' we hauled our food back to th' fire.

"Just in time," Otter said. He had fished out th' clay bricks an' they were lying on a log cooling. We buried our extra fish in hot coals, added more fuel, then turned to th' chore of eating supper.

"If you do this right, you will have your fish to eat in a bowl," I said. I showed th' boys how to crack th' hardened clay on one side and peel it off scales an' all, leaving white meat steaming in th' bottom half of clay. It didn't take them long to catch on an' not much longer till that first batch was eaten. Those boys sure had worked up a real hunger an' couldn't wait 'til th' second batch was cooked an' cooled enough to handle. Little Chief discovered he could use some large sycamore leaves for a pad an' get an early start on peeling clay. To our amusement, they ate four fish each, while Otter an' I had two. Looking at four remaining fish, he shook his head. "If you boys are going to eat like that, one fish apiece isn't going to do for breakfast. Looks like you need to do a little more fishing."

Chief paused from licking his fingers an' said, "We can sure do that, Uncle Otter." He grabbed his pole an' headed for th' vibrating stick. In a moment, he called, "The worms are all gone."

"Move to another spot an' try again," I called.

There was a grunt of satisfaction an' we heard line plop into th' creek.

"How many?" Kit asked as he picked up his pole.

"Three apiece should do," I said.

In a moment, we heard th' second line plunk in an' Otter shook his head an' grinned. It was nearly full dark b'fore th' last batch of fish was cooked an' camp cleaned up. Th' fire pit had burned down to hot coals an' we banked it an' covered it with a big flat rock so it wouldn't get out. Otter showed th' boys how to place fish offal in three places for night creatures to find. I took off my shirt an' filled it with hot fish clays an' the boys led us back to camp.

High excitement of a long ride, an' full bellies, made for sleepy boys. We had a time getting them to properly locate a safe place to sleep out of th' way of horses an' hidden from night prowlers — four legged *and* two-legged kind. In a bowl b'tween two roots of a giant chestnut, we piled dry leaves, rolled th' two up in their bedding, an' laid them to rest. Otter took still warm fish bricks an' laid them against their legs. They were both asleep by th' time we tucked their blankets around their feet.

Wrapped in my blanket, rifle by my side, I leaned against a corner of th' tree and root on one side of th' boys. Otter did th' same on th' other side. It made a snug spot for sleeping, boys b'tween th' roots, me and Otter on each side. It didn't take me long to be soundly asleep with th' boys, though no adult sleeps like a child, I guess.

I awoke to Otter's subdued morning chant an' had a fire started by th' time he returned. Two boys went from full sleep to full speed in an instant. We placed th' bricks by th' fire to warm while we moved horses to new spots. Our fish were just as good an' fresh as th' night b'fore an' made a good breakfast.

"Now, let's see what found our fish bait last night," Otter said. With bows strung an' quivers across their backs, two boys started down th' creek. Otter was good to teach them th' fine points of hunting an' they were good students. I have to admit that I learned a thing or two myself.

We turned down Bull Creek to th' first bait, crawling up the last several feet in case there was some critter there yet. There wasn't, but our bait was gone an' there was a profusion of tracks in th' mud. Otter made th' boys study them an' identify them as 'coon tracks. By paying close attention to size an' markings, they deduced that there were at least five, two adults an' three young ones. He pointed out signs that hinted at how old th' tracks were an' then he had the boys track them through th' woods. It was a long hunt, with boys losing th' trail several times an' us coaching them how to find it agin, but finally it led us to a tall white oak several yards from th' creek.

"They went up the tree, for sure, see the bark chips and scratches on the trunk?" Otter said.

"But that doesn't mean they stayed in *that* tree," I pointed out. "Look around and see if you can see any holes or a nest in this tree or one of these adjoining trees."

It took them a few minutes to find their nest. It was in a hole in th' trunk of th' white oak hidden by leaves an' limbs 'til it was near invisible. I found it first, but didn't say anything, letting th' boys hunt until a stirring of leaves by a young 'coon showed Kit where th' nest was.

"There he is," he called, an' strung up an arrow.

"Hold on, Kit!" his dad called, "we'll leave them alone for now and see what the other baits attracted. Then we can come back and get the 'coons down."

The second an' third baits were upstream from th' mouth of Peckout. We let th' boys lead an' scout th' two locations. There was still a rim of ice around edges of th' creek, but both boys waded in without hesitation an' led up th' creek bank. Their second bait had been scattered around an' nibbled at by a possum an' they decided to check out th' last bait b'fore trailing any possum. Otter nodded in agreement an' they crept on up th' bank. They couldn't find any bait an' casting about finally found traces that told them where it had been. Every speck had been cleaned up an' they were puzzled that there were no signs of what had taken it. Otter spied something in th' grass beneath a tree an' called th' boys over. "What is this here on the ground?" he asked.

"Looks like bird poop," Little Chief said, peering closely.

"Some kind of bird was roosting on that limb up there," Kit said.

"What do you suppose it was?" Otter asked.

"I don't know, but he was big," Chief said, looking at th' roosting on the ground.

"Hey, there's something hanging on that limb," Kit exclaimed. He started to shinny up th' trunk an' I boosted him up to th' first limbs. Th' limb bent under his weight an' what he had seen fell with a plop on Little Chief's cap. "Hey!" he called an' took off his hat. "It's fish gut!" he exclaimed.

Kit swung from th' limb an' dropped to th' ground.

"What kind of bird would eat our bait?" I asked.

"It could have been a hawk," Little Chief guessed.

"Do hawks fly at night?" Otter asked.

"Night hawks do," Kit said.

"They only eat bugs they catch on the fly," Otter said, frowning at his son's lame answer.

"Owls! owls! . . ." Kit began.

". . . it must be an old owl that ate our bait!" Little Chief exclaimed.

"I'll bet you are right," Otter replied. "Owl is too tough to eat and he's gone, so I guess the possum or 'coons are the only things we have to show for our trouble."

"Let's go get them!" both boys exclaimed.

"We know where they are and can get them later, let's look up the creek and see if we can find more game while we are on this side of Peckout," Otter suggested.

"We need meat for camp, maybe we can get a deer or elk before dark," I suggested.

That satisfied th' boys an' we were soon tracking up th' creek bank looking for sign. It wasn't long until they found a place where several deer had come down to drink, then grazed their way back into th' woods. We showed them how to track through leaves an' they were soon on th' trail like two hounds. After a mile or so, Otter stopped th' boys. "They have gone up th' mountain to graze and rest through the day. Most likely they will come back this way a little before sundown for another drink. We'll set up a bower here and wait for them to come back."

Deer seldom use th' same track when moving about unless it's along narrow places where they have no choice, so it was chancy for us to make a bower here since there was no way of telling where they might come down that broad hillside. At least th' boys would learn how to make a proper covert an' we might get lucky an' put it in th' right place.

Making a bower for a rifle hunter is different than making one for a bow hunter an' we showed them how to make both — rifle for us an' bow for them. We picked th' head of a gully that ran down to th' creek. Most likely, we could use th' gully to stalk th' deer if they didn't come within range. The only thing left to chance was th' wind. If we somehow were upwind of th' deer, our labors would be all in vain.

We were ready by midafternoon an' all that was left to do was wait — something young boys find very hard to do. We occupied our time making up riddles we could ask in sign language. Otter napped some an' th' boys became drowsy an' nodded off. I sat watching for some time an' th' stillness made me drowsy too. It must have been some noise that woke me up, but I cannot say what it was. As I opened my eyes, I detected movement of some kind far up th' hillside in a deadfall tree. As I watched, a head slowly emerged from th' dead leaves. Th' doe stood motionless for several minutes. If I had not first seen her movement, I would not see her now, she was so still an' camouflaged. Presently, another head cautiously peered through th' leaves. I pushed against Otter's leg with my toe, not daring to move or make any sound. A slight movement told me he was awake. I heard whispers as he woke th' boys.

By this time deer began nervously stepping out from their cover. Something was bothering them, for they were unusually cautious, stopping to sniff th' air, looking here an' there, mostly over their shoulders at th' deadfall. Eventually, there were three does, two yearlin' deer — one with button horns — and four fawns of this year's crop. Last of all, a buck rose from under th' thickest of th' brush pile an' stepped out into th' open. He wasn't big as some bucks are, only six points on his rack, but you could tell he was th' boss.

Fortunately, th' wind was quartering th' line of their drift toward us so that they would be way past before getting a scent of us — well after th' time that we would shoot. I still couldn't move without giving away our position so Otter set about coaching th' boys on where to git an' when he wanted them to shoot.

In a sudden blur of motion, a panther sprang from a tree overhanging th' deadfall an' in a bound grabbed a yearling doe! He sank his teeth into th' deer's neck an' with a violent jerk snapped it. In th' time it took to do that, th' rest of th' deer had completely disappeared as if swallowed by th' ground.

Otter stood up, "Well, there went supper, boys."

"Wowee," whispered Kit, "did you see that?"

Little Chief just sat there, th' most incredulous look on his face an' didn't say a word. Th' lion stood over his kill a moment, looking all around, then looked directly at us an' gave a long low growl.

"I don't think that was an invitation for us to dine with him," I said.

"No, and I'm about as close to his dinner table as I want to be." Otter chuckled. "Don't make any moves, boys, unless you want to smell that lion's breath!"

Ol' Lucifer crouched low over his kill watching us an' growling low in his throat. I thought he might spring at us any minute, but wasn't much worried since we were a hundred yards away. About three bounds was all he could have lived through with me an' Otter both holding guns.

"I'll shoot first if he charges, Sly Fox, you can have the last shot if it's necessary." I nodded, but events proved out that we didn't have to shoot at all. Presently, seeing that we didn't make any threatening moves, Lucifer picked up th' deer and holding th' carcass as high as possible carried it into th' brush.

Otter laughed. "I never saw the like of that before," he said. "Two things you boys should learn about lions is never to make aggressive moves toward them and if you suddenly meet one, *never* turn your back to him. You could never outrun them. If they can see your face, they are less likely to attack. A third thing is just as important and that is, *don't bother their food*!" He chuckled again.

"I have a good lion story I will tell you some evening," I said.

"Now what's for supper?" Kit asked.

"Looks like it's fish or 'coon," I replied.

Little Chief groaned. "I was sure planning on a big deer steak!"

We turned an' began th' long trek back to camp. This time th' boys stayed much closer to us in th' gloom an' I didn't blame them. More than once I glanced b'hind us to see if we were being followed.

"What will it be, boys, fish or 'coon?" Otter asked as we neared Peckout.

"It's so dark I bet those 'coons are gone," Kit said.

"I think we should fish," Little Chief said. He wouldn't admit he was tired from the day's activities, but I could tell.

Otter grabbed up Little Chief an' carried him over th' creek. I followed with Kit riding on my back. As soon as they were down, they ran to where th' fishing poles were stowed an' I set about vibrating up some bait. When they were taken care of, Otter an' I lifted th' rock slab off our fire pit. That rock was warm all over an' air rushing in caused several coals to glow bright. In a few minutes we had a fire. It was late for fish to be biting, so we baited up our hooks an' helped fish. Not much was biting until I caught a nice catfish. It would be plenty for a couple of us.

"My line is caught on something," Little Chief said. I could see his pole bent as he pulled. The line moved some an' he slowly pulled it toward us. He backed up as his hook neared an' out on th' bank came a large snapping turtle.

"Well, Little Chief, you've caught our supper!" Otter exclaimed. He grabbed th' turtle an' deftly chopped his extended neck, severing th' head. While I skinned my catfish an' cut him up into four pieces, Otter cleaned th' turtle. Cooking over th' coals didn't take long an' it took less time to eat. Both meats were good, turtle bein' all white meat an' tasted faintly muddy, a flavor I enjoyed.

We added fuel to our fire, then replaced th' rock. Letting wood turn to charcoal would ensure that there would be fire enough when we next used th' fire pit. Th' trek to camp was made in total darkness an' two boys burrowed into their bed, almost instantly asleep. Otter an' I tended horses

an' soon turned in. Th' breeze was cold an'
damp an' promised a change.

# CHAPTER 9
## SNOWSHOE DAYS

We awoke to th' sound of popcorn snow falling on trees an' leaves. Th' bole holdin th' boys was totally covered over an' there was no sign that there was any life at all under there. Otter stirred an' kicked off his cover. He motioned for me to be quiet, then left for his morning chant. He must have gone a long way, for I only heard a little whisper of sound from him. Th' boys slept on. Presently I rose an' cleared ground for a fire. Otter reappeared dragging a large treetop. "We can make us a shelter with this," he whispered. I had a fire goin' an' digging through our packs pulled out a generous portion of jerky, which I hung over th' fire. Our one concession to luxury was coffee an' soon it was boiling away. An aroma of food filled th' air an' there was movement in th' bole beneath th' snow. Two heads popped up under th' covers an there was a brief struggle with blankets before their heads appeared.

"Look at that snow, Chief!" Kit exclaimed.

"I'm looking at the food!" Little Chief responded.

"Be careful an' cover up your bed so it doesn't fill with snow," I instructed. They were soon shod an' hovering around fire and food. A cup of hot coffee stayed their appetites long enough for th' leftover turtle meat to get good an' hot.

"Now, we need to make us a shelter over the beds so they don't fill up with snow," Otter said after we had eaten. We got busy an' got a framework up. While the boys cut cedar limbs, we wove them into th' frame an' soon our shelter was done.

The snow had gotten heavier an' gradually turned into big soft flakes that covered that earlier grainy snow. We sat under shelter feeding th' fire an' watching it snow.

"Snow is fortunate for us," Otter said. "Now, we can track much easier. We will stay here another day or two and hunt." Th' boys nodded enthusiastically.

It snowed steadily all day an' we stayed in camp gatherin' firewood an' tending horses. Even in th' woods, snow built up 'til it was six to eight inches deep. It would be even more in th' open. Otter disappeared down th' creek an' in a few minutes we heard him chopping. He returned with six or eight long slim willow limbs. "You boys can learn to make snowshoes while we wait for the snow to stop."

I had heard of snowshoes, but never had seen any an' didn't have any idea how to make them, so I was little help until I saw how it was done. Otter set me to work cutting long strips of leather while he instructed th' boys how to cut notches at regular intervals along th' willow switches. "If you cut too deep, the wood will break when you try to bend it," he said.

When th' sticks were notched, he carefully bent them, wrapping several inches of th' ends together with a portion of leather string so that its shape was like a raindrop. Th' third switch cracked an' split in two. "See here, how this notch at the break is deeper than the others?" Otter asked. "If we had more time, we would soak the sticks in water, then they wouldn't be as likely to split." He set Little Chief notching another stick. "Now be careful how deep you cut," he instructed.

When th' bows were made, he took leather strips and began to weave an open grid in one of th' loops, making it as tight as he could without breaking it, teaching us as he wove. When he had finished showing us th'

151

finer points of his work, he said, "Now the three of you have a loop to weave, let's see what you can do."

The boys enthusiastically took up their task an' I cautiously began weaving mine. I was really embarrassed when my loop broke and th' boys had great fun laughing at my expense.

"You can notch your own stick, now, Sly Fox," they crowed.

I growled at them an' set to notching another stick. I could see why Otter had cut more than necessary to only make four shoes. He lit his pipe an' sat back watching, enjoying our labors, making occasional comments.

We worked on into th' afternoon and snow continued to fall. By th' time those shoes were finished, snowfall had piled on another two or three inches. It was typical of snows in these hills, thick an' heavy, makin' soft swishing sounds as it fell. It was good to watch from a warm dry place.

At last th' shoes were laced an' Otter showed us how to tie them off so they wouldn't come undone. He went over each one making comments an' little adjustments here an' there. "Now, let's put them on and see how they work," he said. With more strings, he laced th' shoes to th' boys' feet.

Little Chief started to walk an' promptly got tangled up an' sprawled in th' snow. Kit laughed, then did th' same thing when he tried to walk. We watched in amusement at their antics trying to learn how to maneuver in th' shoes. Finally, one of them began shuffling his feet instead of lifting them as you would normally do when walking. To his surprise that worked an' it was no time until both boys had caught th' knack of walking with snowshoes. Round an' round th' fire they walked until th' snow was trampled an' packed, then they moved on to undisturbed snow, laughing an' romping until one of Little Chief's laces broke an' he limped back to th' shelter on one shoe.

"Now you see how snowshoes work and how they can help you stay on top of th' snow instead of wading through it," Otter said.

"Hurry up," Kit called. "Let's go down the creek."

"You don't need to wear the shoes out tonight," Otter replied. "You two move the horses in to camp while we cook and we will go hunting tomorrow."

The horses were leery of those strange contraptions th' boys were wearing an' they had some trouble leading them. By th' time they were settled, supper was done an' we ate. With th' fire banked for th' night, we were soon wrapped in our robes, drifting off to sleep.

I awoke some time in th' night to see stars peekin' through low-flying clouds an' noticed that wind direction had shifted, coming out of th' northeast. By morning, it was cloudy again, but snow had quit. We had a quick meal, then th' boys led us out on a hunt. Their first quarry was a rabbit they tracked a long way afore catching up with it. Kit won th' right to shoot first an' zipped an' arrow over th' rabbit's head. Chief's shot burrowed under th' rabbit an' he jumped an' ran several yards b'fore curiosity overcame him an' he stopped, peering over th' snow on his hind legs. Th' boys crept up on him an' their next shots killed him. It turned out to be Kit's arrow that made th' kill an' took some time for us to trample around an' recover their other arrows. We tied th' rabbit high on a tree limb an' continued to hunt.

Soon, we struck tracks of a deer an' they followed its trail a long ways without getting any sight of the animal. Fresh rabbit tracks crossing their trail looked more promising an' it didn't take long to catch up with him. Little Chief got th' first shot an' that's all it took to land another rabbit. In all, they got five rabbits an' found blood on th' snow where another creature caught his rabbit.

With renewed enthusiasm, they trailed th' killer by spots of blood an' tracks until they came to a den under a root of a huge oak tree. Poking sticks into th' hole didn't produce any action so tiring of that, they veered off to find easier prey. They tracked two other rabbits with no luck an' as gloom settled in, we decided it was time to quit an' head for camp.

We discussed th' best route to return to those cached rabbits an' they did pretty good leading us back to them. They struck our trail from a tree where they had hung four rabbits and backtracked to it. Their route to th' first kill struck our trail a couple hundred yards before th' first kill an' they had to double back to retrieve it. It was real work getting back to camp after that. Otter an' I were soaked to our knees from wading snow all day an' th' boys' legs were very tired from unaccustomed walking on snowshoes.

It seemed to take forever to get a fire going and rabbits skinned, but the aroma of two of them roasting raised our spirits an' brought two drowsy boys out of their shelter. Every scrap of meat was eaten an' if there had been another roasted, it would have disappeared just as quickly as th' first two.

Some time in th' night, Kit awoke with leg cramps an' Otter rubbed them until he was relieved an' drifted back to sleep.

The snow had a crust of ice on it in th' morning making snowshoes work better, but th' boys were pretty sore from unfamiliar exercise an' we didn't stray far from camp. We were concerned about our horses getting enough forage so Otter an' I scouted around until we found a bluff that had shielded ground below it so that there was little snow an' they could reach grass easily.

After noon, we hunted again close to camp. Th' icy snow made tracking harder, but the boys caught on quickly an' didn't follow deeper tracks made before th' snow froze, but searched th' surface for fainter sign. They killed two more rabbits an' were disgusted at not finding bigger game.

I knew that Otter wasn't happy that we had only fished an' chased rabbits. He had hoped to have a successful hunt for larger game such as deer or elk, but it hadn't happened. That snow had caused us to spend more time in one camp than he had planned. This would be our fourth night in th' same camp. True, it was a very comfortable camp, but that was part of what was wrong. So far, th' trip had not challenged th' boys' abilities to survive an' live outside th' village.

"It may be that it is a good thing that it has been an easy camp," I said. "They certainly have enjoyed their time here an' they have learned a lot."

Otter nodded an' after thinking a moment said, "We could gain another day of hunting if we stayed here, then returned to the village th' way we came. With a little work, we might get a deer — before that panther does."

"That would be fine with me," I said, an' thus th' stage was set for one of the most memorable events of my life.

# Chapter 10
## Uncle Jerry
## Spends His Peso

*"Probably out of all th' happenin's of my family, this is one o' th' most unusual," Zenas said, settling himself into his rocker. "More than one has told me thet it couldn't happen that a-way an' I've come near t' blows a couple o' times when someone so much as called me a liar. I say this by way of telling you that this is th' truth. I have witnessed th' results with my own eyes. Here's how Uncle Jerry told it:"*

I was awakened by persistent dripping of icy water on my head. Sometime in th' night, th' wind had turned around south, bringin' a thaw. I had been awake for a few minutes when I heard Otter's morning chant. It was unusual in that it was nearby, short an' early, skylight only beginning to gray. He strode back into camp an' called softly, "Get up, boys! You're gonna sleep through the best hunting day of the trip!" He didn't even allow us to fix a breakfast. I only had time to catch up a bag of jerky as I fell in behind them out of camp.

Th' snow had melted a lot an' Peckout was a regular river. Instead of heading downstream, Otter led us upstream, across Low Gap down into Barber's Creek valley. We could see a large clearing ahead when he stopped well within th' shelter of the woods. Th' boys were panting from a swift walk as he explained his plan. "The deer have been laid up the last few days because of the snow. Now that it's melting, they will be out grazing in the daytime to ease their hunger. What we are going to do is lie up down there in the edge of the woods and wait while Jerry cuts way upstream and drives what deer he finds down the valley and hopefully across in front of us. With a little luck, we'll get us a deer or two."

The boys nodded enthusiastically, still catching their breath. I didn't envy them th' wait lying on that ground soaking up cold an' wet. My job was just what I wanted to do — stay on th' move. I took note of landmarks around so I would know when I was near their stand. That clearing looked to be a mile or more long an' I shore didn't want to be between those boys and a deer when it became time for shooting. Back-tracking a ways, I circled around up th' hillside 'til I hit a creek that flowed into Barber's down below. I crept up to th' clearing an' took a peek out from under th' brush. Sure enough, just as Otter had predicted, there grazed a bunch of does an' their young. My next thing to do was to locate th' buck if there was one. I waited an' watched for some time until I was satisfied that there was no buck lurking around. Now my problem was how to get them moving. Too much action on my part would spook them an' no telling which way they would go, but not likely toward our stand. In th' end, I decided to cover myself with bushes an' slowly walk out into th' open like that Digger did at Dennison Bottoms. When I was ready, I stepped out of th' woods an' stood still. One doe looked up an' snorted a warning. Others looked, but seeing no movement soon resumed grazing. I took a few steps toward them but they didn't seem to notice so I showed myself just a little. Another snort, a longer look an' they moved down th' valley a ways. Again I moved and again they watched, then moved away. This time I waited until they had grazed a few minutes before moving again. Deer are intelligent an' curious. They are as likely to stand an' stare at some puzzle as they are to spook an' run if it doesn't alarm them. If you are careful enough, they will not take alarm at your presence. So that was how we moved down th' valley. If they grazed too close to th' woods, I left them alone longer or until they had returned toward th' creek.

It took hours to git them within range of th' boys. I got th' deer just where I thought they could get good bow shots, but they took so long that I was nearly ready to move them agin when th' deer nearest th' woods suddenly sprouted two arrows in its side. I couldn't tell how good th' shots were from my perspective, but th' deer ran several steps, then fell over.

Th' boom of Otter's gun caused everything in th' meadow including me to jump. One deer leaped straight up, came down stiff-legged, an' fell over, th' rest stampeding straight at me. I jumped an' yelled, thinking if they turned, someone might get another shot. Deer scattered everywhere, some heading for woods by th' creek, some turning back an' heading up th' hill.

As they hit th' brush, I heard both boys cry out. Thinkin' a'deer had run straight over their stand, I trotted up toward them, shedding my camouflage. When I pushed through th' brush, Kit was standin' there starin' at Little Chief, who was laid out on his back. "That deer jumped on Chief!" he said.

Little Chief was knocked out cold. Th' skin in th' middle of his forehead had been peeled to th' bone and a chunk of bone th' size of a half dollar still clung to skin that lay across one eye. There wasn't much blood, only a little trickled from th' cut an' ran into his hair.

Otter called from th' clearing, "We got them both, boys, what's taking you so long to get out here?"

"Come here, Pa, Little Chief's hurt." Kit was near tears, his hands shaking an' his voice quivery.

Otter pushed through th' brush, then stopped dead when he saw Little Chief lyin' there with a hole in his head. "What happened?"

"That deer jumped over the brush and kicked him in the head."

Otter knelt an' looked the boy over. We could tell he was alive by his breathing. "We have to cover that hole before we can move him," he said.

I began tearin th' tail off my shirt. It was th' cleanest cloth we had with us. Otter took a piece of it an' gently wiped away blood so we could see better. There were three cuts or tears radiating out from that hole an' the flap of skin over his eye looked like a three-cornered tear you get in your shirt when you hang it on a thorn, only a piece of bone clung to it. Th' deer must have struck Little Chief with one of her front hooves an' then scraped backwards trying to run on. Those hooves are very sharp, I have seen wolves cut to pieces by them. That wound looked very much like a "T" with th' horizontal bar longer than th' upright.

"We have to cover that hole," Otter said more to himself than to us.

"Can we just fold th' skin back over an' stitch it up?" I asked, then realized we had neither needle nor thread.

"No, I mean we have to put something over that *hole* before we close the skin."

"Like what?"

"That's what I don't know," he replied.

He took his possibles bag from his belt an' dumped it on th' ground. There wasn't much there that would work except a flint arrowhead. Otter picked it up an' weighed it in his hand. He held it over th' wound, but it didn't quite cover th' hole. "It's too thick for the skin to come together over it," he said.

I dumped out my possibles an' that silver peso rolled out. With an exclamation, Otter grabbed it an' held it over th' hole. "Just

163

right," he said.

He looked at me as if to question me an' I nodded. "If it fits, use it."

"Take it and clean it up some." He handed it to me an' I rubbed it with my shirttail. Movement against th' leather bag as it jangled along had polished it an' when I rubbed all th' dust an' lint away, it was brighter than when I had gotten it.

Otter was carefully cleaning out th' wound an' when he was satisfied, motioned for me to place my coin over th' wound. Th' skin above th' hole was in th' way and Otter took his knife an' lifted it so that I could slide th' coin under it an' center it over th' hole where the bone was missing. Otter lowered th' skin an' gently rubbed it, pulling it down until th' forehead was smooth above th' cut. It covered almost half of th' coin. We sat back an' looked at it and Otter nodded.

I glanced at him an' was surprised at how pale he looked. Glancing at Otter Kit, I saw that he was as pale an' his lips were tightly pressed together in a thin white line. I'm sure that I looked th' same.

Working together, we put th' other skin in place. I peeled that bone chip off of th' flap over his nose an' folded it up in place. Th' cuts almost met — a lot closer than if we had used an arrowhead — and they looked close enough that we felt they would grow together. I laid a folded piece of cloth over th' wound an' we all breathed easier.

"Wish we had needle and thread," Otter said. "It would come together then."

"How are we going to hold everything in place?" I asked, then I remembered th' limbs I had broken off for my camouflage. Some had been pine an' that sticky sap was annoying. "Wait, I'll be right back," I said, jumping up. Th' sudden move made me so dizzy that I stumbled as I turned away an' I realized how near sick I was. Running up into th' woods, I found a stand of pine an' it didn't take long to find a few broken limbs where rosin had seeped out an' piled up. I scraped off th' freshest an' cleanest an' hurried back to th' blind. "This pine rosin will hold the skin in place."

I folded another piece of cloth into a square an' smoothed a thick layer of rosin on it. We mopped th' wound dry an' I pushed th' cloth down gently. Little Chief groaned. We wrapped his head with more cloth an' tied it in a knot on th' side.

Otter sat back an' sighed. "Good, now what?"

"Let's bleed out those deer an' hang them up, then we can make a litter an' carry Little Chief back to camp."

Otter nodded. "Kit, you stay with Little Chief and call if you need anything," he said.

It felt good to move an' work some of th' sickness out of my system. When we were through, we rubbed our hands an' faces with slushy snow. It was freezing cold but felt good. Otter's color came back an' he looked normal again.

We cut two slender saplings an' trimmed th' limbs off. Taking off his shirt, Otter ran th' poles through th' bottom an' up through th' arms, one pole on each side. I took off th' pullover shirt I was wearin' over my flannel shirt an' slipped it on to th' other ends, so that th' two shirts met bottom to bottom. With Kit cradling Chief's head in his hands, we lifted him into our litter. He groaned again, but he had not yet opened his eyes.

I didn't think that trip back to camp would ever end, but we were finally there an' we busied ourselves building up a fire an' making Little Chief comfortable. While Kit stood by th' litter, we cooked supper, but no one was anxious to eat.

Little Chief was getting restless an' makin' groaning noises when Kit called, "He's opened his eyes!"

When we got to him, he was shivering an' said, "Cold!" We piled on robes, but still he was chilling an' shaking.

"We could heat stones and put them around him," Otter suggested.

"I have a better idea," I said. "Let's take him down to th' fire pit an' put him on that rock slab." I remembered that a few days ago there was no snow on th' big slab we covered that fire pit with an' knew it was still warm from th' fire below. We carried him two miles or more down to th' fire pit. Kit followed with some camp gear packed on two horses. We left th' other two horses at our old camp.

The rock was still warm when I laid my hand on it. We put stones under th' slab to raise it off th' ground some an' laid Little Chief on it, litter an' all. I fed sticks into th' fire pit an' in a few minutes it began to smoke, then we could see a flicker of fire. We kept feeding it slow to maintain warmth in th' slab. Otter gathered some willow bark an' on another fire brewed tea to give to Little Chief. Gradually, th' boy warmed an' his chills stopped. He seemed to ease some after drinking tea an' slept.

No one felt like eating much an' after a while Otter an' Kit rolled up an' tried to sleep. I sat by the boy all night watching an' worrying. Otter got up several times checking on him. Kit slept restlessly; he talked

167

an' muttered in his sleep. Toward morning Otter rose an' went off for his morning chant. When he returned, I rolled up an' tried to sleep some. I awoke to th' aroma of deer meat cooking an' found Little Chief awake an' talking to Kit. Otter had taken th' two remaining horses at our old camp an' retrieved th' two deer we had killed He boiled some of th' meat down into a thick broth an' fed Chief. He ate it hungrily an' we were cheered by his appetite.

That afternoon was spent working up deer meat an' hides. Otter worked instructing Kit an' letting him do much of th' work while Chief watched quietly. He complained of dizziness when he sat up and his neck an' shoulders were very sore. We kept feeding him meat broth and willow tea and it seemed to help a lot. About midafternoon he said, "I'm hot!" so we moved him off th' slab onto a robe close by. That night we all slept much better. I stayed close to Little Chief, but he didn't stir any all night. I cut some steaks for breakfast an' Little Chief said he wanted some. He ate a healthy amount, dipping it into th' broth, an' seemed to relish every bite.

We discussed what we were going to do to get home since we were overdue now an' would be th' cause of some concern. It was decided that we would stay there another day an' let Little Chief rest, then we would start toward home, taking our time an' stopping when Chief had enough. Th' ground was too rough for a travois so he would ride in front of me on my horse.

When time came, we left about midmorning an' took a slow pace up th' valley to Low Gap an' down th' Pine Ridge Trail. I held Little Chief close an' he rested his head on my chest most of th' day. He didn't complain, but I could tell he was tiring by midafternoon so we stopped for th' night. He drank some broth an' tea an' went right to sleep. Otter said we were over halfway home an' should make it there early th' next day. We turned in early.

We came off th' Pine Ridge an' down to th' creek they now call Stout Creek just after high sun. Otter an' Kit took th' packhorses an' rode on ahead to th' village, leaving Chief an' I to follow at our own pace. It was evening when we heard horses coming up th' trail at a good clip an' White Wolf came into view with Morning Starr right b'hind. Little Chief perked up when he saw them an' other than looking a little pale an' having his head bandaged seemed much his old self.

White Wolf took him up on his horse, relieving me an' my horse of th' burden we had carried for two days. I was sore from holding th' boy an' that horse was tired from th' extra weight. We took a long drink at th' creek an' then caught up with th' others. Morning Starr rode beside Wolf an' Chief where she could.

Zilkah was standing in front of th' hut when we arrived an' immediately took charge of the boy. She soon had him in a soft bed of robes feeding him herbal teas an' broths until he protested. It took us some time to tell th' story of what had happened. I was pleased that Chief remembered most of it plainly an' I filled in parts where he was out of it. As soon as I could, I slipped off to my bed an' slept th' sleep of th' dead.

When I went in to see Little Chief the next morning, he was washed an' had a clean bandage around his head. "What is that you have on Little Chief's wound, Jerry? We couldn't take it off," Morning Starr said. I told them what we had done with th' coin an' how we held it together with pine rosin. When Zilkah understood, she smiled an' chattered something I couldn't understand. "She says it is good, but a woman would have had herbs an' needle an' thread for the job." Morning Starr laughed.

Nevertheless, they left th' bandage alone an' let rosin peel off gradually as th' wound healed. It was a chore keeping Little Chief quiet an' in about three weeks he was going without a bandage. Th' flannel pad had been pulled off and you could see th' ends of three scars peeking out of th' stain of pine rosin. Zilkah gently an' sometimes not-so-gently according to Chief's protests washed an' peeled th' rosin off. What appeared was that three-legged scar over a slight bulge where th' coin stood up from th' skull. Over time, bone grew around th' coin an' his forehead appeared normal except for scars. From that time on, he was known variously as Little Star, or Star Chief. People have mistakenly assumed that was how he got th' name Starr, but that was really from his mother's family that had th' name long before he came along.

*"I knew Star Chief when he was a Cherokee chief an' I was a young boy," Zenas said. "He was tall like his Osage father an' th' Cherokees looked to him for leadership. Uncle Jerry had told me about their adventure an' how they had doctored his wound, but I was doubtful until I saw that scar. Star had a way of treating everyone with respect, even little kids, an' he took me up on his lap an' talked to me*

*a while."*

*"Did your Uncle Jerry tell you about his peso?" he asked. I nodded an' he laughed. "I will never give it back to him and so long as I live, I will never be penniless. What do you think of that?"*

*"I think you should keep it!" I replied.*

*"Would you like to feel it?" he asked, an' I nodded. I couldn't tell by feeling that there was a coin there, but I could feel where bone had grown over it and th' edge was perfectly round. They said that when he was angry his forehead turned a deep red except for th' area over th' coin. It stayed pale, a round white spot on his forehead. He came out to see Uncle Jerry not long before Uncle Jerry died, both old men by then.*

*Zenas sat there smiling while I scribbled out the last few lines. "I wonder what these here archaeologists would think if they dug up a skeleton with a 1700's peso imbedded in his skull?" He chuckled.*

# CHAPTER 11
## WEST WITH THE OSAGE

*Spring, 1816*

We whiled away th' winter mostly staying in camp an' it was pretty boring. White Wolf was quite taken by Snowflake an' spent many hours playing with th' child. Little Chief continued to heal an' Zilkah nearly went crazy trying to keep him from overdoing it. She would might-near smother him with attention, 'til I took him out an' he an' Otter Kit played an' hunted along Swan Creek. I spent time with a couple of th' older boys. We would wrestle some or have foot an' horse races, but after a while that got tiresome, too, then we would ride out an' hunt some. Though this was a hunting village, most of th' game had been hunted out nearby an' we most generally ranged far out b'fore finding any sign. But it was a diversion from humdrum days an' we brought back fresh meat most of th' time. We b'gan to see bear sign, which was a sure sign of spring approaching, but we didn't hunt them for they would be skinny after their long winter's nap.

Our last hunt, we got a deer an' when we rode into camp, there was a lot of activity, indicating that something out of th' usual was going on. I put my horse up an' was hanging my portion of venison on th' rack when White Wolf appeared from th' Communal Lodge.

"We have a visitor from the big villages setting the time for the spring hunt. Now, we will have to prepare. The women have to do their planting and we (meaning the men) will have to prepare for the hunt," he said in passing. He hurried on into th' hut an' I follered as soon as I could.

White Wolf was explaining their plans an' there was no small amount of fuss goin' on, for th' call had come late an' these women would be pushed to git ever'thing done in time. It was obvious that a lot had to be done an' quick. Zilkah was digging through stored packs pulling out seed for planting. I was a little surprised to find that they had bean, corn, pumpkin, an' squash seed, all packed to prevent critters from gittin' in them.

"We will never get all the planting done in time" — Morning Starr fumed — "and take care of the children, too."

"I'll be glad to help," I said, not having any pressing duties.

"That is good, Jerry, but this is mostly woman's work we are talking about," Morning Starr said.

"Where I came from, planting was mostly man work an' women helped out." I knew this was agin customs of most tribes, but I didn't much care.

Early next morning I went into th' woods an' cut a large forked limb from a stout red oak. When I had one fork sharpened, I rigged up some harness an' had a decent plow. My horse was broke to plow an' after a refresher course, he straightened up an' plowed right. At th' field, I scratched out a long row as best I could by going over it three or four times. In th' bottom, I laid horse manure an' instructed Zilkah and Morning Starr t'cover it with a little soil, then plant a single bean about two hands apart in th' row. This was new to them, as they had planted ever'thing in hills until now. When other women saw what I had done, they asked me to make rows for them, so I ended up makin' several rows parallel to that first one an' they were happy as spring larks. Only Zilkah an' Mornin' went to th' trouble of using manure.

While we were plowing an' planting, I sent Chief an' Kit to th' creek to cut cane. They protested until I gave them my knife an' hatchet an' told them if they cut a good pile, I would let them drag th' cane to th' garden on my horse. It took longer than I had planned to git to th' cane brake b'cause of th' extra plowing, an' when I did get there, cane was piled boy's head high. We had to make two trips, which helped since each boy had a turn riding. I showed th' women how to make trellises for th' beans to climb an' they got busy making an' improving my construction.

With horse an' plow, I broke up a good section of ground for squash an' pumpkin hills. In each hill, I placed some manure an' th' women planted. I got a lot of teasing from th' other women about th' manure, but I held my peace. Next morning we planted corn in rows an' by evening th' village had finished all their planting, two days ahead of normal planting time. What stature I lost in men's eyes, I gained in women's an' it paid off, as they all saw that I was taken good care of after that. 'Course, I had to win back my status with th' men, an' that took more than one fight. Mostly I won except when they ganged up on me.

■ ■ ■ ■

All was hustle an' bustle for several days after that, for th' whole village was moving. I had assumed that we would go southeast to th' fall hunting grounds an' was excited to learn that this hunt would be for buffalo on prairies west of us.

"When we lived in the east, this time of year was called the Starving Time, for it was when the winter's store of food might run out and there wasn't anything to eat until summer," Zilkah explained. "Many of our people died in the spring, especially the old and the young. It was especially hard on women with child if the food ran out. An' there were many sick babies born then. Now, that we have the buffalo for the spring, there is much less hunger and death among us. It is good that we have come here."

"The only bad thing is that the other tribes are hunting also and there have been clashes with them, especially the Pawnees," Morning Starr added.

Out of th' corner of my eye, I caught Wolf smiling. Having a clash or two with other tribes wasn't bad in a warrior's way of thinking.

Soon everything was ready an' one morning that whole village packed up an' moved off northeast for the tribe's principal towns. Several days' travel brought us to Spring River country at th' edge of th' great prairies.

Here was th' first Osage town I saw, laid out in traditional Osage way, which I will try to describe: A little way outside of town, in this case to th' east of town, was a structure called th' Lodge of Mystery, covered with th' best skins available. It was oriented east an' west with an entrance at both ends. Through the middle ran a line representing th' path of Grandfather Sun an' in th' center was a fireplace. Th' Tzi-Sho Chief was th' peacetime chief an' sat in th' center on th' north side of Grandfather Sun's path. Th' war chief was called Hunkah Chief. He sat on th' south side of th' path facing Tzi-Sho. This is where th' governing body of th' tribe met. It was composed of elders, divided into seven degrees of authority an' presided over by these two chiefs who represented two grand divisions of th' tribe.

The village itself was made up much like th' Lodge of Mystery. Down th' middle running east an' west was a wide avenue, with Tzi-Sho's lodge on th' north side of th' avenue in th' center of th' village. Likewise,

Hunkah Chief's lodge was directly opposite on th' south side. Th' rest of th' village was built around these two, their huts arranged in rows of seven lodges, th' doors facing east to facilitate th' dawn chant.

As I said before, hunting villages had no formal arrangement an' th' layout of th' big villages was mighty interesting to me. I never knew th' meanings of it all, but it was a good way to lay out a town. White Wolf stayed in th' hut of his Uncle Two Calf, who was Zilkah's brother. Th' rest of th' hunting village was absorbed into huts of their kin in town. There was a lot of excitement an' visiting back and forth, folks getting reacquainted an' caught up on th' latest news an' new babies. Star Chief made quite an impression with his new scar on his forehead. Everyone wanted to feel th' coin an' his head got sore from all th' handling 'til Morning tied a headband around it to hide th' scar. As was my custom, I laid my bed outside th' hut an' slept there.

Arrival of th' hunting villages was th' trigger for moving an' in two days, all was ready. Not everyone went, of course, old an' very young stayed b'hind with a goodly number of women.

We had already crossed prairie an' savanna land to get to th' village on Spring River, but after we crossed th' river an' climbed out of th' breaks, we left all hill country b'hind. This was called tallgrass prairie, beings it had more rain than further west, th' grass grew taller. In fact it grew so tall in some places you could tie grass together across th' back of a horse. It was scary to go through these places, b'cause you couldn't see man or beast more than ten feet away, an' to run into either under these circumstances was dangerous.

Mostly grass grew two to four feet tall, depending on how long it had been since it was fired, an' really tall grass areas could be avoided. It seemed that th' prairie depended on fire to renew itself an' nothing was prettier than this country a year or two after it had been swept clean by fire. Real prairie grasses such as Bluestem, Switchgrass, an' Indiangrass had roots that grew deep an' would sprout back after a fire, then there were flowers, such as cone flowers an' lance-leaf sunflowers that could survive fire.

Th' land abounded in game from quail an' prairie hen to elk an' buffalo. It would have been hard for a healthy man to starve in that country. Still, th' village moved on, pausing only to kill a buffalo or elk to feed on as we went. We crossed th' North Fork of Spring River where Coon Creek comes in from th' east an' headed northwestward for th' upper reaches of Little North Fork of Spring River. There, we turned west.

"We are going where the big herds of buffalo are," White Wolf explained, "where we can kill as many as we need for the summer and fall."

West of First Cow Creek, buffalo were more numerous, but still th' village moved on, hoping to find a larger concentration of animals. We had camped for th' night on Second Cow Creek when scouts came shouting that they had found a large herd of buffalo on th' divide between Second Cow an' Lightning Creeks. That caused quite a stir an' after consulting with th' scouts, th' elders d'cided to keep camp right where it was until th' size of this herd could be determined an' if a better campground could be located nearer th' herd.

Next morning, White Wolf an' I rode out with most of th' men to survey th' herd an' locate a good campsite if possible. An hour's ride brought us to th' herd. There looked to be thousands of buffalo scattered over th' prairie grazing an' suckling spring calves. They didn't look to be moving an' it would be ideal hunting if we could get small bunches of them without alarming th' whole herd. We held a conference an' there was much discussion about where to locate a camp. Before they had come to a conclusion, there was quite a detailed map drawn in th' dirt an' a decision was made to locate camp on th' north side of Thunderbolt Creek near a lake. There was plenty of timber an' lake an' creek would provide plenty of water. There was a lot of discussion on how to move camp without alarming th' herd an' it was d'cided to move in stages, half th' village b'fore sunrise an' half after sunset of th' same day.

First, it would be necessary to determine if any other camps were near an' if they were Osage or enemy villages. It was plain to me that *any* tribe other than Osage would be considered enemy! Th' chiefs divided us up in pairs an' gave instructions for us to scout certain areas an' to report back to th' village on Second Cow b'fore three sunsets.

White Wolf an' I were instructed to scout down Limestone Creek to where it meets Lightning Creek an' as far west as Mulberry Creek, then to circle southeastward to Cow, covering th' east side of Second Cow back to camp. With little more talk we moved out an' chiefs an' elders returned to camp. We rode less than a mile before we hit Limestone an' there we split up, White Wolf north of the creek an' me on th' south side. We went slow, looking for sign an' watching th' horizon. A couple of miles down th' creek a gully came in from th' south an' I rode up it quite a ways through trees without finding any signs of life other than animal. Crossing th' gully, I rode back to Lightning without incident.

Wolf was waiting for me, squatting in th' shade of his horse. We rode on an' it was a mile or more b'fore th' creek had water in it. Sunset found us at Wolf Creek without seeing sign of other hunters or camps, so we rode up Wolf Creek a ways an' made camp without a fire. After picketing our horses, Wolf burrowed under a deadfall an' went to sleep. I crossed th' creek an' settled in th' crotch of a huge cottonwood, hidden from th' ground by leaves. We were up b'fore daylight — Wolf giving a subdued chant — and riding just at sunrise. It was a long ride down Limestone an' both of us had trouble finding a place to cross Lightning.

We rode together over th' divide an' down into Mulberry Creek bottoms. Down Mulberry, across Lightning an' over to Wolf Creek, we saw nothing of any manmade sign, but when we hit Wolf, we found a fairly fresh travois trail an' tracks of two horses. We followed th' trail up Wolf until it left that creek an' turned south to Cherry Creek. At Cherry, th' trail turned southwest along th' creek. We had pretty well determined that it was one family an' they were leaving without any knowledge of th' presence of our village.

Near sunset, we watered at a pond beside th' dry creek an' rode up on th' divide b'fore bedding down on open prairie. It was a long dry drag from there to Cow Creek an' we picked up th' pace a bit so we would be back at camp b'fore sunset. We still had a lot of ground to cover, up Cow an' Second Cow an' a lot of it was in timber, which slowed us quite a bit.

Looking at that country today, it's hard to imagine that we made that long ride without seeing another human being. It's just an indication of how empty th' land was at that time. Up Second Cow, we began to pick up other trails, all heading to camp, indicating that other scouts had finished their assignments an' were heading in. Without any more scouting, we headed for camp to get there b'fore sunset. We didn't quite make it, but we were not th' last scouts to come in.

By full dark, all scouts were in except two who had been sent to circle farthest north. We were all sitting at th' Tzi-Sho Chief's hut when they finally rode quietly in. One of them led a horse and th' other had a bandage around his upper arm an' a trail of blood running down to his elbow. We were concerned until he grinned an' held up a fresh scalp. Crossing over from Lightning to Second Cow, they had run across th' trail of a lone hunter on horseback an' followed it. They caught up with th' Pawnee when he made camp an' there was a desperate fight b'fore he was overcome. From equipment they found in camp, they surmised he was out looking for horses, so they hid his body, covered any signs that they had been there, an' continued their scout. Some people have all th' luck.

The elders discussed th' matter some time an' it was decided that Hunkah Chief would send out a war party to follow th' lone trail an' go beyond to see if any Pawnee camps were near. Meantime, since our camp was moving away from th' Pawnee's apparent destination, Tzi-Sho would move camp in two groups to Thunderbolt Creek starting before sunrise. With that decided, all were busy with half th' camp preparing to move, an' a war party prepared to leave after dark, led by th' unwounded scout. White Wolf was chosen for th' war party, but th' elders thought it would not be wise for me to go until I had more experience with Osage ways. Instead, I helped Morning Starr an' Zilkah prepare to move out with th' first half village. It was forbidden to use travois, since they would leave a plain trail, so all gear had to be packed on horses an' most of th' people would have to walk.

We only had time for a little sleep b'fore having to load up an' move. Tzi-Sho sent us off with an elder in charge. Tzi-Sho's wife went with us and would see that their hut was set up when he got there with the second movers. We began to slowly make our way across th' prairie among scattered groups of buffalo. We led horses on either side of our walkers so they would be mostly hidden from th' buffalo an' not cause concern. Th' move was only about eight miles an' by early morning it was over. Women immediately began to make camp, cutting saplings an' building their huts among th' trees along th' creek.

The elder sent several of us out west of th' lake to be sure that we hadn't missed some hunters an' to determine th' size of th' herd there, since that would be th' site of our first hunt. We went west of Grindstone Creek as far as th' headwaters of Mulberry Creek an' saw a considerable number of buffalo but no sign of other camps. Tranquility of th' herd also told us that they hadn't been disturbed by hunters.

*The second decade of the nineteenth century saw the beginning of what has been called the little ice age. It came about primarily because of a series of volcanic eruptions around the world. The first eruption came from an unknown source, then in 1814 Mayon Volcano in the Philippines erupted. In April of 1815, Tambora volcano in Indonesia blew up in what is the greatest volcanic explosion in recorded history. The resulting ash and dust cloud covered the whole earth and caused startling and catastrophic changes in the world's climate. New England in the young United States experienced frost and snow every month of the year 1816 and failure of its crops. That year became known there as "18-hundred-and-froze-to-death." Little is known of the effect the phenomenon had west of the Allegheny Mountains, but it is certain that it was colder. The weather was very unsettled with unusual storms and rains in some places and droughts in others. The Indians noted the diminished brilliance of the sun and the extraordinary sunsets caused by the dust high in the atmosphere and wondered what the portent was. March blizzards on the Great Plains are not unusual, but the intensity of the blizzard of 1816 was unusual and the first event of what was to be the most unusual summer season the Osage tribe could remember. — J.D.*

## CHAPTER 12
## LOST IN A SPRING BLIZZARD

There had been a warm wind out of th' south all day an' we noticed that it was beginning to come more out of th' southwest by th' time we turned back toward camp. High wispy clouds gave way to low gray clouds scudding across th' sky an' getting thicker an' thicker. By th' time we were halfway back, a soft mist was falling that gradually got heavier until it was rain — a cold rain. Now a strong wind was gusting from th' west. It was growing colder by th' minute an' we had no trouble hurrying our horses downwind to shelter along Lightning Creek. We made a hurried crossing, fearing it would rise if we waited longer. This meant that we would have to ford Thunderbolt to git to camp, but it was a smaller stream an' we would take our chances with it.

Someone pointed out that buffalo were bunchin' up an' turning backs to th' wind. Shortly after, I felt a sting of sleet hitting my face. We had ridden out of th' trees, but now we sought their shelter. Sleet rattled through th' trees an' still fell on us pretty heavy. I wrapped my blanket around my shoulders an' head 'til just my nose an' eyes were uncovered. How I wished for a hat with a brim an' I determined to git one as soon as I got a chance.

Out on th' prairie, sleet was so thick you couldn't see half a mile. It got darker an' darker until th' sky was just a gray sheet. I became conscious that sleet wasn't rattling in th' trees an' as we rode out of their cover, great flakes of snow were falling, quickly covering everything.

Tall Oak had been riding out on th' right flank all day an' now he fell in b'side me. "I hope the others didn't leave Second Cow before this hit."

"That would be bad," I said. "Do you suppose they did?"

"Hard to say." He shook his head. "They were probably packed up, waiting for dark, but they may have left early when it clouded up. If so, they are facing the wind and it will be hard to keep the horses going. It will be harder to see the bunches of buffalo. They are likely to run right into one of them and that would be bad!"

"Maybe we should hurry to camp an' try

to find out where they are," I suggested.

As if they had understood what we had said, our horses quickened their pace an' all of us trotted up th' creek. Thunderbolt was still quiet so we turned up it an' crossed at camp.

No one there knew where the other half of th' village was. They could be snug in their shelter on Second Cow or they could be struggling against this blizzard somewhere out on th' open prairie. Trying to find them in this heavy snow would be nearly impossible. It was decided that we would keep all horses up close in case they were needed an' wait. It took me some time to find Morning Starr's hut, but after a few tries, one woman pointed out a house on th' northern edge of camp. I tied up my horse with th' others that were there an' hurried inside.

Did that warm fire feel good! My blanket was frozen stiff an' when I peeled it off my shoulders, it stood on its own for a few seconds. Even my shirt was icy an' my moccasins had a shell of frozen ice an' snow. I crawled under a robe an' changed into dry clothes. Meantime, Zilkah had hung my wet clothes near th' fire an' it wasn't long until they were steaming dry.

"Have you heard any news from the

people on Second Cow?" Morning Starr asked.

"No, we have decided to wait an' be ready to help if it is needed," I replied.

"These spring blizzards can be fierce, but they don't last long," she said. "The danger is in being caught out in the open in one."

Zilkah handed me a bowl of steaming stew. "I hope our friends are safe."

"We are worried that they may have made an early start when it got so dark an' cloudy," I said. Zilkah shuddered an' turned away to wrap herself in her blanket, though I thought it was mighty warm in th' hut.

Star Chief was already asleep an' as soon as I finished my stew, I curled up beside him an' slept too. Th' last few days had been busy with little time for sleeping an' I slept so soundly I lost track of all passage of time. Deep into th' morning, something awakened me an' I sat up wondering what it was. Morning Starr on th' other side of th' fire was sitting up too.

"What was that?" she asked.

"I don't know, something just woke me up," I said.

I was in th' act of lying back down when I heard a long howl, seeming to come from far away. "Wolves," I said, jumping up an' pulling on my moccasins. Outside, th' wind was howling down from th' north an' it was even colder. A check of th' horses found them safe an' secure, but they were alert, facing right into th' wind, their ears pricked forward. Again, that howl came, but this time more distinct an' it wasn't a wolf, but a human voice! I answered with a long "hallo," then hopped on one of th' ponies an' trotted up th' creek an' onto th' open prairie. I couldn't tell if it was still snowing or just blowing, but it seemed that visibility was some better.

Another call came from th' opposite bank of th' creek an' closer now. I answered, then stopped. My pony turned backsides to th' wind an' we both listened. Again that call came an' we continued to call back an' forth and th' caller came closer an' closer. Someone rode out of th' trees an' stopped b'side me. It was Tall Oak. "This is not a good thing, Sly Fox, I think it might mean the people are out on the prairie."

Gradually, a dark form moved out of th' whiteness an' down to th' creek an' we moved down to th' water. Tall Oak called, "Who rides there?"

"It's Wind Son," came a muffled voice, then a moment later, "Is that you, Tall Oak?"

"It is, Son-of-the-Wind, you can cross right where you are."

193

His horse moved forward slowly an' reluctantly entered th' water. He stumbled a time
or two, but made it to th' bank. Tall Oak
took th' horse's bridle to lead him, but he
stumbled again an' I got down to give Wind
Son my horse. When I reached up to help
him down, all I felt was ice-caked blanket.
When he moved, ice cracked an' flaked off,
sounding like little bells as it rattled to th'
ground. I had to pry his hand open to get
th' reins loose. Wind Son grunted an' I
could see he had his teeth clinched. It took
him two or three tries b'fore he could git up
on my horse, even with me boosting him
up.

Without a word, Tall Oak moved off
swiftly, leading Wind Son's horse. I followed
on foot leading a played-out horse. I took
him to our horse's shelter an' gave him hay
an' rubbed him down some. When I got to
Morning Starr's, I saw other figures moving
about. Several left th' hut as I tried to enter
an' they were all in a hurry. Tall Oak had
gotten Wind Son into th' hut an' they were
removing his frozen clothes. Th' fire was
stoked up an' I smelled Zilkah's stew warming. Son-of-the-Wind had a frozen nose an'
cheeks. His fingers were still as I had pried
them away from th' reins an' his feet had a
sick pale look. I was sure his toes were

frozen. Zilkah held a bowl of warm tea to his lips an' he eagerly drank it down. You could see him thaw. While I hurried into my clothes, I listened to th' two men talk.

"Where have you come from?" Tall Oak asked.

"We left too early," came the whispered reply.

"Where are they, Wind Son?" Tall Oak spoke firmly.

"We got halfway before we had to stop the first time." He spoke as if he were tryin' to remember something that had happened a long time ago. "Then we moved on until dark an' fell into a wallow. There was some shelter there an' they stayed. Three of us came on to find help."

Few buffalo wallows are deep enough to offer much shelter an' it would have to be a big one to shelter a hundred people. We had to find them an' find them soon. Tall Oak looked at me.

"The others have gone to get ready to ride an' bring horses enough to carry those that need it. We only need to find out where they are."

"We came due west until we hit Thunderbolt gully, then followed it. They can't be more than four or five miles away," Son-of-the-Wind rasped. "I will show you the way."

"No you won't, we can find them if they stayed near the creek," Tall Oak said. "Our chances of finding them are just as good as yours in this weather."

Tall Oak's wife came in with his gear an' robe an' we heard sounds of many horses approaching. "Where are th' other two that were sent out?" I asked.

"We could not agree on which creek you had camped on so they went on to Lightning Creek. They were going to follow it in hopes of finding you."

A fierce blast of wind hit th' hut an' I felt it shudder. We all looked at each other. It was as if th' weather said, "I have them and you will have to defeat me to find them." Tall Oak rose. "We have to see to the safety of the rest of the tribe before we can worry about those two. They will have to take care of themselves until then. Sly Fox, gather as many of your horses as can make the trip and let's get going!"

I grabbed a robe an' Zilkah handed me a bag of food. Just before I ducked out of th' door, Morning Starr shoved another robe into my arms. "Cover your horse with this, it will help him last longer . . . good luck!"

There must have been twenty men an' fifty horses passing by on their way to th' ford. I tethered up five horses I chose an' fell in line. On th' other side of the creek, we gathered in a circle to decide how to search. That wind was really howling down on us and blowing snow stung any exposed skin. We had to go right into th' teeth of that storm. It wasn't going to be easy.

"If they came straight across to Thunderbolt Creek, and turned down from there, they can't be that far away," Tall Oak shouted above th' storm. "Spread out in a line just far enough so you can see the one next to you and we'll sweep up the creek. Good Walker, you will stay on the bank of the creek, all the others will line up from him. He will go slowly and occasionally fire his gun so you can know where he is. Don't ride too far ahead or get too far behind him if you can."

With that, we began to form our line. I moved way out toward th' end, there being only five or six men beyond me. Good Walker fired his gun to start us moving an' we turned into th' wind. It was one of th' most trying things I had ever done, keeping track of th' man to my left and th' horses headed in th' right direction. They kept pulling off one way or t'other to avoid going straight into that wind. Visibility kept varyin' back an' forth makin' following in a straight line impossible. We would spread out as far as we could — it was never more than thirty, forty feet — 'til we realized our neighbor was just a shadow, then we would move closer in 'til we could see him plainly an' th' process would start all over again. On my end, our track was just a big zigzag line. We walked twice as far as th' straight-line distance we covered with many stops an' starts. Good Walker's gun was sure a help. He told me later that he shot more than he probably should have, but he would keep his hands warm on his gun barrel until it cooled so much they got stiff, then he would shoot again. He had to warm his hands b'fore he could reload.

On an' on we plodded, it seemed like hours, calling an' yellin'. Those horses became more an' more bothersome an' I couldn't blame them much. Mine gave a hard pull an' turned me all th' way around just b'fore Walker fired another shot. I was still struggling to git them turned when a few seconds later I heard a shot coming faintly and far to th' right of our line. Th' men beyond me had stopped when I got turned around an' I called to my neighbor, "Did you hear that?"

"Yes," he replied, "and it came from behind us! Hold my horses and I will ride up the line and stop them."

Well, holding eight horses was sure harder than holding my five, but they calmed down when I let 'em turn tail to th' wind. The men outside of me rode in an' gathered around, turning their horses to th' lee. "Where do you think that shot came from?" one of them asked.

"It sounded like it was way off to the east, beyond our line," replied th' man who had been riding th' end.

Soon th' messenger came back an' th' whole crowd gathered 'round us. "Where do you think the shot came from?" Tall Oak shouted over th' howling wind.

"It sounded like it was off there to th' left, beyond our line," I called back. Others who had heard it agreed.

"Try another shot, Good Walker," Tall Oak called. Th' shot followed an' we held our breaths, listening. Several seconds passed before we heard an answer, so faint it was almost like we felt it instead of hearing. "Where did it come from?"

"Over there!" came a half-dozen replies an' they were all pointing in th' same direction, generally southeast.

"What if it is one of those two that didn't come in, we would be going after two and not the group," someone called.

"That is not likely," Tall Oak replied.

"Son-of-the-Wind said they had crossed Thunderbolt and headed for Lightning Creek."

"They would not be out here this far if they went all the way to Lightning," someone called. "Let's see who this is!"

"Form a line, half on one side of Good Walker and half on the other side," Tall Oak called, "and stay closer together this time. Walker will continue firing. When he shoots, stop and listen, we may have to change directions from time to time."

We lined up an' began walking. It was a few minutes b'fore Walker shot again an' we waited for an answer. It seemed to come from th' direction we were going but it didn't sound much stronger. We started off again. It was getting lighter so our line spread a little. Gradually, th' early morning light grew stronger, but still it was a dark day.

Th' next reply to our shot was stronger but came from more to th' right of our path, so we changed direction. Soon there came a shout from th' end of th' left line. Th' end man had fallen through the snow into a gully.

"That gully flows into Limestone Creek!" someone called.

"If that is our people shooting, they sure

have strayed off th' trail!"

On we plodded, quartering th' wind now, our horses moving faster without snow in their faces. Another shot, then listening, a stronger reply. Plod on.

The next time Good Walker fired, th' reply sounded like it was just over th' next rise, but it was still a ways b'fore we saw anything. Our right line topped a small rise an' we heard them shout an' point to something we couldn't yet see. They broke into a trot an' we quickly followed, converging on some unseen object. As we topped th' rise, we could see, dimly, an object that looked like a stump rising out of th' snow. As we looked, th' object fired a gun, then disappeared.

Instantly, our line stopped an' we all gathered around Tall Oak. Some drew their rifles from their cases. "Why did he disappear?" someone asked.

"It could be a trap."

"Pawnees may have our people and are trying to lure us into range."

Tall Oak studied th' area for a minute, "This *could* be a trap, but I don't think so. If it is, we are at a great disadvantage with all these horses to handle out here in the open. That looks like a wallow big enough to hold the people . . ."

I could see that this was going to be a long discussion if something didn't happen soon an' I couldn't help interrupting, "I will ride up and see who is in there, we are losing time talking about it." With that, I gave my leads to th' nearest man an' without waiting for an answer, I trotted off toward th' wallow. There were muffled hoofbeats behind me an' Good Walker rode up beside me. "You are a foolish impatient man, Sly Fox — and I am just as foolish!" His voice was muffled by th' blanket around his face, but his eyes twinkled.

Glancing back, I saw th' rest of th' men spreading into a line an' walking our way. Every gun an' bow was ready. "Hello-o-o-o the Camp!" I called an' several figures appeared on th' rim of th' wallow. It looked like one or two were women wrapped in their blankets.

"It could still be a trap," Walker said. We spread apart a little an' continued on. Figures became more distinct and we continued calling in Osage until one returned our call an' began running toward us. We came within a hundred yards, well within range, but still no shooting.

"That is Willow, my aunt!" Walker called. "Hold up and let us hear what she says."

"You wait, I'm going on!" I called, never

slacking my pace. Good Walker swore an' pushed his horse on.

When we were in a hundred feet of Willow, she called, "Come on, you laggards, we're cold and hungry! Did you think we were Pawnees? Hurry up!"

With that, Good Walker gave a shout an' rode in circles signaling th' rest to come on up. They broke into a run, but I noticed their weapons were still prominent. I rode up to th' lip of th' wallow an' there was that whole snow-covered tribe huddled in th' bottom.

"Wake up, people, our rescuers are here!" Willow called.

The warrior who had been firing signals fired his gun again an' shouted. Several answering shots came from th' riders. Slowly, they stood an' began dusting snow from themselves an' their things. Other than one or two who showed th' effects of their exposure, th' people were in pretty good shape.

Their horses stamped an' snorted at th' commotion. Only a few forms in th' wallow didn't move an' we had trouble getting these to rise an' move about. Horses were distributed throughout th' crowd an' were soon loaded with gear an' riders. I helped a family of five load their things on my horses an' mount up. As we prepared to join th' line of travelers moving off toward Thunderbolt Creek, a child in a tattered blanket tried to mount up behind one of th' children. Th' mother struck her with her quirt an' snarled, "You will walk, slave, and lead the horse!"

The child moved to obey an' I noticed that she was bare-legged an' her moccasins were worn out. As I rode by, I swooped th' child up an' set her behind me. Protesting loudly, th' woman, Birdsong, rode against my horse an' raised th' quirt to strike again. Quickly, I reached down an' grabbing her foot, lifted an' shoved her off her mount. She fell into th' snow with her skirt flying up revealingly an' her blow landing on her horse who shied an' trotted away. We left her there sputtering an' cursing much to th' amusement of th' crowd around us. Not even her husband, Black Elk, who was as amused as th' rest, offered to help her an' she had to run through knee-deep snow after her horse.

I was surprised that th' slave child who was a Kaw captured in a raid was treated so cruelly. Most captives, especially children, were adopted an' cared for th' same as children born into th' family. This woman was an exception to th' rule and her actions met with strong disapproval.

The child clung desperately to my robe an' it was hard to keep it around my shoulders with her pulling. Finally, I pulled her around in front of me an' sat her in th' saddle in front. She whined in fright until she perceived what I was doing, then sat quietly while I pulled her close an' wrapped th' robe around her. I don't know that I have ever felt a person alive as cold as that child was. I have wondered all my life how she could have survived out there in that wallow. She drew her feet up an' rested them on my knees under th' robe an' they were so cold I involuntarily flinched when they touched me. Gradually her violent shivering ceased and as she warmed, she fell asleep. Nothing but her eyes an' top of her head was visible an' she was so small that a casual observer would have thought I was alone.

Birdsong continued to splutter an' cuss an' once rode to cut us off. As she raised her quirt to strike, her husband, Black Elk, backhanded her so hard she nearly fell again an' with a sharp word sent her to th' back of our little group.

As we rode, th' sky brightened, th' wind died, and snow stopped blowing. Clouds began to break up an' we squinted against unaccustomed brightness. I was surprised that our path was only a little north of due west, but we arrived at th' ford on Thunderbolt a little above camp. Later on when I looked th' land over, I was amazed that we had heard any shots from th' wallow. I can only surmise that we did not go as far north in our search as I supposed an' that sounds carried unusually well in snow-thickened air.

# CHAPTER 13
## THE PRICE OF A SLAVE

At th' ford, Tzi-Sho met us with Birdsong sitting triumphantly beside him. "Sly Fox, you have taken th' Kaw girl?" he asked.

"Yes, Tzi-Sho, I have her here."

"Come with me, then, we will settle this matter."

He led th' way to his hut, which had been built larger than others for th' purpose of having conferences such as this. I followed, carrying th' child. As he went, he motioned to several other men to follow, including Black Elk. Once or twice th' woman tried to say something to th' Tzi-Sho, but was hushed by a wave of his hand.

Inside, we all sat down, Tzi-Sho in his place and th' others around him. I sat with th' child still wrapped in my robe she clung tightly to. It was uncomfortably warm an' stuffy after our trip an' I soon began to sweat. Still, the child held th' robes tightly an' shivered. I realized she was no longer cold, but scared. Tzi-Sho lit a pipe, took several puffs, making smoke offerings to th' east, north, south, an' west. Then he passed to other warriors who made th' same smoke offerings. I was last to receive th' pipe an' I imitated th' others, then handed it back to Tzi-Sho. After he had put it away, he turned to me.

"Sly Fox, you have taken this child from her mother, will you explain why you did this thing?"

I tried to rise to make my explanation, but th' child protested an' Tzi-Sho motioned for me to sit with a wave of his hand.

"I had no intention to take th' child, but th' mother was going to make her walk an' lead a horse when she should have ridden, so I took her up on my horse." Several men who had witnessed th' incident nodded. Th' child lowered th' robe from her face an' shoulder revealing a welt where th' quirt had struck. Tzi-Sho saw, but his expression never changed.

There was a long silence, so long that I became uncomfortable. What had I gotten myself into?

Finally, Tzi-Sho said, "This woman has said that you stole the child, is that true?"

"No," I replied, "I only meant to let her ride an' not freeze to death leading a horse through snow. Th' horse stayed with us an' did not need leading," I added.

Another long uncomfortable silence followed. I wished I had said more.

Tzi-Sho lifted his head an' said, "Child, stand up and take the robe off."

With a whimper, she stood and that robe, thankfully, fell off of both of us. There was a slight stir an' murmur among th' men and th' child stood quietly. I had no way of knowing, but that ragged dirty blanket she wore was the only stitch of clothing that child had on! Her moccasins were tatters with toes an' heels bare. She was dirtier even than any other children I had seen around camp an' her legs an' back showed welts an' bruises where th' quirt had struck time an' again. I felt my anger rise an' clenched my teeth to keep from speaking.

Tzi-Sho turned to Birdsong, "Go bring your other children in, Mother."

She left, returning with her two children. They were wrapped in thick blankets an' Tzi-Sho said, "Please remove your blankets, children."

Underneath th' blankets, they wore warm well-kept clothing an' they both wore moccasins with knee-high leggings.

The Tzi-Sho nodded. "You may be seated

there, children, while I consider this matter."

There was another of those long silences I dreaded so much. Th' naked child sat down in my lap an' I covered her again with th' robe.

Tzi-Sho lifted his head an' said to me, "Sly Fox, I do not believe you intended to steal this child, but only meant to rescue one of our tribe from the storm and cold. For this, we are thankful." Then looking at th' mother, he said, "Birdsong, I perceive that you have been a good mother and wife but that you do not value the one your husband has brought to you from the field of battle. Therefore, because he has valued the child more than you and has preserved her life for the welfare of the tribe, I am awarding the child to Sly Fox."

I drew a deep breath an' opened my mouth to protest. "Shhh!" it was Tall Oak behind my ear.

"He will have to pay Black Elk the value of the child, which shall be set by these men," he said, indicating the ones sitting around him.

Birdsong turned dark with anger an' when she opened her mouth to speak, Black Elk struck her with his open hand. "Be quiet, woman, you have brought shame enough on us!"

Unperturbed, Tzi-Sho said to me, "Take the child into your hut, Sly Fox, and care for her as your own, as we do and as I know the Cherokees do. These men will confer and set the price which you must pay before the next moon. I have spoken and the matter is settled. Now, I am tired and hungry and wish to rest." He dismissed us with a wave of his hand.

Rising was difficult for me, holding th' child clinging tightly an' trying to keep th' robe.

Tall Oak picked up th' trailing robe an' chuckled. "So now you are a family man and still no wife!" he whispered, then more seriously, "What has happened has been coming for a long time. Many a night we have heard our wives whisper about the cruelty of Birdsong to that child. Now, perhaps we can sleep peacefully knowing she will be well cared for — by you!" he chuckled again.

I was speechless. What could I do? How could I care for this child without even a home or tipi to live in an' no woman to help? Outside I breathed in frigid air an' my head cleared some. Th' child wriggled under th' robe so that I could barely hold her. She kicked an' a moccasin fell. Another kick and th' other moccasin sailed an' landed at Birdsong's feet. Then with a scream of anger, she brought that tattered blanket out from under th' robe an' flung it at th' woman. I hurried away with a now-naked child screaming over my shoulder at Birdsong in her language, which no one knew. I hurried toward Morning Starr's hut. She an' Zilkah would know what to do.

"Where are you taking me, Sly Fox?" th' child said in almost perfect Osage — at least it sounded good to me.

"We are going to see Morning Starr an' Zilkah," I replied. "They are my friends."

"Are they Cherokee like you?"

"Morning Starr is. She is married to White Wolf, an' Zilkah is her mother-in-law."

"Where is your hut?"

"I don't have one."

After a pause, "Where do you stay?"

"I stay with White Wolf, but mostly I sleep outside, not in th' hut."

She was quiet for a long time while we walked, then she said, "My name is Kansas."

"Well, Kansas, I am glad to know that you can speak," I replied. "You said not a word until just a moment ago an' I was beginning to think you had lost the ability."

We passed through th' village, Kansas

chattering an' asking a thousand questions. What she had endured in silence she now made up for in talk. As we passed, the women would pause in their work an' nod an' smile their approval. Many spoke either to me or Kansas an' she would always reply, most likely calling th' greeter by name. Many times her parting words were, "I now belong to Sly Fox!"

I trampled on through snow that, true to spring storms, was rapidly melting away under a bright sun and deep blue sky. News of th' happenings must have traveled fast, for Zilkah an' Morning Starr were watching for us an' came out of th' hut to meet us, Zilkah chattering in three languages. I could catch a few words now an' then, but th' gist of it all must have been: "So Sly Fox is now a family man . . . Stand down child and let us see you . . . Oh my . . . *where are your clothes?* . . . Look at you, how *filthy* can you get? . . . I want to see this Birdsong! For every mark you have, I'll give her . . ." she shook two fingers in th' air — to which remark Kansas laughed an' Starr smiled. Kansas began shivering an' Zilkah came to herself. "Here we stand while this child freezes!" She looked at us, eyes flashing. Grabbing up th' robe an' taking Kansas by th' hand, she hurried inside.

Morning Starr laughed. "Well, Jerry, how does it feel to be a father?" Seeing my consternation, she hurried on. "Don't worry, we will help you take care of her. Zilkah and I can use her help."

All I could do was shrug, "I did not intend . . ."

Starr held up her hand. "Don't worry, we will all take care of her and she is welcome here." Then in response to cries coming from th' hut, she hurried in. I stuck my head in to see Kansas standing naked by th' fire an' Zilkah scrubbing away at her dirty face an' body. Little Chief was standing near th' door staring slack-jawed. I grabbed his arm an' we made our escape.

We spent th' rest of th' afternoon tending horses an' gear an' gathering firewood by th' door. By late afternoon, grass was peeking up through leftover snow an' Thunderbolt Creek was roaring. Th' lake was full an' overflowin' into th' creek. Everything dripped. Commotion in th' hut had settled to a soft murmur an' we were hungry enough to risk a peek. Morning Starr an' Zilkah were preparing supper while over on a pile of robes sat Kansas cuddling Snowflake an' playing with her.

Little Chief an' I stared, for she didn't look like th' same person. She was clean an' dressed an' her hair had been deloused, oiled, and tied back from her face. Other than welts an' bruises, her skin was clear an' pink. I noticed again how thin an' starved she looked. There was a fatigue in her eyes, yet she smiled an' seemed at ease. "Come see how well Snowflake can hold my fingers," she smiled at me. Little Chief, pushed by a small jealousy for his sister, hurried over and th' two were engrossed in playing with th' baby.

Zilkah an' Morning Starr seemed subdued an' spoke in murmurs, huddled over th' supper. I slipped out of my wet moccasins an' sat on my bedroll. When Zilkah brought over my meal, she sat by me an' whispered, "She says she is *fourteen* summers, Jerry-harris!"

I started an' almost spilled my stew. "Can't be, look how small she is, she can't possibly be more than ten years old!" I looked at th' girl again. "How long has she been with th' tribe?"

"The raid when Black Elk captured her was two summers ago."

"Two summers! How did she survive that long?"

"Stealing and being fed by others in the village, mostly."

"I have heard of others being treated so,

215

but this is the first time I have seen it," I said, my temper rising, "Do you think she is fourteen?"

"I do not know, it may be that time will tell," Zilkah said rising.

Kansas had already been fed, but now she looked hungrily at my steaming bowl. I motioned for her to come to me. Instead of sitting beside me, she plopped down in my lap, leaning against my chest. She certainly smelled much better! I gave her my bowl an' she ate every drop in it. How could anyone eat in front of a hungry child? She sat th' bowl aside an' chattered happily, though I could only catch a little of what she said. Her skin was almost transparent an' pulled tightly over her bones. She was much thinner than I had first thought, but she was happy an' relaxed. *How resilient children are!* I thought, but if she were fourteen years old, she wasn't exactly a child anymore. Girls of that age in th' village were preparing for marriage an' by th' time they were sixteen or seventeen would be married.

Suddenly, Kansas became quiet an' I felt her stomach contract a couple of times. She jumped up an' ran out th' door an' we heard her retching.

Zilkah shook her head an' clucked, "Too

216

much and too rich." She ladled a thin broth out of a steaming pot as a very pale girl returned an' sat carefully in my lap.

"Sip this — slowly!" Zilkah handed her th' cup.

The thought of more food must have been revolting to her, but Kansas took th' cup an' held it in her hands a few moments before attempting a sip. That prairie hen broth must have been soothing to her, for she eventually finished th' cup. Presently, she began to nod, turned, an' curling up in my lap went sound asleep. I was cramped from sitting still so long an' thankful that White Wolf was not here to see me holding a child like a mother.

Morning Starr made a bed on th' women's side of th' room, took th' child from my arms, an' laid her gently in it. I couldn't imagine that she could have done that with a fourteen year old. Star Chief rolled up in a blanket behind me an' was soon asleep, breathing softly (I never heard an Osage snore). Zilkah, Morning Starr, an' I sat talking softly while th' baby nursed one last time before being put to bed.

"I sure have gotten myself in a fix," I said. "Why did I ever pick that child up?"

"Because she would be dead on the prairie now if you hadn't," Morning Starr said.

"You are too good a man to see that happen."

Zilkah nodded. "Compassion is not a weakness, Jerryharris."

"But what am I going to do with her?"

"We will all care for her," Morning Starr said. "She certainly has spirit, to have lived this long — as she has!"

"Do you think White Wolf will approve?"

"So long as there are two men to bring in the meat and the girl can be a help here, he will."

"I hope so," I said, but I was still concerned that I was imposing on th' family. Still, I could not carry on a household by myself. Th' girl needed to be trained in th' skills of a woman by other women.

Snowflake cooed an' fell asleep, satisfied from her feeding, an' we all turned in. I was very tired from th' events of th' past days. Sometime way in th' night I stirred an' found I couldn't move. Kansas was snuggled tight against my back.

Morning came late for me. Th' household was up an' about, trying to be quiet an' not disturb me. Some weren't trying too hard an' I finally sat up. A cup of tea was thrust into my hand an' I looked up to see Kansas grinning at me.

"Do you always sleep until noon?" she asked.

Suddenly I wanted to give her a big hug as if that would make her well, but she was gone an' a ball of fury jumped on my back.

"Hurry up, Jerry, the river is a mile wide and still rising!" Star Chief was everywhere at once, pushin' my moccasins at me an' throwin' my blanket over my head. "Hurry! Hurry! I have the horses ready!"

Morning Starr handed me a hand full of jerky as I was dragged out th' door by my shirt sleeve. Two horses stood there with saddles on. Th' girth was loose on mine an' while I tightened it, Chief climbed on his horse — and his saddle rolled off, spilling him in th' mud. I righted his saddle an' showed him — for th' third time — how to fasten it securely. He had really done a good job, but was yet too short to force his horse to let his wind out so th' girth would stay tight. Up an' away he rode toward th' creek, which we could hear roaring. It had risen out of its banks an' was washing around th' trees, at least a hundred yards wide, maybe more. It was so high that it backed into th' lake, which was slowly turning a muddy brown from creek water. We rode around th' lake an' downstream about a mile or so looking at th' flood. Little Chief gave a yell an' pointed at a tree floating by. There on a limb stood a red fox watching th' flood like a ship's captain sailing down th' river. We laughed an' as he floated by he looked at us disdainfully. We always wondered where he finally landed.

South of us, toward where Thunderbolt ran into Lightning Creek, th' prairie looked like a big lake that backed up to where Grindstone Creek joined Lightning. We rode down to th' water an' sat watching. Buffalo an' all other animals had been pushed back by rising waters an' were spread out on high ground b'tween Lightning an' Thunderbolt. Way out in th' high waters we could see something standing.

"What is it, Jerry?" Little Chief shaded his eyes an' stared.

"I think it's a buffalo, but I'm not sure."

"Why didn't he get out with the rest?"

"Don't know, maybe he thought the ground he was standing on was high enough." Just then, th' animal raised his head an we could tell it was a horse.

"It's a horse, Jerry!" Chief exclaimed. "Let's go get it!"

"Not a chance, we don't know how deep th' water is," I replied.

"But what will happen to him if we don't?"

"I don't know. Probably, he will stay there

until th' water goes down." Th' horse must have heard our voices, for he turned around an' when his sides showed, we could see a blanket draped over his back.

"Aiee!" Chief exclaimed, "that's someone's horse! Wonder where his rider is?"

Th' horse must have been 400 yards away and I stared hard, but couldn't see anyone. I couldn't get rid of the image of White Wolf under that blanket back at Flee's. There could just as well be someone on this horse's back also.

"Chief, we have to find out if someone's on that horse," I said. "I'm going out there to see an' you wait right here. When I raise my arm an' wave like this, you get back to camp an' tell Tall Oak what we have found. I will raise one arm if th' horse is alone an' I'll raise both arms if someone is out there."

Chief nodded an' I prodded my horse into th' water. It wasn't too deep for a ways, then got deeper of a sudden. I took my moccasins off to try to keep them dry an' th' horse went deeper. He was almost swimming when I turned him to th' left. For a few steps, th' ground was level, then it began to fall off again. I turned him around an' we tried th' right side. Almost immediately th' ground rose an' we continued, angling back toward that horse an' trying to stay on higher ground. By zigzagging around, we were able to approach him without swimming.

When I got close enough, I b'gan talking to him quietly. I didn't know that much Osage horse talk yet, but he didn't seem to mind my Cherokee, he pricked his ears an' watched. We were within about a hundred feet when th' horse lifted his head an' came surgin' through chest high water toward us. My horse stopped an' waited. He whinnied an' nosed th' horse when they came t'gether. By that, I knew they were familiar with each other.

The horse was alone. I took his rein an' sat for a moment looking around, but nothing moved save gentle waves caused by a breeze. I shivered, my legs were freezing, and th' horses were both shivering. I raised one arm to Little Chief an' he hollered an' trotted off toward camp.

Without prompting, my horse turned an' started back to dry land, whinnying softly to th' horse, who followed. I gave him his rein an' he picked his way back without swimming. I don't know how he remembered where higher ground was, but he taught me a whole lot about th' sense of a horse that day, something I have been able to take advantage of through th' years.

When we got to drier land (even in thick sod, th' ground was soggy), I hopped down an' examined th' horse. Nothing was wrong with him, except that he was so cold he was stiff. I started walking back toward camp leading th' two, hoping exercise would warm us all, which it seemed it did. I angled for th' end of th' lake an' presently a group of riders appeared heading my way. Little Chief had made good time getting to camp an' he was ridin' a different horse when he rode up with Tall Oak an' several others.

"That's the horse Hump was riding when we separated," one of th' men I didn't know said. I surmised that he an' Hump were th' other two looking for camp in th' storm. "I went upstream and he went down. That's the last I saw of him," he continued.

"Did you see any sign of him, Sly Fox?" Tall Oak asked.

"The horse was very far out in th' flood," I said, motioning at th' water behind us. "I looked, but there was nothing but water."

"Where could he be?" someone wondered.

"He would have stopped when he got to Thunderbolt Creek, maybe he even started back up it a ways."

"Where would he be now?"

"Probably he and the horse gave out and he sheltered up in the trees somewhere along Lightning or Thunderbolt," another surmised.

"He should have come on after the storm let up."

"May not have if the horse was still down."

"The horse could have run off and left him somewhere."

"He had a buffalo robe with him and it isn't with the horse," said Hump's companion. "It is probably still with him and hopefully he still has his gun."

"Let's ride down to the edge of the water and fire a gun. If he hears, may be that he could fire back to let us know where he is," Tall Oak suggested.

We spread out about a hundred yards apart along th' water's edge an' someone in th' middle fired. We waited, but there was no answer. There wasn't anything else we could do until th' water went down an' it was getting late. Reluctantly we headed for camp, with many a glance backward, hoping that by some good fortune, we would see Hump following. We noted that Hump's horse had soft hooves, indicating that he had been in water or wet snow for some time. He was pretty played out, but seemed to gain some as he walked an' warmed up. My legs were still cold an' I walked to warm them up. It helped, but not by much so long as I had on wet leggings.

Water everywhere slowly receded over th' next days an' though we searched, we never found Hump. Best we could guess by what little sign we found after th' water fell, he had come up Thunderbolt a ways an' made a shelter, but what had happened after that, we didn't know. It was noted that water must have first risen from Lightning Creek behind th' higher ground along Thunderbolt where we found th' shelter an' it was pretty certain that Hump would have been trapped there if he had stayed long. The question never answered was why he stayed after th' storm quit.

I heard a few years later that someone had found a skeleton wrapped in a robe tied high in a cottonwood near where Thunderbolt ran into Lightning. Hump's rifle was in th' robe. Barring an unlikely chance of foul play, Hump must have been trapped by rising waters, tied himself in th' tree, an' for some reason died there. We'll never know why.

When we got back from rescuing Hump's horse, I was called to th' Tzi-Sho's lodge. He was seated in his place and th' men who were to set a price for Kansas were there.

"The price for the child has been set as one horse, Sly Fox, and to be sure the price is fair, the men will pick the horse from your stock."

With that, we left th' Tzi-Sho an' I led th' men to my horses. They looked them over carefully, then picked my best horse an' th' worst horse. I was disappointed that they would have picked th' best an' puzzled that they also took my worst, but didn't say anything. "Now we will go with you to Black Elk," they said. Tall Oak was not one of th' men appointed by th' Tzi-Sho an' as we walked through camp, he joined us. As we approached Black Elk's hut, Birdsong hurried inside an' a moment later, Black Elk came out an' stood by th' door without a word of greeting.

The leader of th' group addressed him: "Black Elk, we have set the price of the slave child at one horse." Indicating my best horse, he continued, "This is the horse that would best equal the value of the child . . ." Black Elk smiled broadly an' nodded, my heart fell. ". . . however," th' man continued, "since it is so obvious that you valued the child so little that you allowed your wife to abuse her, we have judged *your* value of the child to be equal to the value of this horse," indicating my old nag.

Black Elk's smile faded an' his face turned dark.

"Black Elk, this is the decision of the men before you and not any of Sly Fox's doing and you are not to hold him responsible for this action. You cannot refuse the price. This affair is ended." With that, th' lesser horse was led to Black Elk an' we turned an' left without another word being said.

The second day after I purchased Kansas, Black Elk packed up his family an' they left for th' Osage villages. There were those in camp who sympathized with them an' from time to time I got some hard looks. It made me uneasy — not so much for myself, but I was afraid some harm might come to Kansas.

# CHAPTER 14
# THE FIRST BUFFALO HUNT

It took a few days for th' waters to recede an' things began to dry out. There was nothing to do but wait 'til buffalo wandered back an' spread out over th' plain. Crossing Thunderbolt to hunt east was impossible anyway. We whiled away time making everything ready, then we got it all ready again 'til we were tired of being ready.

One of th' men in camp, I don't remember who, had a pistol that didn't work an' I traded for it. I spent most of my idle time working on it an' got it where it would shoot "most ever" time. Otherwise, it was a well-made gun an' I knew a gunsmith or even a blacksmith could fix it up like new, so I packed it away for future use.

Th' bunch who had been caught out on th' prairie fared pretty well. There were frostbitten noses an' cheeks an' only a few lost a toe or two. After a time, their exposed skin began to peel like they had been sunburned. Our camp soon was divided between The Fuzzy Ones an' The Smooth Ones, each group poking good-natured fun at th' other. It provided a distraction from boredom at being stuck in camp.

Kansas peeled almost all over her body. Only her trunk was clear, even one buttock peeled in a spot. Morning Starr cried when she saw how much of her little body had been exposed and th' wonder that she didn't die or lose toes or fingers will stay with us until th' last one of us dies. I can only surmise that th' Good Lord was looking after her in a special way. She continued to grow stronger an' her joyous energy infected us all. She almost completely took over th' care of Snowflake except for nursing, of course, an' would have seen after Little Chief except that he rebelled, being he considered himself too old to be "looked after."

I became Kansas' special responsibility. She took on all th' chores of "taking care" of me, even to th' point of seeing that I was well fed an' properly dressed, all this to th' amusement of Zilkah an' Morning Starr. I enjoyed her company an' constant chattering and found myself looking forward to evenings when we could be together. I continued to sleep inside until White Wolf returned, feeling responsible for family safety.

*"Trouble and thievery did not come from within the tribe, but Jerry was concerned about warriors from other tribes who would sneak into unguarded huts and kill and steal. Since their hut was at the edge of the camp, Morning Starr and Zilkah were particularly vulnerable,"* Zenas explained.

Kansas would go to sleep with th' women, but every morning would find her snuggled up to me, even though Zilkah fussed at her about it an' Little Chief was disgusted that she would sleep on th' men's side of th' hut. Knowing that she must feel some insecurity, I didn't say much, though it did embarrass me some.

Late on th' third day after th' melt, lookouts spied a group riding down from th' north. Most likely it was our war party returning but we didn't take chances. Half th' warriors saddled up an' rode out to meet them, th' other half kept watch from camp. All women an' children were in th' huts. It was a tense few minutes until they were identified as our war party. They came in tired an' hungry on played-out horses. At th' meeting house, they reported that they had scouted far to th' north without finding any camps or seeing any sign. This was unusual, but their general thought was that larger groups had gone further west to hunt. Our group being smaller, we could get adequate meat in smaller herds.

The storm had caught them on th' upper reaches of Pawnee Creek an' they had holed up there. They didn't run into any difficulties on th' way back until after they crossed over th' divide an hit Lightning Creek drainage. At first it was mud, then bunched-up buffalo were in th' way.

The subject turned to th' hunt an' there was talk of moving camp b'cause th' buffalo had moved north. Then someone suggested, "Why not move the buffalo south? So long as the creeks are high, they won't be trying to swim them and they would be trapped between Lightning and Thunderbolt, close to camp."

Several laughed at this, but on second thought it seemed it might work. It was decided that on th' morrow, we would all ride north, cut in b'hind a large portion of animals, an' try to slowly drive them south without exciting them.

Well before daylight we rode up Thunderbolt an' by sunrise we had passed a fair amount of buffalo. We fanned out about 50 yards apart an' started slowly walking south just as th' herd was rising to start th' day. It was touchy work keeping them moving without alarming them an' it took us 'most all day. Finally, we were opposite camp an' Tzi-Sho called us in. Having their meal interrupted left th' animals hungry an' when we left they were busy trying to catch up on their grazing.

"With luck, we'll have several buffalo to butcher tomorrow," White Wolf said as we ate supper. Th' women nodded, knowing that meant a long hard day on th' prairie skinning an' butchering. All was ready before we turned in. Th' women had built their drying racks an' they had their knives sharpened an' ready. Kansas was to keep th' baby an' Star Chief was to help "guard" camp while we were gone.

With Wolf back, I gladly relinquished th' hut to him an' made my bed a few yards north of camp in a stand of cottonwood saplings. Star Chief joined me an' we both tossed a little thinking about th' hunt. He would have raised a fuss to go with us, but knew it was no use. Kansas stayed in th' hut, but it was she who called us in just b'fore sunrise. After breakfast, White Wolf went through th' hunting ritual while I saddled horses. Wolf's buffalo horse was as excited about th' hunt as we were an' pranced an' snorted until Wolf mounted him. Instantly he was off an' I hurried to catch up. I wasn't going to kill today, but watch an' learn — but I took my rifle anyway. Wolf preferred bow an' arrow for buffalo because he could reload much quicker than with a gun.

He picked out a nice cow an' his horse instantly knew which critter to chase. Th' race didn't last long for his horse drew along beside th' cow as Wolf, with his rein in his teeth, notched a long arrow. My attention was on th' horse as White Wolf's shot went home, piercing th' cow's lung. Th' instant he heard th' arrow loosed, the horse swerved so sharply away from th' cow that any rider who didn't expect it would have been thrown. Th' swerve was none too soon, for th' beast hooked those sharp horns only to find air where horseflesh an' man had been an instant before. White Wolf hesitated a moment until he was assured that th' blow was fatal, then he was away after another kill. Th' pace was frantic, repeated a hundred times across th' herd.

In no time a couple hundred or more kills were scattered over th' plain. Women had swarmed to carcasses before th' killing was finished an' were already busy butchering.

There were two or more per carcass an' their efficiency was impressive. It seemed no time before they finished with one animal an' were heading for another. There was a regular highway to an' from camp with youngsters leading horses packed with meat an' hides to drying racks, then hurrying back for more.

Suddenly there was a cry of alarm an' I looked up to see a buffalo thought dead charging after some women. They ducked behind one of th' carcasses an' their pursuer paused in confusion at th' disappearance of her quarry. Good Walker rushed up to finish th' animal, but she turned an' charged this new challenge. It was all he an' his horse could do to avoid th' maddened animal. Circle as he might, he couldn't get in position for a shot. I was near an' rushed to help. As th' two combatants circled, I tried again an' again to get my sights on th' spot just behind th' cow's shoulder that would stop her.

"Hurry, Sly Fox, My horse is tired," Walker called, but th' buffalo kept turning away. "Turn her this way," I called an' Walker reined his horse toward me. Th' cow's side was exposed for a moment an' I fired. It was a lucky shot, for she ran a few steps an' fell over. Cautiously, butchers came out of hiding all around us. One younger woman approached th' cow an' gave it a hard kick in th' belly, just to be sure she was finally dead.

Good Walker dropped from his winded horse. "Thank you, Fox, we couldn't have lasted much longer. Is that your first kill of the hunt?"

"Yes, an' I hope it is th' hardest," I replied as I reloaded.

He soon rode off to some other chore an' I was left to wander th' field. I marveled at th' skill of th' hunters. They used special long arrows an' very few carcasses had more than one arrow in it. Most were buried to th' feathers, which meant that th' arrow had pierced clean through th' animal. Otter told me that he had seen some shots that passed completely through th' animal. That was shooting!

Guns were handy an' every Indian wanted one, but when it came to combat, bow held th' advantage over rifle for a long time, because th' shooter could get off three or more arrows before th' gunman could reload after one shot. It was a long time before rifle gained advantage over th' bow in firepower. When I first came on th' prairie with my old Tennessee long rifle, th' only advantage it held over a bow was accuracy at long ranges. In close combat, th' only way to use th' rifle to advantage was if there were more than one rifleman an' they could keep one gun loaded at all times. Many a frontiersman has come to grief because he couldn't reload in time. Some have escaped death by never firing, only pointing at th' most threat, most Indians being unwilling to sacrifice themselves so another could get a scalp. I guess that's what you would call a Mexican standoff.

By sundown, butchering was complete an' all were gathered at camp. Smoking fires were burning an' th' smell of meat cooking was overwhelming. We feasted that night an' th' next few days th' women spent working up pelts. Wolves, both gray an' th' little prairie wolf we call coyote, vultures, an' other creatures gathered on th' killing field an' their snarls an' quarreling filled th' night. They were so bold as to feed in daylight, hardly moving out of a man's way as he passed by. Flies were so thick you had to keep your mouth closed an' soon th' stench of rotting carcasses made us wish to move.

Hunting was over in this camp, th' herd moving north with greening grass an' we soon followed. Our second camp would be the last before Pawnee country an' we would move from there west for more hunting ground. I was allowed to hunt after that first day, an' did my share of killing. I used my best horse an' he became a good hunter. I could shoot with accuracy from a greater distance than did bowmen so we didn't have to dodge horns so much. Our problem came when my first shot didn't kill, then we had a long run while I reloaded for a second shot. That horse got to where he could tell when th' kill was made an' he would break off an' wait while I reloaded and found another target. We could only get two or three kills b'fore he was played out an' couldn't keep up with th' buffalo. Those fellows were slow t'git started, but once they began running, their speed was impressive. It was a rare horse that could outlast a running buffalo.

Midsummer found us well out on th' prairies an' our trip back to th' village took several days. We had captured a lot of wild horses an' broken them to ride an' pack. They were very necessary for th' trip home. I caught and gentled a pony for Chief an' one for Kansas. They were very pleased.

We arrived at th' village tired but happy at a successful hunt, though I detected among th' men a certain disappointment that there wasn't a horse stealing campaign against th'

Pawnees. When we left for our hunting village, they were planning a war party an' urged me to go along with them, but I declined, feeling I must help White Wolf an' family get back home.

The change in little Kansas was most amazing. She fleshed out, grew stronger an' healthier through th' summer. Where she was energetic before, her energy became almost boundless. I think she must have grown a head taller over that time, but it was plain that she would always be a small person. By th' end of our hunt she was helping butcher instead of carin' for Snowflake, who was left with Little Chief, much to his disgust.

A lot of White Wolf's neighbors stayed at th' big village a few days, but Wolf was anxious to get back to th' woods, so with Otter an' Tall Oak and their families, we left early one morning an' a few days later rode into th' old hunting camp. That is, what was left of th' old camp. Almost every hut had fallen in. Not a few of them held new occupants — th' four-legged kind. Instead of moving, th' women set about burning the old huts in a big brush pile. In almost no time, three new huts appeared where old ones had been and th' families settled in.

Early th' third morning, th' women gathered up baskets an' set off for their gardens. We were preparing to go out an' hunt when Kansas came running into camp. "Sly Fox! Sly Fox! Morning Starr needs you!" she called, then turned an' ran back down th' trail. Coming back, she stomped her foot an' demanded, "Are you coming?" then turned an' disappeared.

Wolf an' Tall Oak chuckled. "Better go, Jerryharris before you get into more trouble."

I mounted an' rode up th' trail, stopping under th' trees at the edge of th' garden. Zilkah and th' rest were out in th' garden looking over everything an' chattering. Morning Starr looked up an' called, "Get down, Jerry, and come here."

I walked down beside bean rows where th' vines had grown all over their trellises. They were heavy with beans already matured, some beginning to dry.

"Look over here at *our* beans!" Morning said.

There was a big difference in th' rows of beans I stood in an' Morning Starr's row, which we had fertilized with manure. Their vines were profuse an' held twice as much fruit.

"Now you can see what row planting an'

feeding th' seed can do," I said.

"It's sure that we will be saving the horse manure from now on!" she replied. "Thank you for the help!"

Zilkah called from th' pumpkin patch, "Come see the pumpkins and squash!"

We walked up th' rows to th' end. Th' darker green of th' leaves showed plainly which hills had been fed with manure. Vines ran everywhere and squash was noticeably larger than th' others. A dozen large pumpkins lay turning orange in th' late summer sun. I saw dark green melons peeking through th' leaves an' anticipated their sweetness.

Th' women were excited at th' differences my methods had made an' thereafter were diligent to use them in their gardens. When th' missionary William Requa came among th' Osage a few years later, he found some of th' tribe practicing improved farming an' with these people as a nucleus he established a segment of th' tribe along th' Neosho River that became known as Requa's Band. They practiced farming an' animal husbandry that gave them year-round comfort an' security quite apart from th' rest of th' tribe.

# Chapter 15
## Betrayed by a Neighbor

*"Uncle Jerry used t' tell me that a year with th'
Osage was about all he could stand." Zenas
chuckled. "In th' fall of 1816 he took Kansas
an' went back to Sam an' Grandma Ruth's. I
'spect there were some things happened he
didn't talk about that helped him make up his
mind. Anyhow, this is what he told about those
times."*

It was only a few weeks after we got back to
th' hunting camp that they began talking
about a fall hunt. There was a lot of discussion about where to hunt an' when to go
an' some of it wasn't too congenial. Usually, I would find somewhere else to be
when th' topic came up. Being a guest, I
didn't think it was my place to enter into
those discussions an' some of th' others
made it plain that they felt th' same way. I
told Wolf that I would go wherever he
decided, regardless of anything else.

One morning when I went out to tend th' horses, I found an arrow sticking in Kansas' pony. It wasn't deep, having hit a hip bone, but it had bled some an' would be sore for a while. There were some marks on th' shaft an' when I showed it to White Wolf, he said it was Black Elk's. Otter agreed. After I got over my mad enough to think about it, I realized that if he had gone to th' trouble to come all this way, he wasn't going to stop with just shooting a pony. He meant to do harm to me or Kansas or both an' knowing th' Osage temperament, he wouldn't worry about hurting anyone else who got in th' way. I could tell Wolf an' Tall Oak were concerned, so we got our heads t'gether an' I asked them to look out for Kansas while I looked for Black Elk.

It wouldn't be easy finding that Injun, but I had to try. I started hunting by making a circle around camp, looking for sign. It took most of a day but I finally found what I was looking for on th' opposite side of camp from White Wolf's hut. There in th' grass was a mark where someone had stood for some time. When I stood in th' same place, I could plainly see th' entrance to Wolf's hut. That was th' only sign I could find, an' even it might not mean a thing. I backed off away from camp an' walked another circle.

I had no idea where th' watcher had gone from there. Probably if he had been there more than once, he would have used different routes coming an' going. If I was going to catch this rascal, I would have to set a trap. There wasn't a trace of sign out of everyday traffic, so I came back to th' place where I had found sign. Back in th' woods a ways was a big white oak. If I could get up into that tree without being seen, I could see anyone who approached camp from this side.

Getting into th' tree unobserved proved surprisingly easy. Th' next best thing to no sign at all is too much sign, so we drove our horses under th' tree a couple of times when we took them out to graze. Th' third evening, I was on a horse with my gear an' when we went under that tree, I swung up on a limb. High up, I made a nest an' hid myself as best I could. By prearranged signal, Wolf told me that he couldn't see me so I knew I was well hidden. Now, all I had to do was wait an' watch.

It got pretty chilly after sunset an' it was a long cramped wait with not a sign of th' watcher. All day I stayed in th' tree, waiting. It was some entertaining to watch th' activities in camp. People came an' went on their errands, children played an' I learned a lot about their games just sitting in one place an' watching. I had never had a chance to play much, especially after we were captured, and their games were fascinating.

By turning my head just a little, I could see th' doorway of every hut an' who came an' went. After a while, I could account for everyone in camp an' where they were. It got to be a game I played with myself. I would close my eyes, name as many as I could, where they were an' what they were doing, then check myself to see if I was right. I got pretty good at it. By evening, I could name everyone in camp, where they were at th' moment without making a mistake.

It was another long, uneventful night. Nothing bigger than dogs an' possums moved about below. Just before dawn, adults came out of th' huts an' disbursed for their morning chant. I watched with interest where each went to their private places, feeling a little bit like a nosy spy. As they started their chants, I closed my eyes an' recited where each one was. I was scanning th' huts when a silhouette of a man passed inside one of th' doorways an' I thought for a moment that I had missed one of the neighbors, Lynx an' where he was chanting. Yet, when I looked at his spot he was there! I could feel th' hair on my neck crawl. If Lynx was there, who was that in his hut? Carefully, I looked over th' camp. Every man was accounted for! There was an extra man in th' camp. Black Elk wasn't hiding out in th' woods and th' reason I couldn't find any sign was because he was in Lynx's hut right here in camp! My head swam, I shuddered, an' broke out in a cold sweat. How many times did Black Elk watch me pass that hut, or watch Kansas as she went about her day? Just yesterday I had watched as Kansas passed within ten feet of that door.

So, Lynx was helping Black Elk. I hadn't known him much, but he had always been courteous to me, though maybe a little distant. I got angry. I was being betrayed by someone in camp. Now it was up to me to do something about it, but what could I do?

It came to me that I could not say anything to Wolf or Tall Oak or Otter because they had to live here with these people long after I was gone. No, whatever I did would have to be kept secret from all others. Th' question of why Elk had not already attacked us bothered me. Thinking back, there were several times when either Kansas or I had been within his grasp an' he had done nothing. It must be that he wanted us both together. Well, if that's th' deal, we could draw him out easily enough. All we'd have to do is to show ourselves together an' lure him out after us. It was at that moment that I knew that I had to return to Little Red River country, I could not deal with Black Elk and stay. Carefully, I slipped down to th' bottom limbs of th' tree an' when Wolf drove our horses under, I jumped down.

"Did you see anyone, Sly Fox?" he asked.

"Just people in th' camp," I replied, "and I know every one of them."

Wolf laughed. "I'll bet you do," he said.

Instead of sleeping in th' place I customarily slept I moved after dark an' slept in a different place every night. It was a couple of days later after I had made some preparations that I announced my intentions at th' evening supper. Mealtime was th' only time I felt it was safe for us all to be together an' I was careful to stay inside th' hut — and armed. As we were sitting around visiting before turning in, I said, "I have been thinking that I should get back to Little Red River country an' my kin. My sister's baby should have been born an' I wish to see them all."

It was very still for a moment, Zilkah an' Morning looked surprised, then sad. White Wolf was weaving a leather rope an' studied his work carefully. Finally, he spoke, "You know, Sly Fox, that you are more than welcome to stay with us as long as you wish, but I know that you miss your people. It is good that you have family and you should be close to them." I suspect that he knew what my intentions were, but he didn't say anything about them — ever.

Kansas was wide-eyed and, I thought, a little scared. "You will go with me, Kansas, I wish you to know my people." She beamed an' nodded. By that, I knew she would be happy to go.

"I would be very happy if you stayed with us," Zilkah said, "but I know how you love Ruthie and Jesse."

"Aside from blood kin, you — and we — have been through much together," Morning Starr added. "Still, I will miss you like a brother."

"We will all miss you and Kansas," Wolf said. "I suspect Snowflake will be lost without her here."

I nodded; it was about as much as I could do at that moment, with all that was welling up in me.

"When do you think you will leave?" Wolf asked.

"I would like to leave day after tomorrow."

"Oh, but that is too soon!" Starr exclaimed.

"I know it is soon, but I think that to go quickly would be easier for all of us. It is not like we will never see you again," I added.

Little Chief had been taking all this in an' suddenly gave a yowl. "I want to go with you and see Riley and Jesse!"

Morning Starr laughed. "We all want to go and see Riley and Jesse — and Ruth and Lonza and all the rest, but we have to stay here for the hunt."

She could have added that it would be dangerous right now for an Osage to travel into Cherokee country. Th' two tribes were arguing over their hunting grounds an' there had been some violence. I felt safe enough here in camp, but I would be in real danger around larger Osage villages where I was not known. That was another reason for getting back to Cherokee lands, something we all knew but didn't talk about.

There really wasn't much packin' to do to get on th' trail an' we could have left th' next morning as far as that goes, but I wanted to be able to say my "goodbyes" to my friends in camp an' have one day just for visiting. I also wanted to give Black Elk time to prepare for our leaving. I was going to have to deal with him somewhere on th' trail. I only hoped to have an advantage when that time came. I went to sleep late thinking about how I was going to take care of Black Elk without getting Kansas hurt or losing my hair in th' process. Several times that night I woke in a cold sweat, wondering what to do, but nothing came to me.

I spent all day just visiting an' saying goodbye to my friends while Kansas stayed close to th' hut an' Snowflake. She was gonna miss that baby an' Morning Starr was gonna miss her help. To see her now, you would hardly suspect that only a few months ago she was a starved waif nearer dead than alive. I was proud that she had carried more than her weight in her time with us. Still, I was anxious to get her out of this Osage influence an' into more genteel ways of Ruthie an' th' Cherokees.

There was a lot of talk about th' trip an' I got lots of advice on routes I could take. Each time I discussed it with someone, I indicated that I would take Fallen Ash Trail down th' north side of White River, then somewhere east of th' disputed hunting grounds I would cut south to Little Red River country. This way I knew that Black Elk would know our intended route.

Zilkah an' Morning Starr had been busy cooking all day an' about midafternoon they called us to eat. Other families gathered with us an' we had a feast. There was squash, beans, ahuminea, mounds of stan-inca bread, an' lots of deer meat.

I have to say that th' Osage excel in feasting an' this time was no exception. I had long ago given up trying to keep up with them an' that made me victim of many a joshing. This time, I limited my food intake for a deadly serious reason. I had to be sharp an' especially alert th' next few days — our lives would depend on it, along with a lot of luck.

Late in th' evening, people b'gan drifting off toward their huts an' I knew everyone would sleep soundly that night. Everyone, that is, except me an' Black Elk. Gathering my bedroll, I said goodnight an' headed off toward my customary sleeping place. I laid out my bed an' then crept out into th' woods an' around to Lynx's. I couldn't be sure that Black Elk would come out through th' doorway or through th' hut wall some-wheres else, so carefully an' quietly I strung a small string around th' house three or four feet from th' walls an' about six inches above ground. It was strong enough t'give a tug when someone struck it, but would break an' not give away what it was. I wrapped myself in my blanket an' set against a large blackgum tree facing th' hut door with each end of th' string tied to my wrists.

I didn't worry about being seen in that pitch-blackness, but if I was alert, I might see th' door open up by th' backlight of th' fire. My only other hope was that th' string would betray any movement I couldn't see.

I was so keyed up I don't think I even blinked for a long time. Gradually, my eyes adjusted to th' darkness an' I could make out th' bulk of th' hut ten yards away. If I was lucky, I might even see Black Elk as he came out. I didn't have long to wait. About th' time all was totally still in camp, th' curtain drew aside an' a man slipped out of th' door. In about ten steps he was gone in th' blackness an' I could breathe agin.

It was a funny thing, but I felt relieved that my stalker was out an' on th' hunt just as I had supposed. After I wound my string in, I crept off. Even though I was pretty sure where Black Elk was headed, I didn't feel safe sleeping on th' ground, so I climbed that big old oak tree an' settled into th' crotch I had spent two nights in. Soon I was asleep.

It was still black when I climbed down an' gathered up our horses. Before th' dawn chant was over, I had our little gear packed, loaded, an' was ready to go.

Not much was said as we ate. Kansas sat an' rocked Snowflake gently an' didn't eat. We finished an' I stood up an' there was a rush of talk, everyone trying to get their last words out at once.

"You should have good weather for traveling today," White Wolf said. After all the time I had known him, I felt a tug at our parting.

Zilkah, then Morning Starr hugged me an' wished us good travel. Kansas held Snowflake close. There were tears running down her cheeks, but she didn't say anything until Morning Starr hugged her close, then she sobbed an' hugged her tight. I may have sounded a little gruff when I told her to come on an' mount up, but it was either that or shed tears too. When she was seated, I handed her th' lead for her pony that would have to limp along b'hind her.

I had one foot in th' air preparing to mount my horse when Little Chief trotted into th' yard on his pony. "I'm going with you to see Riley an' Jesse!" Little Chief yelled. His face was red an' th' white of his scar stood out on his forehead.

"I wish you could, Star Chief," I said, "but you will have to stay here an' help your father with the fall hunt. With me gone, he will need a hunting partner if your mother an' sister eat well this winter. In a year or two, I will bring Riley an' Jesse an' we will all go on a hunt together, maybe buffalo hunting."

"My father hunts well enough for all of us and doesn't need my help!"

"I think he does, remember last year we nearly ran out of meat an' you an' I had to go hunting? It could happen again an' they would go hungry if you were not here to show them where we got that deer."

His determination faltered a little. "We-l-l . . ."

"I *will* need help on the hunt, Little Chief," Wolf said. "You are big enough to hunt now and there is much you must learn. Come, now, and we will plan the hunt together. I need to know where you found the meat last spring," White Wolf's voice was low but firm.

"We-l-l I will stay, but I won't tell you our secret hunting place unless we get real hungry! It's only for emergencies, isn't it, Jerryharris?"

I pretended that something called my attention away to hide a smile. "You're right, Chief, only in an emergency." I clucked to th' horses an' with a wave we were off, heading for th' Fallen Ash.

"You can ride with them to the edge of

253

the camp, Chief, but don't go past the creek," White Wolf said.

# CHAPTER 16
# THE REVENGE OF BLACK ELK

How do you plan for an ambush? There are a thousand ways, each dictated by conditions you find yourself in — an' most of your well-laid plans don't work when time comes to use them. Black Elk had a good eight hours' head start on us an' I expected him to attack this first day out. He would be anxious to attack us an', too, didn't want to be much further away from Osage villages. I wanted to frustrate him an' delay his action for a couple of days until I had an advantage. I was glad no one rode with us, for as soon as we were safely out of sight of camp, I cut across an' headed due south to White River. It was low this time of year so we had no trouble crossing out of sight of th' customary ford. I steered back to th' south trace an' pushed th' horses hard, making no effort to hide our trail. I planned to go straight through those disputed hunting grounds to the Village at Bear Springs.

From there, it should be a safe trip to th' Little Red River Valley as there was a lot of traffic between villages.

Now we would see how determined Black Elk was to get revenge on us. He would wait most of th' day in his ambush, then back-track to th' village. Depending on how far out he laid his trap, we could be more than a day ahead of him b'fore he found our trail. I didn't expect him to give up easily. If I could draw him deeper into th' woods, maybe he would lose some of his caution an' that would give me an advantage. He was a big man even by Osage standards an' I knew I could not best him physically, so I had to outsmart him.

I didn't know if I should tell Kansas or not an' debated with myself quite a bit afore I d'cided to get her prepared without telling her of any specific danger. Where she could, she rode beside me. She was rather quiet for a while, getting over th' goodbyes, but being on her way to a new place soon excited her an' made her curious about a hundred things. Being raised on open plains, th' woods closed in on her an' she was a little scared of them. I remembered having to get used to them when we got back from th' plains. I loved deep woods an' hills an' would have been happy to spend all my life in them. Those forests were some different than they are today. Virgin timber was mature an' there were some trees so big it would take half a day to ride around 'em. They reached up a hundred feet an' more, mostly without a limb within 30 to 40 feet of th' ground. More vigorous trees had squeezed out others an' they were spaced far apart, sitting up on mounds that had built up around their roots over th' years. Had woodcutters taken time to count th' rings, they would have found some of those trees to be 300 to 400 years old. Most places now nothing's left of those trees 'cept mounds.

There wasn't any underbrush in th' woods, it was like a park where th' ground was combed an' curried an' you could see plainly. Overhead th' canopy was almost solid an' sunshine had to fight through to reach th' ground. Mostly, it didn't. Some would say it was gloomy, but not me.

Deep woods was mostly free of animal life except for birds an' squirrels an' they was high in th' trees. What wildlife was there was mostly traveling from one open spot to another. These open places were due to storms or fire an' once th' trees were elimi-nated, they would grow up in th' most profuse vegetation you could imagine. I guess seed from all those plants must have laid dormant for years an' years waiting for something to happen to give them a chance to grow — an' when they got th' chance, did they ever grow! This was where food was for forest creatures an' this was where they congregated, mostly. That's where th' best hunting was.

But there's something about th' openness of th' plains an' that high blue sky that's downright intoxicating. Sometimes I'll just set an' look at th' world with no obstacle b'tween me an' th' horizon. Turning around an' looking all around me, it seems that th' ground rises in every direction an' I'm in th' center of th' world. Oh, it can be hot, an' it can be cold, an' it can be dry but there's water if you know where to find it. An' back then game aplenty — so much that you had to be careful not to step on 'em nor get run over by 'em.

I never get tired of looking at th' night sky out there. It never is dark if th' clouds are gone an' many a night I've traveled by starlight, following my shadow. When th' moon is full, you can read a paper by it — if you had one — an' you can see to th' horizon plain. We used to sit on some hill at night an' watch game coming out to graze.

You could see white antelope tails shining all around. They were like little white lights, some bouncing an' playing an' others just moving around as th' other end took on graze.

You haven't lived until you've watched thunderheads build an' move across th' plains. Boy, are they monstrous things! Up in th' morning, they start building over th' hills an' by afternoon, they're big enough to start movin' out over th' plains, flashing an' pouring th' coldest rain you ever felt — so cold that sometimes they were ice. It'd turn th' ground white an' wash into gullys an fill them up with hail 'til they were level with ground around them — takes hours to melt.

Th' lightning's some dangerous. Sometimes you can see a bolt come out of th' top of one of those building clouds an' strike th' ground fifty miles away in clear air. I've run miles to get out o' th' way of one of those monsters. You could find a gully to hide from th' lightning, but then you'd have to worry about flash floods. Hail, cold rain, floods, wind, an' lightning, those clouds are best viewed from a distance! Long 'bout sundown, th' clouds are spent with tops spread across th' sky like an anvil top. Way off down at th' bottom there'd still be flashes an' you could hear her still rumbling, but most of th' violence is gone out of her an' all that's left b'hind is th' sweet smell of rain on th' prairie an' maybe a rainbow. After sunset, th' tops shine in th' sun, turning all colors an' shades. Even in full dark, they still shine with some mysterious glow. By morning, they'll be gone an' th' whole process will start over agin. There's nothing like God's creation, mountains, plains, woods, or grass.

Th' silence brought me out of my thoughts, Kansas had asked a question an' was waiting for me to answer an' I had no idea what she had said. "What's that, Kansas? I was a hundred miles away."

"I said, do you think the bears in these woods are mean?"

"Well, I don't see any bears an' I suppose if they are here, they would be just like any other bear, mean when they are hungry or have cubs an' happy when they are full. Our biggest danger out here is from th' two-legged kind of animal an' we should be prepared for them one way or th' other." Reaching down in my possibles bag, I brought out a large knife an' sheath. "Tie this around your waist an' carry it at all times while we're on th' trail. You'll find it comes in handy for a lot of things *and* may be necessary to defend yourself. I will teach you how to fire a gun an' when we get th' chance, I will get one for you."

Her eyes grew wide. "You will give me a gun?"

"Why, yes, why not?"

"Because I am a slave."

"No! You are no longer a slave! You are as free as I am and I will take care of you like you are my child — or sister — or friend!" I stammered.

She looked at me in wonder. "I am free?"

"Yes, mostly so, except that you must stay with me until it is safe to take you back to your people."

"My mother and father and brothers are dead; that monster Black Elk killed them!" Her teeth were clinched an' she trembled with fury. She hung her head an' her eyes filled with tears. "You are my only family now and I want to stay with you."

There was a lump in my throat I couldn't quite explain an' I reached over an' lifted her onto my saddle. Th' heft of her surprised me, she had really grown since that first time I had lifted her onto my horse. Sitting there sidesaddle, she held on to me tight an' laid her head on my chest an' sobbed. I hadn't much experience with girls, but I was beginning to find that they were a different creature an' I kinda liked some of th' differences. I guess I was kind of like clay in her hands, for my heart was always soft toward this child — and I'm pretty sure she already knew it!

"You may stay with me as long as you like," I said. She was very still for a long time an' gradually relaxed her hold on me. I realized that she was asleep.

One of th' horses nickered an' I came out of my thoughts with a little start. Kansas stirred a little, then lapsed back into her sleep. This wouldn't do. I couldn't be distracted from my watchfulness so long as there was danger around — and any time on th' trail in those days was dangerous. In th' bottom of a little swale, I stopped to let th' horses drink. Kansas hopped down an' took th' reins of her horse an' mine while all five horses lined up to drink. "Stay here while I take a look around," I said an' trotted back up th' trail. Looking carefully over th' hill, I could see a long ways through th' trees along th' trail we had just come. Nothing moved an' I watched for several minutes until I was satisfied no one was close. Ahead, th' trail looked clear an' there were no places handy for an ambush. I guess I thought by taking all those precautions, I could make up for th' lapse of th' last few minutes.

Soon we were back on th' trail an' I was back to being alert to things going on around us. "Kansas, we have to be alert at all times, no telling when trouble might pop up. Where you can, I want you to ride on my right side a step or two behind me. It's your job to look out to th' right an' ahead for anything that might be unusual an' I will cover th' front left, an' behind. When we talk, we will be very quiet about it an' we don't make any sudden moves or startle th' horses."

"I understand, Jerryharris," an' she dropped back a step or two.

We rode in that manner until mid-afternoon. Where th' trace went across burns or through windfalls, we took th' lesser traveled detour around them to avoid any possibility of ambush. We waded down a small branch until well out of sight of th' trail, then stopped to rest an' eat. I gathered wood an' started a fire an' Kansas pulled out th' cookware an' warmed beans an' jerky an' tea. We ate heartily, sopping up th' juices with staninca Zilkah had sent.

Back on th' trail after a couple of hours, we rode until sundown, then b'fore full dark moved off th' trail an' made camp. There was no fire. We ate cold jerky an' th' rest of th' bread. We picketed our horses at th' edge of an old burn where they could graze, then I made a bed of cedar boughs under a cedar where th' lower limbs touched th' ground. We were well hidden there an' soon fell asleep, Kansas pushed against my back. Twice in th' night I checked on horses an' looked around, but all was quiet.

There was just a crack of light in th' east when we awoke. A small fire and some hot food got us ready for th' trail. We watched th' sun rise from horseback. Our 24-hour head start was up an' I wondered how soon Black Elk would find our trail or if he would even try. It could be that Lynx had scouted around an' found our trail. That would save a lot of time for Elk. Would Lynx join Black Elk in th' chase? I wondered. It was a possibility I couldn't afford to ignore. I pondered leaving th' trail an' striking out cross-country, but that would slow us an' we could not hide our trail. We would be alone an' vulnerable, where on th' trace, we might meet with some of my people an' be safer.

We would stick to th' trail an' push our horses hard one more day. With luck, that would get us to Bear Springs. Kansas would be safe there an' I could watch our back trail.

But luck wasn't with us, Kansas' pony was

so sore he could hardly walk. There was no question about leavin' th' horse, Kansas would have stayed with him.

Now I value an' take good care of my horses, but I have avoided any overly sentimental attachments to any of them. If they come up lame an' I'm in a tight spot, I'm leaving them to their own devices. They're probably better off anyway, but I knew it was no use asking Kansas to do th' same. Had our situation been more desperate, I would have insisted on leaving th' pony. Even th' other horses became restless an' tried to pick up th' pace.

And so we limped along at a walk, stopping to rest often. Th' pony was game an' tried hard to please Kansas. His wound had closed an' I couldn't find any infection, but th' muscles of his leg were as hard as iron an' I suspected th' bone was sore too. Th' result of it all was that we only made about ten miles that whole day.

That meant that if Black Elk was on our trail he had gained about 30 miles on us an' would only be a few miles b'hind. He would catch us b'fore we got to Bear Springs. I got angry, a cold hard anger that made me want to do something. We had changed trails to throw him off an' run hard to git away (an' that rankled) yet it was more than likely that he was back there bearing down on us to catch us b'fore we got to safety. An' for what? B'cause he had lost face? B'cause his wife was a mean woman that abused helpless children? Was that enough reason to want to harm innocent people? If he was still chasing, I guessed it was. Well, I wasn't gonna let him get us without a fight. He might win, but he'd know he had been in a fight if I had anything to do with it!

Th' trail had now reached Bear Creek an' ran upstream toward th' springs. We turned off at Barren Fork an' waded up th' creek some distance, then up a gully that came down from th' right. This was th' last gully b'fore you get to Walnut Creek. It was a steep climb to th' top where it comes out on a bench b'low th' mountaintop. Over against th' slope up th' hill we found a seep with some water still running. We made camp here an' I climbed up to see how th' land lay an' where th' trail was from here. All I could see was th' ridge dividing th' gully we had come up from that first gully we saw on Walnut. Beyond that was Bear Creek an' th' trail. I guessed it was a couple of miles as th' crow flies.

Back at camp, I helped Kansas set things up, then dug out that pistol I had traded for. I dry fired it a couple of times an' it looked like it might work, so I put a new flint in th' lock an' loaded it. Then I checked out my rifle t'make sure it was in working order. Kansas watched nervously as she heated supper. When she had it ready she came an' sat by me as we ate.

"What are you going to do, Sly Fox?" She had a worried look on her face. She already knew something was wrong.

"We won't get to Bear Springs before Black Elk catches up with us, so we are going to have to fight him," I said, forgetting for th' moment that I had not told her we were being followed.

She started and almost spilled her bowl. "Black Elk? He's following us?"

"Yes, he was hiding in Lynx's hut waiting to kill us both."

She thought this over for a moment. "Is he far away?"

"I am not positive that he followed us all this way, but we can't be too careful. He left camp th' night before we did an' went down Fallen Ash Trail to ambush us, that's why we changed to th' Bear Springs trail an' rode so hard th' first day. I didn't say anything for fear of scaring you." At that she kicked my leg.

"I am not a child, Jerryharris, I have been fourteen summers!"

I looked carefully at her. It sure was hard to b'lieve, but she was stunted some by th' bad treatment she had been through, then had grown some through th' summer. Maybe she was fifteen, but she was still small for her age an' she didn't show any signs of being a young woman.

"Fourteen summers?"

"Yes and you had better believe it!" She had risen an' stomped her foot for emphasis.

"Sit down an' I will tell you what I have planned."

She sat b'side me an' took a deep breath to hide her fright. "Are we going to have to fight, Jerry?"

"Yes, I think there is a good possibility that Lynx will be with him."

"Lynx is the son of Black Elk's uncle, I have heard Elk speak of him."

"That makes it more likely that he will come too. What I plan to do is cut across to our back trail an' try to catch them by surprise. I want you to stay here with th' horses. I will give you my rifle for protection in case I don't succeed."

"No," she shook her head, "I will go with you!"

"No, Kansas, you would be in great danger an' I am going to have to move fast if I catch them. You need to stay with our horses. If there are two of them, I may not be able to keep one of them from getting to you in a fight. This way if they beat me, only one of them will be able to look for you, I will see to that!"

She thought a moment, shook her head silently, an' got very still. Then she squeezed my arm an' said, "All right, Jerry, I will do as you say. What do you want me to do?"

"I want you to build a little rock fort around this seep. Then I want you to bed down in it with th' rifle. If Elk or Lynx come to you, you will know that most likely I am dead. I want you to wait until they are nearly on you, then shoot them. What you have to do is point th' gun at them by looking down th' sights like this, then pull this hammer back to here an' sque-e-e-ze th' trigger. Hold steady until the gun fires. If you miss, you will have a moment to run or get your knife out an' fight."

I was surprised at her calmness. It must have been because she had never been in a fight an' didn't know how serious this was an' how great her disadvantage would be.

I looked up at th' sky through th' white oak we were sitting under. It was a young tree an' its first limb was only about twelve feet above us. As I studied it, an idea came to me an' I looked around for just th' right log for my purposes. A huge chestnut tree nearby had lost a big limb an' a ten-foot section of it was just what I needed. I dragged it back to camp, then got rope from our packs and tied equal lengths to both ends of th' chestnut log. With the other ends tied to a limb of the oak tree, I made a swing that had a ten-foot horizontal seat hanging about three feet above ground, one end hangin' over th' seep. In the center of th' log, I tied a third rope, ran it over a limb of a tree behind th' oak, an' pulled it until th' log swung back as high as it would go. When I turned th' rope loose, my log swung down over th' seep an' ground in front of it. It was heavy enough to take out anyone who stood in th' way, even a man as big as either of those Osages.

Kansas saw my plan an' smiled. I pulled th' log back up an' anchored th' end with a slipknot to a tree just on th' other side of th' seep. With a stick, I marked out where Kansas was to build her wall. "Just remember that your wall cannot be any higher than this stick an' when you pull th' rope, keep your head below th' rocks," I said.

She smiled. "Do you think I might miss with the gun, Jerry?"

"Have you ever shot?"

"No."

"Then I think missing is a good possibility, but whoever you shoot at will dodge or stop an' you will have time to loose the swing." I got up. "I have to go now, if I don't come back by noon tomorrow, follow th' trace to Bear Springs an' tell people there that you want to go to the Village on Middle Fork, that you belong to Wash Fishinghawk. They will know him an' you will be safe. You may have to give someone a horse to take you to them."

She nodded, wide-eyed an' silent. I stuck th' loaded pistol in my belt, took my bow an' quiver, an' trotted off along th' bench. As I rounded th' head of th' next gully, I swung northeast an' runnin' downhill an' walkin' uphill, made it to a dry Charlie Creek. This I followed down until it crossed th' trail.

I watched for a while an' it was quiet. Our tracks on th' trail were plain, then I picked out two sets of unknown tracks on top of ours! It wasn't very likely that anyone besides Black Elk an' Lynx would be travelin' th' trail. At any rate, I couldn't take any chance that it wasn't them, so I followed.

By th' trail, it was four or five miles to Barren Fork an' it would be pitch-dark before they got there. They couldn't follow our trail in th' dark, so they would have to stop soon. Maybe I could find their camp. My tracking got harder an' harder as light failed an' I finally couldn't see th' trail at all. Back off th' trace a ways, I sat on a log an' thought about my situation. Somewhere b'tween here an' Barren Fork, Black Elk an' probably Lynx were camped. They would be off th' trail, hidden but they could be close enough to hear or see if anyone passed in th' night. I could creep forward slowly in hopes of hearing or seeing something or I could stay here all night an' pick up in th' morning. There was a risk that I might pass them in th' night an' wind up ahead of them or worse yet stumble into their camp an' git caught. Passing them would not be so bad so long as I knew it b'fore they did, but they would find my tracks an' I would lose what little advantage of surprise I had. I couldn't afford t'go any further, th' risks outweighed the advantages. At th' same time, Elk would have to stop for th' same reasons.

Sliding off th' log, I rested my back against it where I could see th' trail, but at least as long as it was dark, no one would know that I was there.

I didn't intend to sleep, but I awoke with a start. Some noise had wakened me. I listened, barely breathing. A hoof clinked against a rock, someone was coming down th' trail from Barren Fork. His pace was erratic, he would stop a while, then come on. I became convinced that it was a horse without a rider. Sure enough, it was a horse loose from his hobbles grazing his way up th' trail, probably moseying back home.

An idea struck me an' I snared th' horse as he passed. He snorted his displeasure, then settled down an' followed me. A little further down th' trail, a bush brushed my leg, just what I was hunting for. I tangled th' rein in th' bush an tied th' rope out of sight so it would look like he had just gotten tangled up while grazing. Back a ways, a big limb overhung th' trail an' I found th' tree an' climbed up, settled in th' crotch, an' waited for sunrise.

There was just a hint of gray when I crawled out over th' trail. I didn't have to wait long until someone came trotting along th' trail. I got ready, then froze. As he turned th' bend, he spied his horse an' came on, eyes on th' horse. He was just past th' limb when I jumped. As I landed on his back, I swung an' th' pistol struck him just b'hind his ear. Lynx fell like a limp rag. What was I to do now? I had no enmity against him. If my kin was on th' warpath I would help just like he was doing. He was still as death, only soft breathing told me otherwise.

I made up my mind not to kill him, but I had to keep the man out of our fight. With th' horse tied close, I hoisted Lynx's limp body on his back an' tied his feet t'gether underneath th' horse's belly with th' hobbles. A piece of rein fastened his hands tight around th' horse's neck. Lying that way, Lynx would not be able to free himself. I took th' flint out of his gun an' put it in his possibles bag. Hanging his gun on th' horse, I led him down th' trail a ways, then hazed him on his way. He would be home in a day an' someone would find Lynx, safe but mad as a hornet. I didn't think he would be back.

Now, to find Black Elk — no — I thought, let Black Elk find me! He would get tired of waiting an' come to see what had happened to Lynx. There was too much light for me to pull th' tree limb trick again, I would have to find another way to get to him. It occurred to me that I could shoot him with his own arrow, but at that time in my life, I didn't cotton to ambushes. I sure didn't want to fight that man with me on th' ground an' him on his horse. Any hand-to-hand combat had to be short an' to my advantage, for he was too strong for me to whip.

I found a bushy sapling growing by th'

trail an' pulled it down until its bare trunk lay across th' trail. Snuggling down under brush, I waited. It seemed hours b'fore I heard a horse approaching. Just when he started to step over th' sapling, I let it fly into th' horse's face. He reared straight up an' Elk fell, trying to hold on to th' rein.

I swung my pistol hard. He dodged an' my blow hit him high on th' shoulder with a crack. His left arm went limp, but he swung upward with his right hand, th' knife he held cutting a long gash in my ribs, but not hitting anything vital.

Black Elk sprang to his feet, his face contorted with anger an' hatred. "Now I will kill you, Stupid Fox," an' he sprang at me, knife held low. His thrust missed, but his momentum carried him into me an' we both fell. I rolled to his left out from under his body, then scrambled onto his back. With one useless arm an' my weight, he couldn't get up quickly enough.

"That was your last chance, Black Elk!" an' I slid my knife between his ribs, high up. Slowly he sank facedown. There were a few gurgling breaths an' he was still.

I lay on his back, expecting him to rise again, but he never did. Then th' world went black.

# CHAPTER 17
## FOURTEEN STITCHES

When I awoke, th' sun was high, th' horse cropped leaves nearby, an' my side felt like it was on fire. When I tried to stand, my shirt tore away from my chest and I felt a warm gush of fresh blood. Black Elk's back was covered with blood — it was mine. I needed help an' fast. A few strips of buckskin cut from Elk's shirt wrapped tightly around my chest seemed to stop th' bleeding. I took a few shaky steps toward th' horse an' his head snapped up. He looked at me an' was turning his head to move away when I spoke to him, "Hold, little horse, I need you." He stopped an' gave me a curious look. I continued talking an' slowly walking toward him. Just as I reached for th' rein, he jerked away an' took a few steps.

"Hold still!" I called, then blacked out again.

When I came to, th' horse was standing

over me, th' rein lying across my arm. I slowly moved my other hand under my body an' gripped th' rein. "Now, little horse, I have you!" But it was a long time before I had enough strength to stand. One or two steps exhausted me.

Th' horse sort of dragged me along until we came to a large boulder lying by th' trail. On my third try, I got on top of it an' threw my leg over his back. He b'gan to move off an' I held on. At last, I seated myself an' lay on th' horse's back. I was able to turn him up Barron Fork b'fore I passed out an' when I came to, he was standing in water before th' gully. I turned him an' we were well on our way b'fore I realized it was th' wrong gully. I didn't know where we were, but I let th' horse keep on climbing. On top, I recognized th' bench an' that we had come up th' first gully. A turn right and a couple hundred yards would get us to camp. Last thing I remembered was turning th' horse . . .

I don't know how long I was out of it, Kansas says it was three an' a half days. That's hard for me to b'lieve, but I guess I'll have to take her word for it. What brought me up with a start was th' sound of a gun going off almost in my ear. I jumped, tried to rise, an' felt a sharp sting of pain in my ribs. It wasn't until I lay back down that I opened my eyes. There sat Kansas beside me, th' gun stock under her arm, smoking barrel b'tween her feet.

"It knocked me down," she said in Kaw an' I'm sure she was talking to herself.

I tried to laugh, but it hurt too much. "I forgot to tell you about that." My voice was just a croak.

"Oh-h oh-h," she whispered, "you're awake! I shot at a deer, but it ran. How are you feeling? Do you hurt? Do you want a drink? Is your fever gone? Can I get you something to eat?"

I could only smile an' groan. Her hand was cool on my forehead an' I knew I had a fever. I opened my eyes an' saw her face bending over me.

"I thought you would die." Tears welled up in her eyes.

"Too ornrey to die . . . you need to reload th' gun."

"I don't know how, Jerry."

I tried to sit up, but couldn't. "You can do it, I'll tell you. Get my horn an' bag."

In a moment she was back, sitting close to my side. I didn't even feel like opening my eyes. "Under th' barrel is a stick, pull it out. Now put a rag from th' bag through th' slot in th' end an' run it down into th' barrel a couple of times to clean it out."

"That's done."

"Now take th' cap off th' end of that horn an' pour about two thimbles full of powder down th' barrel."

"What's a thimble?"

"O-h-h-h . . . well, fill th' cap with powder two times an' put it down th' barrel." A sudden thought hit me, "Where's th' fire?"

"It's outside, Jerry, we're safe."

I heard her fill th' caps an' pour powder down th' barrel. "Now, shake it down by tapping th' stock on th' ground." I lay still a moment an' must have dozed off a little.

"What's next, Jerry?" I jumped.

"Take your piece of rag out of th' stick, wrap it around a ball, an' ram it down tight against th' powder."

"There! Is that all?"

"For now. Does th' flint in th' lock look good?"

"I think so, should I see if it will spark?"

"No, no, that would fire th' gun!" It sure was hard to talk without moving, but my body was resisting movement at th' moment.

"Lean th' gun up close by where th' barrel doesn't point to anybody or anything living an' where you can grab it quick if you need to."

She scrambled up an' in a minute she was back with a cup of tea of some kind. I drank, coughed, drank agin. It was strong an' hot an' felt good going down.

"What is that?"

"Sassafras with some willow bark boiled in it. It will help your pain." She put th' cup to my lips again.

"You said you shot at a deer? How far away was it?"

"About ten horse lengths." Indians didn't know yards an' feet.

"That's pretty close, do you think you hit it?"

"I don't know, it fell down, then jumped right back up and ran."

"Sounds like you hit it. Go out where it was an' see if there is any blood."

She scurried off an' in a moment called, "There is blood here . . ." then from some distance away, ". . . I see it! I see it! It's lying by the woods! I'll get a horse and bring it back." She was running back.

By keeping my body straight an' inching up on my elbows, I was able to sit up an' push back against th' bank. I was inside th' rock fort, an' could barely see over th' top of th' wall. Kansas' head bounced by, an' in a moment she hurried past leading a horse.

"Get a rope an' drag th' carcass back to th' oak tree," I called. She made no reply. In a few minutes she was back, th' soft sound of a body dragging over th' grass.

"Can you throw th' rope over a limb an' hoist th' deer up?"

"We didn't have many . . . trees on the prairie . . . I can do better with it . . . lying on the ground," she said between grunts as she positioned it like she wanted.

I couldn't see much of her over th' wall, but I listened an' we talked as she worked.

"How did I get here?"

"I found you lying on Elk's horse out on the bench."

"But how did I get in th' fort?"

"You walked, don't you remember?"

"No . . ." I must have dozed off, ". . . when was that?"

"When was what?"

"How long ago did you find me?"

"Three days ago."

"Three days?"

"It was midafternoon. The horse was still a little wet from wading the river and your blood was running down his side. I talked to you and you slid off the horse right here by the fort and I helped you to the bed."

"Did I talk?"

"Yes . . . you told me you had killed Black

Elk, that he had cut your side, and that you had tied Lynx to his horse and sent him home . . . and that he never did even see you."

"I don't remember . . ." I drifted off to sleep.

The smell of meat roasting an' liver frying woke me up. "Are you through butchering?"

"No, but I will stop soon and we will eat."

It hurt to stretch my neck, but I could feel my cut an' tell it had been stitched up. "When did you sew me up?"

She giggled. "While you were asleep that first day. A couple of your ribs down low were cut but the cut wasn't that deep up high. You have lost lots of blood and that is what is making you so weak. The cut wasn't that bad, just long — and deep down low. If he had hit you one rib lower, the knife would have gone into your vitals and you probably would have died."

"I guess he didn't have time to turn th' knife so it went between th' ribs."

"You are very lucky, Jerry." Her voice faded away. I slept again.

"How many are there?"

"How many what!" Her head popped over th' rocks. She brushed her hair back with th' back of her wrist, her hand holding a bloody knife.

"How many stitches?"

". . . Twelve . . . no, fourteen. I couldn't stop on thirteen, that's an unlucky number to my people," she looked at me an' giggled. "The cut was so wide in th' middle I could lay my finger in it and I had to push it together to get the stitches in. You didn't even move, so I put the extra one where the cut was the widest."

"I don't remember feeling a thing." I drifted off again an' next thing I knew she was sitting by me with a bowl of cut-up meat an' liver. With a stick, she speared th' pieces an' fed me. I felt awful silly being so helpless, but moving my arms any pulled my side an' I didn't want that.

"I will have some good broth ready by morning. It will make you stronger."

"May I have a drink of water?"

She dipped from th' tiny pool under th' seep an' gave me a gourd full.

"Where did you find a gourd?"

"Down the bench a way. There must have been a camp there once."

She made me eat all of th' liver. "It is good for your blood," she said.

When I woke again I was still sitting up a little an' it was pitch-black. I could smell th' fire faintly an' see a few stars through bare limbs of th' oak. *Thank goodness it hasn't rained,* I thought. Kansas was snuggled under my arm against my good side, her hand on my arm. If I moved, she would know it. I wondered if she had slept like that every night. Next thing I knew it was morning. Kansas stirred an' looked up at me.

"Are you hungry, Sly Fox?"

"Why, yes I am!" a little surprised.

She sat up an' pulled my arm around her, squeezing it tight. "I'm glad you are back!"

"Me too. What are we going to do?"

"We will stay right here until you are well enough to travel." She nodded her head to emphasize her determination.

"I hope it's before we eat all of that deer." I chuckled — carefully.

"Why? Don't you think I couldn't shoot another one?" she rose, hands on hips an' trying to hide a smile.

"When I'm well, I'll teach you to shoot an' you can learn to miss them like I do."

"Humph!" She was off stoking up th' fire, getting breakfast ready.

I had gradually slumped down in th' night an' carefully pushed myself back up. Was th' pain a little less? I would have to walk some today. Hot tea relaxed me an' I slept after breakfast. I woke about midmorning. All was still.

"Are you there, Kansas?"

There was no answer an' I decided to try to stand. Th' deadfall was still tied up an' I could reach th' rope. It was tight enough that I could pull myself up by walking my hands up th' rope until I could put my feet under myself an' stand. It wasn't until then that I realized I was barefooted. *Well never mind,* I thought an' carefully ducked under th' rope. My first steps were stiff an' faltering, but I got better as I went. I could see Kansas over by th' edge of th' bench. She had a big bundle of long poles cut for her racks to dry meat on. I was halfway to her before she saw me.

"What are you doing running around?" she said as she came with th' poles.

"I came to help you cut poles."

"Well you're too late, I'm done. Are you hungry?"

"A little. I'll be back after I take a walk behind those bushes."

"Don't be too long, and don't fall!" She hurried on to camp.

We ate an' I watched her build her drying racks awhile. I delayed th' pain of lying down as long as I could, but I got so tired an' my head hurt so that I had to rest. Walking myself down th' rope helped a lot, but th' exertion hurt an' my side felt damp when I was down. My hand came away from my side with blood on it. Not much, but I really didn't have any to spare.

I awoke to th' aroma of supper cooking. There were different smells I couldn't quite identify until she came to me with a bowl of steaming greens with deer bacon.

"I found some poke the frost hadn't bitten and cooked us a batch," she said. It surely did hit th' spot with me an' I finished th' bowl.

Our camp was on th' south side of th' mountain an' pretty warm, catching that early fall sun. It would be good — so long as it didn't rain. I had picked th' site quickly thinking it was temporary an' we would be gone in a day. As time wore on, I became more an' more aware that any rain would turn our fort into a pond an' be very uncomfortable.

Th' cut healed quickly but I was still very weak, I suppose from loss of blood. We enjoyed our camp for a week more, then one night th' wind switched from north to south an' I knew it would soon rain. It was cloudy when we got up an' by th' time we had broken camp, a light rain was falling. We rode quickly down th' creek before it had time to rise an' rode into th' Bear Creek

Springs Village midafternoon in a heavy rain.

# CHAPTER 18
# BEAR CREEK SPRINGS

The village at Bear Creek Springs was large
— about three hundred people lived there,
but not a person was to be seen when we
rode in. Th' only sign of life was smoke
pushed out of tipis an' washed to th' ground
an' a pack of dogs yappin' at our horses'
heels.

We were halfway through th' village b'fore
a single soul braved th' rain to see what all
th' fuss was about. A short very round
person wrapped up in a robe stepped out of
a large tipi. It could have been a young
person not grown to full stature, I couldn't
tell with only nose an' eyes showing, but as
soon as he spoke, I knew it was a man with
an unusually deep voice.

"Who goes there on such a day as this?"
he asked.

"I am Jerry Harris of th' clan of Wash
Fishinghawk returning to the Village on
Middle Fork."

"Fishinghawk! How is that old bird?" his voice boomed.

At that, a woman stuck her head out an' called, "Bring them in here out of the rain, John Watie, and you can talk about Wash Fishinghawk all night if you want!"

"Yes, yes, do come in! You can put the horses behind there and bring your gear in here."

Kansas was down an' had our pack unloaded b'fore I could gather up all th' reins an' leads. I tied them to some trees where they could get under their shelter an' hurried as much as I could to th' tipi.

Inside, th' warmth surrounded me like a blanket an' I was suddenly very tired an' sleepy. Kansas an' th' woman looked up from where they had been talking.

"Why, you are sick!" th' woman exclaimed. She was a little taller than th' man and her hair was streaked with gray.

She hurried to me as Kansas explained, "He lost a lot of blood in a fight with an Osage and has not recovered yet."

"Osages!" John Watie exclaimed. "We know all about those dogs! Where did you meet up with them?"

"On th' north trail just north of Barren Fork," I replied. I wanted to lie down, but had to stand until invited to sit.

"A-a-h-h," Watie nodded. "We have seen your handiwork, but why did you leave that carrion to stink up the trail?"

"He was too hurt to do anything with that murderer," Kansas broke in vehemently, lifting my shirt to show th' cut.

"Ask our guests to sit, John, and let me examine this wound," Rebecca Watie (for that was her name) said.

"Yes, yes, do sit down, sit down!"

She led me to a couch. "Don't sit, lie down here and let me see that wound. Mm-mmm," she hummed as she looked an' lightly touched around th' cut. "Fourteen stitches! From the second rib all the way up above the nipple! You did a good job sewing him up. I couldn't have done better myself, even an extra stitch here where it was needed."

I grunted. "That extra stitch was so she wouldn't stop on an unlucky thirteen stitches."

Rebecca nodded. "That is good also." She left an' I didn't rise as good manners would have dictated. In a moment she returned with a bag of sweet-smelling salve she gently rubbed over th' scar. "This will help it heal."

"You have a nice trophy there, young man," John Watie said, smiling.

"He didn't turn his knife or I would have

been killed."

"Oh, that was no mistake, he intended to carve you up until the loss of blood made you too weak to fight, then he would have pulled your entrails out and left you to die a slow death," John said.

Kansas shuddered. I patted her arm. "But he didn't get th' chance."

"The men found only one wound in his side, the fight must have been short."

"I broke his shoulder before I killed him," I said.

"Aaahhh, a neat one-on-one fight, I would say."

"There were two of them, Black Elk and Lynx," Kansas said. "Jerry tied Lynx to his horse and sent him home."

John Watie's eyes widened. "Two? You have done very well, Jerry Harris, the people will be proud of you . . . but you should have killed them both!"

"I had no quarrel with Lynx, he was part of th' clan I lived with."

"You lived with the Osages? We must hear more of this story . . ." his voice faded away an' I slept.

I awoke some time in th' night right where I had laid down. Kansas was rolled in a robe on th' floor beside me. Th' patter on th' tent told me it was still pouring down an' its music lulled me back to sleep.

Th' smell of good food cooking brought me awake next morning an' I sat up. Kansas was dishing up a bowl of stew an' brought it to me. John Watie was gone and th' rain was still falling. I was glad we left th' fort on th' bench.

"You have slept well, Jerryharris, that is good." Rebecca smiled.

After I ate, I started to rise, but Kansas pushed me back. "I have cared for the horses and they are fine," she said. "You stay right here and rest."

"Yes," Rebecca said, "John has gone to see some of the other men and I expect you will have company soon."

I sat back an' watched th' women as they moved around th' tipi an' talked. They sent an occasional question or comment my way, but mostly chatted with each other. After a while, I dozed. I was awakened by th' sound of several people entering th' tent an' looked up to see Watie an' several other men removing rain-soaked blankets. I stood.

"This is Jerry Harris, who was named Sly Fox by an Osage seer," John introduced me to each of th' men. "He has lived with the Osage and I think he has quite an interesting story to tell us." I shot a glance at Kansas, someone had been talking!

We sat down an' without further ceremony, I started with th' rescue of White Wolf at Flee's Settlement an' Morning Starr an' Zilkah at Blowing Cave an' told them th' story of our journeys. There were some questions, but for th' most part the men listened an' nodded without comment.

When I finished, one of th' men said, "We have seen where you fought the Osages, how you jumped from the limb and got one of them and where you caused the sapling to flash in the face of the horse and fought the other. We saw where you caught and mounted the horse, but we lost your trail after that. Did you go up Barren Fork?"

"Yes, then we climbed th' hill to th' right to th' first bench and camped at a seep we found there. We — Kansas — built a rock wall around th' seep and we stayed there until rain forced us to leave. Then we came here."

Another man spoke, "We have had much trouble with the Osages, had it not been for your fight with the two, we might suspect that you are a spy against us."

"My mother was Cherokee, a Fourkiller. I was raised Cherokee and my allegiance is to th' Cherokee. However, I believe it is possible to live peaceably among many tribes if they will allow it. You now know th' reasons for my ties to White Wolf an' I think they are just. Morning Starr is Cherokee an' lives peacefully among th' Osage. I would hope th' two tribes can settle their differences an' live as good neighbors."

"We would hope the same thing, but that does not seem to be the Osage way," John Watie said.

"Then let us defend our people until they understand that we will not shrink before them," I said.

The men looked at one another an' nodded agreement. "We believe you, Sly Fox, and welcome you to our village."

"Thank you," I said. "We will move on as soon as we can. I am anxious to see my people at the Village on Middle Fork."

"There are some people here from the Village at the Forks who will be returning there soon. It's only a short way from there to Middle Fork. I'm sure they would welcome you to ride with them."

"I would like that," I said, looking at Kansas, who smiled.

I didn't get around th' village much, Rebecca an' Kansas would not allow me to, but John an' I sat outside in th' sun an' many people came by to make acquaintances. They seemed impressed that I had fought two Osage an' won. One visitor was a widow who had recently lost her husband to an Osage party. Her hand was just healing where she had cut off her little finger in mourning. I had not seen this old custom among th' Cherokee before. Th' custom had died out in th' Eastern Tribe, an' John said only a few of th' Western Tribe still practiced it.

The third morning we were there, I looked up an' saw a familiar figure approaching. It was Isaac Tenkiller. He had a big smile on his face as he held out his hand in welcome.

"I have heard so much about this great warrior Sly Fox that I had to come see him for myself. Now I find that it is only Jerry Harris of the Middle Fork and the long hunt."

"How are you, Isaac, have you herded any elk lately?"

"No, those were the last ones we have seen for a while. There is too much hunting for the elk to be comfortable with and they have moved way up the Buffalo River for now. It may be that they will never come back," he shook his head sadly.

"How are Running Quail an' Bluebird?"

"They are fine, Running Quail is here with me and Bluebird has married and has given me a fine young grandson. She lives with her husband at the Forks. Running Quail will be here as soon as I tell her who this Sly Fox really is." He laughed. "We are planning to leave for the Village at the Forks the morning after tomorrow. Do you think you will be going with us?"

"Yes, I would like to. I have a slave girl, an' six horses. If you need th' loan of a packhorse, you may use one of mine."

"We have heard of your girl Kansas, she is a Kaw?"

"Yes, I rescued her in a blizzard and th' chiefs said she was mine for a purchase price. I freed her an' she has stayed with me because th' Osage had killed all her people."

"It may be that they think twice about taking slaves when we make slaves of some of their people." Isaac was frowning. "I must hurry back and tell Quail who you are. She will be mad if I delay long," he laughed.

They must not have been staying very far away, for soon I saw Running Quail hurrying our way.

"Jerryharris is it really you?" she called. She gave me a hug that almost made me wince. It was a real joy to see her an' she seemed just as pleased as I was. We talked awhile an' I called Kansas out to meet her. We sat an' talked for a while longer before she had to go.

"I have much to do before we are ready to leave. We are so glad you are traveling with us!"

"Yes," I replied, "it may be that we will hunt a little along th' way."

She smiled. "I would like that."

"I have offered Isaac a spare packhorse if you need one."

"Thank you, it may be necessary. I have gained many skins in trading here and I am not sure I will get them all on my horse."

"A light load for two is better than a heavy load for one, just come an' get it when you are ready."

"I will come for it tomorrow evening, then," she said, as she hurried away.

"Isaac has family living here," John Watie said. "He moved to the Forks when Running Quail's father died there an' she needed to care for her mother. There are many with kin in both villages an' even at the villages on the Arkansas River, though I do not see how they live in those flatlands. If they stay there long, they will grow webs between their toes!" He smiled. "We have always been people of the hills."

I nodded. "I am not happy in th' river lowlands, but I like th' western plains — so long as I can get into some hills often."

"I have only been to the prairies once. At

297

first I didn't like them, but there was something about them that that grew on me and I find myself with a yen to see them again."

"Yes," I said, "I will go back. It may be that Kansas will want to visit her people an' I would take her there."

"Such travel used to be common, but that all changed when the white man came. Now we are crowded and pushed together and there is conflict and war between the tribes. To travel now is dangerous."

We sat for a long time in silence, John Watie no doubt remembering how things were when he was young an' me remembering my days in th' Tennessee hills with Ma an' Pa. I thought about our trip west, life on th' island. I wondered what happened to Samuel an' if we would ever see little Joseph again. I would not know him now that he has growed an' he probably would not remember me at all. When Ruthie prayed, she always mentioned th' two boys an' asked for their safety. I will always believe that Sammy escaped to safety an' lived a long life, "Something only eternity will reveal," Ruthie said. There were such empty places in our lives, but there were also many places filled by special people like th' Fourkillers, Ruth an' Sam Meeker, even

Kansas now had a special place. It would be hard to be without her around.

Th' next day passed quickly an' pleasantly. I felt stronger an' rested. Rain had freshened th' fall air, even th' horses were restless. Kansas' pony seemed much better an' we decided he would make th' trip in good shape.

We left Bear Creek Springs under one of those crystal clear skies. Th' trail led us southeast an' soon we came out on high ground with rolling hills an' open prairie. Big tall mountains were to th' west. They looked inviting. By evening we were back in hills an' camped that first night by a spring just past Clear Creek.

There were twenty-one adults in our group an' I never knew exactly how many kids, all th' way from papooses hanging from their mothers' saddles to boys an' girls on th' edge of being adults. They swarmed here an' there along th' train and it's a wonder we didn't lose some of them.

"It may be that we did," sighed Kansas after that first day as we were eating supper, "and the parents didn't say anything for fear someone might find the rascals."

I had to laugh. Even if she were fourteen summers, she was still a youngster, but th' events in her life had matured her beyond her days. She worked hard to care for me an' I bore up under it as well as I could, knowing that it made her feel needed and useful.

It was hardly dark when I rolled up in a robe an' was soon asleep. Sometime later, Kansas pulled some of th' robe away and snuggled up close. She was already up when I awoke in th' early gloom. I felt lazy an' ashamed that I hadn't waked up earlier. Horses were in an' packed except for our cooking utensils. *I am going to have to pick up th' slack,* I thought, *she can't do it all th' whole trip.*

It wasn't long until we left th' ridge top an' entered th' breaks of th' Buffalo. Th' trail went down a dry gully to Mill Creek an' down that to th' bottoms, where we turned downstream until we were past high rock cliffs that lined th' south side of th' river. It had been a dry summer an' th' rain we had only brought th' river up to a trickle. We had no trouble crossing just above Bear Creek. Now this is th' second Bear Creek, th' one that runs into th' Buffalo River, not th' White River like th' creek at Bear Creek Springs.

This Bear Creek valley is one of the most picturesque valleys in th' Ozarks. Th' hills are made of white chert an' come down steeply to th' valley floor. In places they are so steep an' rocky that very little or no vegetation grows on them. In moonlight, they have a special glow that makes them look like silver an' they properly carry th' name Silver Hills. There is very little soil mixed in th' gravel bluffs an' they are continually sliding off, especially in wet weather. In lower reaches of th' valley, th' bottoms are wide an' fertile an' game back then was plentiful. Some of th' side canyons were gentle enough to provide good graze an' shelter.

Our trail traveled Bear Creek bottoms over twenty-five miles until they narrowed then were no more, just steep hills cut right down to th' channel. Here, we left th' creek an' climbed out on a ridge, one of those razorbacks that fell off on both sides, Bear Creek to th' west an' upper reaches of Middle Fork to th' east.

"Too far and rough for a trail down Middle Fork," Isaac said. "It's closer to go to the Forks then across to Middle Fork Village than it is to follow the river from here."

A little later we turned due east an' made dry camp th' fourth night above Archer's Fork Valley. I was getting pretty tired by then. I would walk to ease th' pain in my side until I was too tired to walk anymore, then I would ride until th' pain was intolerable. Kansas kept fussing over me until I got grouchy with her, then felt bad about it. We got into camp a little late an' camped by Isaac an' Quail. I must have been a sight, for Running Quail came over an' gave me a bowl of strong tea to drink. It eased my pain an' I slept.

At breakfast, Isaac said, "We will go down into the valley today and camp in the bottoms for a few days while we hunt."

Our descent into Archer's Valley was steep but not too rough an' by noon we were down. Th' bottom was narrow an' heavily wooded but a little ways down th' creek it opened up. Here th' train stopped an' made camp on a pretty stretch of th' creek. Kids were already splashing an' yelling in th' creek even before any horses were unloaded. As soon as tipis were up, women and girls disappeared down th' creek to bathe, for it had been three days since they had enough water to wash in.

Most of th' men swam an' bathed with th' youngsters. I sat on a large rock in water up to my armpits an' soaked a few minutes. It was my first bath since Bear Creek Springs an' it felt good. I didn't stay long after I washed my hair, for just sittin' in that clear water was cold. When Kansas got back from her bath, she found me asleep in my robe. I slept until supper, got up an' ate a steak, and slept again. Th' only thing I remember was when Kansas lay down against my back. I didn't waken until th' sun hit my face an' our hunters were long gone. It made me feel bad that I wasn't hunting with them, but I would have only been in th' way, not being able to shoot a gun or even pull a bow.

Kansas made a big meal an' I ate hearty. She found a shady spot by th' creek an' led me to a log an' made me sit there while she tried riding her pony for th' first time. He must have been feeling pretty good, for he hopped a little when she got on. He trotted some, but she didn't let him run any, which was probably good. When she had turned him loose back into th' herd, she came back satisfied she would be riding him in a few days.

"When do you think we will get to the Village at the Forks, Jerry?"

"Don't know, did Running Quail say how long they were going to stay here?"

"She said maybe ten days or more if the hunting was good."

Th' women were all out cutting cane for drying racks while youngsters were playing an' fishing in th' creek. We watched their antics a few minutes.

"I don't want to stay here that long, Kansas, what do you think about us staying a day or two an' letting th' horses rest, an' going on alone to th' Forks?"

"That will be fine with me, Jerry," she had a little smile on her face, but didn't say a thing about me needing th' rest.

"We will ask Isaac tonight if he thinks it would be safe for us to travel alone."

"It should be safer than the country we have just come through," Isaac said when I asked him. "Nothing is sure, but not many war parties would venture this close to the villages. The bears seem especially fat here with much mast, so I think we will stay until we have enough."

We set our sights on leaving th' third morning, Kansas saying th' horses should be well rested by then. I noted that she had not looked at th' horses when she decided that.

Early next mornin', there was much excitement among th' youngsters. They had found a bee tree an' were determined to get honey by themselves. Soon we heard multiple axes sounding out a ragged rhythm on th' trunk of a large blackgum tree not far from camp.

There was much traffic b'tween tree an'

mothers who were dispensing advice on how to do this or that in th' art of gathering honey. Eventually we heard a crash as th' tree fell — partway. Th' cutters had misjudged th' fall of th' tree an' it lodged firmly in th' crotch of a nearby oak. More traffic to camp for advice.

One of th' mothers called out, "Sly Fox, will you please go see what these youngsters have done and show them how to get that honey?"

So I walked out to th' tree. A dozen kids were standing around two older boys who were discussing their next move with their fists. I watched a moment an' decided that these boys were too evenly matched for a decision coming from them anytime soon.

The hive was high on one side of th' trunk as it lay. It would be easy enough to shinny up, reach around, an' dip out honey. Th' hole was small an' it would take a small hand to get inside. I instructed th' half-dozen kids who had followed me to gather wood for a fire b'neath th' bee hole. Two girls were sent to camp to find small spoons with long handles for dipping an' containers to hold honey. Seeing some action taking place, th' fight observers joined us. I sent two smaller boys to coat themselves in mud. One of them had a younger sister who "could do anything he can do" who went with them an' all three of them came back well coated.

By now th' fire was going good an' I looked up to find th' two combatants had joined us. One had a bloody nose and th' other had an eye slowly swelling shut. I assumed they had come to a decision about what was to be done next, but they didn't offer it. I sent them to cut some green cedar limbs for th' fire an' we soon had white smoke rising up into th' tree.

Now I instructed my mud roosters to shinny up th' trunk and try to dip out honey. Up they went, little sister close b'hind. Two more mudhens appeared from th' creek an' I sent them up with pots to hold th' honey. They were a comical sight, five kids coated in mud dipping honey out of th' hive. There was only an occasional yell from a sting an' they did well until dried mud started flaking off. Number One harvester, being in th' line of fire, b'gan to get stung an' started yelling for th' other four to back down. Number Two also felt a need to retreat, but Sister had not been stung an' would move only after a sting or two. It was too much for One an' halfway down th' tree, he bailed out followed by Two an' Sister. They hit th' ground scrambling for th' creek. Numbers Four an' Five, holding pots, stayed on th' trunk well out of bee range.

To my surprise, One, Two, an' Sister came back recoated in mud anxious to continue th' harvest. Keeping things fair, I let Four an' Five lead th' harvest with One, Two, an' Sister b'hind. When th' yowls got too loud, retreat was sounded. As Four, Five, an' One sprinted for th' creek, I felt a tug on my pants leg an' looked into th' eyes of mudhen Number Six. She was followed by Seven through Twelve lined up b'hind. Each had a spoon an' various sizes of pots.

After that, it was only a matter of managing th' flow of climbers. By th' time we got back around to a disgusted One, there was a continuous parade of Mudhens b'tween th' bee tree, th' mud, and camp, triumphantly carrying pots of honey an' comb to their mothers — after paying th' manager a small tax in his honey pot, that is. Several returned recoated an' carrying empty pots from mothers who were not so fortunate as to have honey harvesters in camp.

All in all, it was a busy an' productive day. I'm sure that any observer downstream wondered at th' slug of muddy water that drifted by over th' next few days. They would have noted that there were a number of dead honey bees floating by.

That night, every household partook of th' fruits of th' Mudhens. I placed th' bee tree off limits explaining that th' bees had shared their honey (an' stings) with us an' that we must leave enough for them to live on through th' winter. Running Quail told me later that th' tree furnished honey for several years, each time it was harvested by spoon-wielding Mudhens.

I know from experience that it takes a long time to replenish lost blood. Even though my side was healing nicely, I was still weak. Th' honey harvest, though a lot of fun, wore me out an' I dragged into camp that evening tired an' a little sore from laughing so much. Kansas had been busy helping jerk bear meat an' rendering fat all day. She was tired out too so we both turned in early. I wished I had a tipi for her, but even if we had one, she would have left it to curl up against me where I slept outside. It took me a long time (an' some aging) to get used to sleeping inside of anything with a roof.

Word had gotten around that we were going on to th' Village an' some older people asked to go with us. In th' end there were several grannies an' young ones in our group. Kansas was th' proud owner of a fine bearskin robe, a gift from Quail. We took two packhorses loaded with meat, fruits, nuts, an' furs for Bluebird to store.

The valley of Archer's Creek was quite different from Bear Creek valley. This was sandstone country an' pretty rocky away from th' bottoms. They were narrower an' in some places steep hills an' bluffs came right down to th' creek with hardly room for a trail along its banks. We would cross that creek half a dozen times a day, sometimes wading a good distance on solid rock or rocky bottoms before we could climb th' bank. Still, it was a beautiful valley with tall cliffs an' rocks inviting th' adventurous to climb. Game was plenteous from th' sign we saw. There was more than th' usual panther sign; I suppose rocks gave good shelter for them an' deer ample feed. We heard their screams nightly an' th' horses stayed nervous th' whole trip.

We made a leisurely trip of it because of th' older ones, stopping a little after mid-afternoon an' fishing for our suppers. Th' creek was full of fish, black bass, rock bass, goggle eye, an' bream an' we had fun catching them using grasshoppers for bait. The air was crisp an' turning leaves made th' hills shine. Some hard maples were so bright they glowed red or yellow in th' sun. Leaves falling on th' still waters made little boats that skittered here an' there with a light breeze. Some had dragonfly passengers. Kingfishers dived for minnows from over-hanging limbs an' robins, finches, an' red-birds sang high up in th' sycamores an' willows. Even th' call of th' crow high an' fast disappearing was pleasant.

We came upon a buzzard roost high on a rock cliff an' watched them launch an' circle in unseen wind currents higher an' higher until th' top birds were no bigger than dots. There must have been a hundred of them an' we watched their circling dance a long time. Th' most elegant fliers, of course, were eagles. There were many along th' creek, nests high on some inaccessible ledge. Old-timers told us they had been occupied for many, many years.

It was th' third day of th' trip that we entered th' upper reaches of the Village at th' Forks an' almost th' first person we met was Bluebird. She was large with child an' somewhat heavier than when we met on Hartsugg Creek three years b'fore. I was surprised she knew me on sight, but then I guess I hadn't changed all that much. She was pleased at th' sight of th' packhorses' loads an' she an' Kansas were soon unload-ing an' storing th' plunder while I tended th' horses.

# CHAPTER 19
## HOMECOMING

Th' closer I got t' home, th' more urgent
was my need to get there an' we only stayed
with Bluebird one night. I left Running
Quail th' packhorse she had been using as a
gift and a rising sun found us crossing Pee
Dee Creek on th' trail to the Village on
Middle Fork. Kansas had saddled her pony
an' was riding him for th' first time since he
had been shot.

It seemed to take forever to make those
ten or so miles to Weaver's Creek, but we
rode into th' yard around noon. Ruthie was
just coming from th' spring with a bucket
of water. She stared from th' porch a moment, then squealed an' dropped th' bucket
an' ran to meet me. I forgot about my side
when she jumped into my arms an' we
hugged. There were tears in her eyes an'
mine were kinda misty when she stood back
to examine me.

"I do believe you have grown some since

you left us!" She laughed, wiping her eyes on her apron tail.

Two whoops from th' corner of th' house told me Riley an' Jesse were approaching an' we went down in a heap of arms an' legs, Sippie licking my face an' yipping.

"What's going on here?" Sam's voice boomed. "Looks like you boys have caught another rascal, was he in the corn crib?" He laughed, shoving boys here an' there an' lifting me out of th' dust. "How are you, Jerry? Welcome home. Have you brought a wife, too?" said he as he turned an' lifted Kansas off her horse as if she were nothing an' stood her down by me.

I felt my face flushing. "No, this isn't my wife, this is Kansas, a Kaw who I have adopted. She's just fourteen summers," I added a little lamely. "Kansas, this is Sam Meeker an' my sister, Ruth. This is Ruth's son, Jesse, an' this is Riley, th' son of Lonza an' Lydia Fourkiller."

"And Jerry, this is your niece, Sarah." Laughing Brook stood by my side as I turned an' beheld th' sweetest little blue-eyed cherub you have ever seen. I greeted Laughing Brook as best I could with a baby b'tween us an' she handed her to me. I turned back to show her to Kansas.

"You don't seem surprised, Jerry," Sam

boomed.

"I think I knew about her before you did." I grinned at him.

"Well, I'll . . ." he stood there open mouthed as th' rest of us laughed. "Might have known." He grinned. "I'm usually the last to know what's going on around here."

"You're usually the one *making* the goings-on around here." Ruth laughed an' hugged Sam, his arm going affectionately around her waist.

"She is a beautiful baby," Kansas said shyly in her broken Cherokee.

"Thank you, Kansas," Ruth said, taking her arm an' leading her to th' house. "You must be tired after your trip. Come in and we will eat." Laughing Brook took little Sarah back an' I began to unload th' horses.

"Let the boys do that, Jerry, and we'll visit a minute before we eat," Sam said.

I had seen Wash round th' corner from his house an' sit in one of Ruth's chairs on th' porch. He stood when we approached, as tall an' erect as ever. "Welcome home, Jerry!"

"Thank you, Grandfather, it's good to be home," I said, taking his proffered hand. His grip was strong an' warm.

I heard a step an' turned to see Lydia an' Lonza step up on th' porch. A chubby Rising Sun followed across th' yard, calling to her "Iley," th' best she could pronounce "Riley."

Sippie, wagging his tail, moved to intercept her b'fore she got under th' horses' hooves.

"Welcome home, Jerry," Lydia said an' gave me a big hug, Lonza patting my shoulder an' reaching for my hand. "We were just wondering about you last night and wishing you were here," he said. "Mother said you were closer than we thought. She seems to always know . . ."

". . . And she told me this morning we needed to make room for two more at the table today, have you brought someone with you?" Lydia inserted.

"Yes, I have adopted a girl who was a slave to th' Osage." I said. "She has gone inside with Ruthie an' Grandmother."

"I will go meet her," Lydia said, moving to th' door.

"You will have much to tell us, Jerry. The weather is mild, we should all eat in the arbor this afternoon and give you time to talk," Fishinghawk said.

A breathless Jesse jumped up on th' porch, Riley pulling little Sunshine along b'hind.

"Jesse, go tell the women I said we will all eat under the arbor this afternoon," Wash said.

314

Sticking his head through th' doorway, Jesse yelled, "Ma, Grandfather said we will eat under the arbor today!" We all laughed as Sam shook his head.

Laughing Brook came to th' door. "Jerry, come in here and let us look at your wound."

"What wound?" Lonza asked.

"Come to think of it, you *do* look a little peaked." Sam squinted at me. "There's blood on your shirt, what have you been into without me, Jerry Harris?"

"It was just a small argument with Kansas' old owner." I tried to shrug it off.

Kansas came out an' pulled me into th' house. "There's fresh blood on your shirt, Sly Fox. We need to look at your side."

"Sly Fox?" I heard Sam say as th' door closed.

Ruthie was drying her hands an' looking at me with concern as Kansas led me to a chair b'side Laughing Brook an' lifted my shirt for her to see. Lydia drew a deep breath. Laughing Brook's hands were cool an' tender as she probed my side, I guess looking for telltale signs of infection.

She nodded. "It looks good to me, you did a nice job sewing him up, Kansas, thirteen stitches?"

"Fourteen," we said in unison.

"Thirteen would have been bad luck," I added, not being able to suppress a grin. Kansas' foot pressed on mine.

"From the bottom of your ribs to your pap, no wonder you look so pale," Ruthie said behind me, hugging my head to her breast.

"He lost a lot of blood and has been slow to gain his strength back," Kansas said.

"I should think so," Lydia said.

"We can fix that with some special foods," Grandmother said. "You and I will go to the woods tomorrow and find the herbs while Ruth cooks us some chicken broth."

"I feel fine, just a little tired," I protested.

"Tomorrow we will remove every other stitch." Laughing Brook ignored me, talking to Kansas as if she were in charge of me instead of t'other way 'round.

Kansas nodded an' carefully washed th' scar. She lowered my shirt. "I will get you a clean shirt, Sly Fox," she said an' hurried out th' door.

"Sly Fox?" I heard that question again from two voices this time.

Grandmother waved her hand. "We will all know in due time, now the boy has to rest." She led me to Ruth's room an' said, "Lie down and rest, Jerry, and we will call you to eat." I surprised myself by doing as she said an' must have slept a good three hours before Ruth called.

A fresh shirt was lying on th' bed an' I put it on. It seemed people were gathering from all directions when I stepped out of th' door. There were even some of my friends from th' village in th' crowd. Th' table was piled high with food an' I wondered how so much could have been done in such a short time. It looked like Sam an' Lonza had built a large stone fireplace by th' arbor an' two whole deer roasts were being turned on a spit.

After a few moments of greeting visitors, Sam's voice called out, "It's time to eat, friends. As is the custom under the arbor, we will all eat together." (He said this to indicate that women an' children would eat at th' same table an' time as th' men, which was not th' ordinary custom, men usually eating first, then others.) "Now, we will say grace before we eat."

I looked up in surprise. Sam Meeker was going to say a blessing? Sure enough, he bowed his head an' prayed: "Father, we thank Thee for this day and for bringing Jerry safely back to us. Thank Thee for little Kansas and her watch-care over him. Now we thank Thee for this feast you have given us. Bless the hands that have prepared it for us. Amen."

I looked around an' noticed that even guests from th' village had bowed, it was just like th' white folks' gatherings back in Tennessee an' I marveled at what Ruthie had done in this community in th' time she had been here, for I knew it was her handiwork. Kansas stood close by me, uncomfortable with all these strangers an' strange customs. I smiled an' whispered, "Little Kansas?"

"I may be little to Sam Meeker, but he's the only one!" she retorted.

That was th' best feast anyone could have imagined. We ate an' talked an' laughed for hours. It grew late, th' sun sinking toward Buffalo Hump when we were all full except th' boys, who were bottomless. They kept coming back for more until Ruth an' Lydia shooed them away with dire warnings if they returned. A few minutes later, Kansas nudged me an' I looked to see a hand furtively feeling over th' table top for leftover cornbread. They had sent Rising Sun to hide under th' table an' scavenge for them.

"Jerry, you have to start when we parted on the long hunt and tell us all that you have done since," Lydia said. "What happened to you and White Wolf when you met the Osage?"

So I told them about our meeting an' that Otter an' Tall Oak were friends from Wolf's village; how we moved to their camp, then went on to White Wolf's village an' about th' birth of Snowflake.

"You didn't tell them about how you got your name," Kansas said accusingly.

"Tell us, Little Kansas." Sam smiled. "I know 'Sly Fox' won't give us all the details."

So she told them in her broken Cherokee-Osage-Kaw how I got my name an' I helped her by interpreting words she stumbled on. I was surprised she knew so much about that event; Morning Starr or most likely Zilkah had told her. Th' family enjoyed her quaint telling of th' tale as much as the events. It was plain that they had accepted Kansas into their circle an' that she was welcome. ". . . she hit him with her cane an' said, 'Jerryharris, you are a sly fox and that shall be your name!' " They all laughed. "And that is how the two named each other. It was the talk of the Osage for some time. I heard about it before I knew Jerry."

. . . So that was how she knew about it! Happenings like that make great stories among th' tribes an' are told over an' over. I have heard stories an' legends that had to be hundreds of generations old, but they are told accurately an' th' same way each time they are told, regardless of who th' teller is. This is an amazing thing among peoples with no written history, for them to remember th' stories from generation to generation without variance or addition. Th' white man scoffs that th' spoken word can be reliable but I have found that many times his *written* word is subject to error, fabrication, and inaccuracy . . .

". . . I do not know the whole story of how Sly Fox lost his peso, so I will learn about it with you." She looked at me expectantly.

I told them about our hunting trip an' how a deer kicked Little Chief in th' head an' how we fixed him with th' coin. Riley an' Jesse listened wide-eyed and open-mouthed. "Little Chief has your peso in his head?" Riley asked.

"It may be that we should all carry a silver coin in case of an accident," Jesse said solemnly.

"In your case, you should carry a silver plate!" Ruthie said as we all laughed. Th' exploits an' mishaps of those two boys were becoming legendary. Hardly a week passed without some momentous event involving them.

"How did it come about that you became — were adopted — by Sly Fox?" Wash asked Kansas. So she told th' story of how she came to be a slave an' about th' blizzard on th' plains. Tears ran down her cheek when she told of how I had picked her up out of th' snow an' she leaned her head on my shoulder. I saw Laughing Brook smile and nod. They all laughed when she told of how I had tipped Birdsong into th' snow, showing her "big bare ass" as she put it. She knew a lot about th' conference with th' Tzi-Cho that only Tall Oak or Otter could have told her.

"The blizzard did not come here," someone said, which is a characteristic of Ozarks weather. It seems that these storms wash against th' mountains an' are deflected northward, leaving our hills to bask in mild weather.

"Tell us about the buffalo hunt, Jerry," Lonza requested. Kansas got up an' left as I began to talk. They all listened as I told of th' hunt, Jesse an' Riley were especially attentive an' interrupted with a dozen questions.

"I want to see that!" Jesse whispered in awe.

"Me too!" Riley's eyes were big in th' light of th' fire.

A mound of fur with Kansas' legs came into the circle of light. "I have made robes of the first kills Jerry made," she said to my surprise. "There is one for you, Grand-mother, and for Lydia and Ruth. I have kept one for myself." She smiled shyly.

*"Th' women were pleased an' all three — I should say four — robes served them many years. Rising Sun now has both robes from Laughing Brook an' Lydia, an' I saw Ruthie's spread across Sarah's bed a ways back," Zenas added.*

"You still haven't told how you got that cut, did you skip that part?" Ruth asked.

"He hasn't gotten to that part yet, and I don't know all of it, either!" Kansas frowned at me.

I told them how Black Elk had shot Kansas' pony an' how I had discovered him in Lynx's hut; about our trip an' how I had sent Lynx home tied to his horse. I didn't want to tell that I had killed Elk, but Kansas interrupted an' told that part herself, how I had come back to th' fort bloody an' lying on th' back of Black Elk's horse. Her story of sewing me up an' th' fourteen stitches made them laugh. She gave Wash an' Brook greetings from John Watie an' Rebecca an' they were pleased th' Waties were doing well.

The men were glad to hear that we had traveled with Isaac an' Running Quail an' that they were well. It was dark and very late, our friends from th' village said their "goodbyes" an' disappeared down th' trail. Rising Sun an' Sarah both had long been curled in their mothers' laps asleep and both boys kept rubbing sleepy eyes. I was suddenly very tired an' needed to lie down. Kansas brought my bedroll an', as th' others scattered, unrolled it right there in th' arbor. Ruth protested that I should at least sleep in th' cabin, but she understood my aversion to sleeping under a roof — especially in good weather such as then. Taking Kansas in hand, she departed for her cabin an' I never heard th' door close b'hind them. I only vaguely remembered Kansas snuggling to my back 'way in th' night. It was an old familiar story. I slept long an' well.

# CHAPTER 20
# THE FIGHT AT
# HALF MOON MOUNTAIN
# 1817

Winter with its rain, snow, and ice came on early that fall of 1816 an' we spent many days cooped up in cabins. It seemed that I was especially affected by th' cold. It soaked into my bones an' I found myself seeking warmth by th' fires more than I ever had. Laughing Brook said it was because of my loss of blood an' that as I gained it back I would lose my cold nature, an' she was right. By spring, I was back to my old self again, bored with inactivity, ready to *do* something.

That "something" turned out to be plowing an' spring planting, while my buddies laughed as they passed on their way to th' spring hunt. I noted that some of their families were gaunt an' pale from lack of food, while th' Fishinghawk clan had come through winter with food aplenty. Wash saw to it that widows with no kin an' even some of th' poorer families were fed. More than one of them came an' watched our spring planting an' several moved out of th' village along th' bottoms where they too could plant garden plots. Most were successful, but one or two proved too lazy to help their wives an' ended up hungry th' spring of '18.

"It takes some people time to learn." Wash sighed.

I noted that his provisions for th' lazy ones tapered off quite a bit th' next year an' by th' spring of 1818 they were back at their bottom plots more determined to farm than b'fore. Eventually, there was a large portion of th' village raising food an' becoming less an' less dependent on th' hunt for survival. In this, we had come full circle as a tribe, for planting an' harvesting was once our people's way of life.

It was ironic an' maybe a little sad to me that these were th' people who left th' eastern tribe b'cause they wanted to continue their old ways of hunting an' gathering, yet they couldn't move away from th' fact that there was a better way an' they were reluctantly forced to accept it as th' pressure of other tribes depleted wildlife.

Kansas fit into our family as though she was always meant to be there. She more than did her part of daily work, practically taking over care of Rising Sun an' Sarah.

Though her health had improved greatly after I took her in, I was surprised at th' way she continued to improve under Ruth's care an' a more varied diet of vegetables with her meat. It was almost as if she blossomed along with those spring flowers.

Ruth was dismayed when she found that Kansas was slipping out to sleep with me an' convinced her that a growing young lady did not do such things. She still took care to see to my affairs, watching th' horses, washing my clothes, an' making sure I was served at table, but she became more coy an' modest around me an' to tell th' truth, I was relieved. I was shocked when I accidentally walked in on her one day as she bathed by th' fire. She really was well developed an' must have really been fourteen or by then fifteen summers!

She learned Cherokee quickly an' became quite proficient with it. At th' same time, she taught Jesse, Riley, an' Rising Sun Kaw an' Osage words an' phrases. We all had to learn th' other languages just to be able to communicate with th' kids. Ruth began to teach all of th' children *an'* Kansas the English language an' after a while, she b'gan teaching Kansas to read. Add to that th' fact that there were many French an' Spanish words used an' our village was quite literate in th' languages.

With Jesse an' Riley both sleeping out with me, now, th' bedroll was quite full. Sometimes I had to sneak away an' roll up separate from those young mules to get some sleep. Jesse was ten years old an' Riley nine, but to look at them an' th' things they did, you couldn't tell that there was a minute's difference. Whatever one did, th' other would do or die trying. Around Weaver's Creek, it was as if they had three homes an' it was all th' women could do to make sure that they were watched an' fed properly. It was a common custom for one or th' other mothers to call out her son's name at mealtime an' if th' boys were at th' other home or at Laughing Brook's house, someone would sing out, "they're here" an' all would be well. It was not uncommon for those boys to eat twice if there were good or special things on tables. For this, there were mild reproofs, mostly tongue-in-cheek. After all, they were growing boys.

The long hunt of th' fall of 1816 had been troublesome for th' Cherokee. They found many Osage hunters in their former hunting grounds, which by treaty were now th' property of th' Cherokee. There were several clashes an' parties of both tribes were robbed of their winter's provision by parties of th' other tribe. Almost all these clashes resulted in bloodshed an' several Cherokee hunters were killed. There was a shortage of food in th' spring of 1817 because of all th' trouble, an' people in th' three Cherokee villages suffered.

With th' Osage gone west for their spring buffalo hunt, things were pretty quiet through summer an' early fall. However, when th' long hunts began, trouble redoubled. There were more trespassers in Ozarks hunting grounds than before. A band of Delawares an' Kickapoos moved in an' established a village on Crooked Creek (they call it Yellville, Arkansas, now), well within Cherokee land. There were also several new bands of Shawnees, Peorias, Delawares, an' Piankashaws living along th' north side of White River who crossed th' river to hunt. Th' result was poor hunting for all an' unrest grew.

In spite of th' fact that most of th' Osage tribe had gone west again in th' fall to hunt, most Cherokee anger was directed against them. Th' first of October, word came by runner that Cherokee warriors were to meet at Bear Creek Springs for a campaign against th' Osage. Lonza an' I would not go because of our Osage friends an' Sam decided not to go because of us, so we all stayed home while a lot of men from th' village went. Some people understood our position but there will always be those who do not or will not recognize reluctance of one to make war on his friends.

Over six hundred warriors gathered at Bear Springs, mostly Cherokee, but there were some Delaware an' Shawnee warriors as well. They traveled west into Osage territory, finding most of their camps an' smaller villages deserted. On th' Verdigris, they attacked a large village finding only old men, women, an' children. To their credit, th' Osage put up a stiff fight, but being vastly outnumbered, they were soon overcome. Their bloodlust up, th' Cherokees killed all they found, including women an' children. Then thoroughly looting an' burning th' village, they broke up into small bands an' slunk away with over a hundred captives.

Meanwhile, things were far from quiet on Middle Fork. Two weeks after th' warriors left, a party of Shawnee an' Peorias came into th' village disgruntled at a poor hunt an' determined to plunder th' village of its provender. Being somewhat isolated, we were unaware of events until late that night when a terrified young boy banged on Ruth's door. I heard him from my bed by

329

th' chimney an' with my gun crept to th' corner just in time to see someone admitted into th' darkened house. I listened to his story standin' by th' door.

Sam stuck his head out an' said, "Jerry, go get Lonza and Wash. Tell them to bring their guns and all th' folks over here. *Don't show a light!*"

It didn't take long to summon th' family an' we listened as th' boy told his story: "It was after noon when we saw these men coming into the village. They were Shawnee and Peorias, Mother said, about twenty of them. After they had looked around a little, they told us to gather our horses and bring out our food to load on them. No one moved to obey them and they started shooting at us. Several fell and the rest of us ran. The boys watching the horses saw what was happening and ran the horses down the river. They got away before the Shawnees could catch them.

"Mother grabbed the baby and I took my sister and we ran for the river. We hid in the brush until they started looking for us there, then we swam down the river. Mother got an arrow in her shoulder but we all got away. When it got dark she sent me to see what was happening. I found the village quiet and the Shawnees gone. People were gathering back to the village. There were several bodies still on the ground. I told Mother and she is going to the village. She said to come here and see if you were unharmed."

Sam looked at Wash, "What should we do, Grandfather?" It was he as head of th' family who would determine our action.

Grandfather's face was pale, but his jaw was set an' his eyes flashed anger. "We must see that the village is safe, then we will pursue the raiders."

With that all of us made ready. We gathered medicines an' wrappings while Kansas readied th' two babies. It didn't take us long an' as we stepped out of th' doors, Riley an' Jesse brought up our horses. I noted with satisfaction that both had their bows strung an' ready. They could do damage if given an opportunity.

Our trip was done quickly an' as quietly as possible, more quickly than quietly, I think. Nearing th' village, we saw a large fire in th' town house an' people moving about. In th' darkness, I stumbled over a body as we approached. We could hear keening in various parts of th' village. People in th' town house were huddled in little groups talking in low tones.

Wash was th' picture of strength an'

331

authority as he walked in an' looked around. He motioned for four or five elders to join him an' they conferred quietly for some moments.

As th' men departed on some errand, he looked up an' spoke in a strong voice, "Listen, people, the criers are going through the village to gather everyone here. Gather the wounded at the back of the house so we can treat them as they need it."

He nodded to Laughing Brook an' our women moved to set up an' help those that were hurt. It took a few minutes for people to gather. Wash was stern an' determined, even sending people to get mourners who refused to come at th' call.

"Drag them if you must, but get them here!" he demanded.

When all were gathered, he stood an' spoke, "We have been attacked by murderous cowards who would kill women and children and steal their food. We must avenge this outrage and retrieve our winter's food. When that is accomplished, there will be time for proper mourning for the dead and wounded. Until the council says it is time, there will be no mourning or burial ceremonies."

There was dead silence for a moment an' Wash looked around th' room. "Where are the horse herders?" Four young men stood in various places around th' room. "You have done well by saving the herd," Wash said. "Now bring the horses into the village so we may be ready to ride when the time comes."

The four left on their mission. While they were gone, Wash gathered all th' men an' asked questions. From them, we learned that there were twenty or twenty-four warriors with most of them mounted, that they had loaded every horse an' some few horses they caught in th' village with as much plunder as they could carry, an' left about an hour before sunset after setting several fires. People were able to return an' put out th' fires before they did too much damage. Three older boys had followed th' raiders. They reported that they had taken th' river trail an' it looked as if they were staying on it.

"There is hardly any place they could leave it for a long ways with those pack-horses," Lonza said. "They would have a hard time traveling that trail in the dark, so they would have to camp soon after sunset."

One of th' scouts spoke up, "We followed them to Little Tick Creek and it was getting too dark to go any further."

Another spoke, "The next place to camp

would be where Lost Creek comes in from the south."

There was quiet for a moment while we thought. "If they camped at Lost Creek, or say they even got to Meadow Creek or the bottoms between, we could have a good chance of catching up with them before they got to Half Moon Mountain," Wash said.

"But the trail is so narrow and the mountains so steep that one or two of them could hold an army off while the rest escaped." I was surprised that Sam knew so much about th' country.

One of th' scouts spoke up, "If some of us went over the mountain by the Chimney Rocks and followed the ridge we could get down to the trail west of Half Moon before they get there." I was impressed that th' young man held enough respect for his elders that he didn't finish sayin' th' obvious.

Wash completed th' plan. "We will split into two groups, one following up the trail and one riding as hard as they can to the trail west of Half Moon in hopes that they might get ahead of the enemy."

Quickly, he split us into three groups, th' youngest boys an' old men would stay with th' village; six young warriors, an' me, were to ride th' ridge with Sam, and th' rest to follow th' trail.

"You who are to stay with the village have the responsibility to keep the women and children safe. As soon as you can, take them to the cave in the pedestal rock valley and keep them there until we come to get them. You who are riding with Sam pick your best horses and ride as hard as you can. If they haven't passed you on the trail, set up an ambush in the narrows on the north side of Half Moon. The rest of us will follow the trail and try to push them into your trap. We will follow close enough to hit them from behind when you start firing. Now let's move!"

Some of us heard that last sentence on th' way to our horses. Every man of us was handed th' reins of his fastest horse, saddled an' ready, by women folk who had heard th' conference.

Kansas gave me my horse an' whispered, "Be careful, Sly Fox!" as I mounted.

We splashed across th' ford at a run an' headed up th' trail to the Village at the Forks, then turned right up th' mountain. Some of th' boys would have run th' whole way, or at least until their horses give out, but Sam held them back, showing them how to make th' best time without ruining their horses. As it got lighter, we picked up our pace an' when we slid down th' mountain to th' river, our horses were winded, but not hurt.

While we watered an' tied our horses in a canebrake, Sam looked at th' trail, "They haven't passed by here," he said as he came back. "Let's wander down the river and find a good place to trap them." Pointing to th' best rider, he said, "Bring your horse."

About a mile downstream, th' river washed straight into a bluff, then turned a right angle along th' foot of a solid rock bluff. Here was a small open flat on th' inside of th' bend, then th' mountains pushed right down to th' river, sqeezing th' trail between th' mountain and the cut bank.

Sam looked over th' layout an' made his plans. Looking at us, he asked, "Who's the best shot in this bunch?"

The boys grinned an' all pointed to th' least one of th' bunch, a skinny kid not as tall as his Tennessee rifle. "Tiny can hit anything in range if he can find a rest for his gun," one of th' boys said.

"Good! Tiny, you take Sly Fox and climb the bluff above that whorlly hole and find a good place that looks down on the trail. I want you two to wait until the first two Indians have almost gone back into the woods at the west end of the meadow, then shoot them. Don't miss — and don't shoot a horse if you can help it! Now, who is the best bow shot?"

The boys grinned an' again pointed at Tiny, who grinned too.

"Next best."

"Those two," Tiny spoke for th' first time, pointing to one called Bull Calf and a heavy set boy called Silent with a strong bow as tall as he was.

"You two get up there on the side of Half Moon where you can see and shoot the third and fourth men in the line after Tiny shoots, then shoot anyone as the opportunity arises."

The two nodded an' turned as if to go. "Wait until I have laid it all out," Sam said.

To Redhorn, th' boy with th' horse, he said, "Do you remember above the bend where the trail was right against that cut bank?" At th' boy's nod, he continued, "Ride back there and block the trail with brush and anything you can find high enough that a horse can't jump over. Then hide in the bushes this side of your block. If a rider comes through, shoot him, if pack-horses, catch them and tie them up."

Turnin' to th' last boy, Noah, who was th' largest of us all, tall an' heavily muscled, Sam said, "You and I are going to get under that cut bank and give a surprise to the last ones in the meadow when the shooting starts!"

Looking at us all, he said, "Many a warrior has been accidentally killed by his own men in a battle. Look that you don't make the same mistake. Put yourself where you won't have one of us in your line of fire. Make your shots sure. These are mostly seasoned warriors and we are badly outnumbered. We have to depend on surprise and the followers to be close by when the fighting starts." Then he handed me his rifle. "Tiny can't carry two rifles, but you can. Set up where he can shoot first, you shoot close behind, then while you reload, Tiny can shoot again. After that, one of you be reloading while the other is shooting. Try to have one gun loaded at all times. Let's go! Hurry, we don't know how close they are!" he called as we departed.

Tiny an' I followed in th' dust of Noah's horse back up th' trail, then waded across th' river above th' bend where it looked like we could climb that steep an' rocky hill. By grasping saplings an' roots, we were able to reach a spot above th' bluff, then slide down to the ledge above th' river. We could see th' whole meadow an' th' trail from end to end. There was no prop for Tiny's gun, so I left him on watch an' scrounged up a large flat rock just the right height for a man to rest his gun on. While Tiny set it in place, I quickly gathered several more large rocks an' soon had a wall with a couple of holes we could shoot through without being exposed. There was a gully to our left an' that ledge turned an' followed it. We were almost to th' corner. It was a good place for an' ambush. Our first shots were only about 150 yards an' th' whole meadow was within 300 to 350 yards long. Hopefully, we would not have that long a shot to make.

We could hear Redhorn building his barrier for a while, then all was quiet. I could see Sam an' Noah sitting under th' cut bank. They had stripped to their breechclouts an' their faces were streaked with red clay. It looked like Sam was sleeping. Those two bowmen had disappeared completely an' I had no idea where they were.

"Do you see where Silent an' Bull Calf are?" I asked.

Tiny nodded an' pointed with his chin. "They are on either side of that black gum, about fifteen feet apart." I still couldn't see them, but made note of where they were.

Th' ledge was warm an' we were soon sweating. I felt it trickle down th' hollow of my spine an' soak into my pants. A large drop collected on the tip of Tiny's nose an' dripped to th' rock. There was a wet place where it hit. I shore wished I had a drink.

As it usually turns out in those cases, we had a long wait. You can think of a hundred things you could be doing to improve things an' won't b'cause action could start th' next second, so you sit there an' wait.

We talked over our plan of action an' got things set between us, then waited some more. It was after midmorning b'fore something stirred on th' trail. I saw Noah an' Sam get up an' crouch under th' overhanging bank, but after that first stirring, something we felt more than heard, nothing moved. I had just relaxed some when a packhorse walked out of the woods an' started across th' little meadow. He stopped to crop some grass an' a man with a long pole poked him on, then faded back into th' brush. As any horse would do, he walked a few yards an' b'gan grazing again. This time the man came out an' b'gan hurriedly driving the horse across th' clearing. A few yards b'hind, another man appeared an' then close b'hind him came a whole line of horses an' men.

It occurred to me that th' whole train might not be in th' meadow b'fore Tiny an' I would have to begin shooting. Sam could be right in th' middle of th' line with enemies ahead an' b'hind, whichever way he turned.

"Tiny, Sam, an' Noah might be in the middle of the train when you shoot. Make your second shot the last one you can see in the line."

Tiny nodded, he was already sighting th' entrance into th' meadow. Then he took up his second rifle an' sighted on th' lead man. I began counting men as they appeared, 19, 20, 21 . . . They were still coming.

Th' train was hurrying across that open space. I could almost feel that crawly feeling running up my back — th' way *they* must be feeling right then. Number one was at th' edge of th' woods, one more step an' he would be gone. Tiny fired. In quick succession, I fired on th' second man an' he too fell, his horse bolting down th' trail b'hind th' first. Almost th' same instant I fired, th' third man sat down hard with an arrow through his neck. I don't know how he did it so quickly, but Tiny's long tom rifle boomed an' a man at th' other entrance to th' clearing threw up his hands. I was already loading as fast as I could, watching th' fight. Two more went down in quick succession with arrows in them. I tried to count 5, no 6 down? Forget it, fool, I said to myself, shoot! I took a quick shot at a man running for th' woods where Bull an' Silent were an' missed. Th' point of an arrow suddenly protruded from his back an' he stumbled, spun an' fell on his back, th' arrow pushed backwards into him.

Th' spang of a bullet hit our rock wall an' whistled on over our heads, another spattered hot rock on us as Tiny fired. Sighting through my gun loop in th' rock wall, I saw that a horse was down an' two or three men were crouching b'hind it. A shout from th' river an' I saw that some Shawnees had jumped off th' bank into th' shallows. Others were running back. None got past Tiny an' I.

Side by side, Sam an' Noah charged th' ones in th' river with two sharpened poles. "Lances! I should have known," I said. Tiny chuckled. Man, he was cool for a kid in th' middle of a battle. One of th' warriors in th' river raised his musket to fire at Sam an' Noah. I fired an' he dropped his gun, falling facedown in th' water. Sudden firing down th' trail told us that our men had caught up with th' train. Help was on th' way.

Th' clearing was empty save for panicky horses an' those men huddled b'hind th' dead horse, all others had jumped into th' river or run back down th' trail. Suddenly th' two bowmen, naked an' painted, burst from th' brush with a yell an' dashed for th' river, jumping off th' bank behind eight or ten facing Sam an' Noah. Arrows flew both ways. I saw Bull take one in th' leg, but he kept firing an' advancing.

Two bullets ripping into our rock wall brought me back to my work. Th' ones b'hind th' horse were firing at us. I could see a leg an' foot over th' packs an' taking careful aim, I fired. When th' smoke cleared, th' leg was gone.

Tiny was sighting at someone in th' river. "Get out the way, Silent," he muttered, then fired. A man just in front of Silent crumpled. Silent threw us a look, an' returned to his fight.

"They're getting in our line of fire, Tiny, let's get those b'hind th' horse." Another gun boomed at us an I could see th' barrel of th' rifle glint. I aimed just down th' edge of th' barrel an' fired. A scream told me I had done damage.

Sam an' Noah's rush brought them through th' enemy, one or two falling an' they joined up with Bull and Silent. They backed up to th' bank an' th' Shawnees began to close in. Tiny fired an' th' last man in th' river with a gun fell. Fighting was hand-to-hand now an' Tiny continued to shoot when he got a chance.

There was a war cry from upstream an' we saw Redhorn, naked an' painted, riding down th' river straight for th' men around our friends. Laying low on his horse, he plowed right into th' crowd, firing his musket under his horse's neck an' scattering the enemy. Then turning, he drove back through, stopping between th' two combatants an' turning to face th' enemy, most floundering in deeper water.

Sam was not to be stopped an' charging, he struck th' nearest warrior in th' head with his pole an' he sank. Noah an' Silent charged too, knives in hand. Bull leaned against th' bank, shooting at any target he saw.

There was a shout from th' trail an' our men burst into th' clearing, running to th' river, unaware of th' ones behind that dead horse. "Watch the dead horse, Tiny!" He was already aiming. Two men stood up from th' horse, rifles aimed at our men on th' bank. Four rifles boomed almost simultaneously and both enemies fell. To our chagrin, three of our men fell, one headlong into th' river. There were a few more shots from th' bank into th' river, then silence. Nothing moved b'hind th' dead horse. Noah an'

Silent lifted our man out of th' water. He moved feebly; hopefully, he would be OK. Th' two fallen on th' bank didn't move.

It was eerily quiet. Tiny an' I stood up an' instantly, a half-dozen guns swung up. We dived behind th' rocks as a rifle boomed. Th' bullet struck rock b'hind us. I heard talk, but didn't move until Sam called, "You can come out now, Jerry, we won't shoot!"

Cautiously, we looked out to see all watching, not a gun raised. Now we could stand. Our trip down th' bluff wasn't as hard as going up an' we both made short work of it, falling into th' cool river an' drinking deep as we cooled our bodies. Water stung my face an' when I wiped it, my hand was bloody. Something stung an' I pulled a piece of rock out of my cheek.

"Looks like we took some hits," Tiny said, lifting his arm to show blood mixed with th' water running off his elbow. Both of us had cuts an' holes where splintered rock had hit us.

Th' ones on th' bank were at work collecting horses an' tending th' wounded. Th' arrow through Bull's leg had already been removed an' his leg wrapped tightly. He was a little pale around th' gills, but grinned at us as we came up, "Good fight," he said. "Too bad you weren't down here to join in the fun!"

Tiny sniffed, "I saved your rear end — twice!"

A look at th' other wounded explained why three had fallen at two shots. One bullet from th' enemy had gone clear through one man an' hit th' one who had fallen into th' river. It had knocked a hole in his backsides just below th' waist an' had pushed th' leather shirt he was wearing into his back. When they pulled th' shirt out, th' ball came with it. It hadn't even penetrated th' shirt! He would be all right, just sore for a while.

Others hadn't been so fortunate. Besides two fallen in th' meadow there were three in th' woods where th' following men had fought. Six or seven were wounded, two seriously.

Sam an' Noah were sitting on th' dead horse nursing their wounds, none of them seemed serious, though they both would need a stitch or two here an' there. There was a red welt across Sam's chest where a ball had plowed an' Noah had a big knot over his left eye.

"You should have been down here to join the fun." Noah grinned, showing a missing tooth an' bloody lip.

"Aww, we weren't painted for th' party, so

we stayed away," Tiny drawled.

"We were too busy drawing fire away from your sweet rear end," I added. I glanced at th' bodies behind th' horse. Besides th' two Tiny an' I shot, there was a third one with a shattered leg lying in a big dark patch where his blood had run out. His friends hadn't even tried to stop th' bleeding.

". . . And saving it to get busted another day!" Tiny said.

"You two did very well," Sam put in, "though some of those shots came pretty close. Overall, I think the plan worked very well. Good job, all of you!" He slapped Noah on th' back an' Noah winced.

Redhorn rode into th' meadow leading two packhorses that had bolted down th' trail. He dropped down an' examined his horse for damages, but found none. There was blood running down his leg where it had been slashed by a knife or a limb.

"Good work, Redhorn, you probably saved us from a good beating," Sam said.

"You didn't think you could have *all* the fun without me, did you?" he grinned. "Looks like you and Tiny have a pox," he said to me.

"Just rocks splattering," I replied. "Next time, someone else can do th' sharpshooting, Tiny an' I are going to be in th' middle of things."

"Oh but you *were* the middle of things," Sam said. "You started it off and you finished it from up there. Why would you want to be down here in the blood and grime getting shot and cut up?"

Wash Fishinghawk an' Lonza walked out of th' woods. There was a bloody rag tied around Wash's head, but he had a scalp tucked under his belt. Lonza carried two guns, a rifle an' an old musket that had left its good days far behind. He had three bullet holes in his clothes, but none had drawn blood. His pants leg was torn to mid-thigh where his leg was bandaged. I noted two scalps under his belt.

After surveying th' field a bit, Wash gave some orders an' th' men began to clean up. Several waded into th' river an' pulled bodies out, nine dead an' one wounded in th' shoulder. Th' water was dark with blood.

"How many were there?" someone asked.

"I counted twenty-one coming out of th' woods an' there were more coming," I said.

"There are twenty-five counting the wounded one," one of th' men said. "Soon he will be joining his friends," he added menacingly.

"I think we have something better for him to do," Wash said. "Bind up his arm and bring him to me."

When he was bandaged, th' whole party gathered around Wash. The man was a strong-looking Shawnee maybe thirty years old, proud an' defiant. Wash stared at him for a long moment until th' man looked down. Motioning to th' six of us sitting an' standing around Sam, he said, "Do you see these six young men?" he signed. Th' brave looked at us sullenly.

"They took on your whole party, six boys and one warrior (I thought he could have better said five boys and *two* warriors, but I wasn't ashamed to be named with these boys!), and defeated you almost single-handed. These are boys left home from the war party to tend horses and look after the village you and your companions attacked, killing women, old men, and children and stealing their winter's food and horses, grown warriors who would go behind a warrior's back and attack and rob his wife and children!" He spat. "Now you alone remain and all you would have gained is lost. Instead of sending you to your companions, we are going to send you back to your people with the news of how six Cherokee boys have destroyed the rest of your party and only you remain because we had mercy on you, though I suspect the more merciful thing to do would be to send you after your friends." All this, he said in sign language, for none of us knew th' Shawnee tongue.

"Waugh!" th' men responded in agreement. Such would shame a warrior far more than capture an' death by an enemy.

"You will watch and see how the Cherokee treat their fallen enemies, then we will take you back to your home beyond the White River to tell your people what happens when you trespass on Cherokee hunting grounds and attack their villages." To th' rest of us he said, "We must bury these away from the river, for our children and wives will be drinking and washing in these waters."

We unpacked several horses an' loaded th' bodies on them. Someone knew of a crevice between a large boulder an' th' bluff up th' mountain a ways an' we laid out th' bodies there. Most of them had been scalped an' th' rest of them would have been, but Wash prevented it. Taking their own blankets, we covered th' bodies, then buried them under dirt an' rocks. Next, we cut brush an' laid over th' grave to discourage scavengers. Th' Shawnee watched in silence, then with us all watching quietly, he sang th' Shawnee Death Song.

"Now," Wash signed, "we will take our five fallen warriors back to the village for burial and these seven will escort you to the White River," indicating Sam an' th' six of us.

# CHAPTER 21
## BACK TO WHITE RIVER

We returned to th' meadow an' prepared to depart, th' men with th' packhorses to th' village an' th' seven of us north to White River with our prisoner. After a good meal, we packed provisions for our trip on one of th' horses, and walked up th' trail to retrieve our horses an' move on.

Redhorn took some good-natured ribbing for his trail blocking. He had done a good job of it an' it took us a little time to clear it. Th' horses had rested an' were impatient to move. We watered them again an' struck a leisurely pace up th' trail, Sam leading with th' Shawnee walking behind him, his good arm tied to th' rope around his waist an' tied to th' horn of Redhorn's saddle.

Th' trail was rough an' got rougher as we went. We left th' river at Trace Creek where th' valley widened some an' followed Trace an' Begley Creek up to th' divide where we crossed over into th' Buffalo River watershed. This was rough country, with many steep mountains an' bluffs an' we tried to stay on th' ridges as much as possible. Though he tried valiantly, th' Shawnee was too weak to walk th' whole way.

"We're going to have to let him ride or he won't make it," Sam said, so we divided th' packhorse's load among us an' put him on th' horse in th' middle of th' train. We crossed th' Buffalo below Water Creek and th' travel got easier — a little. Bearing northeastward, we reached White River some miles below th' Shawnee villages.

"Now the question is how are we going to deliver this man to his people?" Sam asked as we sat around th' fire after our supper.

"More importantly, how do we get our message to them without knowing the Shawnee tongue?" Bull Calf put in, licking his fingers.

"Or losing our hair," said Silent.

"This is going to require thought," Sam said. "I wonder if there are any Cherokees living among the Shawnee." He punched th' Shawnee who was dozing beside him an' signed th' question. "No," th' warrior replied, then as best he could with one hand, he indicated that there were Shawnees there who could speak Cherokee.

"Good!" Sam exclaimed. "Now the only

thing we have to do is get them over here."

"Without losing our hair," Tiny mimicked, an' dodged a swing from Silent.

"We will have to do some scouting tomorrow an' see what we can do," Sam said. "Now that we are this close, we will have to be very careful that we aren't taken by surprise or don't lose our prisoner. Be extra vigilant on your guards tonight."

With that, we turned in except for th' two on first watch. Four hours of sleep an' Tiny shook my shoulder for duty. "There are boogers in the bushes," he whispered.

It was quiet, but I was uneasy — it felt as if I was being watched. I tried to put it out of my mind, reasoning that it was just my nerves, but th' feeling persisted. I moved around a lot an' so did Silent. It was obvious he was bothered too. Toward th' end of our watch, I passed close to him an' before I could say anything, he said, "Where is he?"

"Don't know."

"He's circled the camp twice, but I can't get sight of him."

"I haven't seen him, just felt he was there," I replied.

"Let's turn out the next watch early and we'll trap him."

I shook Noah awake. "Your turn," I muttered, then whispered, "Someone's out there. Silent and I are going to trap him. Don't shoot us!" Silent had wakened Bull Calf in th' same manner.

Pretending to go back to sleep, I crept out of my bedroll an' crawled into th' bushes. Flat on my belly under a thick cedar, I lay an' watched. Someone was there, I could smell him, but where? Maybe by lying very still, he would come to me. Th' moon sank b'hind a bank of clouds in th' west an' if it could have, it got darker. Now I had to rely more on my ears than my eyes.

Bull Calf had been walking a circle around camp an' it was time for him to pass. I heard th' softest scrape on th' grass an' strained to see what was making noise. A shadow passed b'tween me an' th' coals of th' fire. It wasn't one of us. In a moment, th' shadow crossed th' light returning th' way it came; movement stopped a moment, then th' figure turned an' came straight toward th' tree I was under! He rolled under th' low limbs an' almost ran into me b'fore I grabbed him, clamping my hand over his mouth.

He bit me. I had hold of a small person who was kicking an' flailing like a catfish on a hook. I finally got a lock around his neck where he couldn't use those teeth an' my other hand under his belt, I pushed him into th' ground an' crawled out from under th' cedar.

"Got him!" I called.

In a trice, Sam was up an' throwing sticks on th' fire. "Bring him into the fire, Jerry, and let's see him."

Noah an' Bull Calf came in from different directions. "Herded him right to you, didn't we?" Noah grinned.

"Yeah an' if I had known about his teeth, I would have 'herded' him right back to you!" I shook blood off my fingers.

Bull Calf grunted. "Be still and let us see you. Here, have a piece of meat."

Instantly, th' boy stopped struggling an' grabbed th' meat, eating voraciously. He was barefooted and naked save for a breech-clout. He finished eating an' reached for another piece of meat.

"Go slow or you will be sick," Sam warned.

"I haven't eaten in four days," he said. His fluent Cherokee surprised us, but we didn't believe he hadn't eaten in four days.

My grip on him slipped a little an' he twisted loose, but instead of running, he sat down an' began eating any food he could reach. He looked to be about twelve years old.

"Who are you, boy, and where did you

come from?" Sam demanded.

"I am Bet from Bear Creek Springs, and you," pointing a grimy finger at me, "are Sly Fox who has a slave named Kansas. The Osage stole me, but I gave them much trouble so they sold me to the Shawnees who named me Slippery Elm."

"Should have named you Beaver Teeth," I muttered, shaking blood from my throbbing fingers again.

"I ran away from the village over there four days ago. They can't catch me. If they do, I'll get a beating sure," he added.

"Stay with us and they won't catch you and we will take you home," Redhorn said.

"Are you alone, Bet?" Sam asked.

"Sure, no one would come with me."

"Are there other Cherokees in the villages over there?"

"The Peorias up on the hill have one they bought when the Shawnees bought me. There is another older Cherokee who is married to a Delaware living up the river a ways, but she isn't a slave."

"Can you speak Shawnee?" Tiny asked.

"Yes, my Shawnee mother taught me."

"Looks like we have an interpreter," Tiny said.

"It also looks like we have a Shawnee who speaks from the side of his mouth," Sam jerked sharply on th' Shawnee's rope.

Bet saw th' prisoner for th' first time. He stopped chewing an' his eyes got big, "Sa-a-y, that's Cloud Man from our village! He went on the long hunt last moon."

"He robbed our Village on Middle Fork, but we caught him," Tiny replied.

"Where's the others?"

"They're dead."

"All of them?" Bet was incredulous. Th' boy was silent a moment. "My Shawnee father was with them. He was a good man, only beat me twice."

"He won't do it again," Bull Calf said.

"Would you like for us to take you home to Bear Springs?" Sam asked.

Bet nodded enthusiastically. "Sure would like to see my family an' the boys back there! I was hoping the Cherokee army would come up this way and get me."

*So they have heard about th' raiders,* I thought. *This could work for our advantage.*

"We have to return this Shawnee and leave a message. Will you translate for us?"

"Sure, as long as I don't have to cross the river."

"We can work that out," Sam said. To th' rest of us, he said, "Let's eat and decide what we are going to do."

We ate in silence, each deep in his own

thoughts. As he finished, Sam looked around an' asked, "What do you think we should do, men?"

"One thing we *shouldn't* do is let ourselves get drawn into a trap," Bull Calf said.

"We should be cautious, but not show any fear," Noah said.

"I think we should trade the prisoner for the Cherokee slave they have," I said.

"That might work, but they would have to get him from the Peorias," Sam said. "That might take too much time."

"Her," Bet muttered through a mouthful.

"It wouldn't take too much time if they believed there were a few hundred warriors behind us," I said. Th' others nodded.

"You're right there." Sam rubbed his chin.

"Suppose we call for a chief and elders to come over for a parley and told them what we want, let them see the prisoner, and tell them they have just a little time to bring the slave to us or we will wipe out all the villages," Redhorn proposed.

"They would be full of questions about how we caught this one and we could tell them when they brought the slave back."

"How did you get across the river, *Slippery Elm*?" Silent spoke for th' first time.

"Stole a canoe and paddled."

"Where is it now?" Noah asked.

"I pulled it up in the bushes over there."
A generous piece of jerky pointed th' way.

"That's enough food, you'll be sick," Sam
grabbed th' meat away.

"One of us could take Slippery Teeth here
and meet the chief in the river to make
negotiations," I suggested. "The rest of us
could cover them from this side. If they are
out on a long hunt, there won't be many
left in their villages and maybe not many
guns."

"We'll let you go, Sly Fox, you seem to
have a relationship with the boy," Bull Calf
chuckled.

"Then it's set, let's go!" Sam said jumping up.

Bet led us to his canoe. He an' I got in
and th' others shoved us off. There were
women washing on th' bank an' I paddled
up near enough for them to hear as they
stood an' stared at us, gesturing an' jabber-
ing.

"Tell them that I have a message for their
chief and I need for him to come here at
once," I said to Bet.

We had no way of knowing what th' boy
said to th' Shawnees an' he used a lot of
latitude in how he interpreted what we said.
This is th' way he told us afterwards what
he said: "Mothers, this warrior has a mes-

360

sage for the chief and elders. Tell them to come to the river now or *our* army will wipe out all the villages!"

We pulled back to th' south side of th' river. It was a longer shot from th' north bank. I was surprised at th' energy that was put into summoning th' chief. It was only a few minutes until three men appeared. I paddled back an' when we were within a few feet, I told Bet to tell them that we had Cloud Man our prisoner and that we would exchange him for the Cherokee slave th' Peorias had.

This is what th' little scamp said, "Fathers, there is an army of hundreds of Cherokees coming from the south. They have promised that if you do not have the Cherokee slave girl the Peorias have and two fine ponies here immediately, they will cross the river and wipe out the villages and all the people. Those seven young men have killed all of the hunters from our village save Cloud Man standing there on the bank, who will be given in exchange for the slave and the horses. You must hurry, they are anxious for war!"

Th' women on the beach listened an' there was much shouting as they ran for th' village. Th' chief looked at our prisoner and th' others standing on th' bank, then gave instructions to two boys standing there. The boys quickly mounted an' galloped away, one for th' Peorias' village and th' other down th' river.

"Where is that one going?" I asked th' scamp.

"He's going to get two horses," he replied offhandedly.

"What for?"

"We have to ride *something.*"

"Did you tell them to get horses?"

He only nodded. My suspicions were aroused. "What else did you tell them?"

"Only what you said to tell them, Sly Fox," he shrugged his shoulders.

I was surprised at what was happening on th' far shore. People began streaming out of the near village an' up th' trail to an upper village, even as th' boy was returning from there, a girl clinging to him as he raced down th' hill, followed by a crowd of Peorias. A path opened for him through th' Shawnee women an' children an' he came on at full speed. When th' crowds met, there was confusion an' milling for a moment, then all th' people ran up th' hill save for one woman who continued following boy and slave, screaming an' crying.

At almost th' same time th' other boy ran into sight with two ponies in tow. They met with the chief and after a talk, an elder set the slave girl on one of th' ponies. With the spare pony in tow, she rode into th' river, soon swimming for the other side, her Peoria mother crying and screaming on th' shore. Quickly, we put Cloud Man in th' canoe an' held it until th' horses were out of th' water.

As he struggled to paddle with one arm, Bet shouted at th' men standing on th' far shore, "There, you children of a bitch wolf, you have your man-squaw of a warrior who can't whip a Cherokee boy; you child stealers who won't face your foe, who sneak around and steal from women and take their babies. Go steal some Osage babies who will grow up to be real warriors! It may be that they will fight the Cherokee for you. Your women are better warriors than you are!" and with many other words that we could not understand, did he exhort th' hapless Shawnees. No wonder their animosity grew toward Cherokees!

"Grab that boy and let's get out of here before they are mad enough to follow!" Sam said.

Noah grabbed th' boy an set him on his pony an' Tiny pulled th' pony into th' woods while th' rest of us made a leisurely exit, th' girl led by Redhorn. She told us she was six summers, her name was Antelope (Bet contemptuously called her Little Mouse, a name she hated), an' had been stolen from Bear Springs at th' same time as Bet. There were others stolen, but they were still with the Osage. She immediately chose Redhorn as her guardian an' was with him or Bet constantly.

Bet showed a disdain for her typical of a boy his age, but from time to time, we caught him taking care of her. They were both filthy an' lousy and th' first chance we got *they* got a good scrubbing, but that came later, our present need being to travel far an' fast b'fore th' Shawnee found out they had been tricked. We headed west, traveling fast an' camped that night on a small branch in Crooked Creek valley.

"The Shawnee will expect us to go to the Bear Creek Springs Village as directly as possible and that is what we have done so far. After we eat we will wade down to Crooked Creek and find a rock shelf to climb out on and head south."

"We could take the children home with us and get them to Bear Creek later," Bull Calf said.

"We may do just that," Sam agreed.

"Our next job is to find a place to wash these two or they can follow us just by using their noses," Redhorn said.

"Or listening for us to scratch!" Tiny added.

Bet was grinning defiantly. "No one is going to give *me* a bath if I don't *want* one!"

He walked toward th' food packs an' as he passed, Silent grabbed his breechclout, spun it off him, and threw it into th' fire all in one motion. Noah grabbed one arm an' leg an' swung him up where Bull Calf grabbed th' other arm an' leg an' they hustled him to th' branch.

"Watch his teeth," I called, following.

Th' two waded into th' branch an' dunked Bet under. That stopped his yelling an' he came up spittin' an' sputterin'. I waded in right b'hind them an' as he came up, I b'gan rubbing him vigorously with a hand full of sand. Tiny was on th' other side scrubbing away. He must have gone barefooted a long time, for his feet were as hard an' callused as leather.

Every time Bet complained or started to yell, we dunked him again. We were almost done when Silent waded in with a sharp knife and began shaving his head. Bet was so nervous about that blade that he stood still an' didn't complain. Soon he stood in th' branch, naked, pink, shivering. and bald as an onion.

Sam stood on th' bank watching an' laughing. He tossed Bet a shirt, "Here, Slippery Elm, put this on and when you're ready for a bath, let us know. We know where there is a nice warm spring that will work fine for baths."

One of th' things we admired about Bet was that he wouldn't be intimidated. Probably why he was not so valuable a slave to th' Osage women. It didn't look as if th' Shawnees did any better with him either.

"I'll get you all for this," he said, an' we believed him.

"Be careful what you say," Bull said. "I'd hate to see you get your new shirt wet first thing." He lifted th' tail an' Noah gave him a wet slap on his bare butt.

"Ye-e-o-ow," he yelled.

"There, we now name you Redhand!" Noah said looking at his handprint. Th' name stuck an' we used it whenever he got out of hand or started to misbehave. Th' memory of that slap made him more careful about how he acted.

Someone threw a blanket around his shoulders an' we all walked back to th' fire. To our great surprise, there sat Antelope washed an' dressed in one of Tiny's shirts, combing her newly washed hair.

"You won't cut my hair off, will you?" she

asked Silent, lip quivering. Silent shook his head an' smiled.

"He only cuts the hair of lousy boys who talk too big, Little Sister," I said.

"We will take good care of your hair, Antelope," Bull Calf said.

Sam looked at both of th' young ones. "It is important that you keep clean. We will all bathe often on this trip and you will bathe when we do. Keep your hair combed and when we get to the villages, the women will have things to rid you of the nits. I don't think Bet will have that problem for some time if ever again!"

With that, we broke camp, even taking th' precaution of throwing our ashes in th' branch an' scattering th' rocks we used. It was fortunate that Crooked Creek was low and wading it was easy. We moved slowly upstream in single file, trying to stir up as little muddy water as possible. With luck, it would be gone soon an' any followers would not find it . . . with luck. That was our greatest need at th' moment. Soon we came to a shelf of solid rock on th' north side of th' creek. Sam led us out of th' water an' stopped.

"Silent, take the boy and go up the creek on the rock. Hide your trail off the rock as best you can and follow the creek until you find another rocky place to the water, then wade back down here past this rock until you see one of us waiting on you on the south side."

Silent nodded an' was on his way, leading Bet's horse.

Sam moved back down th' creek an' we followed in th' failing light. At a wide sandy beach, he waded out of th' water an' into the woods. Tiny was th' last in line an' without a word, stopped his horse in th' water and waited on Silent.

Well into th' woods, we stopped an' cut some cedar an' willow limbs. It was almost an hour b'fore we heard Tiny an' Silent leave th' creek. We stepped off a rock into th' creek an' starting underwater, brushed out all tracks back into th' woods. It would be hard for anyone to find our trail, but we well knew that there were *some* few who could, though it would take precious time.

We turned off Greasy Creek up one of th' gullies, climbing an' hoping we would find some ridge to ride for a while. Near th' top in pitch-dark, Sam stopped an' we slept until morning.

A short climb in th' morning brought us out on a divide an' it proved to be a ridge that ran south for several miles, easy going, but no trail. We nooned by that sugar loaf mountain at th' head of Tomahawk Creek. It was a long rest, for there was good graze an' our horses needed it. Tomahawk was twisty an' rough an' it was near dark when we got to th' Buffalo. Upriver a ways we found a place where th' bluffs stopped on th' south side an' crossed.

Even without it being a bluff, that hill was steep leaving th' river an' Sam said, "I don't relish climbing that in th' dark, not knowing what is up there or if we will wind up in a box and have to come back down, let's find a good place and camp."

Back in th' edge of th' woods, a huge sycamore had fallen, th' log near as tall as a man. Debris from floods had washed up aginst it, but th' back side was clean an' we built a fire there that couldn't be seen from either side of th' river or through thick brush. There was some grass b'tween th' log an' th' river so we staked our horses there.

During th' night, th' river rose an' we found our horses needing all of their ropes to stay out of water. "Good," Sam said. "Anyone following will have a hard time crossing."

In th' time it took for us to be ready to move, water had risen another foot an' it would soon be washing against th' log. Our only way out was straight up th' mountain. It was a hard climb on foot, sidling around th' steepest parts an' pullin' th' horses along, but we came out on another razor-back that ran generally southward. Our horses were glad to get a blow an' we were glad to ride again.

Th' end of that ridge gradually sloped to a valley that ran east of the Devil's Backbone an' through wide prairie-like valleys to Trace Creek. There, we picked up th' trail to the Village at the Forks. Other parties were moving along it an' we felt safer.

People at th' Forks had heard of th' raid on our village an' our battle. They knew we had been on our way to White River an' welcomed us. They sent a runner to Middle Fork to tell them we were safely back an' would be home soon. Women took Antelope in hand an' she soon reappeared, her hair glistening and nit-free, in a dress, with moccasins on her feet. She thanked Tiny for th' loan of his shirt, then tripped happily off with a young woman who had agreed to keep her. Slippery Elm refused all offers of aid, including moccasins, an' stayed with us.

There was a party there from Bear Creek Springs an' they agreed to take th' two young ones back to their families for us. Bet would have stayed with us in spite of mandatory baths but we insisted he must go to his people. We left their two Shawnee ponies with them an' they were happy about that. They left th' same morning we did, Slippery Elm promising to return an' little Antelope waving happily from her pony's back.

I don't know how many times I have crossed Pee Dee Creek headed home after being absent, but it was always a welcome signpost along th' trail an' it always seemed th' burdens got lighter after passing that creek. We parted company at Weaver's Creek, th' five headed for th' Village, me an' Sam headed for home. As usual for Laughing Brook, our arrival was anticipated an' we all sat down to a great meal before a gently crackling fire. It was good to be home.

It must have been a week later that th' war party came in. Criers brought th' news that there would be a celebration at th' Meeting House that evening. Of course, we all attended. There was a great feast an' th' warriors strutted about with their scalps under their belts. After th' meal, several men stood in turn an' told of their adventures and exploits on th' warpath, displaying their grisly trophies. I noticed Sam twisting an' squirming in agitation an' several times he made to rise only to be restrained by Ruthie's gentle hand on his arm.

Finally, th' last man had spoken and th' crowd was about to break up when Sam jumped up an' in his booming voice called, "Hold, friends, there are other warriors here who have not spoken."

There were more than a few nods from th' women, lips compressed, jaws set.

When all was quiet, he continued. "While our warriors were away, our village was attacked by a large Shawnee and Peoria hunting party. Several of our people were killed resisting their attack while five young men, Bull Calf, Tiny, Noah, Silent, and Redhorn, led the village to safety. The enemy plundered the village and set it afire before retreating up the river trail. These boys led the women and children back into the village and helped put out the fires.

"When pursuit was organized, they were in the forefront and volunteered to race up the mountain with Sly Fox and me in an effort to get ahead of the enemy and stop his escape. They were successful in setting up an ambush and these six young men who were deemed too young and inexperienced to join your war party proved they were warriors that day by stopping the Shawnee and accounting for over half of the kills of the enemy.

"In addition to that, they took the remaining Shawnee survivor back to his village and secured the release of two Cherokee slaves in exchange for him. Those slaves were brought back to the Village at the Forks and are now safe with their families at Bear Springs." He looked around angrily at th' crowd, picking th' war party in particular, I thought.

"Some of us chose not to go with the war party because of previous friendships with the Osage. For that we were called cowards and other names. When you were displaying your trophies, I noted that many of them were gray or showed streaks of gray in them. Others were from children. Only two were the scalp locks of Osage warriors."

Stooping, he picked up a bag an' dumped out a pile of scalps. Taking one up, he held it a moment, then threw it to a war party warrior standing near Tiny. "Look at that scalp and take note that it is the lock of a Shawnee warrior. Now, give it to Tiny, he fired the first shot and killed the first warrior, then killed several others, saving some of us from being killed."

Another scalp he threw to a warrior behind me. "Does that look like an old woman's scalp? Give it to Sly Fox, he killed the second, a Peoria, with the second shot. He too shot several others during the fight." Tossing out two more scalps, he said, "Give those *warriors'* scalps to Bull Calf and Silent, they each killed several warriors with their bows, one that was charging them, and they stood firm, then they charged across the battle ground, Bull Calf with an arrow through his thigh, and came to the aid of two of their companions who were fighting eight or ten Shawnees in the river."

He had to restrain his anger when he tossed th' next scalp. "That trophy is for Noah, who stood with me in the river and charged those ten Shawnee warriors armed only with a pole lance. His charge was so determined that I had to work hard to keep up with him."

He picked up th' last scalp from his bag an' stood a long moment. It was quiet, deadly quiet, in that room. "This last scalp is for Redhorn, who worked alone to block the trail to see that no one escaped our trap, then charged his horse through the enemy surrounding us in the river and broke their attack. Without his action, which he didn't have to do, one or two of us would not be standing here tonight."

He glared out at th' crowd an' I know he

picked out every war party warrior this time. "These are the real warriors of this village, the ones left behind who gave of themselves, even in the face of death and came to the aid of their kin and clan, not bringing home a single trophy, but deserving even more than they have gotten here. I will put my life in their hands anytime, for they are men."

He sat down. It was quiet for a moment, then a great shout arose from th' crowd, even some of th' war party joining in. We received many thanks from th' men an' hugs from th' women. Sam stood off to one side with Ruth an' I kept a wary eye out for him. He had publicly scorned a bunch of men an' made some enemies that night. Privately, several of th' war party came to him an' said he was right in saying what he had and that they were ashamed of what they had done on th' warpath. Others held a smoldering hatred for him an' more than one tried to exact retribution, even to trying to ambush him a time or two. We six took it upon ourselves to protect him without his knowledge. We succeeded in foiling at least one attempt to kill him.

Whenever there was trouble with invaders or miscreants, th' seven of us worked together an' became quite a team of fighters.

We had many adventures.

*"Now that I have told you about their first adventure together, I'll tell you what Uncle Jerry said about th' natures of those five warriors. Sam being married an' several years older had other priorities an' responsibilities. Th' six of them ran together for several years an' had many scrapes, most of which they came out of on top." Zenas chuckled.*

Tiny fit his name, never being very big. He was a scrappy fighter an' could outwrestle all th' others except Bull Calf. Being just as wiry an' a little bigger, I could hold my own with him an' it was a question of which one would win in any one bout. We were undoubtedly th' champions of th' village an' more than once bested wrestlers from the Village at the Forks.

The boys from th' two villages would meet somewhere an' have all sorts of competitions. To be honest, the Village at the Forks boys had an advantage, being larger an' greater in number. Us boys on Middle Fork were always underdogs, but that had its advantages an' we enjoyed th' challenges. I don't think anyone ever equaled Tiny's accuracy with bow or gun. It seemed th' longer an' more difficult th' shot, the better he was. His vision was legendary an' he could see things both far an' near that th' rest could not see. Where others would watch for movement to discern things, Tiny saw th' still targets. As a result he was a great hunter an' on th' warpath he invariably got th' first shot — an' kill.

He was fearless an' many times got himself into tights that we would have to rescue him from, often being bloodied in th' process. We had a saying that he was born under a wandering star, for he never stayed in one place long. I saw or heard of him all over th' west as it was in those days, from Utah to Missouri an' all points between.

Many years later, Tiny was killed when a party of Pawnees caught him out on th' prairie alone. He took refuge in a wallow an' we found much Pawnee blood around him. Later, one of th' attackers told me that out of ten, Tiny had killed four of them an' wounded two others before they got him. They couldn't believe he was th' only one in th' wallow an' respected him so much that they didn't scalp or mutilate his body. "He was a fine warrior," were th' Pawnees' parting words.

Bull Calf was a horse of a different color. He was big th' first time I saw him an' stayed big his whole life. When he was a boy, strangers would take him as being older than he really was because of his size. In reality he was th' second youngest in our bunch after Noah. When I say he was big, I don't mean fat, for there was little of that on his body. I've seen him single-handedly lift th' back of a wagon that was hub deep in a bog an' push while th' horses pulled it out of th' mud. When it came to hand-to-hand competition or battle, no one ever beat him. Loud an' jolly at play, he was silent an' deadly at war.

When they got over their awe of his size, he was a great favorite with women. Once he held a woman on each knee an' roared with laughter while they fought over him. He ended th' fight by hugging them like a big bear an' left with one under each arm, their b'hinds showing an' their kicking feet a good two feet off th' ground. Th' end of his bachelor life came when he was captured by a beautiful an' statuesque Osage woman nearly as tall as he was. They eventually settled in Indian Territory an' raised a house full of kids who got rich on th' oil beneath th' old home place. Bull never saw any of th' riches, being long gone, but I doubt that he would have cared for them anyway.

■ ■ ■ ■

Noah was th' smart one. He could use his head an' get himself out of tights when th' rest of us would have to fight our way out. Many's th' time he stood aside safe an' sound watching us get our rears whipped for no reason he could fathom. Now don't think by that he was cowardly for he wasn't an' in deadly combat he was a demon. His vision of th' battles we were in an' quick wit to anticipate th' enemy's next move made him our leader an' we called him War Lord.

He was fascinated by things mechanical an' became quite a gunsmith. He could take an old used-up gun an' make it a weapon again. He was a mechanic back when they called mechanics blacksmiths. Years later he did much to bring machinery to th' reservations in Indian Territory an' teach people to use them.

His place on th' west bank of th' Neosho River became our meeting place in later years when we no longer ran in a bunch. Tiny an' Redhorn, who never settled, could often be found there when they were not on one of their rambles.

It wasn't because he was a man of few

words (though that he was) that we called him Silent. It was because he was th' best hunter an' stalker any of th' rest of us ever knew. I have seen him stalk a grazing deer an' cut it with his knife before th' deer gave notice that he was near. Unbelievable, an' I don't blame you if you doubt it.

More than once he has approached an enemy close enough to touch them undetected. In one of our war games with the Village at the Forks, he crept up on a boy sitting on a log an' cut th' thong holding up his breechclout without being detected. When th' boy stood up his clout fell off to th' glee of all.

His skill could instill terror in th' enemy. One night he went into a Pawnee camp an' slit th' throats of every other sleeping warrior without being caught. In th' morning we watched as th' camp awoke an' found themselves surrounded by dead companions an' panicked an' fled. We enriched ourselves with plunder, including horses left behind.

Once he captured a sentinel of an enemy camp an' freed one of our men who had been captured, placing th' sentinel in his place. Imagine their surprise an' anger when they found one of their own men trussed up an' gagged in th' place of their prisoner.

Th' best rider in our bunch was Redhorn. Many a slower horse won a race because of his skill in riding. Never very big, he was strong an' quick an' it seemed he could read a horse's thoughts before he acted. He was a great horse breaker an' trainer, though not very popular with th' range rancher because he refused to use th' rough methods of th' bronc buster. Bronc Ruiner, he called them. With th' advent of barbed wire, th' needs of th' rancher changed an' not being so needful of a big herd of horses, Redhorn's gentle breaking method became preferred an' he did a thriving business.

While he lived in the Village on Middle Fork, he helped develop th' Cherokee Pony into a breed desired all over that region. They couldn't be beat for stamina an' bottom. When paired against similar ponies in a race, they were a formidable force.

His riding skill came into its own when he was hired as a scout for th' army. After his long riding became known, to his disgust he spent more time as a message courier than as a scout. Eventually he quit th' courier business, moved to th' southwest, an' hired on as a scout for General Carlton. He kept his riding skills under cover an' satisfied himself with scouting in New Mexico an' Arizona.

*"It wasn't th' last battle Uncle Jerry was in by a far cry,"* Zenas said, after I had leaned back and begun massaging my writer's cramp away. *"He narrowly missed Custer's debacle on th' Little Horn in '76. He didn't have much truck with Custer after what he had done on th' Wichita. Grandma Ruth had a letter from him telling about that so-called battle. One of th' things I remember he said was that th' General was going to get a lot of soldiers killed an' sure 'nough he did!*

*"Oh, by th' way,"* he exclaimed, *"th' 'Paches at White Mountain knew about th' Little Horn battle three days after it happened. Soldiers at Stanton didn't believe them until it was confirmed to them a week later. Never did find out how they got th' news so fast. Maybe smoke signals or mirrors, but nobody ever found out."*

# CHAPTER 22
## OUTLAWS AND WINE
## 1818 TO 1820

*"I'm gonna tell you about a couple of places on th' Middle Fork that are unique an' then about a scrape Dad an' Riley got into," Zenas said as we settled in for another tale.*

*"I guess it's been th' same story from th' Atlantic to th' Pacific; Pilgrims settled in th' northeast an' it wasn't long until people started spreading west. First t' go were mostly outlaws an' those who couldn't get along with their neighbors for one reason or another. Some o' them were good people who loved th' wilderness, but on th' whole, first were th' lawless. Later, more decent people moved in behind them an' settled up th' country proper. Uncle Jerry an' Grandma Ruth had experiences with both kinds an' here is a tale or two about those times an' people."*

A couple of miles south of Weaver's Creek an' Buffalo Hump was an unusual valley th' Cherokee mostly shunned because they thought it was haunted. We simply called it th' Pedestal Rock Valley, but they now call it Williams' Valley after th' first white settlers there. From th' north, you first come to a rock bluff that runs along th' north edge of th' valley with solitary boulders an' some on little pedestals sitting on top of it, but when you descend to th' valley floor, there are several tall pedestals an' other strange rock formations.

About halfway down th' valley is a dry cave, not very deep under th' mountain. Th' floor was powdery dry dirt several feet thick. In olden times a large boulder had fallen from th' roof an' on top of this rock was a large grindstone where th' occupants ground their grains. I say occupants, because no one knows who they were, having left many years before Osage or Cherokee moved into th' area. It was obvious that they had farmed th' valley an' on top an' lived in th' cave.

There is an X chiseled in th' wall of th' cave indicating that someone was buried under it, an' digging around, you could find bones, teeth, an' an old green trader's glass along with some arrowheads. As a result of that X, people said it was haunted an' avoided th' place as much as possible — except for us boys, that is, we loved playing in th' valley, climbing bluffs, an digging through th' dust. Still, it was a strange place, dark an' forbidding at times an' then bright an' inviting at others.

It was to this cave that Wash had directed th' village to seek refuge when th' Shawnees attacked, but th' women being in a high state, refused to go. Instead they went to Indian Rock House, which was another cave not far away. It too was an interesting place, where people had lived long ago. They had dug footholds into th' rock bluffs so you could climb up an' down with ease an' legend claimed that writing on th' cave wall tells of an Indian who was killed in th' cave. I don't know why th' women didn't think *it* was haunted. We always loved visiting those places as boys an' had many a mock battle an' games on th' rocks.

Along about 1819 a few white men began to trickle into th' country. They were rough people who enjoyed life without structure or law an' they caused a lot of trouble. One of them set up a saloon at his cabin an' others gathered there an' drank an' caroused. There was more than one run-in with them. They traded their liquor for furs an' pelts, generally cheating th' unwary Indian. If they couldn't cheat him, they would get him drunk an' steal his furs.

Things got so bad that th' elders told them all to leave th' country, this being Cherokee territory an' they had no right here, but they were laughed at an' threatened an' chased off.

In Council, it was decided that th' matter had to be handled firmly an' Sam was given th' job of seeing that th' wishes of th' elders (an' th' people) were carried out. A day or two later, Sam met one of these men on th' trail to th' village an' told him he had twenty-four hours to quit th' country.

The man laughed an' being a big brawler, swung at Sam. To his surprise an' dismay, he found that Sam was not a typical Indian who didn't know how to fist fight, but was a brawler of th' first order. In no time, he was thoroughly whipped an' Sam, his ire up, said, "Your time is up an' you will leave right now!" Whereupon he escorted th' man to his hovel, gathered his things, an' sent him on his way, to th' sound of fire crackling through th' roof of his shack. He was escorted by six young braves who saw him safely delivered to th' north side of White River, never to be seen again on Middle Fork.

When word of this got out, a couple of those two-legged snakes slithered off to th' east, hastened by strange sounds an' noises that followed them clear to Flee's Settlement. It might be stated here that their stay there was also short-lived, they deciding that a more settled life back east was better for their health.

Still, there were a dozen or more rascals left an' it became th' mission of the Seven to rid our country of them. Two carousers lived on th' trail to the Village at the Forks where upper Weaver's Creek crosses. They were charging Indian travelers a toll for th' privilege of wading th' creek to cross. One evening, Tiny came along from the Forks carrying a sack of goods. As he approached th' creek, one of th' men met him.

"Whur yuh going, little boy, y' mama know yo're out here by yoresef?" he sneered.

"I'm on my way home on Middle Fork," Tiny answered, smiling.

"Let's see whut air y' got in that there bag." Th' man grabbed th' sack from Tiny's hand an' began poking through it. He pulled out several items an' tossed them aside, poking a handful of pemmican into his mouth as he dug further.

"Whut's all this grass doing in th' bottom?"

Tiny seemed alarmed. "Don't dig in there, it's where I keep my pet rattler."

"Right y' air, a Injun carrying a snake around in his bag! I aingt seen a buck yit whut wasn't skeert to death of a little ol' rattler," he said as he dug through th' grass. Suddenly, he yelled an' dropped th' bag. Attached to his finger was a small timber rattler. Slinging th' snake off, he yelled again, "Ye-e-e-o-o-w, I been bit!"

His partner who had been lolling by th' cabin taking in all this ran to th' creek. Too lazy to wade cold water to his partner's aid, he called, "Whut air ye hollering 'bout, Jed?" him knowing full well that his friend had been bitten by a snake.

At that moment, Noah "happened" along from th' east, unnoticed. Just behind Lazy, he called in a loud voice, "What's wrong over there?"

Lazy jumped an' spun around, just as Noah "accidently" bumped into him an' spilled him into th' creek. Feigning regret an' apologizing profusely, Noah reached down to give th' man a hand, but when he was halfway up, their hands "slipped" an' th' man was doused into th' stream again.

Meanwhile, Tiny had grabbed Jed's hand an' choking off th' circulation to his bitten finger was hurrying him across th' stream. Jed was so distraught he didn't notice Lazy One falling again an' stumbled into him.

Trying to keep his footing, he stepped square in Lazy's chest an' walked over him pushing him to th' bottom an' hurrying on to th' cabin.

He brought up short when he saw Redhorn an' Sly Fox sittin' on th' bench b'side th' door.

"What is the matter, men?" Sly Fox asked lazily.

"This man has been bitten by my pet rattler," Tiny said, a look of worry on his face.

"Let me see." Redhorn leaned forward, but didn't seem too concerned. " 'S a snake bite, a-right, what have you got to treat it with?"

"Nothin, nary a blessed thang but that jug setting thar," Jed whined.

"Oh! Well, here, take a drink." Sly stuck his finger through th' jug handle an' as he swung it up to th' victim, it smashed into th' bench, shattering. "Oh my," Sly was dismayed, looking at th' ring an' jug neck swinging from his finger.

"Whut 'dyuh do?" Jed shouted. "Whut 'dyuh do?"

"It must have hit the log an' broke," Sly said. "Sorry."

Redhorn had risen, an' examining th' swelling finger said, "There's only one thing we can do now if your hand doesn't wither or you don't die."

"Whut's thet?"

"We have to cut the finger off."

Jed's eyes bugged. "Cut it off'n my *hand*?" Sweat beaded on his forehead an' under his eyes.

"Yep, cut it plumb off an' in a hurry."

"Bring him over here to th' splittin' stump," Sly called from th' wood pile. Thumbing th' axe, he said, "This axe is awful dull, do you have a sharp hatchet there, friend?" This to Noah who had just walked up with the soaked Lazy One.

"Yep, I always keep it sharp." Noah pulled his hatchet from his belt.

All business now, Sly Fox commanded, "Lay that finger down here!"

Whimpering, Jed laid his hand on th' stump.

"How many of those do you want me to chop off?"

Jerking his hand back, Jed carefully folded his good fingers an' laid his forefinger on th' stump.

"Why, that's his trigger finger," Tiny said.

The up-swinging axe stopped. "You're right, friend," Sly said. Shaking his head sadly he brought th' axe up again, "That's too bad."

He began his chop an' just before th' axe

struck, Jed's hand jerked away, an involuntary act of self-preservation.

"Looks like someone's gonna have to hold Jed's hand still." He looked around.

"Not me!" chorused Noah, Tiny, an' Redhorn together.

All eyes turned to Lazy standing there shivering, caked mud peeling off his back an' rolling down. "Not me!" his eyes widened when he realized his position.

"Who else would be best fit to aid this man an' save his life, but you, his friend?" Noah asked.

"That's right," Tiny said.

Redhorn nodded solemnly. "You would always be 'the man who saved my life' to Jed here."

Lazy shuddered.

"Hurry up, man," Sly Fox commanded. *"This man is dying!"*

Reluctantly, Lazy took Jed's arm an' holding his wrist rigid with one hand, th' other behind his elbow, they laid th' finger on th' stump.

"This time, Jed, close your eyes and you won't know when it hits," Tiny suggested. Jed squeezed his eyes tight an' so did th' Lazy One.

"Now, Jed, I'll honestly tell you that this is gonna" — wham! went th' axe severing th' finger cleanly just beyond th' first knuckle — "hurt!"

The severed finger rolled away across th' stump an' Jed's knees sagged. Lazy got th' dry heaves an' turned away, pale as death. A little trickle of blood oozed out of th' stump of a finger, then th' vessel spurted, pulsing with Jed's heartbeat.

"Better bandage that quick," th' amputator said authoritatively.

Tiny produced a rag an' in no time th' hand was tightly bound in a large bandage, no doubt larger than need be.

Now, in fairness to Jed an' th' Lazy One, I have to say that under normal conditions a toughened frontiersman would not react in this cowardly way when it became necessary to do such as was done here, but both men, being th' bullies they were, an' quite dissipated by drink, didn't at that moment have th' constitutions to stand up to th' crisis.

*"I've seen a man take an axe an' chop off his own thumb when he got bit by a big rattler,"* Zenas added. *"And he did it hisself before any of us around him could move to help him!"*

The two victims of th' caper sat pale an' spent by th' stump while th' four innocents looked on. "You best seek medical help to get that hand healed up," Tiny said.

"Jist whur'd yuh git this here medical help in this country?" Lazy asked, his slow mind recovering from th' shock and beginning to suspect a plot — which it was except for th' amputation, which came along as a result of Jed's intemperate behavior.

Sly Fox rubbed his chin. "I hear there's a good Indian doctor at Shawnee Town up on Crooked Creek. You could be there in a couple of days if you had horses."

"We could borry horses from Nick at th' tavern," Jed said.

"That's a good idea," Noah said. "We will go with you as far as the Village. It isn't far from there to th' tavern."

*[I might add that th' word "tavern" is used very loosely here to describe a split log bar set between two stumps in th' yard of Nick's hovel. — J.D.]*

So it was that th' six started out on th' trail to Middle Fork, Noah an' Sly Fox gallantly carrying th' two white men's muskets for them, an' sharpshooter Tiny bringing up th' rear with Redhorn. Shortly, a rider appeared coming hurriedly from th' Village leading two spavined horses. They stopped to rest an' visit as was th' custom.

"Where are you going with those horses,

friend?" Noah asked to th' "stranger," who looked a lot like Silent.

"I'm going to trade these at the Village at the Forks," said th' rider, "I found them roaming th' woods an' no one at Middle Fork claimed them."

"Sa-a-a-y, those look like Nick's horses!" th' Lazy One took a closer look. "They *are* Nick's!" He looked accusingly at th' rider. "Did you steal them horses?"

"I-I-I found them in the woods," th' rider stammered.

"Woods, my rear," th' suddenly righteous frontiersman said. "You *stole* those horses!"

"Those are Nick's horses?" Sly asked.

"Sure as shootin'!" Lazy said, an' Jed nodded. "Sure as shootin'," he agreed weakly.

"This may be fortunate for you," Noah said, raising his gun muzzle to bear on th' rider. "We were just going to Nick's to borrow his horses so this poor fellow can go seek medical help for his snake bite."

"These are my horses," th' rider stammered weakly. "I found them."

"*Stole* 'em!" Lazy corrected.

"You're sure of that?" Tiny asked.

"Sure!" th' two whites chimed.

Sly Fox reached over an' jerked th' leads from th' rider's hand while Noah an' Redhorn stepped closer, their guns raised. Tiny grabbed th' rider's gun from th' saddle where it hung.

"This is really fortunate for you, here are the horses you need an' there is the trail to th' Forks an' Bear Springs. It's only a jump from there to Shawnee Town an' the doctor," Sly Fox said.

"You can pick up your gear at th' cabin an' be on your way tonight!" Tiny added.

The pair hesitated. Sly pushed th' leads into Lazy's hand. "Take them an' be on your way! We will help you pack your gear an' I saw two saddles hanging in your cabin. We will tell Nick that you have recovered his stolen horses an' will return them to him after you see the doctor."

"If you don't get that hand treated, it could turn into gangrene an' you would lose your arm — or worse," Noah warned.

"We'll do it!" Jed spoke.

"Those are my horses!" th' rider said weakly.

"Turn around an' go back, friend," Sly said firmly, "lest we take you before the Council for stealing from the white man."

Reluctantly, Silent turned his horse an' rode back down th' trail.

"Back to the cabin!" Tiny said triumphantly.

The packing at th' cabin was done quickly

an' th' gear soon stored behind th' saddles. Of course, th' plunder from th' toll enterprise was too bulky to haul on two horses so th' young Indians assured th' men that they would cache th' things in a safe place until their return.

Happily, they escorted th' riders to th' Forks, where they "found" that a group of warriors were on their way to Bear Springs an' would be glad t' see that th' two were safely delivered an' then escorted on their way t' Shawnee Town.

After th' two whites had moved on their way th' next morning, th' young men let it be known that whatever had been appropriated from th' people was at th' cabin an' could be retrieved on th' next visit that way. Silent rode into town leading four horses an' th' boys were soon back home.

While being treated at Shawnee Town, Jed an' Lazy got word that Nick had discovered that it was they who had stolen his horses an' he let it be known that there would be stern retribution if he ever caught up with them. With that in mind, they retreated further north beyond th' White an' it was rumored a few weeks later that they had gone up th' White River Trace to St. Louis.

Most of th' people got back their things except for th' furs that had been traded in for whiskey. With a little fixing up, th' cabin became a way station an' provided needed shelter for travelers for many years thereafter. You might have noticed that Bull Calf an' Sam were not participants in th' removal of those "ferry" keepers. They were on a more risky mission I'll tell you about.

# CHAPTER 23
## SILVER BULLETS

Nick Row wasn't a big man, but he wasn't a small man either; he wasn't a loud man, but he wasn't a quiet man; he wasn't a black man or a white man or a red man; his coloration was what we called swarthy. He wasn't a dirty man, but he wasn't clean. He was a man who worked very hard at being lazy, preferring th' more devious shortcuts to his gains than th' longer honest routes. He was a killer. Not one of those honest in-your-face killers, but a sneak killer who took his victims unawares an' unseen. Every man was his friend — and he killed a lot of his friends. No one ever saw him kill a single person, his victims just showed up dead or else disappeared, never to be seen again, an' th' legend was that death followed Nick Row like rain follows a cloud. He was feared by all who knew him, but never respected. He seemed content with this or he just didn't care. His great talent was drawing th' dregs of society to him, cultivating their friendship, an' using them in his many devious schemes. A portion of every ill-gotten gain from th' enterprises of these vassals found its way to his pockets.

He didn't simply drift into th' Little Red River country, he suddenly appeared, his shanty an' saloon looking as if they had been there many moons. A few drifters were with him an' more came in, like flies drawn to carrion.

Sam Meeker realized early that Nick was th' linchpin that held th' lawless ones together an' if he was eliminated, all others would move on when they found that staying was unprofitable or detrimental to their health an' well-being. *But how do we rid ourselves of this man?* he asked himself. A frontal assault would not do, there were too many defenders an' Slick Nick would not be caught in a stand-up fight. If he couldn't be run off or scared off, he would have to be lured away, but how? Sam puzzled over this for many days, then something he heard about events way down in th' Arkansas valley gave him th' germ of an idea. It cost him dearly, but soon he was th' secret possessor of two of those silver pesos floating around th' village.

A constant need in th' villages was lead

an' powder. They came primarily down th' trace from St. Louis, but th' discovery of galena north of White River made lead more readily available. Seizing th' opportunity, Sam began importing lead an' soon had a brisk trade established. He would bring lead down, an' with th' loan of one's lead mold, would mold bullets for his customers. Soon business was so good that he started trading with Cherokee an' Choctaw villages along th' Arkansas River. Every few months, he would make th' trip there with a load of lead bricks an' trade. It was there he heard tales of a red-headed woman an' her secret mine an' th' settler who ignorantly molded his bullets out of a vein of pure silver.

When he made these trips to th' south, he would hire one or two of the Seven to travel north an' secure more lead so it would be on hand when he returned. Th' boys loved th' travel an' adventures it brought an' usually more than one made th' trip just for th' fun of it. For a few days after his return, Sam was flooded with orders for bullets an' worked steadily at th' forge.

Not long before th' boys had closed the ferry, Sam returned from th' south to his usual backlog of orders. A couple of whites had ordered balls an' when they came to get their order, Sam showed them a couple of "special" balls he had molded for them that were harder an' had a special shine to them. "Makes them easier to dig out of the carcass than the regular lead balls," he said. He was so eager for them to try the new "premium" lead, he even accepted a jug of wine in trade, something he refused to do normally.

*"A tale hangs on that jug that I will get to later."* *Zenas chuckled.*

Leaning on Nick's log bar that evening, th' two were laughing about th' ignorant Injun's claim of "premium lead" for his bullets. As usual, Nick's ears picked up th' conversation an' as usual, he seemingly paid no mind to it.

Later when th' two were sleeping off their indulgence, Nick was seen placing their muskets an' horns in a safe place. In doing so, he spilled one of th' bags of balls an' with a curse retrieved them from th' ground. Later in th' privacy of his hut, he examined two of th' balls he had palmed, one made of th' regular lead an' one of th' premium lead. Th' premium ball was definitely shinier an' when he tested hardness with his teeth, it was harder than a lead ball. Nick studied th' ball thoughtfully, it was only a little lighter than th' lead, but what was it made of? Certainly not lead, not zinc either, he thought as he pulled a couple of coins from his pocket. His lucky peso shone in th' candlelight an' he stared at its polished face. Silver! That ignorant Injun was makin bullets out of silver!

Th' initial flush of discovery soon faded to cold thought. How could he get ahold of that silver? He could buy up all th' premium bullets th' Injun had, but that could be only a drop in th' bucket to what was really there. Somewhere there was a vein of silver, probably north of th' White River, where he gets his metal. That had to be it. Some Injun had stumbled on to a vein of pure silver an' was selling it for lead! If he found that mine, he'd be fixed for life, but how to do that without raising a bunch of questions an' before someone else discovered th' truth? He would have to think on that.

Later as he passed th' two sleepers, two bullets with slight tooth indentions fell from his pants leg where he had spilled th' others, right where they were found in th' morning light.

A few days later, Nick Row sent his bullet mold over to th' forge, with th' request for bullets, a few of which should be th' premium lead. His errand boy returned with th' order an' th' sad news that th' bullet man was all out of th' premium lead.

"But," said a sweating Sam, "I will be going for more lead next week and will bring back more of the premium because there has been a great demand for it."

Nick took th' bullets an' put them away, but th' knowledge he had gained remained on his mind where he had already stored knowledge of th' route Sam took in going to th' lead mines. Early next morning, he packed some gear, loaded his plunder on a packhorse, an' sauntered down th' trail toward Flee's, leaving his saloon to th' care of a not-so-trusted assistant.

Nick turned off th' trail to camp that evening an' when he left camp th' next morning, he was th' Delaware Indian they called Rowdy. His route was north across th' White River, then west on th' Fallen Ash Trail. He left Fallen Ash where it crossed th' river an' continued up th' river, spending one night with th' Osage on Swan Creek, where he learned that Sam Meeker had passed through a couple of days b'fore.

Th' trail from there to th' mines on th' upper James River was well marked an' he hurried on. Th' center of trade for th' lead mining district was a squalid little village on th' banks of th' James where men of all

403

tribes an' makes gathered to trade for th' precious metal. It was an unspoken law that enmities were set aside in th' trading area an' Osage, Delaware, Piankashaw, Kickapoo, White, an' a half-dozen other tribesmen mingled warily among th' traders.

Rowdy spent a day wandering among dozens of traders looking for th' "premium" lead, but it wasn't to be seen. Even a few discreet inquiries brought him nothing, an' evening came without success. Some had seen Sam Meeker in th' village, but he had passed on north, saying he would be back in a couple of days. Rowdy learned that he usually traded at th' mines somewhere in th' rough hills between Pine Run Creek an' Cave Springs an' so it was that morning found Rowdy trudging up Pine Run looking for th' fabled silver mine.

At noon he happened upon a lone Indian cooking his meager meal. Upon his hail, Rowdy was invited in by th' miner. His blackened hands an' arms marked him as a lead miner, though th' whites of his eyes did not yet show th' discoloration that came with lead poisoning. Rowdy tried to engage him in conversation, but th' Indian was a man of few words an' Rowdy finally gave up an' ate his meal in silence.

His meal over, th' miner rose an' grunted

in broken Delaware, "You want lead?"

Hardly paying any attention to him, Rowdy nodded his head. "I need special lead."

"Shiny and hard?"

Rowdy couldn't help a sharp look at th' miner. "Yes, the premium lead."

"I have premium lead in my mine."

Rowdy ducked his head an' lifted his cup to his lips to hide any hint of excitement that might show through his feigned disinterest. "I might buy."

Th' miner disappeared into th' brush while Rowdy leisurely drank his coffee. In a few minutes he emerged from th' woods with a small leather bag. He poured a hand full of bright crudely refined blobs of th' shiny metal. Rowdy took one an' examined it, biting it to test its hardness. "It looks good, but I am looking for much more than this," he said, replacing th' nugget.

"How much?"

"Enough to fill my packs."

The miner grunted. "Too much, no have."

"I must have it very soon," Rowdy said. Then he whispered, "We go to war with the Pawnees."

The miner nodded. "Pawnees bad." Looking at th' bulging packs, he speculated on how long it would take him to mine that much silver. "Take ten days to mine that much, one horse can't carry it."

"I know," Rowdy said impatiently, "but that is too long to wait, can you get help to mine it?"

"No one knows where mine is but me."

"You mean you won't get help?"

The miner nodded.

"But I have to have it soon. Can I help you?"

"No."

Rowdy knew by th' firmness of th' reply that he would not be helping th' miner. He shrugged, "Then I guess that I will have to wait ten days. I will go get more horses an' meet you back here on th' morning of th' eleventh day."

Th' miner nodded an' squatted before th' fire, pouring another cup of coffee. He watched as Rowdy unloaded th' four packs.

"You may have what is in these packs as a partial payment. What do you want for a pack full of lead?"

The miner studied a moment. "Two horses per pack plus two more."

"Too much." Rowdy shook his head.

The miner just looked at him.

After a minute, Rowdy offered, "I will give you two horses a pack and no more."

The miner didn't seem interested in trading. "Too bad," he said rising an' tossing th' dregs into th' fire. A small cloud of steam arose, smelling of coffee. "I have given you th' contents of the packs," he said, opening them an' spilling th' contents on th' ground, furs, an' fine leather garments, finely tanned skins, "which could easily be two horses. In addition when I come back, I will bring two horses per pack."

This caused some chin rubbing by th' miner. He idly rummaged through th' nearest pile of goods, noting th' value thereof. "Two horses plus one?"

Sensing negotiations nearing an end, Rowdy was firm, "No." There was a long silence, then Rowdy began to repack th' goods.

"As you say." Th' miner seemed very reluctant, but a glint in his eye betrayed his satisfaction with th' trade.

"Good!" Rowdy replied, rising. Now that th' dealing was done, he was in a hurry to be gone. "It is a long ride to th' horses. I must be going if I am to be back in eleven days. I will meet you here then. You may keep the packhorse an' I will return with seven more." Quickly, he was up an' away hurrying his horse back down Pine Run.

The miner sat by th' fire a minute an' didn't look up when he heard footsteps an'

Sam Meeker squatted by th' fire. "Did it go well, Bull Calf?"

"Very well, I suppose, we got these packs full of plunder and the horse. He will bring me seven horses when he returns."

"Take what you have and don't ever plan on seeing any more horses," Sam snorted.

"It's just the same, he won't ever see seven packs of the prime lead." Bull grinned at th' thought.

"Silver," Sam corrected, though he knew Bull Calf didn't understand th' value white men put on th' metal. "A hundred horses wouldn't equal th' value of those four packs full of silver."

Bull Calf shook his head. He was puzzled by th' excitement stirred up by this new substance.

"Now, Bull Calf, I am going to follow Nick Row from now until he returns here and I bet he will be back before two sunrises. Don't let your guard down one minute. He is a sneak killer who specializes in ambushes. I don't think he will try to kill you until he knows where your mine is. I will tell you when he returns by giving three owl calls in the night like this . . . or if it is daylight, I will give three crow calls like this . . . When you hear, answer by chopping on the log four times with your axe.

Continue with your routine and lead him to the mine. Don't make it too easy for him to follow, that will make him suspicious. As soon as you get in the mine, prepare yourself to be attacked. We don't know how he will do it, but I would imagine it would be as you come out of th' mine instead of him going into the dark after you."

Bull nodded. "I will stay here by the camp until I hear your signal."

Without another word, Sam slipped into th' brush an' worked his way to th' trail. He trotted along until he heard a hoof click against a rock, then faded into th' woods. Another sound told him that Nick was moving away from him an' he cautiously continued following. Several times he caught glimpses of man or horse on th' trail ahead of him. At sundown, Rowdy stopped to camp. He staked his horse out in grass after watering him an' proceeded to make a fire an' eat.

All th' while, Sam watched. When it looked as if he was going to stay in camp, Sam worked his way around to th' horse an' tied a long horsehair string to th' rope near th' anchor stake. Playing it out several feet into th' brush, he tied th' other end to his wrist. If Rowdy moved in th' night, he would know it without having to stay awake all night watching for a movement in that blackness. Both men rested well that night, but long before daylight, th' string tugged Sam's arm an' broke. Rowdy was on th' move.

Now was th' time for extreme caution. Sam had to rely on his ears to keep track of Rowdy. Any slip-up now would ruin th' whole plan, yet he couldn't let th' man get away an' stalk Bull Calf unawares.

True to his predictions, Rowdy moved back up th' trail toward Bull Calf's camp, Sam following at a safe distance. Light was just beginning to gray th' eastern sky when Nick pulled off th' trail an' hid his horse in brush by th' creek. He would be safe there until needed.

Dawn was streaking th' sky when Bull Calf heard th' crow. After a few minutes, he casually picked up a stout stick an' laid it over th' trunk of th' fallen tree. It took him four chops to cut it in two an' he tossed th' pieces onto th' fire. Presently, he picked up his rifle an' moved into th' woods. He traveled some distance going northeast, then suddenly turned northwest on a shelf of rock. Fortunately, Rowdy was near enough to see him turn or he would have lost a lot of time trying to find where Bull had left th' rock.

After walking a mile or more, Bull turned down a gully that ran back to Pine Run. At th' creek, he waded across, up over th' hill, an' down into Big Spring Hollow above th' spring. There, he jumped off a shelf of rock into th' bed of th' gully an' disappeared under th' overhang.

Was this th' mine, or was th' miner skittering along under th' ledge to lose anyone who might be following? Rowdy's heart raced, an' sweat popped out on his face. He had to know an' now, else lose th' chance of finding that mine today. Quickly, he moved to th' ledge an' lying prone stuck his head over th' edge. Nothing moved upstream or down. Th' miner had disappeared. Rowdy cursed to himself but didn't move, his eyes taking in every detail of th' gully. A gravel rattled toward th' spring an' he saw leaves move contrary to th' wind, still he didn't move. Presently, another sound came to him, very faintly, he could hear th' metallic chink-chink of metal on rock. Th' mine was near!

Walking along th' ledge, he followed th' sound until he was directly across th' creek from it. With a grin of satisfaction, he lay down on th' ledge, his rifle pushed forward under a buckberry bush.

The hammering continued steadily for

some time, but Rowdy was content to rest where he was. Sooner or later, that miner would have to reappear an' when he did, he would get his last glimpse of daylight in this world. Rowdy grinned at th' thought, *A silver mine an' it will soon be all mine!*

He watched Rowdy stalk Bull, saw him crawl under th' buckbush an' wait, now Sam had to decide how he would keep th' killer from ambushing his friend. To climb th' hill behind him would be risky because he could not keep Rowdy in sight th' whole time. It would also expose Sam to detection since th' coverage was sparse an' th' hill steep an' rocky — hard to traverse quietly. Floods that occasionally washed down th' gully had worn down to bedrock an' washed it as clean as if Ruth herself had swept it. If he was careful, Sam could walk under th' shelf out of sight until he was directly under Rowdy. All he had to do was reach up an' grab th' barrel of th' rifle to spoil his aim an' maybe even capture th' weapon.

Sam sat down an' removed his moccasins, then gently lowered himself into th' gully. It was only a few feet until he could see th' gun barrel protruding over th' rock. Slowly, ever so slowly, he approached, counting th' steps as he carefully made them, 1, 2, 3, 4,

5 . . . 23, 24, 25, 26 . . . one more step an' he would be there . . . 27. Sam hardly dared to breathe, he felt smothered from th' exertion an' shallow breaths. It took him a long time to catch up. He heard Rowdy take a deep breath an' move a little. Th' barrel extended further from th' ledge. Raising his arm, Sam measured th' distance to th' barrel. He would have to take a step outward then jump to reach it, but it could be done. Now there were two listening to th' measured chink-chink of Bull's hammer. Sam decided that when it stopped, he would act without waiting for Bull Calf to appear.

The sudden quiet of th' hammer brought Sam out of his thoughts an' into action. Taking a step, he leaped just as Rowdy lifted th' rifle. Sam's fingers slapped th' barrel, but it had moved too high for him to grasp. His momentum carried him into th' open as Rowdy sprang to his feet with a curse. Instantly, his rifle came down to bear on this new target as Sam scrambled on his hands an' knees to regain th' shelter of th' shelf. *Kaboom,* th' sound of two black powder reports slapped against th' rocks an' reverberated down th' gully. Sam was thrown forward on his face, his right leg suddenly frozen in place an' numb.

Nick Row's face showed amazement as he felt th' warm flood of blood washing down his shirt. He looked down at his chest an' watched th' rock slowly rise to meet him. He rolled over on his back an' both hands could not stop th' flow or th' burning deep inside his chest. He relaxed, feeling detached an' light. The pain was gone an' he seemed to rise into th' air high above th' gully. Looking down, he saw his body lying on th' shelf, th' body lying in th' gully an' smoke from th' other rifle rising from th' bushes across th' gully where th' mine was. Somehow, he knew before he saw what had happened. He watched as he rose, an' th' miner dropped into th' gully an' ran to th' prone body. Sam Meeker moved an' rolled over. How had he known who it was an' that he wasn't dead? This was wondrous, look how beautiful th' world is from up here! Suddenly, a vast hot blackness engulfed him an' his soul gave a great shudder. "NO! NO! NO! NOT THAT!" he screamed . . .

As Nick Row fell, Bull Calf jumped into th' gully an' ran to Sam. He was lying partially on his side, his right leg drawn up so that his knee propped him up. "Sam, are you hit?" Bull Calf called, then was disgusted with himself for asking th' obvious.

Sam groaned, "My leg's cramped up."

Carefully, Bull rolled him on his back, but that intensified his pain so that Sam quickly rolled himself back on his left side, his knee still drawn nearly to his chest. Leaning over his body, Bull Calf saw th' blood soaking th' back of Sam's leather leggings. There was a long cut in th' leather down his right buttock revealing a furrow in th' flesh about two inches long.

"You've been hit in th' rear, Sam. Looks mostly like a graze, nothing vital was hit, but you won't be sitting down for a while."

Sam groaned, "Oh no, not that again!"

"NO! NO! NO! NOT THAT!" Nick Row screamed, his voice seeming to come from far away an' high above. Both men jumped an' a horrible chill seemed to shake them to their very souls. Bull Calf rose an' sprinted across th' gully to his rifle, forgetting for th' moment that it wasn't loaded. Turning, he brought th' gun up, but Rowdy's body hadn't moved from where it had fallen. "Must have just died," he said, then realized he held an empty gun.

"Better reload," Sam advised.

"That voice seemed to come from far off

an' high up," Bull Calf said. "Are you sure it was Rowdy?"

"It was his voice all right, but it did seem far off. This has happened before with others, I've been told. A scream like that is called the Second Death."

Bull Calf felt th' blood drain from his face an' a chill ran through his body. He shuddered.

Sam was beginning to feel better an' his leg gradually relaxed. A careful attempt to move it caused another cramp an' he lay back, trying to relax again. "I have to stand up."

Bull helped him stand an' th' restored circulation allowed his leg to relax. A tentative step or two showed that he could move — carefully. Th' buttock was beginning to burn an' sting. He pulled th' torn leggin' over th' wound, an' with a handful of moss from th' ledge pressed against th' wound, began limping up th' hill.

"Do you want me to run an' get a horse?" Bull asked.

"I don't know how I would mount an' I would have to ride through these woods standing up," Sam answered. "I expect that I would be as well off walking."

They made their slow an' torturous way up th' hill an' down to th' Pine Run.

Gathering th' horses, they rode back to th' mines. People wondered as they approached why th' man was riding standing up, an' their wonder turned to grins when Sam passed by an' they saw bloody leggin's an' buttock.

Bull found an Osage woman who agreed to sew up Sam's wound. Thankfully, she had a steel needle an' some thread, but she seemed to take pleasure in puncturing Cherokee buttocks an' took her time doing it. Sam was just as determined not to show discomfort an' it was a battle of wills amusing to watch. Eventually, she finished, thinking it was over too quickly while Sam thought it took her forever. She refused payment an' they parted with many thanks for her charity.

"It was payment enough to puncture a Cherokee buttock!" she muttered to her husband. He almost laughed out loud.

It took a couple of days for Sam to trade for th' lead he needed. They discussed what they would do with th' plunder Nick had, then decided to return it to th' village an' give it to any original owners who could identify their work. By th' time they left early on th' third day, Sam's wound was much better, but not good enough for him to ride comfortably. Thus, he rode standing or sitting on his left side until it became tiresome. Walking was out of th' question, since his pace was too slow. So it was that they made their painful way back to th' village, bypassing Bear Springs an' th' Village at the Forks for reasons obvious. Home was a welcome sight. Sam was th' "butt" of many a jest from his unsympathetic friends, though Ruthie gently assured him that they were glad th' wound wasn't more serious.

Time passed at th' tavern an' Nick Row did not return, whiskey ran out, an' men grew restless. Then one day one of them hurried up from th' village with news that he had seen Nick's horses in th' village herd. He wasn't believed until others had confirmed it for themselves. It didn't take much thought to realize what had obviously happened an' by ones, twos, an' threes they began slipping away. Th' last two left, glancing furtively over their shoulders at some specter that seemed to follow them. Th' tavern soon burned to th' ground, that log bar smoldering long after th' rest of th' fire had died.

Word spread among th' flotsam washing along th' frontier that the Village on Middle Fork did not countenance outlaws an' rowdies. Therefore, it was avoided by those sorts for th' most part an' th' second more settled pioneers, who appreciated civility an' peace, were attracted to th' area.

# CHAPTER 24
# A BOTTLE OF TROUBLE
## 1818 TO 1820

*"This tale is best told in th' words of Grandma Ruth, though I have heard it from many others through th' years," Zenas said, then he chuckled. "I might just throw them all together an' give you all th' details as given by Grandma an' Grandpa Sam, Aunt Lydia an' Uncle Lonza, th' boys, an' others!"*

We knew nothing about th' plot Sam had hatched and th' *real* reason for their trip until they returned, Sam riding high in th' saddle. I knew when Sam came in with that bottle of wine he had gotten for bullets that we should have gotten rid of its contents at once, but he set it up high on th' mantel an' I let it stay. It stayed there untouched except for my dusting for over a year.

Jesse an' Riley became curious about th' bottle an' its contents. We discussed the dangers of alcohol and its exaggerated effect on our race and warned them to stay away from all drink. This they seemed to take in, but I was still uneasy about th' presence of that poison in our home.

*"Pa an' Uncle Riley told me th' 'fishing trip' came about in this way:" Zenas said.*

We had seen what whiskey had done for white men and how it had made Indians crazy and do funny things so we thought it would be fun to do that ourselves. Besides, it was a grown-up thing to do and we were nearly as big as any of them. We have always argued about who hatched up the plan, alternately taking credit or blaming the other, depending on the audience. The final result of *that* being that *both* of us shared blame equally, which is mostly the just thing to do. Curiosity got us. One of us would ask the other, "I wonder what it tastes like?"

The other would say, alternately, "It smells good," or "It smells bad," which only tended to heighten our curiosity.

One day we came in when Ma/Aunt Ruth was gone and with a chair climbed up to examine the bottle closer. We smelled the cork. It smelled. We were just about to take a sip when we heard someone coming. By the time Ma/Aunt Ruth opened the door, we were wrestling on the floor and she chased us out of the house.

One would jab th' other in th' ribs an' ask, "Did you smell that?"

"Yeah, it stunk!" or "Yeah, it smelled good!"

"Did you taste it?"

"No, did you?"

"I think I got some on my tongue."

"No you didn't, I saw you!"

"Did too!"

"Did not!"

"Did too!"

"Did not!" and on and on until violence resulted, the winner having the last "Did too" or "Did not" and the vanquished muttering th' opposite under his breath.

It wouldn't be long until the question was burning us again and we began plotting how to get a taste of forbidden fruit.

While Sam was gone on a trip north to the lead mines, one of us came up with the idea of stealing the contents and leaving th' bottle full of water so no one would suspect. We carefully laid our plans and gathered equipment we needed. Mondays were wash day and the women would be out and busy with the wash, so we made plans to strike then.

Sunday night, we asked for permission to spend the night fishing Monday night after the washing was done. This was approved by the Powers and we worked very hard helping with the wash Monday. On one trip for firewood, we sneaked through the back door and quickly got away with the contents of the bottle, replacing most of it with water, so that, though mostly water, it would at least smell like the real thing.

"Let's take a drink now," said one.

"No! They'll smell it and we'll be in trouble," the other replied.

"No they won't!"

"Yes they will!" The argument stalled before blows were exchanged when Ma/ Aunt Lydia called from the fire, "Where's that wood?"

Wine went into a hidey-hole and we didn't think about it the rest of the day until the washing was done and dried. Soon we were released from our chores and in the shortest time were loaded and ready to go, a large bag holding cold biscuits an' jerky, and down in the bottom safe and secure lay the wine.

We found a secluded little cove on the river where there was good fishing and most important, out of sight. Our first order of business was to test the waters and see if anything was biting. It was just so-so, not great, but not discouraging. Being established in our fishing, one of us produced th' wine an' two cups. We sat and fished and sipped wine. It was strong and fiery and neither one of us would admit that we didn't like it.

When we had enough fish for supper, we fried them up in bacon grease and sat down to a meal of fish and wine.

That shore was a big bottle, an' it seemed to git bigger as we drank. Funny things b'gan to happen and we laughed and laughed. Jesse fell in the river and Riley fished him out with his pole.

"Looky what I caught," he crowed and laughed 'til he fell down. "I'm gonna cook him for supper," he said, and stumbled to the fire. Th' skillet handle was hot when he picked it up and he dropped it into the fire, which promptly flared up and singed his eyebrows off.

Jesse laughed hysterically, rolling on the ground. "You look so funny without eyebrows."

"Let's see what *you* look like without them." Riley held the pan with its flaming contents under Jesse's chin. The acrid smell of burning hair filled the air and Riley watched Jesse's hair curl and blow away.

"How do I look?" he asked.

Riley laughed hysterically. "Like me!" He

sat the pan down and ran his hand over his forehead.

Jesse began to laugh. "You painted your head black!"

Seeing black soot on his hand, Riley painted a circle on his cheek. "I'm a warrior going to war!"

His strut around th' fire was just a stagger and Jesse laughed until tears rolled down his face. Scraping soot off the pan, he painted his face and joined the dance until he was so dizzy he fell into the bushes. Riley screamed with mirth.

Emerging from the bushes, Jesse stumbled over the bottle of wine and sat down clumsily. He picked up the bottle and took a long drink. The last thing he remembered was seeing Riley downing the remainder of the wine.

He awoke shivering in a cold drizzle, his face streaked with soot and water. When he sat up to see where he was, his head swam and his stomach rebelled. He lay back with a groan and shuddered in a wave of nausea and cold. Slowly and cautiously, he crawled to his pack, his head swimming. Fumbling into the blanket he found there, he rolled up in it and soon fell into a troubled sleep to be awakened by the sound of Riley retching.

"O-o-o-o-h-h, I think that wine was poisoned," Riley groaned.

"Don't yell!" Jesse held his throbbing head.

Riley threw up again, and Jesse did the same. For a long time they lay there in the rain, fighting waves of nausea and shivering.

"We have to get help," Riley whispered.

"Where?" Jesse asked. "Our Ma's 'll kill us!"

"O-o-o-h," Riley groaned and closed his eyes. "Do you think we're gonna die?"

"I would have to improve to," Jesse whispered, to himself more than to Riley.

They both drifted into a troubled sleep only to be awakened by Sippie's insistent nosing and snuffling. He sneezed to clear the stench from his nostrils and sat down looking at Jesse and whining in concern.

"Go 'way, Sippie," Jesse groaned.

At the sound of Jesse's voice, Sippie happily wagged and licked his face, glad that his boy was alive after all. He turned his attention to Riley, licking his face until his tongue was blackened.

"G'way, Sippie," he groaned, covering his head with his blanket.

Sippie whined, then curled up against Jesse's back and slept. Warmed by the dog, Jesse too drifted off to sleep.

It was midafternoon when two blanket-shrouded figures stumbled into Laughing Brook's cabin. "Grandmother, we've been poisoned," a muffled voice whined from the first blanket.

Brook hurried to the boys, but one sniff of them told her what the poison was. She stood back, hands on hips and studied them. The blankets were wet and filthy, covered with the dirt they obviously had been rolled in; the boys were streaked with black and reeked of rotten alcohol and vomit.

Pretending concern, she said, "What do you think you have been poisoned with, did someone poison you?"

"No'um," Riley murmured.

"Did you eat spoiled meat?"

"No'um," again.

"What did you eat?"

"We just had fish last night," Jesse groaned and sat heavily on the floor.

"The fish was fresh, wasn't it? You cooked it thoroughly, didn't you?"

"Yes'um," came the twin replies.

Laughing Brook reached down and raised Jesse's head an' looked at his face in seeming concern. "If it wasn't something you ate, could it have been something you drank?"

"It — could — have — been . . ." his voice trailed off uncertainly.

"Was it something you drank, Riley?" she said sharply. "I have to know if I am going to help you!"

"Yes'um, I think it was."

"Was it water?"

"N-o-o-o . . ." His voice trailed off.

"Tell me *now!*" Brook demanded.

"ItwasPa'swine!" Jesse confessed in a rush of honesty.

There was a long pause as Laughing Brook sighed in supposed relief and looked at the two wretches reproachfully.

"The wine Sam had on the mantel?"

"Yes'um," came the twin replies.

"You drank it all?"

"Yes'um."

"Last night or this morning?"

"Last night. Please, Grandmother, are we gonna die?"

"Well you ought to!" she glared at them.

"Can you fix us before our Ma's find out, they might kill us and we don't feel like it right now," Riley whined.

"I think I can, but it will be hard to hide this from your mothers," she replied. "I can mix you up an antidote that will remove the poison from your bodies." She hurried about the room gathering up two large mugs. "I will be right back," she said leaving the cabin door open as she left. The place needed airing out. At the spring, she pulled out the morning's milking and stirred th' cream in that had risen to the top. Pouring both mugs full, she noted with satisfaction that each had a goodly amount of cream rising. At the house, she set the mugs close to the fire, stirring occasionally. When it was warm, she gave each boy one and said, "Drink this up, all of it, and go home, it should act soon."

She set the empty mugs on the table and practically pushed them out the door, almost running them into their mothers, who had come to see Laughing Brook.

"What's wrong with them, stay up all night fishing?" Ruth asked, watching the shrouded figures retreat to their respective homes.

"No, I don't think they were up all night, but maybe most of it." Laughing Brook was smiling broadly. "They think they were poisoned."

"Poisoned!" Lydia was alarmed, then calmed at Laughing Brook's smile.

"Not really, they just got drunk on Sam's wine."

*"Drunk?"*

*"Sam's wine?"* the women exclaimed.

"Don't worry, I gave them an antidote." Laughing Brook smiled.

"What is your antidote for wine poisoning, Grandmother?" Kansas asked.

There was a small smile tugging at the corners of Brook's mouth. "Warm milk."

*"Warm milk!"* the two mothers chimed.

"Yes, then I sent them home."

*"Oh no,* we just cleaned!" Ruth said in alarm. Already, she was turning toward the door.

"Don't worry, they won't get there before it acts," Laughing Brook said serenely.

Ruth stopped with her hand on the door.

Lydia, who hadn't said anything, giggled. "Mother! Shame on you!" she said in mock severity.

Ruth giggled, then laughed, and the three women broke out in hilarious laughter while Kansas looked puzzled.

"I don't know when I've laughed so hard," Lydia sat weakly, wiping tears with the tail of her apron.

"I don't understand what's so funny," Kansas said.

"The boys drank up the wine that Sam had sitting on the mantel and got very drunk," Ruth explained. "This morning when they woke up, they were sick, so they came to Grandmother for healing."

"The wine is such that if the boys had drunk water, they would have been drunk again," said Lydia, "so instead, Mother gave them milk, which will sour on their stomachs and make them sick again — very sick."

"And that is funny?" asked Kansas, still puzzled.

"You must know that wine and strong drink are very bad for our people, don't you?" Laughing Brook asked.

"Yes, Grandmother, I do."

"Well those two rascals disobeyed all we have told them and all they have seen about the bad influences the drink has on people and stole the wine. They drank it all up last night."

"*All* of it?" Ruth asked.

"Oh my," Lydia said.

Laughing Brook nodded. "And got very sick. I gave them the milk for two reasons, to purge the poison out of them and to teach them a lesson about fooling with strong drink. They will soon be over the sickness, but I hope they will not soon forget what happens when they drink that poison."

"I see," said Kansas, a smile of relief crossing her face. "I will go see how they are doing."

"Tell Jesse we are having his favorite meal of cornbread and sweetmilk for supper,"

Ruth called.

"You wouldn't!" Lydia laughed.

It wasn't hard to follow Jesse's trail to the house and when she got there, he was sitting on the edge of the porch, head in hands and elbows on knees to hold himself steady.

"How are you?" Kansas asked.

"We got poisoned and I think Grandma's medicine poisoned us again," he said without raising his head.

"Yes, I know, I followed your trail here. She gave you a purgative to get the poison out of you."

"Well it sure did that, I'm empty now."

"I will go see how Riley is. Your mother is having cornbread and sweet milk for supper."

Jesse groaned and heaved.

*"Kansas found Riley in about th' same condition as Jesse. It was a day or two b'fore th' two were back t' normal"* — Zenas was still laughing at the tale — *"but I have t' say that both boys had a lifelong aversion for strong drink that they must have passed on to their children, for none of us were ever attracted to it and most were teetot'llers.*

*"Grandmother Laughing Brook knew lots of remedies an' medicines for different things. I'll tell you one more thing as Grandma Ruth told*

us and then we will be done — for today, that is!" he grinned.

Little Sarah and I were helping Laughing Brook shell peas one day and Sarah was playing on the floor, chasing Sippie's tail when she stopped and toddled over to me on her chubby legs. Lifting my blouse, she began to nurse.

"Isn't she getting close to weaning time?" Laughing Brook asked.

"Yes, she is!" I answered. "She eats from the table now but I can't get her to forget about the milk."

"I have a cure for her," Brook said.

"It's not to put bitterweed on the nipples, is it?"

"No, this is much more gentle than that, it convinces the child to quit on her own."

"I'm almost ready to try the bitterweed," Ruth sighed.

"Try this and see if it works." Laughing Brook went to the fire and removed one of the pots sitting on the curb. To Ruth, she said, "Take some of the soot and paint your nipples black — don't be sparing — now see what happens."

Later that afternoon when Sarah got the yen for another nursing, she crawled on her mother's lap and lifted her blouse. The sight of the blackened nipple stopped her and she reached for the other breast, but it too was black! She tentatively touched it, drew back, and looked at them both, gave one a little pat and returned to her play. That was the last time she offered to nurse and Ruth was amazed and pleased.

"So easy!" she exclaimed.

That night when Sam came in, he noticed the soot smudges on Ruthie's blouse. "Weaned Sarah, did you?"

"You knew how?" Ruthie asked, incredulously.

"Sure."

"Why didn't you tell me?" she demanded.

"Figured you knew — didn't you?"

"Hummph!" was the only reply he got.

# CHAPTER 25
# KANSAS RETURNS
# TO HER PEOPLE
# 1824–1825

*"After th' wars with th' Osages th' Federal government moved in t' keep peace. Fort Smith was established at th' mouth o' the Poteau River on the Arkansas about 1818, an' by 1820 an uneasy peace had settled b'tween th' two tribes. Uncle Jerry an' Aunt Kansas were married in 1822, mostly due t' Aunt Kansas' persistent devotion t' Uncle Jerry. Grandma told us all about it once, but I will bypass that tale for th' time being."*

Uncle Jerry had gotten into raising an' breeding horses with Speaks Softly an' they had a brisk trade going, as they say. They were getting low on brood mares an' agreed that their horses needed some new blood to improve th' stock. Jerry had seen many herds of wild horses on th' plains an' determined that it would be a good source of stock at little or no cost. Things had been pretty peaceful b'tween th' tribes an' so he decided to go to th' plains in what's now eastern Kansas an' catch horses. At th' same time, he could fulfill his promise to take Aunt Kansas back to her people.

They left in early March, 1824, an' traveled th' old familiar trails north. Th' camps on Swan Creek had long been abandoned, White Wolf an' his clan following their tribe west into Kansas.

Jerry an' Kansas moved on northwest toward Kaw territory an' found th' village in early April on the Kaw River somewhere west of where Topeka is. Th' tribe was in deplorable shape, having been driven west an' south by whites an' Indians an' decimated by war an' disease. There were no more than 2,000 of them led by White Plume. Kansas could find none of her kin among them. It was a very sad time for her an' they didn't stay there long.

*"This is what Uncle Jerry told me about th' rest of th' trip," Zenas said.*

We moved southwest an' camped on Horse Creek, so named for th' abundance of wild horses that roamed there an' along th' two Rock Creeks. Th' third night we were there, a party of Pawnees stole all our horses except th' one we had kept saddled an' close. Kansas wanted to fight them, but I knew it was useless since we were so out-numbered. If we had harmed one of them, they would have hunted us down an' killed us, so I put her up on th' horse an' we made our escape riding double.

We returned to camp next day an' found it pretty well plundered, except for th' gear an' food we had cached up in a tree. They would have taken that also if it had been light enough for them to see it. I was pretty sure they had left th' country in a hurry, an' not wantin' to leave Kansas there alone, didn't follow them. We picked up camp an' moved east to a box canyon on th' east side of West Rock Creek. There would be water here for a couple of more months an' it was a good place to pen up any horses we caught.

Catching those horses now b'came more complicated with only one horse and saddle. Running them into a trap was out of th' question, at least until we caught an' broke a horse or two. Here is where Kansas' knowledge came to th' rescue.

"When the horses first appeared on the plains, our people could not buy them from the tribes that had them and didn't know how to catch them without riding. A young man determined that he would walk the horses down, so he went out on the prairie and found a likely group. There were several good-looking colts in the bunch. He began following the herd, not allowing it to rest or eat or drink. At first, when he appeared, they ran off a mile or so and began feeding while the stallion kept watch. Soon he saw the young man approaching and gave the alarm. Off they went this time running a little longer. Again, the man approached and again they escaped.

"The third time he appeared over the hill, the herd became alarmed and took off. Now, they were all nervous and kept watch for the persistent creature. All day he walked behind the herd until the young ones were too tired to run any more. They began to fall out and the boy had an easy time capturing them. Each was hobbled and left for later, the boy continuing his pursuit. When night came, he returned to the young horses. They were too tired and hungry to resist and followed along quietly to a pen he had built in a box canyon.

"His friends seeing what he had done now joined him in the enterprise, some helping follow the horse herd in relays and some caring for the captured colts, getting them tamed and used to people.

"They had the good fortune of catching a

couple of the mares who had followed their young to the pen. The walkers followed the herd day and night, not allowing them to rest, eat, or drink. By the fourth day they were exhausted and began falling out of the little herd. One by one they captured the mares and led them to the canyon and water and grass. Now, it was the distraught stallion that followed the mares and soon he was captured, only they kept him tied and separate from the mares, knowing that he would try to free them if he could.

"It was only a matter of training and breaking the horses until they became tame and there was many a mishap on the way to accomplishing that. We could find a herd out of all of these that we liked and walk them down and catch them."

Jerry looked at Little Kansas an' wondered if she was strong enough to walk after a herd of horses. Yet he knew that to walk down a herd with their horse would wear her out an' they needed her fresh an' strong at all times because of th' danger from hostile parties an' buffalo herds.

"Are you sure you can do this?" he asked an' was immediately sorry he had said it.

"I can walk as far and as long as you can, Jerryharris! Sly Fox should know this!"

With a wry smile, Jerry said, "All right,

my little lady, let's ride out and see if there are any close we would want to catch."

On th' divide between th' two Rock Creeks there must have been a thousand horses, each stallion guarding his herd, jealously challenging any other stallion that would come too close or try to steal one of his mares. All morning they rode through an' around th' herds until Kansas had found th' one with th' horses she liked. She was especially fond of one white filly in the bunch.

With th' horse, they hazed th' bunch further up th' divide toward Gun Barrel Hill where water was less abundant. Jerry took some food an' water an' an extra pair of moccasins an' b'gan following th' herd. Kansas found a hill an' sat in th' shade of the horse, watching.

Wild horses have a range they are familiar with an' their instinct is to stay in that range, so long as th' forage is good an' water available. When out of their range, it's their desire to return to it as soon as possible. Thus it was with this herd an' they kept circling about to their range, th' result being that they walked in big circles five to ten miles in diameter, returning to their range, then being driven out by th' persistent walker. At noon, being nearby, Jerry signaled

440

for Kansas an' she took up the walk. It was Jerry's plan that she would not walk the horses in th' night. Off she went b'hind th' horses, who were now well alarmed at th' creature stalking them. All evening an' into th' dusk she followed them. Some of th' colts began lagging b'hind an' th' mares with them, th' stallion, a big (for wild horses) roan with splashes of white, driving them an' nipping at their rumps until th' mares were forced ahead, leaving their colts to follow. Jerry had to ride several miles in th' gloom to find th' group an' when he did, he instructed Kansas to go to a certain tree in a draw an' rest for th' night, with th' horse picketed nearby.

Mile after weary mile, Jerry followed th' horses, keeping track of them by starlight an' sound until th' moon rose making work easier. Near midnight, he came upon a colt standing exhausted an' with a lead, pulled him on to where there was water an' there hobbled him, leaving him to rest an' drink.

On they went, another, then another of th' colts giving up an' being hobbled by water. At sunrise, Kansas found him an' traded places. Jerry followed the back trail, picking up colts as he went. It wasn't hard to put halters on them an' for the most part they followed along behind th' horse quietly until they were released in the box canyon pen, hobbled, to drink an' rest. He rested all day, occasionally rubbing his weary legs, then took up th' chase as th' light failed. All through th' second night they walked until th' sun rose an' th' walkers traded places again. Jerry let Kansas follow th' herd most of th' day since they were now going at a slower pace, some with hanging heads an' dragging steps.

It occurred to him th' third day that th' horses might be tired enough to drive into th' pen with th' added incentive of th' now recuperated colts calling to their mothers. Putting th' leg weary Kansas on th' horse late that afternoon, he said, "I think that they are tired enough to drive into the pen now. Let's herd them back down the divide and see if we can get them in. When we get close, ride ahead and open the gate and then don't let them run past it when I run them down the creek."

With fresh legs on th' ground an' Kansas on th' horse, they pushed th' little herd harder an' instead of circling them through th' high ground, they pushed them west toward West Rock Creek an' th' pen. As they neared, Kansas veered off an' riding hard around th' head of th' box canyon, came up to th' gate from th' south. When she heard th' herd nearing, she threw down th' gate an' backing out of sight south of the gate, waited an' watched.

The horses were puzzled; while th' man-walker had pushed them hard, he now slowed down an' they took up a shuffling walk, looking longingly at th' creek, but being forbidden to approach it. As they approached th' mouth of th' gully, a horse an' rider appeared in front of them waving a blanket. Their only escape was up th' gully an' th' lead mare, hearing her colt's knicker, turned an' raced to him. Even b'fore th' last lagging horse was through, Kansas was racing for th' gate. In a moment it was closed an' th' horses were trapped in th' little box canyon b'fore they knew it.

Jerry jumped on th' horse an' called, "Let us through." Inside th' pen, he quickly located th' stallion an' roped him. There was still plenty of fight in him an' Jerry had to choke him down so he could put hobbles on him. He released th' choking rope an' sat on th' horse's neck, rubbing him an' talking calmly to him, th' horse quivering at his touch, but gradually calming as he became familiar with th' man an' caught his breath. Finally, th' two-legged tormentor got up an' the horse struggled to his feet fighting th' unfamiliar hobbles. Th' smell of water caught his attention an' for th' first time in three days he drank. Green grass, water, an' rest! The pursuers were no longer pushing them along. Quietly, Jerry removed the hobbles from th' colts an' they ran to their mothers.

". . . Eighteen, nineteen, twenty, twenty-one mares, one stallion, and ten colts! That's a good herd, Jerry!" Kansas called from the gate.

"Yes, if we live long enough, we can break them and take them home!" he replied. He led their mare out an' stripped off th' saddle. After a good rubdown, he turned th' tired horse loose in th' pen.

Kansas returned from camp with food an' blankets an' they went to th' creek an' soaked their tired feet.

Kansas sniffed, "I haven't had a bath in four days, Jerryharris, and I'm going to, right now!" She rose an' stripped off her dress an' leggings an' waded into th' water. Jerry watched his lovely wife a moment, then joined her in th' water. With sand from th' bottom, they scrubbed th' grime of three days of hard work off of each other. Kansas washed her long hair while Jerry watched, then they lay on a blanket in th' soft grasses an' dried, too tired to move.

Late in th' night, Jerry awoke to find

himself covered with a blanket an' the still naked Kansas sleeping quietly, his arm for a pillow an' snuggled closely to him. *How different she is from th' scrawny tyke I pulled from th' snow so long ago an' who had slept snuggled to my back those many nights,* he thought. *How fortunate it was that I found her!* He pulled her closer an' drifted off into a deep sleep.

"Ow! Ow, ow!" He awoke to Kansas' cries of pain. "My legs, my legs!" She was rolling on th' blanket, her legs drawn up in cramps.

"Your legs are cramping, let me rub them!" He sat up only to have both his calves convulsed in cramps. "Ow, ow," he cried falling back an' rubbing his legs, every attempt to move bringing fresh spasms.

"Rub my legs, Jerry!"

"I can't move, mine are cramping too."

Tears were welling in her eyes.

"Stand up and they will stop," he said.

"How can I stand when I'm dying?" she said angrily.

Jerry chuckled. "Ow, it hurts!" He rolled over an' got on his knees. Slowly he stood an' th' cramps faded as blood circulated through his legs. Bending, he took Kansas under her arms an' lifted her up, hugging her close to his chest, her head on his shoulder. As the circulation was restored, her legs gradually straightened until they completely relaxed, her feet still a good six inches from the ground. "You can put me down, now, Jerry, they are well," she whispered.

"I don't think I *want* to put you down," an' they sank to the blanket an' covered up again.

Th' sun was a big ball on th' horizon when they next rose, cautiously to avoid a recurrence of th' cramps. In clean clothes for th' first time in over a week, they went about setting up a more permanent camp. Just inside th' pen behind some cottonwood saplings, there was an overhanging rock ledge. Jerry dug into the wall an' floor, making a little den large enough for two people. He piled rocks around th' opening for a wall. Later he would build a high rock wall across the mouth of th' gully an' forming a wall for th' western side of th' den. Now, they had a place of refuge in case of attack, well hidden an' not likely to be found. It would be easy to defend an' with a little water an' food, attackers could be held off for a long time.

Kansas set up camp on a small bench to th' north of th' gully. It was just large enough to make a comfortable camp warmed by th' morning sun an' shaded from the heat of the afternoon sun by th' tall cottonwoods along th' creek. As soon as breakfast was over, Jerry climbed up above th' pen an' studied th' horses. Kansas soon came an' sat by him.

"Look at that little white filly, isn't she pretty?"

"Sure is, she'll make a valuable trade," he teased.

"That's *my* horse and you'll not be trading her!"

He chuckled. "How much will you give me for her?"

"*Give* you?" she elbowed him sharply in the ribs, "That's not your horse and I gave plenty walking her down so *we* could catch them all!"

He laughed softly, "You are right, Little Kansas, it belongs to us both an' I think you should have the filly for yourself."

She didn't like th' "Little" part, but allowed Jerry to call her that for it was his term of affection for her. Rarely did he use the name in th' presence of others.

They sat long in th' warmth of th' morning sun studying th' herd an' discussing th' attributes of th' individuals. Th' stallion was still struggling with his hobbles an' trying to find a way to escape with his herd, but there was no way out but the way in an' that was securely blocked.

"I suppose I should break him first," he said.

"Will you bring me the white filly? I want to tame her."

"I will, but there is something I need you to do while I break the horses."

"What is that?"

"We can't gentle-break them, there isn't enough time, so I will have to ride them tame. If one of them throws me, we could lose the saddle. You are going to have to take the rifle and shoot the horse if it throws me and begins to run away."

"Oh, that would be bad after all the work we had catching them."

"It would be even worse if we lost that saddle. We couldn't finish breaking them and would have to turn them loose."

"I suppose I could do that if I had to, but I wouldn't like it!"

"I wouldn't either, but it will be necessary. If you don't knock the horse down your first shot, you will have to reload fast to get another shot before he is out of range."

"I can reload faster than anyone," she said.

"We will lay out the right amount of powder and ball and patches so that you can be even faster."

"When will we start?"

"This afternoon, I think. I will go get your filly and we can work with her until we are ready to eat, then we will begin by breaking the stallion."

Th' little filly was hard to catch. She knew right away that Jerry was after her an' kept well away from him. It wasn't until Jerry mounted his horse an' ran with th' bunch that he caught her. He pulled her to th' gate where Kansas waited with a halter. She was so wrapped up with getting th' filly used to her voice an' hands an' leading her with th' halter, that she forgot all about eating. An amused Jerry cooked th' meal.

"Put th' filly up, it's time to eat," he called.

Kansas looked up surprised, then put th' filly in th' pen an' hurried to the fire. "I didn't know what time it was," she said, breathless from her trot up th' hill.

Jerry grinned at her. "What are you going to name your horse?"

"I don't know, but I'll think of something after I get to know more about her."

After the meal, Jerry found his old dirty clothes an' put them on.

"Peuwee! Why are you putting those old dirty things on?"

"Because the horse will be easier to break if he smells the same person around him

449

every time. I won't change or wash until the horses are broken."

"Don't expect me to snuggle up to you as long as you smell like that!" she snorted in disgust. Jerry grinned.

It wasn't hard to catch th' hobbled horse an' Jerry put a halter an' blindfold on him before removing th' hobbles. Across the creek was an open flat an' that was where they planned to break horses. Kansas climbed a knoll at th' edge of the woods an' sat down with th' rifle propped on a forked stick she would use as a stand.

With th' tame horse necked to th' stallion, he handled an' talked to him, rubbing him all over except for his lower legs. At first, th' horse quivered an' trembled at his touch, but presently, he became used to it an' th' soft voice an' stopped resisting. Th' horse blanket was th' next step an' he tried to buck a little at that, but th' tame horse restrained him. Jerry put it on an' removed it several times, sometimes flapping it against his sides, all th' while talking to him quietly. Soon it was time to try th' saddle an' that was a new experience altogether. Even with restraints, th' horse managed to throw off th' saddle a couple of times before accepting it.

Now came th' risky part of tying th' girths

under his belly. There being no gentle way of doing this, Jerry fought th' horse an' tied it tightly, then he led th' two horses around th' clearing. It took an hour for th' horse to settle down an' accept the lead. He removed th' blindfold an' led th' horses some more. Seeing made it as bad as if he had never been led an' another hour of hard work finally calmed him down enough to handle.

"Now for th' real work to begin," Jerry called an' he slipped th' blindfold over th' horse's eyes again. He released th' tie to th' mare an' she trotted off a ways an' began to graze. Kansas caught her an' led her back to her station on th' hill.

At first, Jerry just leaned on th' saddle, th' increased weight causing th' horse to shy away. When he was used to that, at least a little, he tried lying across th' saddle. Finally he was ready to sit in th' saddle. Th' blind-folded stallion stood trembling as Jerry sat talking to him until he was reasonably calm.

Th' blindfold came off an' the horse blinked a moment. When he realized he was free from restraint, he determined to rid himself of all th' other impediments to his freedom, th' man on his back being th' first thing that must go. Lowering his head, he gave an angry squeal an' leaped high into th' air, twisting an' kicking, trying everything in his limited knowledge to rid himself of this unaccustomed burden. Nothing worked. Every move he made failed to dislodge this demon riding him, yet he tried until he was exhausted.

As a last resort, he headed for th' trees, planning to rub th' man off under th' limbs, but a strong pull on th' halter lead caused him to veer away an' he ran down th' open ground until his sides were foaming with sweat. Gradually, he came to a walk an' th' rein pulled him around until he was walking back toward th' horse an' woman on th' hillside. He jumped when he heard the unfamiliar sound of th' woman call, "I think I can ride him now."

"We'll see what you think about that in the morning." Jerry chuckled.

He guided th' docile horse to th' pen. Tying him to a stout sapling, he removed saddle an' blanket an' with fragrant grasses rubbed him down, all th' while talking to him. For a change th' horse stood still, this rubbing thing was pleasant! That finished, Jerry stood by his head stroking his neck an' talking softly. *Maybe this wasn't so bad after all,* the horse thought, then he remembered the riding an' his anger flared. The hand on his neck sensed th' change an' th' voice became sterner, "Now don't get rambunctious with me or we'll do it all over again right now."

He didn't understand th' words, but th' tone relayed th' message adequately an' he relaxed. The man led him to th' creek an' he waded out a ways in the cooling water to drink some, but th' man didn't let him drink too much. Back at th' gate, the hobbles were tied on, this time with a little more rope between th' legs for a more comfortable stride. Into th' pen he went gladly for a little rest an' graze.

Kansas called from th' fire an' Jerry pulled his weary body up th' hill to a warm meal. Even before full dark, he was rolled up in his blanket asleep. Th' stars told him it was near th' middle of th' night when he awoke. That familiar body was tucked tightly against his back, only this time there were two blankets between them. Jerry grinned an' drifted off to sleep again.

And so it continued day after day, Jerry riding broken horses in th' mornings to keep them accustomed to their new task, an' breaking a new horse every afternoon. The pace was grueling, each horse presenting new challenges to th' trainer an' he enjoyed th' work, though his body protested.

He was only thrown twice an' both times they were able to retrieve th' precious saddle because of Kansas' marksmanship. She cried th' first time she had to shoot because th' four-year-old mare was one of th' prettiest of the lot. Jerry had to drag th' mare off on th' prairie well out of sight after he had saved th' hide. Th' second mare she shot gladly, for she was a vicious animal always fighting th' lead mare for dominance an' in general causing unrest among th' herd. By sunset, she had skinned the carcass out an' th' next few days were spent making smoked jerky out of th' troublemaker. Th' tanned hide became a soft furry foundation for their bedroll.

Kansas helped Jerry by riding some of th' broken horses when he rode, but it was awhile before she could ride th' stallion. She continued to work with her filly an' some of th' others, getting them used to being around these strange human captors. Th' white filly soon became tame as a kitten, following her around camp an' getting into all kinds of mischief. Kansas was calling her to "come here, you rascal" so often that it became her name. Come Here You Rascal had the run of the camp whenever possible, then spent most of her time in th' pen at th' gate watching th' activities an' calling to be set free.

It is a testimony to th' kinship of man an'

horse that a horse can be taken from th' wild state an' become trained an' attached to man with such relative ease. A horse's dedication an' loyalty to man is such that he will give his life without complaint in service to his master. It's not that th' horse is a dumb brute as some inexperienced an' insensitive men will assert, but th' horse is a very intelligent animal, smarter than any of man's other domesticated animals — and many a man that rode on his back! Many owe their lives to this companion, whether it was as a warning of intruders, a finder of water or th' homestead in a blizzard or dust storm, or bolting from a mine, the miner following an' cursing only to hear th' mine collapse behind him. Horse, mule, or jack-ass, from th' dawn of time they have been th' (mostly) willing servant of man an' a good companion to boot.

It took th' couple over six weeks to break th' horses to th' point that they were reasonably assured that they could keep them together on th' trail. Th' first big obstacle to overcome was going to be getting them through th' wild horses without losing them. A couple of th' older mares, too old for much service, Jerry had turned out, but they had hung around th' pen so much that he finally let them back in where they seemed content to stay so long as the rest of th' harem was there. In th' end he broke them too, thinking they would serve as pack-horses, which they both did faithfully until too old to function anymore. They spent their last days contentedly with th' lead mare an' stallion in th' pastures of the Little Red River bottoms.

After a few weeks, Jerry had put a bell on th' lead mare an' th' herd became accustomed to hearing it. One day he saddled her up an' with Kansas riding an' he bareback on the stallion let th' two older mares out of th' pen. Kansas rode off, th' bell ringing, an' th' two loose horses followed without hesitation. The stallion fell into line just as was his custom, guarding th' rear an' seeing that the little parade moved on. Th' surprising an' encouraging thing about th' trip was that when they got back to th' pen, th' other horses were lined up along th' barrier as if they would have followed if allowed.

"I think they are ready for th' trail," Jerry said as they ate their supper.

"Well, I'm certainly ready for you to take a bath and change clothes!" Kansas sniffed.

He had noticed that she avoided standing downwind from him, but he knew that if th' horses smelled any difference in him when he trained them that it would mean real trouble. Later, when cowboys were rough-breaking horses, the bronc buster didn't even change his underwear when working with a new horse. Some say that the horse has a better nose than a dog. There is ample evidence that this is true, some horses following a trail unseen by th' lingering scent of th' pursued.

White man's horse didn't like th' scent of th' Indian an' conversely, th' Indian's pony shied away from th' scent of a white man. Of course, th' Indian did th' same, it probably being true that on th' whole th' frontier white man was dirtier an' smellier than th' Indian.

"I'll take a bath this afternoon, but I think I should wear the dirty clothes at least a few days when we start out on th' trail."

"That will be all right so long as you stay downwind from me!"

Jerry laughed an' dug a precious chunk of Ruth's lye soap from th' pack, stripped, an' headed for the creek. "Don't you touch those dirty clothes," he called back, laughing.

"You don't have to worry about that!" came the reply.

He came back pink an' clean, th' soap diminished by a goodly amount an' fish in th' creek abandoning th' pool for a while. Dressed an' relaxed, they sat in their favorite spot an' watched th' horses.

"They have about grazed the pen down and we are going to have to move them out very soon," Kansas observed.

"Do you think you could be ready to move by moonrise tomorrow night?"

"Yes, that will be plenty of time to pack," she replied.

"I want to get out of th' horse range before we travel in daylight. It may not be much of a problem with us along, but I don't want some stud thinking he can steal a mare or two from us."

"I should think you would be more concerned with the two-legged thief."

"Most of those thieves are west of here on their summer buffalo hunt, but they will be returning soon an' are sure to find where we have camped. We need to get a good lead on them or they will track us down an' try to take our horses. I'll breathe a little easier when we get into Osage country — a little, but not much."

They spent th' rest of th' afternoon an' next morning packing. It was surprising how much they had accumulated while breaking horses, but Kansas had worked hard when she could, gathering the fruits an' herbs of the plains an' had a good start on a winter's supply of meat in th' mean mare's flesh.

They rested an' slept th' afternoon away an' by th' time a full moon arose, th' packs were loaded on the old mares, the lead mare was saddled for Kansas, an' Jerry had a blanket on th' stallion. Jerry opened th' gate an' their herd fell in line behind th' bell mare. It took a couple of hours to get them lined out properly, but they soon got the idea an' being glad to be out of their confinement, followed along at a goodly pace. They headed southeast toward th' Neosho River an' Osage country.

*"They had a couple o' adventures going home an' I'll tell you about them th' next time we get together," Zenas said, rising. "Right now, I want to show you something before you go." He led the way to the barn.*

*There on a sawhorse suspended by wires from the rafters in the tack room hung a saddle. Zenas removed the dust cover and revealed a very old and scarred saddle. There was a long scar across the seat and a bullet hole through one of the stirrup straps, about .50 caliber, I would say.*

# Chapter 26
# All the Way Home
# 1824–1825

It was bright moonlight that we rode into that night. We could see th' different groups of horses scattered over th' plains, some feeding an' some resting. Kansas wove her way through them keeping as much distance from th' bunches as possible. Stallions came out to watch this herd moving with riders fore an' aft. Some of them snorting an' challenging th' stallion, some returning to their herd an' moving them away from this unfamiliar parade. I had to hold th' stud back from accepting th' challenges.

At the far edge of th' prairie we came upon a herd under attack by lobos an' prairie wolves. The horses were circled around their colts an' fended off intruders with hoof an' teeth. I normally left nature alone to solve its own problems, but for some reason, I rode to th' aid of th' horses. The stallion knew how to fight wolves an' flew into them with teeth an' hoof, putting them on th' run. Th' herd ran too, its stud nipping at th' laggards as they escaped over th' plain.

All except two, that is. In th' middle of what had been th' protective circle lay a mare an' over her stood a colt, his head hanging, ears ragged an' bloody from th' attacks of th' wolves. Apparently, th' herd had come to th' rescue of one of their members too late, for she was dead. Th' colt was too spent to run with th' herd an' would soon be dead when th' wolves returned. I had dismounted an' was just about to slit th' colt's throat when Kansas called, "Don't, Jerry, let's take it with us."

"How can we do that? It's too beat up to walk with the herd an' we don't have a wagon to put him in."

I may have been a little sarcastic with that reply an' Kansas' reply was sharp, "You would kill a horse just because he had bloody ears? Look at how pretty he is and how long his legs are. He will be a runner someday!"

"Someday if he lives."

"*I* will see that he does!" she replied, an' I could tell that there was going to be no other alternative but to try to take th' colt along.

"It might work if you take him up on your

saddle."

"That is good, bring him here."

I couldn't get th' colt to walk. There didn't seem to be much wrong with him but he must have been that tired. Kansas tried to ride over, but the smell of blood spooked the bell mare an' th' rest of th' herd was getting restless, so I picked th' colt up an' carried it to Kansas an' th' bell mare. Kansas had to get down an' hold th' mare. I let her smell th' colt an' she calmed some, but didn't like it at all when I tried to put th' colt across her saddle.

Kansas led her to a nearby tree an' positioned her by it where she couldn't shy away when I loaded the colt on th' saddle. I tied his front legs together an' ran th' rope under th' mare's belly, despite her objections, an' tied th' hind legs together.

Kansas led her a ways until th' colt quieted down an' th' mare was more comfortable with her burden. I sat Kansas on th' horse b'hind th' saddle an' we were soon gathered up an' on our way. I had been awful nervous that th' herd would run when we stopped, but without th' hobbled stallion's leadership, they stayed near an' fell in line when th' bell mare moved again.

Th' sky was turning gray when th' moon set an' we kept on moving all day. We rode th' divide south of Duck Creek until it became a narrow ridge, then found our way down one of th' gullies to Badger Creek, where we stopped late in th' evening. Th' herd was tired an' ready to rest after watering in th' creek an' spreading out in th' flat to graze.

I was surprised th' wounded colt had made it through th' day tied like he was, but he did. He was pretty wobbly when I got him down but he soon recovered enough to walk to th' creek an' drink. He had grown pretty tamed to Kansas. I could hear her talking to him most of the day an' I don't guess there was a moment when she wasn't touching him, being's she had to hold th' reins over his back. She took him to the creek an' washed his ears an' the blood off. The ears were pretty tattered. I knew we would have to trim them up after they healed a bit.

We caught up one of th' mares that had an older colt an' let th' little one nurse. He soon had all her milk an' I tied a sheet of buckskin over her teats so her filly couldn't suckle. It would take a few days for th' older horse to wean away an' th' mare seemed glad to nurse the wounded colt.

Th' whole herd was pretty tired after their inactivity in th' pen an' then th' long walk we had taken. After they had grazed awhile, we hobbled them an' picketed them for th' night. We let them graze awhile next morning.

Kansas had named the new colt Tatters because of his ears. He recovered quite well overnight an' now she had two colts following her around camp. Come Here You Rascal was jealous, but her nips an' complaints didn't deter Tatters.

I saddled Tatters' new mother for Kansas to ride since the bell mare would be pretty fatigued from her extra load. They led off, Kansas with a lead on th' bell mare just in case, Tatters trotting along one side an' Come Here You Rascal on th' other. It was quite an amusing parade.

Our pace was slower the second day to allow th' horses to work out some of th' soreness an' get more trail hardened. The Neosho bottoms were off to our right an' we stayed high up on th' divide, crossing th' upper reaches of such feeder creeks as Dry, Plum, Troublesome, an' Logwater where they were small an' easy for th' herd to cross. We stayed that night on East Hickory Creek, picketing th' horses back up under th' trees away from th' water.

I rode th' stallion several days in a row to make sure he was good an' tired an' didn't have ideas of breaking away for th' home range. As long as we had him an' th' bell mare under control, I felt that th' herd would remain docile an' follow, which turned out to be th' case.

From then on, we rode in easy stages making fifteen to twenty-five miles a day. It was like a homecoming of a kind when we crossed Lightning an' Thunderbolt Creeks. We could see th' lake we had camped by as we passed an' spent th' night on the upper Limestone. We were now in Osage territory, but didn't see any of them. Th' buffalo herds were not numerous enough to sustain a hunt by the tribe an' I surmised that they were hunting further west.

We crossed over into Missouri territory sometime an' stayed on th' prairie as much as possible. I was extra wary now b'cause of th' increased numbers of people, mostly from tribes not favorable to the Cherokee. Nights were a struggle, for I was awake most of th' time, standing guard. Twice we came up on white farms with corrals where th' farmers let us keep our horses. Both times I gave them one of th' lesser colts as pay when we left. Then we pushed hard to be out of range of them if they got any ideas about needing our whole herd.

We stayed above th' breaks of White River

almost to Galena. I had hoped that Sam Meeker would be there on one of his lead trading trips, but no one had seen him for a while. In a stroke of luck more welcome than gold, we caught up with Strongbow the Silent an' Redhorn just beginning their return trip with a load of lead for Sam. I had not seen a more welcome sight for a long time. Kansas an' I both were near exhaustion from th' lack of sleep an' constant strain of watching out for th' herd. With four of us, th' job was much easier.

We crossed th' river over into Cherokee country under sullen eyes of tribes living in th' bottoms. After crossing, two Shawnees chased after us, bent on mischief of some kind. It took an arrow through the leg of one of them before Strongbow could persuade them to turn back.

There seemed to be a surplus of lovely young women at Bear Springs Village an' we almost lost Redhorn to a two-legged filly with long eyelashes an' a short skirt. He reluctantly came with us when we left but with th' promise that he would return. Miss Eyelashes even rode a ways down th' trail with us.

The Village at the Forks was some different. Heavy storms in th' hills north an' west had caused both streams to flood an' th' bottoms had been inundated several feet deep. Th' people retreated quickly to higher ground an' were scattered for a time. When th' waters receded, there was little left of th' village, but the flood had cleansed th' ground an' deposited a thick layer of new soil an' humus on th' bottoms an' the new soil restored lost fertility. The new crops were greener an' th' corn taller than ever.

A runner sent the night before met us at Pee Dee with Speaks Softly's sons an' Jesse an' Riley an' we had a great time on that last leg of th' trip.

We turned th' herd into Speaks Softly's corral, except for Bell Mare, Come Here You Rascal, Tatters, an' his adopted mother, all of whom were claimed by Kansas an' would not have left her even if we had tried to separate them.

Th' boys were quite taken by the two colts an' even though they were nominally Kansas' property, they assumed th' primary role of training an' caring for the two. True to her prediction, Tatters became quite a racer, proving himself to be faster than any horse in the three villages an' the pride of th' tribe in races with other tribes.

Th' addition of th' herd to our stock greatly improved bloodlines an' went a long way toward perfecting th' Cherokee Pony line. Though they were a smaller horse, they possessed great stamina an' endurance (bottom, as th' western cowmen call it).

March 5, 1825, our first child was born an' we named her Brook Kansas Harris after Laughing Brook.

*"There were two more descendants of th' first Kansas in th' family that carried th' name, th' last one being Sarah Kansas Halpain. It is a testimony of th' great character o' that first Kansas that th' name lived on for three more generations."* Zenas sat in deep thought for a few minutes as I finished my notes and as I looked up, he said, *"I could tell you a lifetime o' tales about Uncle Jerry, but that wouldn't get me down t' mine an' Pa's trails. If I live long enough an' you are interested, I'll go back an' tell you some o' th' events in his life — at least th' ones that would bear telling without revealing too many family skeletons!"* He laughed.

*Later, reading over my notes, I marveled that one man and one woman would travel through that hostile country alone and capture, train, and return through the wilderness with a herd of mostly wild horses. It was striking to me that after leaving the Kaws way up on the Kansas River, they did not see one other human until they had returned to Missouri. All that country and not a road, not a fence, not a house, and not a person. Amazing!*

In Book III, a restless Meeker family resumes life on the trails with adventures on the California Road with Captain Marcy, the Cherokee Trail, and the Santa Fe Trail. Zenas Leonard Meeker is born and begins his life on the trails as well.

# ABOUT THE AUTHOR

**Jim Crownover** grew up in the woods and on the streams of central Arkansas where much of this story takes place. He spent many hours walking fields picking up arrowheads and other artifacts possibly left by some of his ancestors. He has a keen interest in history, especially that of the west and southwest. Early, he became interested in the everyday activities of the pioneers and explorers and the oral histories of the day. This has led him to concentrate his attention in this book to the "minute historical accuracies . . . entirely devoid of importance" to Bernard DeVoto, but full of the drama of life of the time.

Jim lives in the small community of Elm Springs in northwest Arkansas.

The employees of Thorndike Press hope you have enjoyed this Large Print book. All our Thorndike, Wheeler, and Kennebec Large Print titles are designed for easy reading, and all our books are made to last. Other Thorndike Press Large Print books are available at your library, through selected bookstores, or directly from us.

For information about titles, please call:
  (800) 223-1244

or visit our Web site at:
  http://gale.cengage.com/thorndike

To share your comments, please write:
Publisher
Thorndike Press
10 Water St., Suite 310
Waterville, ME 04901